EROTIC LITERATURE

EROTIC LITERATURE

TWENTY-FOUR CENTURIES OF SENSUAL WRITING

Edited by Jane Mills

HarperCollins*Publishers*

This book is published in Great Britain by Bloomsbury Publishing Limited under the title *Bloomsbury Guide to Erotic Literature*.

FIRST EDITION

Design by Fielding Rowinski

Library of Congress Catalog Card Number 92-52543

ISBN 0-06-270057-X

93 94 95 96 97 98 10 9 8 7 6 5 4 3 2 1

Printed in Hong Kong

CONTENTS

Acknowledgements

I have been helped by many friends as well as by numerous librarians and booksellers, particularly those at the British Library and the London Library, and at Compendium, Editions des Femmes, Gay's the Word, the Owl Bookshop, and Silver Moon Bookshop. I wish to thank the following for their references, ideas, advice, support or love (none of these being necessarily exclusive): Parveen Adams; Bill Anderson; Lisa Appignianesi; Pete Ayrton; Jennifer Baker; Rosie van der Beek; Ruth Bundey; Margaret Blumen; Carmen Callil; Sarah Carpenter; Julie Christie; Julie Clarke; Wendy Collier; Wendy Cooper; Mark Cousins; Kevin Crossley-Holland; Robin Davidson; Rosalind Delmar; Sira Dermen; Bernard Enlander; Manuel Escudero; Susie Figgis; John Forrester; Jessica Fraser; Monica Furlong; Jacqui Glanville; Trevor Glover; Mick Gold; Asli Göksel; Jonathon Green; Trevor Griffiths; Fred Halliday; Gareth Humphreys; Keith Jacka; Nick Jacobs; Margaret Lally; Kathy Lette; Denis MacShane; Brian McGill; Marilyn Minet; Jan Montefiore; Toni Morrison; Richard Neville; Geoffrey Nowell-Smith; Katey Owen; Ursula Owen; Luisa Passerini; David Pirie; Cathy Porter; Gary Pulsifer; Peter Pringle; Ann Quinlan; Barbara Rennie; Geoffrey Robertson; Marsha Rowe; Linda Semple; Jennifer Silverstone; Joan Smith; Elaine Steel; Liz Stoll; Jennie Stoller; Juan Carlos Valdovinas; Gerard Valentine; Marion Virgo; Marina Warner; Francine Winham. They may not have been aware of it, but Katrina Forrester, Katrina and Imogen Gold, Alexander Halliday, Lucy and Angelica Neville, Piers Pennell, Julius Robertson and Russell Saunders were all important to me in the writing of this book. I would also like to thank Sheffield Hallam University for enabling me to finish it.

Sandra Ferguson deserves a medal for her research but will have to make do with my gratitude and this acknowledgement. Likewise Charles Onion who checked my drafts and spent many hours searching for books and remained cool and unbothered for even more hours at the photocopy machine. My thanks to my editors, Kathy Rooney and Louise Speller, for their understanding and patience. And sincere thanks to Jonathon Green who donated large quantities of his enthusiasm and skilfully designed data-base information. I want to express my admiration for Angela Carter who generously shared her knowledge when she was very ill; she is hugely missed. To Dee Dee Glass, Maxine Molyneux and Margaret Mulvihill who came to my rescue at various stages throughout the writing of this book in a variety of ways, I would like to express love as well as thanks. And special thanks and love to Margaret Walters for her scholarly criticism, for sharing her knowledge of art history and for reading, commenting and advising on the manuscript in all its drafts.

My sister Carolyn would have enjoyed this book; I dedicate it to her memory, to my sister Ruth, and to Ruth Bundey who gave me the love of a sister when Carolyn was murdered.

INTRODUCTION

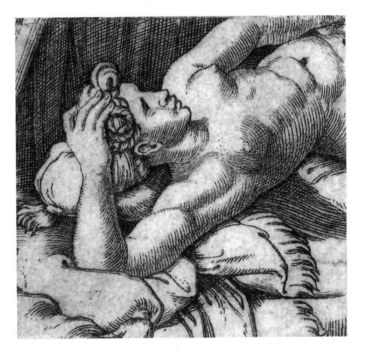

From *Postures* Marlantonio Raimondi

The Language of Desire

Socrates calls Eros a Sophist, but Sappho calls him 'weaver of fictions'.

Maximus of Tyre (Greece, 1st century)

'Imagine a city where there is no desire. Supposing for the moment that the inhabitants of the city continue to eat, drink, procreate in some mechanical way; still, their life looks flat. They do not theorize or spin tops or speak figuratively. Few think to shun pain; none gives gifts. They bury their dead and forget where . . . Now and again a man and a woman may marry and live very happily, as travellers who meet by chance at an inn; at night falling asleep they dream the same dream . . . but it is unlikely they remember the dream in the morning. The art of storytelling is widely neglected.

A city without desire is, in sum, a city of no imagination.'

Paraphrase of Aristotle (Anne Carson, *Eros the Bittersweet*, 1986)

The common properties of language and sexual love are captured in the opening lines of an ancient Sumerian love poem: 'Because I uttered it, because I uttered it, the lord gave me a gift'. The gift is sexual desire. From the same period the courtship between the goddess Inanna and her lover begins, 'The word they had spoken/Was a word of desire.' As the American writer Anne Carson states in her illuminating essay *Eros the Bittersweet*: 'It is nothing new to say that all utterance is erotic in some sense, that all language shows the structure of desire at some level.'

To the ancient Greeks the verb *mnaomai* had the meaning 'to give heed, to make mention' and also that of 'to court, woo, be a suitor'. And the goddess Peitho had charge of rhetorical persuasion, as well as the arts of seduction. In earliest metaphor it is 'breath', 'wind' or 'wings' that move words from speaker to listener as they transport Eros or his arrows from lover to beloved. This trope is present in most ancient creation myths, as in this Pelasgian myth, lovingly described by Robert Graves:

'In the beginning, Eurynome, the Goddess of All Things, rose naked from Chaos, but found nothing substantial for her feet to rest upon, and therefore divided the sea from the sky, dancing lonely upon its waves. She danced towards the south, and the Wind set in motion behind her something new and apart with which to begin a work of creation. Wheeling about, she caught hold of this North Wind, rubbed it in between her hands, and behold! the great serpent Ophion. Eurynome danced to warm herself, wildly and more wildly, until Ophion, grown lustful, coiled about those divine limbs and was moved to couple with her. Now, the North Wind, who is also called Boreas, fertilizes; which is why mares often turn their hind-quarters to the wind and breed foals without the aid of a stallion. So Eurynome was likewise got with child.'

(*The Greek Myths*, Vol. 1, 1955)

From the Orphic creation myth in which Eros is introduced we learn that Eros is the same colour as the honey words spoken by lovers: 'Night, a goddess of whom even Zeus stands in awe, was courted by the Wind and laid a silver egg in the womb of darkness; Eros . . . was hatched from this egg and set the Universe in motion. Eros was . . . golden-winged.' (Graves, op. cit.) And from the New Testament we learn that language and creativity are inseparable: 'In the beginning was the Word.'

The written word has a similar effect to the uttered word. 'As the vowels and consonants of an alphabet interact symbolically to make a certain written word', writes Carson, 'so writer and reader bring together two halves of one meaning, so lover and beloved are matched together like two sides of one knucklebone'. The following description of Pythagoras at work makes clear the erotic implications of the written word: 'He took pains over the geometry of letters, forming each stroke with a geometrical rhythm of angles and curves and straight lines.'

It is the written word that breathes sexual desire into Dante's adulterous Francesca in *The Divine Comedy* (completed 1321). 'Tell me,' the poet asks her, 'how, and by what, did love his power disclose/And grant you knowledge of your hidden fires?' The damned woman replies:

> One day we read for pastime how in thrall
> Lord Lancelot, who loved the Queen;
> We were alone – we thought no harm at all.
>
> As we read on, our eyes met now and then,
> And to our cheeks the changing colour started,
> But just one moment overcame us – when
>
> We read of the smile, desired of lips long-thwarted,
> Such a smile, by such a lover kissed away,
> He that may never more from me be parted
>
> Trembling all over, kissed my mouth . . .

'Among the dark gods of the psyche', writes Allan Rodway in his essay *The Erotic Novel – A Critical View* (1975), 'Eros is a power so commanding that few novels could be classified as wholly unerotic'. The novelist, like the poet, woos the reader, causing Francesca to cry out, 'The book and its author was our pimp.' In the nineteenth century, like Madame Bovary and Jane Austen's impressionable young heroine in *Northanger Abbey*, Pushkin's heroine in *Eugene Onegin* experiences something very similar:

Tatiana is besotted by romantic fiction:
with what attention she now
reads a delicious novel,
with what vivid enchantment
drinks the seductive fiction!

. . . sighs, and having made her own
another's ecstasy, another's melancholy,
she whispers in a trance, by heart
a letter to the amiable hero.

And what would Mr Justice Charles, who presided at the trial of Oscar Wilde and who maintained that Charles Dickens wrote 'the most wholesome literature' and 'never wrote, so far as I know, a single offensive word', have made of novelist Eudora Welty's mother who 'read Dickens in the spirit in which she would have eloped with him'?

What the lover wants from love and what the reader wants from reading are very similar experiences, both embodying a reaching out for the unknown. 'What is erotic about reading (or writing)', Carson explains, 'is the play of imagination called forth in the space between you and your object of knowledge. Poets and novelists, like lovers, touch that space to life with their metaphors . . .'. At the core of desire is imagination, and imagination is at the core of metaphor. It is essential to sexual love and to the activity of reading. Words, like Cupid's darts, ignite desire in readers and lovers and cause a sensation that is both sweet and bitter. The hunger for knowledge is like the hunger for love. The reader, like the lover, desires what she or he does not (yet) have; the Greek word *eros* also denotes 'want', 'lack' and 'desire for that which is missing'. Erotic literature can be seen as one of the recognizable attempts of humankind to find her or his missing half.

What is erotic literature?

'. . . there is to the erotic some connotation of . . . mystery.'

Jan Morris (*The Independent*, 1992)

'Without secrecy there would be no pornography.'

D. H. Lawrence (*Pornography and Obscenity*, 1929)

The disruptive power of Eros to cause pain, to induce madness, to subvert, has been recognized in most cultures throughout history, although nowhere has it been considered so dangerous as in Western cultures imbued with strong Christian notions of original sin. Were erotic literature to be divided into its many sub-genres and traditions, one very large, and largely twentieth-century, sub-genre would exist of writings by academics, critics, lawyers, clerics, novelists, dramatists, psychologists, politicians, poets and pundits who have attacked or defended any or all of the various sub-genres of erotic literature, in particular what has come to be called 'pornography'. To this end, literally tons of type, huge lakes of ink, and, more recently, millions of megabytes have been used in attempts to tease out the meanings of the words 'erotica', 'pornography', 'obscenity' and 'literature'. As German academic Ludwig Marcuse, author of *Obscene: The History of an Indignation* (1965) wrote, 'when we are at our wit's end in the search for the identity of a concept, we usually pursue the origin of the word'.

The origins of the word 'erotic' are easily traceable: it entered the English language in the seventeenth century via the French *érotique* from the Greek word *erotikos* which derives from *eros*, meaning 'sexual love'. But that's about the only aspect of the word on which dictionaries agree; when it comes to semantics, matters become rather more complicated. The *Oxford English Dictionary* (*OED*) defines 'erotic' as: 'Of or pertaining to the passion of love; concerned with or treating of love; amatory', and its nineteenth-century cognate, 'erotica', as 'matters of love; erotic literature or art'. If only it were that simple. The *Concise Oxford Dictionary* (*COD*) hints at why the subject should arouse passions other than the sexual by adding: 'esp. tending to arouse sexual desire or excitement'. *Webster's Dictionary* has no quarrel with this, but narrows the *COD*'s definition of 'erotica' by adding connotations of pleasure and excellence or merit that are not necessarily present in a notion of sexual desire: 'literary or artistic items having an erotic theme, esp. books treating of sexual love in a sensuous or voluptuous manner'. It instructs the reader to 'compare Pornography'.

The etymology of 'pornography' is complex. The *Oxford Dictionary of Etymology* tells us that it derives from the Greek *porne*, meaning 'prostitute', and *graphos*, used in the sense of 'writing' or 'describing'. The lexicographers of Webster's were more correct in translating *pornoi* as harlots; within the ancient Greek hierarchy of prostitution, these slaves who worked in brothels were placed at the bottom and the term became one of denigration when applied to other women.

According to the *OED*, 'pornography', a mid-nineteenth-century neologism, first appeared in an English medical dictionary, which defined it as: 'a description of prostitutes or of prostitution, as a matter of public hygiene'. This surprising medical element presumably refers to the new profession of psychiatrists who 'captured' images of female sexuality on camera. It was thought at the time that nymphomania could be detected in facial expressions and poses. The term 'pornography' quickly acquired a non-scientific (or 'hygienic') usage: 'Descriptions of the life, manners, etc. of prostitutes and their patrons; hence, the expression or suggestion of obscene or unchaste subjects in literature or art'. 'Pornographic', in terms of literature or art, is defined as 'that which deals in the obscene'. *Webster's* circumvents the need to define 'literature' or 'art' by defining pornography more luridly as 'a depiction (in writing or painting) of licentiousness or lewdness: a portrayal of erotic behaviour designed to cause sexual excitement'. Then, as if acknowledging the futile circularity and sophistry of so many legal and literary arguments, it instructs, 'compare Erotica'.

'Licentious', 'unchaste' and 'lewd' are all broadly synonymous, but each possesses slightly different connotations of moral indignation which are not immediately present in 'erotica' – except, of course, to those for whom sexual arousal is a matter for disgust. Deriving from the Latin *licere*, 'licence', meaning 'liberty of action', entered the English language in the fourteenth century. Over the next 100 years its meaning shifted from 'formal permission from authority' to 'excessive liberty'. By the sixteenth century it denoted 'deviation from normal form'. In the context of this book, *Webster's* gives its current meaning as 'marked by lewdness'.

The etymological history of 'lewd' is equally fascinating and is highly revealing of the history of what came to be called either erotic or pornographic literature, depending on the point of view. The Old English word *laewede*, meaning 'lay, not clerical' may be connected to the Latin *laicus* (unlearned). In the thirteenth century it took on this meaning, manifestly demonstrating the Christian Church's attitude towards its flock. Later, however, it came to mean 'low, vulgar, ignorant, ill-conditioned, lascivious and unchaste', finally arriving at its current sense of 'lascivious, indecent, obscene'.

The origins of 'obscene' have been a subject of much debate and fanciful imagination. The *Oxford Dictionary of Etymology* maintains that it entered English via the French in the sixteenth century (when French erotic poetry greatly influenced the English poets of the High Renaissance) from the Latin *obscenus*. Originally, 'obscene' was probably a term of augury, meaning 'ill-omened, abominable, disgusting, indecent'. In the nineteenth century it was thought to originate in the Latin *scena*, meaning 'stage', getting its sense from the grotesque phalluses worn by ancient Roman actors. Following the same etymological path, but arriving at an opposite conclusion, the English sexologist Havelock Ellis (1859–1939) proposed that 'ob-scene' meant 'off the scene', since indecent or salacious behaviour did not happen on stage in front of a Roman audience. Yet another theory suggests it derives from *caenum*, meaning 'dirt, filth, mire, excrement', and also used as a vulgarism for 'penis'; in the plural it was a coarse term for both 'prick' and 'arse' (the phrase *obsceno verbo uti* means 'to tell a dirty joke').

The epithet 'obscene' is used today as a label for anything which arouses moral or aesthetic indignation or disgust. It is also a term used by censors, or would-be censors, for any writing, object or display they would like banned. The crime of obscenity was first established in England in 1727, when a judge declared that publication of a book entitled *Venus in the Cloister* (which would almost certainly have been called 'pornography' had the word yet been invented) constituted a common-law misdemeanour because it tended to 'weaken the bonds of civil society, virtue and morality'. This new crime was not used again until 1763, when the House of Lords declared *Essay on Woman* (a licentious parody of Pope's earlier *Essay on Man* (1733–34)) by the political radical John Wilkes, to be 'a most scandalous, obscene and impious libel'. The word 'libel' comes from the Latin *libellus*, the diminutive of 'book' (so an obscene libel involves not speech but 'a dirty little book').

The obscenity law made little initial impact on the then limited circulation of erotica, but when cheap and trashy material flooded the market in the early nineteenth century, Victorian prudery increased and led to the passing of the 1857 Obscene Publications Act. This empowered the police to take books before local justices to have them forfeited and destroyed for obscenity. The crime was defined by Chief Justice Cockburn in 1868 as follows: 'I think the test of obscenity is this, whether the tendency of the matter charged as obscenity is to deprave and corrupt those whose minds are open to such immoral influences, and into whose hands a publication of this sort may fall.' 'Deprave' means 'to make morally bad, to pervert, to debase or corrupt morally'; 'corrupt' means 'to render morally unsound or rotten, or destroy the moral purity or chastity of, to pervert or ruin a good quality, to debase, to defile'. The law encompassed not only likely readers but any possible reader and was applied to any 'purple' passage, regardless of the context or overall message of the book.

Other European legal codes followed suit with varying degrees of success, and imperial powers imposed their values on their colonies. In the United States the First Amendment posed a problem to censors since it stated: 'Congress shall make no law . . . abridging the freedom of speech or of the press.' But this did not stop the nineteenth-century guardians of morality from passing a statute in 1865 which outlawed the sending of 'any obscene, lewd, lascivious, filthy book, pamphlet, picture, print or other publication of a vulgar or indecent character . . .' through the US mails. Using entrapment, America's foremost crusader against pornography, Anthony Comstock (1844–1915), a special agent of the US Post Office, prosecuted over 3,500 individuals (although no more than 10 per cent were found guilty) and destroyed more than 160 tons of allegedly obscene literature. But by the early 1900s his enthusiastic puritanism was losing favour with the American public. When Comstock's crusade included an attack on George Bernard Shaw's *Mrs Warren's Profession* in 1905, the play became a smash hit and 'comstockery' became an international joke at the expense of the United States.

In Britain the banning of erotica had a similar effect in popularizing authors, some hitherto unknown, to an increasingly literate population. But Cockburn's test of obscenity, which focused on how a book affected the most vulnerable members of society (as determined by zealous policemen and Oxbridge-educated judges) meant there could be no defence of literary merit. The arguments of liberal British writers and publishers culminated in the 1959 Obscene Publications Act, which maintained that erotic writing could be divided into two classes – 'literature' and 'pornography'.

The 1959 Act liberated many a volume of erotica from the pyre, but it perpetuated the notion that 'literature' was quality stuff while 'pornography' was shoddy by continuing to confuse the question of social and moral desirability with that of literary merit. Lying not far beneath this confusion was a sense of disgust, and perhaps fear, of sexual arousal. American critic and novelist Susan Sontag attempted to unravel this confusion in her essay *The Pornographic Imagination* (1967) in which she pointed out that 'so long as pornography is treated as a locus for moral concern' it becomes impossible to regard any pornographic book as an interesting and important work of art.

The confusion between social or moral desirability and literary merit has a history which predates Aretino, who is widely regarded as having 'invented' pornography in the sixteenth century. Plato's reproach to Homer for his purple passage between Hero and Zeus provided a very early example of the debate on the seemliness of writing about Eros in 'high' literature. And when English medieval monks were discouraged from reading bawdy verse, the moral concern (or need to control, perhaps) felt by the Church authorities for their more junior members clearly coloured their literary judgement. Thus, Enea Silvio de Piccolomini banned the erotica he had written in his youth on becoming Pope Pius II in 1458. The Catholic Church, at first concerned to protect its members from heretical literature, then focused its attention on the disruptive power of Eros. In the secular world the aesthetic and erotic pleasure derived from the 'luf-talkynge', the ecstatic verbal dalliance of the practitioners of courtly love, may have seemed perfectly harmless to those at the receiving end of a troubadour's song, but Dante's Francesca in the *The Divine Comedy* (completed 1321) blames her depravity, corruption and loss of self-control on her erotic reading matter.

That erotic literature was popular during the medieval and Renaissance periods there can be no doubt. *The Romance of the Rose* (see page 97) was a medieval bestseller, as were several versions of Arthurian romances whose attraction was doubtless, in part, the treatment of illicit sex. While England during the late Middle Ages and Renaissance periods failed to produce a writer quite as bold as many of the French and Italian erotic writers of the period, Shakespeare's *Venus and Adonis* (see page 137) was probably the first book frankly merchandised as erotica in England; by 1636 it had reached thirteen editions.

Catholicism during the Counter-Reformation and Protestantism in the hands of zealous Puritans clearly played a large part in encouraging the questioning of literary quality in erotic prose and poetry. In most cases moral purpose could be used to justify the most purple of passages, which is just what the early Christian fathers did to explain away the potentially embarrassing presence of the sexually arousing 'Song of Solomon' (see page 40) in the Bible.

As morality, especially middle-class morality, became increasingly codified, the confusion increased about the place of Eros in literature. In the sixteenth century Aretino's style of erotic writing (see page 117) which had initially served entertaining and sometimes didactic purposes gradually became a vehicle of satirical protest against the authority of the Church and State, and ultimately against bourgeois morality. Similarly, eighteenth-century 'pornography' was a realistic portrayal of genital or sexual behaviour which deliberately violated widely accepted moral and social taboos by its graphic presentation of sexual activities.

Erotica emanating from the aristocracy could be condemned as exemplifying the excesses of a class whose political power and moral stranglehold on the populace was waning. The introduction of obscenity legislation from the mid-eighteenth century testifies to a growing sense of moral indignation. The educated middle classes could accept the erotica of the past more comfortably than anything produced in their own time. The ancient Greek and Latin of an Archilochus or a Catullus, even the medieval Scottish dialect of William Dunbar's erotic satire 'The Tretis of the Twa Marriit Wemen and the Wedo', were enough to elevate these writers to the ranks of 'high' literature. But a contemporary writer who showed no classical education was immediately suspect, as Robert Burns (see page 208) was to discover. Wordsworth's judgement on the literary merit of the *Merry Muses of Caledonia* was stern: 'He must be a miserable judge of poetical compositions who can for a moment fancy that such low, tame and loathsome ribaldry can possibly be the production of Burns.'

In the preface to *The Picture of Dorian Gray* (1891), Oscar Wilde expressed a very different view: 'There is no such thing as a moral or an immoral book. Books are well written or badly written. That is all'. With these words he was proclaiming art to be independent of the sexual morality or immorality of the age in which it is written. 'I am quite incapable of understanding how any work of art can be criticized from a moral standpoint', he wrote in reply to a hostile review.

As well as believing art and ethics to be quite separate, Wilde also distinguished erotica from pornography in terms of literary and artistic merit. '. . . I take it, that no matter how immoral a book may be,' challenged his prosecution lawyer, 'if it is well written, it is, in your opinion, a good book.' Wilde replied: 'Yes, if it were well written so as to produce a sense of beauty, which is the highest sense of which a human being can be capable. If it were badly written it would produce a sense of disgust.' This criterion of whether a book affords aesthetic satisfaction in addition to sexual arousal lies at the core of attempts to define the terms 'erotica' and 'pornography'.

Readers generally show greater tolerance for 'art' or 'literature' than for hack work, being influenced by what they think the author intended. For example, a writer suspected of exploiting prurient interest for financial gain is unlikely to be as highly regarded as one with an apparently 'loftier' purpose. And yet a connotation of the profit motive was present in the nineteenth-century coining of the word 'erotica', just as much as it was in the neologism 'pornography'. While certainly courting legal trouble, Victorian publishers and booksellers doubtless found the tag 'pornography' helped sell this sub-genre of erotica (and indeed, still do). The term 'erotica', and its many euphemisms, such as 'facetiae', 'bawdy', 'curious' or even the bizarre 'kruptadia', were applied to writings of a sexual nature – either explicit or implicit – in an attempt to circumvent obscenity charges which might lead to heavy financial penalties and also, one suspects, to attract a better (i.e. wealthier) class of reader. The distinction between the two genres becomes blurred when seen in this light.

The contemporary French essayist, novelist and art historian Alexandrian maintained that there was no difference between eroticism and pornography.

'Pornography is the description pure and simple of carnal pleasures, eroticism is this same description but evaluated as a function of the idea of love or of social values. . . . It is very much more important to make the distinction between the erotic and the obscene . . . eroticism is all that makes the body desirable, displaying it in all its brilliancy and vigour, awakening an impression of health, of beauty, a delectable game; whereas obscenity evaluates the body differently, associating it with dirt, infirmity, scatological jokes, filthy words.'

(*Histoire de la littérature érotique*, 1989)

But, like the terms 'erotic' and 'pornographic', the concept of obscenity is not a constant, as D. H. Lawrence noted:

'What is obscene to Tom is not obscene to Lucy or Joe, and really, the meaning of a word has to wait for majorities to decide it. If a play shocks ten people in an audience, and doesn't shock the remaining five hundred, then it is obscene to ten and innocuous to five hundred; hence the play is not obscene, by majority. But Hamlet shocked all the Cromwellian Puritans, and shocks nobody today, and some of Aristophanes shocks everybody today, and it didn't galvanize the later Greeks at all, apparently. Man is a changeable beast, and words change their meanings with him, and things are not what they seemed, and what's what becomes what isn't, and if we think we know where we are, it's only because we are so rapidly being translated to somewhere else.'

(*Pornography and Obscenity*, 1929)

On Editing an Anthology of Erotic Literature

'People who feel themselves secretly attracted to different temptations are eagerly bent on removing these temptations out of other people's way.'

Ernest Jones 1879–1958 (biographer of Sigmund Freud)

'An anthology is like all the plums and orange peel picked out of a cake.'

Sir Walter Raleigh (1861–1922)

The word anthology comes from two Greek words: *anthos* meaning 'flower', and *-logia* meaning 'collection'. The problem facing the editor of any anthology is that what is to one person a magnificent bouquet, to another is a poorly arranged posy of poisonous weeds. In other words, even if one characterizes a genre in terms of its formal properties and function, its actual reception will inevitably depend upon the individual response and cultural values of its readership.

As they trawl through millions of words on their chosen subject, anthology editors face numerous problems – not least of which is the ghostly presence of a faceless future reviewer waiting to deride inclusions and condemn omissions. Unless the subject is extremely narrow, no anthologist can hope to cover every single word ever written on the chosen subject. This one nearly gave up in despair on several occasions, but no moment was so dark as when she discovered the complete works of George Sand ran to 105 volumes.

Certain decisions about how to limit the scope of the material have to be taken early on. Is the anthology to be organized chronologically or thematically? Does the whole of a poem have to be included? Can passages of prose be sprinkled with dots to indicate omissions? Should an extract be the best example of a writer's work or can it simply be a good example of a particular genre or sub-genre? Should racist, misogynist, ageist or any other politically incorrect tendencies be permitted? Should badly written or examples or 'low' literature be included in order to show a range of writing and styles? Can the inclusion of a poor translation be justified? Can the exclusion of pop song lyrics or screenplays be justified? Can an internationally renowned work in the field be excluded on the grounds that most readers will know it anyway? Should prose translations of poems be permitted? The considerations are endless. And for every piece of writing included, several others have to be jettisoned.

The publisher's brief for this anthology was alarmingly large: a chronological ordering of erotic literature from Plato to NATO by writers female and male, gay and straight, throughout the world. The only subjects my editor suggested excluding were rape and child sexual abuse. It was left to me to define 'erotic' and 'literature', which raised problems discussed earlier in this introduction. The few existing anthologies on the subject were of limited value; the criteria for selection were seldom clear, although I began to appreciate why. I bombarded friends, acquaintances, scholars and experts in particular fields with requests for their favorite erotica, but often to little avail. I would spend days, sometimes weeks, tracking down their recommendations only to stare at their hot tip in amazement and conclude if that was what turned them on, there's nowt so queer as folk.

Clearly, I had to come to some decisions about what constituted erotic literature. Far from narrowing my field, I began by making it impossibly wide. Fiction and poetry were two givens, but I spread my initial research net over medical and scientific textbooks, sex education, psychoanalytic case studies and theory, religious tracts, journalism, popular music and screenplays, as well every genre of fiction, including crime, science fiction, popular romance and the bonk-buster. I also delved into history way beyond Plato, discovering, to my delight, some ancient Sumerian poetry which remains my personal favourite.

Authorial intent to arouse sexual desire in the reader proved to be a red herring. How could I decide what produced a genital response in another epoch or culture? A Japanese lover in the Middle Ages would, I suspect, have been bewildered by Robert Herrick's seventeenth-century view expressed in 'Clothes Do but Cheat and Cozen Us' (see page 156). In the eighteenth century James Boswell found *Fanny Hill* 'most inflaming', while twentieth-century critic George Steiner merely laughed, finding it a 'mock-epic orgasm'. Angela Carter's advice to me was succinct: 'I would steer clear of de Sade as he is more emetic than erotic.' I agreed, but I didn't act on it. If I hadn't already suspected, it became transparently clear that it takes all sorts or, to quote D. H. Lawrence, 'What is pornography to one man is the laughter of genius to another'. After wading through the arguments for and against pornography I came to agree with Susan Sontag that it is not helpful to separate pornography from the realm of literature and that the stimulation of sexual desire can be a legitimate aim of high literature as well as pornography.

This opened up a vast field of research and I sat for days in the British Library ordering up nineteenth-century books with titles like *Lady Bumtickler's Revels, Colonel Spanker's Experimental Lecture, The Story of a Dildoe* and, a favourite of students of Victorian prurience, *Raped on the Railway: A True Story of a Lady Who Was First Ravished and Then Flagellated on the Scotch Express.* That there are relatively few examples of obvious pornography in this anthology may well be because I do not find this library atmosphere conducive to sexual desire. And while I know that millions of men and many women find modern pornography sexually arousing, I have included none that is deliberately marketed as such. Perhaps this is because I, or modern publishers, have somehow internalized the widely prevalent view that 'yesterday's smut is today's erotica', as declared in the banner headline to an article on the subject in a recent *New York Times.*

I admit to other equally idiosyncratic reasons for the inclusion or exclusion of various works or authors. While not in total disagreement with the notion of political correctness, I had to disregard it as a criterion for selection. To have proscribed rape would have meant dropping Shakespeare's *Venus and Adonis,* for example. Similarly, to ignore child sexual abuse would have meant the exclusion of a powerfully erotic passage from Nadine Gordimer's *The Conservationist.* At one stage I was tempted to ignore Henry Miller, whose misogynistic novels I find not just anaphrodisiac but highly repellent, but was dissuaded by an eminent feminist publisher who remains grateful to Miller for introducing her to her own eroticism. I am also grateful to Toni Morrison who, when I asked her what she considered to be the most erotic novel of the twentieth century, introduced me to *The Garden of Eden* by that well-known Dead White European Male, Ernest Hemingway. Regrettably, it was not possible to include all the extracts I would have liked. Copyright restrictions and exorbitant permission fees also played an important part in the final selection.

Given that I define erotica in its widest sense – anything that is about sexual desire whether or not it was written with the intention of arousing desire in the reader (Nathaniel Hawthorne's *The Scarlet Letter* (see page 235) is, to me, an example of unconscious erotica from the nineteenth century, for example) – I am very aware of certain absences. I decided to exclude drama and screenplays because without the visual input clearly intended by the writer they seemed to me to suffer when compared to the fiction and poetry. Modern popular songs

– indeed, most words that were set to music – are excluded on the grounds that most of them seem to shrivel when deprived of their musical score.

I also decided to exclude erotica that might be classified as sex-manual instruction. (As the author of a matter-of-fact sex education book who has been told by many of the erotic pleasures they experienced while reading it, this was a tough decision.) Non-English language erotica also presented a problem; if this anthology appears to be overly Anglo-centric, it is because it was not always possible to get adequate translations. On occasions, as with D.H. Lawrence for example, I decided not to select a passage from a well-known work, in this case *Lady Chatterley's Lover* (1928), partly because I wanted to demonstrate the breadth of the author's erotic literary vision, but also, I confess, out of perversity. I reluctantly also made the decision to exclude personal letters and journals. This was especially sad in the cases of James Joyce (to his wife) and Virginia Woolf (to her sister) which I highly recommend to erotophiles.

As for the absence of science fiction, crime novels (the American thriller-writer Sarah Schulman came close), erotica from Scandinavia (although twentieth-century Norwegian novelist Knut Hamsun's *Victoria* deserves inspection), aboriginal or white Australian literature, or omissions from anywhere else (being a Turkophile, I was especially sad to find myself excluding some of the mildly erotic Turkic religious poetry I came across), all I can say is that I tried, honest. But I didn't find any that fitted my own parameters. Of course, like most people who construct hard and fast rules, I also broke them from time to time.

Before I became fully convinced of the need to limit my material, I wanted to organize the extracts thematically rather than chronologically. I was enjoying tracing the ways in which, for instance, kissing had been treated over the years, from Catullus's beautiful poem 'Vivamus, mea lesbia . . .' and, across the centuries its various translations and imitations (including those by Louise Labé, Johannes Secundus, Ben Jonson, Byron, and Sir Richard Burton), through Robert Herrick's 'Kisses Loathsome', which begins, 'I abhor the slimie kisse . . .', to the 1950s folk song by Jonathan Denwood entitled 'T' Ragman's Kiss':

Quoth frisky Mag, Ah's thurty-five
An hevn't hed a man;
Yit Ah's as fir as owt alive
An kittle ta t'bean;
Ah's full o'luive fra top to toe,
Wid me theer nowt amiss,
Ne doot o'that, said ragman Joe,
An gev her gob a kiss.

I also became intrigued by the theme of the comic-erotic. There it is, wilfully strong, in ancient Greece and Rome from writers such as Aristophanes, Catullus, Apuleius and many epi-grammists, and then it disappears until the High Middle Ages, with Boccaccio and Chaucer leading the way for other lesser erotic comedians. During the early sixteenth century Rabelais (see page 123) kept the comic fires of sexual desire burning, but there is again a hiatus until the late Renaissance. This theme comes into its own with the erotic satires and many of the outrageously bawdy novels of the seventeenth and eighteenth centuries, but relatively little of nineteenth-century erotica was very funny. Of course, much of the anonymous vulgar poetry throughout the ages was often (intentionally) hilarious, but it clearly failed to perk up much of the mainstream erotic/pornographic publishing trade. It was something of a relief to find that among what seemed to me a preoccupation, if not obsession, with perversion and death in the twentieth century, the comic-erotic once again reared its silly head. I remembered, for instance, literally falling off a chair with laughter when first reading Terry Southern's *Blue Movie* (1970). On reading it again, I was distressed by its misogyny (being wiser and more sober), but still I laughed.

The list of possible themes which could have given me the opportunity to explore constant or changing obsessions over the ages was almost endless: breasts (female); buggery; chastity; class; death; defloration; dildo; fantasy; fear; flirting; food; foot fetishism; frustration; guilt; homosexuality; impotence; incest; infidelity; instruction; love; male castration fear; masturbation; medicine; misogyny; mother/child eroticism; old age; oral sex; organ size; orgasm; pederasty; perversion; prostitution; religion; science; sex education; sexual intercourse; shame; sodomy; unrequited love; virginity; voyeurism; zoophilia. Doubtless I could have come up with many more. But I was eventually persuaded that a chronological approach would best serve my purpose.

The point of this book is not simply to provide the reader with pleasure (although it would be sad if it failed in this respect), nor to present a self-help guide to ways in which sexual pleasure can be experienced (although most of the extracts give more than the odd clue). A chronological ordering enables the reader to learn the ways in which, synchronically, across different cultures during a certain epoch the genre has been defined and how, diachronically, it has developed and become redefined over the years.

In the introductions to each epoch I could only hope to give the broadest of indications as to the context in which the selected extracts have been written and read. I am also very much aware that the extracts themselves can give only the most tantalizing of invitations to the reader to delve further. In any anthology, whatever the subject, be it literary references to tap-dancing, taxidermy, or toe-sucking (the colloquial term for which, incidentally, is 'shrimping'), there will always be a sense of *interruptus* as an extract comes to an abrupt end. This became glaringly obvious as I slashed through passages of erotica which may or may not have been intended to arouse sexual desire in the reader. With some writers it seemed almost not to matter much where the passage I selected began or ended (de Sade, for example). But with some of the long passages or poems, cutting them down proved to be both impossible and unbearable (Thomas Nashe's 'Choise of Valentines' from the sixteenth century and Christina Rossetti's 'Goblin Market' from the nineteenth, in particular), so in the interests of producing an anthology that covered as wide a spread as possible, I left them out altogether. I decided not to introduce each extract with a short précis of 'the story so far', as some anthologists elect to do; this always seems to me to be unsatisfactory and just a little absurd.

So, in my defence, I can say only this: the reason for including each of the selections in this book is that someone, somewhere, at some time has found them, or the activity described, to be erotic. Finally, almost two years of my life would have been unbearable had I not discovered that many writers clearly believe love, sexual desire and the imagination to be compatible. For me, that triangle, like the shape of Eros's bow when the arrow is drawn, involving the heart and the mind as well as the genitalia, constitutes the erotic.

Sources

Myths abound about the difficulties of getting access to erotic literature. In fact, it is not a problem for anyone showing a serious interest. The basis of the British Museum collection in London was the bequest of 15,229 books from the leading Victorian erotophile, Henry Ashbee, who used the pseudonym 'Pisanus Fraxi' – an anagram of the Greek *fraxinus*, meaning 'ash tree', of *apis* meaning 'bee', and a scatological pun ('piss', 'anus'). Ashbee's three-volume erotic bibliography is a stunning blend of scholarship and idiosyncratic comment. It was updated in 1936 in the *Register Librorum Eroticorum* by 'Rolfe S. Reade' (actually Alfred Rose), who drew upon a wide variety of previously published bibliographies of erotica from several countries. It is available in several public libraries in the UK and the USA.

Until fairly recently the British Museum stored its 20,000 volumes of erotica in what is known as the Private Case. These were excluded from the main catalogue, making it impossible for any but the most determined and knowledgeable of scholars to call them up. The key to gaining access was a book by Patrick Kearney entitled *A Guide to the Private Case* (1981). Today, access is relatively simple. Kearney's book is on the librarian's desk, new titles are now automatically catalogued, and old titles are slowly being transferred. Once the books are delivered (some are now on microfiche) the reader has to promise faithfully to use only a pencil or word processor, and to sit at a specially designated table under the eye of the librarians. This arrangement is not, as some readers have fantasized, to protect the atmosphere of the library from the pollution of self-abusing pornophiles but rather to protect the precious volumes; erotica attracts a greater number of thieves and graffiti artists than most other literary genres.

The largest collection of erotica in the world is held in the Vatican Library in Rome, which has over 25,000 volumes. The largest American collection was started by the sexologist Dr Alfred C. Kinsey and is now held at the Institute for Sex Research at the University of Indiana, Bloomington. The 15,000-volume collection known as 'Delta' (the Greek symbol for 'woman') at the Library of Congress, Washington, is based on material confiscated by the Post Office and Customs, which makes one grateful to the nineteenth-century prude and censor, Anthony Comstock. The large public collection in Europe, known as 'L'Enfer' (Hell) at the Bibliothèque Nationale in Paris, was begun under Napoleon; one of the three co-authors of its bibliography, compiled in 1913, was the erotic poet Guillaume Apollinaire.

ANCIENT
WORLD

From *Postures* Marlantonio Raimondi

Sumerian, Egyptian and Hebrew Literature

In 1951, while working in the Istanbul Museum of the Ancient Orient, Sumerian expert Samuel Noah Kramer came across a small tablet of cuneiform script. His description of the awe, tenderness and excitement he felt as he realized what he had found read like the beginning of a love affair:

> 'When I first laid eyes on it, its most attractive feature was its state of preservation. I soon realized that I was reading a poem . . . which celebrated beauty and love, a joyous bride and a King named Shu-Sin . . . As I read it again, and yet again, there was no mistaking its content. What I held in my hand was one of the oldest love songs written down by the hand of man.'

(History Begins at Sumer, 1958)

Kramer was to unearth yet more riches, but none more powerfully erotic than the clay tablets which revealed the story of the goddess Inanna. These were inscribed sometime around 1750 BC, but parts may be much older. The section known as 'The Courtship of Inanna and Dumuzi' (see page 30) begins with the sexual awakening of Inanna by her brother, the sun god Utu: 'Brother, after you've brought my bridal sheet to me, who will go to bed with me?' She is at first appalled by his choice of the shepherd Dumuzi and angrily expresses her preference for a farmer. At first the couple argue but when Dumuzi likens himself to Inanna's beloved brother, her desire for him is at last aroused. Their lovemaking is described in richly erotic imagery; to press one's neck close to another, to put one's hand on another's and to embrace are all Sumerian expressions for making love.

The poetry from the New Kingdom period of ancient Egypt (*c.*1570–1085 BC) is the earliest surviving example of secular love poetry. Its erotic imagery, which does not greatly differ from that of the earlier religious poetry of ancient Sumer, recurs in erotic literature from many different cultures throughout history. The image of the vagina as a luscious fruit was also a favourite of the ancient Greeks, notably Sappho (see page 38) and Diodorus Zonas, and is also at the very heart of the Biblical story of Adam and Eve. In the twentieth century this same image can be found in D.H. Lawrence's 'Figs' (see page 302). Another image of the vagina – as a trap in which the penis is caught like a fish or bird, with its implicit connotations of castration – appears in countless medieval Chinese erotic poems.

In one Ancient Egyptian fragment, feminine erotic sensibility finds first expression: 'How sweet it is to enter the lotus pond to do as you desire, to plunge into the water and bathe before you, to let you admire my beauty with my dress of sheerest royal linen all wet and clinging and perfumed with balsam. I join you in the water and catch a red fish which lies quivering and splendid in my fingers.' The power of delicate, rich clothing on the female body to arouse male sexual desire is a constant theme in Oriental erotic literature (see *The Confessions of Lady Nijō*, page 101). Although it did nothing for English Renaissance poet Robert Herrick (see page 156), modern-day organizers of Wet T-Shirt competitions presumably have some inkling of what this unknown ancient Egyptian female poet meant.

'The Song of Songs' (or 'Song of Solomon') is, perhaps, the best known, and certainly one of the most beautiful erotic love poems ever written (see page 40). Although its author is unknown, there is no reason to suppose it could have been the licentious King Solomon of Israel (*c.* 1015–977 BC) who is mentioned as the lover. Some historians believe it to be an ancient liturgy of a fertility cult, others a secular love song written by an educated man of high rank with some knowledge of the Persian court. It may have been written before 450 BC, perhaps during the reign of Atartaxerxes II (404–359 BC). However, scholars who believe the poem describes the relationship of Yahweh and Israel date it to the second half of the fifth century BC. If, as is most likely, the book is composed of several love lyrics, the folk songs of a poetic pastoral people, it may be considerably older.

That this manifestly erotic account of physical love between two lovers before and after their marriage, with no mention of God, should be included in the Old Testament has long puzzled theologians. The English feminist historian Marina Warner explains how it was justified:

> 'Because first Yahweh and then Christ appear as bridegrooms, and because the Virgin was identified with the Church, the bride of Christ, it was possible for rabbinical fathers to read the passionate poetry of "The Song of Songs" as an allegory of God's love, and for later Christian exegetes to identify the lover of the Song with Christ and his beloved with the Church, each Christian soul, and the Virgin Mary. From the point of view of Western literature, this was a fateful and fortunate decision; but it remains astonishing that an ascetic religion should have included in its sacred canon a text so remarkable for its undisguised sexuality.'

> (*Alone of All Her Sex*, 1976)

Ancient Greece

The erotic imagery in the earliest surviving literature of ancient Greece is altogether more prosaic than anything in the earlier Sumerian, Egyptian and Hebrew poetry. Homer's most common expression for sexual intercourse is 'to be united in love', which he uses of friendship as well as of love-making. The only mention of sexual desire in the *Odyssey* (850–800 BC) is where Penelope, adorned by Athena, parades before her would-be suitors: 'And thereupon their knees were loosened and their hearts were enchanted with love [*eros*], and they all prayed to lie in bed with her.' The metaphor is put to infinitely more powerful use by Alcman two centuries later (see page 38).

Homer's strongest erotic passage (see page 36) comes as a lull between battle scenes in the

Leda and the Swan Fiorentino Rosso

Iliad (*c.* 700 BC) where Hera, ever anxious to support the Greek army, decides to divert the attention of her husband Zeus from the fighting by seducing him. When the two divinities finally mate, Homer writes with a sensuousness that remained unequalled until the time of Sappho one hundred years later. The intercutting of scenes of sex and violence – a device also employed in medieval Arthurian romances, perhaps nowhere more effectively than in *Sir Gawain and the Green Knight* (see page 107) – is clearly not the invention of twentieth-century producers of 'slice 'n dice' movies, which deliberately set out to excite sexual arousal by closely associating sex with violence.

When Hesiod (eighth century BC) describes the creation of woman in *Works and Days*, we learn of Zeus's specifications: 'He told golden Aphrodite to pour attractiveness over her head and cruel longing for her and cares that devour the limbs.' It was this painful longing and these cares that the Greek lyric poets such as Archilochus (see page 37) made their concern. Unlike the surviving work of earlier writers, Archilochus called upon his own experiences for his material. He expresses for the first time what it feels like to be the victim of erotic desire: 'Wretched I lie, lifeless, pierced through the bones by grievous pains.' The imagery is from war; the lover is a dead soldier pierced by a spear. The penetrating pain pre-echoes Cupid's darts, the spear and thorns in Christ's body as erotically experienced by medieval women mystics and, in the twentieth century, the infibulation of O's labia in *The Story of O* (see page 316), and the razor-like activities of a credit card on the naked bodies of two women in Bret Easton Ellis's *American Psycho* (1991). Eros, god of love, and Thanatos, god of death, have long been close companions in the history of erotic literature.

Plato (*c.* 427–347 BC) rated the woman poet Sappho so highly that he referred to her as 'the tenth muse', but within a few centuries of her death Sappho's name was surrounded by scandal. Tales of her suicide leap into the sea from the Leucadian rock because of her unrequited love for the ferryman, Phaon, were a later androcentric, homophobic invention, as was the allegation that she was a prostitute. Debate about her sexual preference has at times tended to obscure appreciation of her poetry. As a woman writing about both women and sexuality, Sappho violated patriarchal rules that demand silence from women in the public (male) sphere and insist a woman's sexuality must be defined by her father or husband.

With one certain and one possible exception, Sappho's reputation rests on mere fragments. But lines of considerable erotic impact emerge from her remarkable use of language, including alliteration, the poetic stanza form (which came to be named after her), and the care she took over the use of consonants. In the one positively attributed full poem that exists, she completely avoids the hard consonant *b* and plays with the liquid *l*, *m* and *n*. All conspire to deliver lines of considerable erotic impact.

Portraying the erotic impulse as an assault both mental and physical, Sappho was the first to express the oxymoronic notion of 'bitter-sweet'. Homer had used the less complex 'sweet longing,' which was to echo down the ages until, perhaps, the twentieth century, when sexual continence became a relatively rare event in erotic literature. To the ancient Greeks, however, this oxymoron meant that when Eros stirs the senses, decision is impossible, action a paradox, and love and hate converge all too easily. 'I'm in love! I'm not in love!/I'm crazy!

I'm not crazy!' writes a bewildered Anacreon in the late sixth century BC. 'When I look at Diophantos, new shoot among the young men, I can neither flee nor stay,' despairs an anonymous poet in *The Greek Anthology* (compiled in the tenth century AD). But one of the most startling descriptions of the exquisite pain and havoc wreaked by Eros comes from Sophocles in a fragment of 'The Lovers of Achilles' (see page 39) written in the fifth century BC.

The eroticism of the early Greek lyric poets suffered a decline as the form itself was used in choral works where the required themes permitted little of the erotic impulse. In the fifth century this impulse emerged most strongly in the dramatists of the period. Fragments of a lost fifth-century BC play by Aeschylus, for example, treat Achilles and Patroclus as homosexual lovers. The erotic content of Sophocles's *King Oedipus* and *Electra* written in the fifth century BC was appreciated long before it was (re)discovered by Freud. The disastrous aspect of Eros, when love and hatred become closely intertwined, was made bleakly clear in the *Medea* (fifth century BC) of Euripides. But in the comedies of Aristophanes fresh life is breathed into Eros. Athenian comedy was astonishingly wide in its range – from low lyrics and high comedy, through knockabout farce and obscenity to vulgar jokes.

The Greek Anthology comprises two collections of epigrams drawn from all over the Greek-speaking world, ranging from the seventh century BC through to the renaissance of Greek culture in Byzantium in the sixth century. Many of the epigrams are sexually explicit and misogynistic. Although the majority are heterosexual, it is clear from the male homosexual epigrams that while the Greeks had no word for 'homosexual', there was widespread acceptance of the fact that men might be either straight or gay or both. Poets like Strato (see page 56), Automedon (see page 43), and Meleager (see page 43) all wrote of both male heterosexual and homosexual desire.

The homoerotic literature of ancient Greece reveals that there were, however, some prescriptions concerning certain forms of male homosexual love and love-making. The legitimate, socially acceptable form involved a man and a youth – the *erastes* and the *eromenos* respectively. As boys (along with women, slaves and foreigners) did not qualify for citizen status, the relationship was definitely not one between equals. The Greeks believed that while an active male homosexual role was natural, adult males have no inherent desire to be the passive partner; for a man to allow himself to be sodomized was the extreme expression of passivity and could be punished by the withdrawal of citizenship.

Also to be found in *The Greek Anthology* are examples of pornography in its literal and value-free sense of 'writing about prostitutes'. Automedon's 'Turkish belly-dancer' (see page 43) may, in fact, have been an entertainer, putting her a couple of notches above the *pornoi* – slaves who worked in brothels and who lacked status even among other prostitutes. At the top of the prostitutional hierarchy was the *hetaera*, literally 'companion', the Greek equivalent of a courtesan. Asklepiades, whose epigrams combined the themes of the love elegy and the bawdy drinking song and transformed the epigram into a vehicle for personal poetry, was no stranger to the world of the *pornoi*. His 'devil Hermione' may be a married woman (and therefore 'respectable'), but Dorkion seems to possess the street wisdom of a 'working girl' (see page 39).

The erotic poetry and drama of ancient Greece was largely a male preserve with women competing with beautiful young men as the objects of affection (or, on occasions, hatred; see 'To A Randy Old Woman', page 47). Sappho, of course, stands out as a remarkable exception to this rule although there were others. Women writers chose their own themes – often focusing on love which to Nossis, the third-century poet from Locri, was the greatest good: 'Nothing is sweeter than love, all other blessings/Come second to it. I have spat even honey/From my mouth . . .' Elephantis and Philaenis are thought to have written erotic poetry and prose in the same century. Although nothing survives of Elephantis's work she is reputed to have written in explicit detail about nine positions for sexual intercourse. A few fragments of erotic prose, possibly in diary form, survive of Philaenis, who is thought to have come from Samos, an island renowned for its female prostitutes. The first-century Greek poet Meleager, author of some exquisite erotic epigrams, described the female poets of ancient Greece as 'few flowers, but these few, roses'.

Ancient Rome

Latin erotic literature, which dates back to Laevius's *Erotopaegnion* and the Fescinnine verses of Ennius (*c.* 329–169 BC) of whose works virtually nothing survives, tends to lack the joy and intensity of feeling that characterized the erotica of ancient Greece. It tipped towards the light-hearted, the amusing and the bawdy. By the end of the Empire erotic literature was recognized as having a purpose beyond its religious or literary value. In the second century, for example, Suetonius records that Emperor Tiberius (42 BC – AD 37) at his luxurious retreat on Capri 'had several chambers set around with pictures and statues in the most lascivious attitudes, and furnished with the books of Elephantis, that none might want a pattern for the execution of any lewd project that was prescribed to him'.

Influenced by the Greeks and by the Etruscans of several centuries earlier, phallus-worship in which sexuality was linked with the cult of the fertility gods, was an important part of Roman religion and a constant subject for writers and artists. The Romans came to see the phallus as a powerful talisman against the evil eye, as the mosaics, stone carvings, wall paintings and amulets found at Pompeii testify. A collection of first-century epigrams known as the *Priapeia* affixed to the statues of the god Priapus suggest that not all Romans took the cult completely seriously. According to the privately printed English edition of 1890, these epigrams are '*Facetiae* . . . the collective work of a group of *beaux esprits* who formed a reunion at the house of Macceus, the well-known patron of Horace, who amused themselves – Martial, Petronius, and others, possibly Catullus, Tibullus, Cinna and Anser' (see page 44).

Lucretius, however, took religion and erotic desire seriously. In his major work, *De Rerum Natura* (see page 41), he aspired to popularize the theories of the Greek philosophers Democritus (fifth century BC) and Epicurus (*c.* 341–270 BC) in order to attack conservative religious belief. Central to his erotic ideal is the Venus of procreation, not the Venus of pleasure – although, Dryden's seventeenth-century translation magnificently reveals the erotic pleasure in the text (see page 169). Lucretius's erotic sensibility was to prove unacceptable to the fourth-century ascetic St Jerome (see page 78), whose counter-attack was based on the claim that Lucretius committed suicide after being driven mad by a love potion administered, according to the nineteenth-century English poet Alfred Tennyson, by his wife. In the twentieth century, however, Lucretius received high acclaim from atheist revolutionaries: in Russia he was assimilated into Marxist theory; in France he was the only Latin poet in an anthology entitled *Les Classiques du peuple.*

Before Catullus (*c.* 84–54 BC), colloquialism in Latin poetry had been largely confined to comedy and satire, but with great originality and daring Catullus personalized the Roman love epigram by using direct, often coarse, language on erotic subjects ranging from pederasty to incest. He has been greatly admired, censured and censored for this by moralists ever since. If Catullus could write bluntly about sex, he could also infuse his verse with an intimacy and profound understanding of the complexity of desire. His celebrated literary treatment of the kiss, 'Vivamus, mea Lesbia . . .' (see page 44), was to exert great fascination on subsequent erotic poets, who continually translated and imitated it. Across the centuries these have included Louise Labé (see page 124), Johannes Secundus (see page 124), Robert Herrick ('To Anthea'), Ben Jonson (see page 154), Lord Byron ('Oh! might I kiss those eyes of fire . . .'), and the nineteenth-century erotophile Sir Richard Burton. Much of Catullus's verse was devoted to the married Clodia Metelli or 'Lesbia', the obsessional love of his life. Perhaps more than any of the other great Latin poets, his writing was imbued with passion and, at times, hatred: 'I hate and I love. And if you ask me how, I do not know: I only feel it, and I'm torn in two.' Sappho would have understood.

Horace, widely considered a master of satire and irony in the Augustan (or Golden) Age of Latin literature in the first century BC, took the personalization of poetry and the colloquial mode a step further than Catullus. His series of *Epodes*, a genre of slight but vitriolic attacks on individuals first introduced by Archilochus, form an amorous autobiography, recording a succession of mistresses and several boys. Disgust towards the sexually active older woman and impotence – two common themes in Latin erotic poetry – are combined in one particularly brutal epigram (see page 46). Hell clearly knows of a fury greater than that of a woman scorned: it is a man scorned by too few inches of his own erectile tissue.

In his first-century BC epic poem the *Aeneid*, Virgil treats the scorned, abandoned woman infinitely more kindly. Virgil's description of Dido's passionate love for Aeneas, which culminates in betrayal (see page 45), has a sweetly gentle and insistent eroticism tinged by pathos. Shakespeare was to treat a similarly betrayed and abandoned Venus much more cruelly (see page 137).

The foremost erotic poet of the next period was Ovid, whose wicked mixture of humour, sensuality and explicit sex, barely disguised by a (mock) didacticism, made him hugely popular in pagan Rome, but did not endear him to the early Christian fathers. Interest in him revived in the eleventh century – both Chaucer and Boccaccio borrowed shamelessly from him – and later no self-respecting Renaissance poet could remain unenthusiastic. The late sixteenth and early seventeenth centuries were England's 'Ovidian Age'; the erotic poems of Thomas Lodge, Christopher Marlowe, William Shakespeare and others were all indebted to him, and echoes of his lines can even be found in Milton.

Unlike his contemporary Propertius, who could write of mutual love between woman and man (see page 47), Ovid, in *Amores* (see page 48) and *Ars Amatoria*, reveals himself to be a man for whom women are fundamentally sexual objects and preoccupied to the point of obsession with priapic functionalism. 'Take away the high poetic finish, the sophisticated wit, the brilliant instinct for parody,' writes Peter Green, 'and what remains, far less coarsely expressed, is, in essence, the attitude of Henry Miller as formulated in his *Tropic* novels: women . . . reduced to their ultimate vaginal function – or as mere grit in the poetic oyster' (*Ovid: The Erotic Poems*, 1982).

Ovid's *Metamorphoses*, however, are written in a different strain (see page 50). The love story of Echo and Narcissus has a liquid eroticism which made it one of the most popular classics in medieval times. The erotic possibilities of metamorphosis fascinated the Roman poets, as it had the ancient Greeks, whose gods similarly transmogrified into different forms, and the fascination extended to poets in subsequent epochs. Later, in the second century towards the end of the Roman Empire, Apuleius used this idea to satirical purpose in *Metamorphoses* (otherwise known as *The Golden Ass*) to attack corruption among the priests and bogus doctors of his day. In the fourteenth century, attracted by its carnal explicitness, most of which is based on the assumption that no woman's virtue is unassailable, Boccaccio personally transcribed *The Golden Ass* with his own hand and borrowed three stories from it for the *Decameron* (see page 104), while others appeared in the sixteenth-century French erotic text *Les Cent nouvelles nouvelles* (see page 111) and elsewhere. But of all the tales within *The Golden Ass*, that of Cupid and Psyche is one of the masterpieces of erotic literature (see page 57).

Apuleius borrowed one of his tales, a sardonic caricature of a society seeking an escape from boredom in debauchery, from Petronius's *The Satyricon*, written in the first century. Both texts are regarded as the forerunners of the picaresque tradition, which was to culminate in the amorous adventures of *Tom Jones* (1749) in the eighteenth century. Surviving only in fragment form, *The Satyricon* is a comic account of how Priapus takes his revenge on two male homosexuals who have offended him by making them impotent. It too was a source that future erotic writers were to delight in and plunder. The story on page 53 appears to have originated in China, and then been imported into Greece from Syria; it was later retold by three giants of French erotic literature – Pierre de Bourdeille, La Fontaine and Voltaire. Put to a somewhat different purpose, it also appeared in Bishop Jeremy Taylor's *The Rule and Exercises of Holy Dying*, a popular English seventeenth-century book of piety.

Coming at the end of this period was *Daphnis and Chloe* by Longus (*fl.* third century AD), possibly a Roman who wrote in Greek. Distinguished by its pastoral character, *Daphnis and Chloe* was described many centuries later by Goethe as 'a masterpiece . . . in which Understanding, Art and Taste appear at their highest point, and beside which the good Virgil retreats somewhat into the background'. However, in the nineteenth century, Elizabeth Barrett Browning's otherwise unconventional heroine Aurora Leigh dismissed it as an 'obscene text'. *Daphnis and Chloe* belongs to a group of love stories written in the late second or early third century known as the *Erotici Graeci*. This important collection includes stories by Heliodorus, whose *Aethiopica* influenced Sir Philip Sidney's *Arcadia*, Xenophon of Ephesus, and possibly the author of the conjectural Greek original of the Latin *Apollonius of Tyre*, the earliest source of Shakespeare's *Pericles*.

The later years of the Roman Empire were characterized by an increasing debauchery and licentiousness, particularly during the reigns of Tiberius, Caligula, Nero and Domitian. The moral atmosphere was criticized by Martial, Juvenal and Petronius among others. Subsequent moralists pointed accusing fingers at the Romans' free attitude towards sexuality as the cause of the eventual break-up of the Empire. This view conveniently ignores the fact that such debauchery was merely symptomatic of the political and economic chaos that brought the Roman Empire to an end.

To the ancient Greeks, Eros had been a deity invested with great power. As Sophocles wrote in *Antigone*: 'Invincible Eros, you swoop down on our flocks and watch, ever alert, over the fresh faces of our maidens; you float above the waves and across the countryside where the wild beasts lie. Among the gods and mortals, no one can escape you. Whoever touches you is at once thrown into delirium.' But a certain taming of Eros becomes discernible as the ancient Greek civilization progressed: in the art of the first classical era Eros is a beautiful young man with a slim and perfectly proportioned body; in the art and literature of the later Hellenistic and Roman periods he has become a chubby infant. An anonymous Byzantine (*c.* 500–600) epigram found on a small bath and included in *The Greek Anthology* cuts the once powerful god down to size: 'Do not ridicule the small./Little things can charm us all./Eros was not big at all.'

By the end of the Roman Empire, Amor, the great and sacred god with all-consuming bittersweet powers was replaced by a prank-playing small boy, as described by Apuleius in *The Golden Ass*: 'She [Venus] at once called her winged son Cupid, that very wicked boy with neither manners nor respect for the decencies, who spends his time running from building to building all night long with his torch and his arrows, breaking up everyone's marriage. Somehow he never gets punished for all the harm he does, though he never seems to do anything good in compensation.' In phallocentric ancient Rome an increasingly jokey Priapus, no longer a 'great god' with a mysterious religious cult, but a domesticated and frequently unreliable lord of lust, had been allowed to usurp Eros.

Anon. (Sumeria)

*Poem recited by the annual brides of King Shu-Sin (c. 4000 BC).
Trans. Samuel Noah Kramer*

Bridegroom, dear to my heart,
Goodly is your beauty, honeysweet,
Lion, dear to my heart,
Goodly is your beauty, honeysweet.

You have captivated me, let me stand tremblingly before you.
Bridegroom, I would be taken by you to the bedchamber,
You have captivated me, let me stand tremblingly before you.
Lion, I would be taken by you to the bedchamber.

Bridegroom, let me caress you,
My precious caress is more savoury than honey,
In the bedchamber, honey-filled,
Let me enjoy your goodly beauty,
Lion, let me caress you,
My precious caress is more savoury than honey.

Bridegroom, you have taken your pleasure of me,
Tell my mother, she will give you delicacies,
My father, he will give you gifts.

Your spirit, I know where to cheer your spirit,
Bridegroom, sleep in our house until dawn,
Your heart, I know where to gladden your heart,
Lion, sleep in our house until dawn.

You, because you love me,
Give me pray of your caresses,
My lord god, my lord protector,

My Shu-Sin, who gladdens Enlil's heart,
Give me pray of your caresses.

Your place goodly as honey, pray lay (your) hand on it,
Bring (your) hand over like a *gishban*-garment,
Cup (your) hand over it like a *gishban-sikin*-garment.

Anon. (Sumeria)

From **'The Courtship of Inanna and Dumuzi'** (*c.* 4000–*c.* 2000 BC).
Trans. Diane Wolkstein

> The word they had spoken
> Was a word of desire.
> From the starting of the quarrel
> Came the lovers' desire.

The shepherd went to the royal house with cream.
Dumuzi went to the royal house with milk.
Before the door, he called out:
> 'Open the house, My Lady, open the house!'

Inanna ran to Ningal, the mother who bore her.
Ningal counseled her daughter, saying:
> 'My child, the young man will be your father.
> My daughter, the young man will be your mother.
> He will treat you like a father.
> He will care for you like a mother.
> Open the house, My Lady, open the house!'

Inanna, at her mother's command,
Bathed and anointed herself with scented oil.
She covered her body with the royal white robe.
She readied her dowry.
She arranged her precious lapis beads around her neck.
She took her seal in her hand.

Dumuzi waited expectantly.

Inanna opened the door for him.
Inside the house she shone before him
Like the light of the moon.

Dumuzi looked at her joyously.
He pressed his neck close against hers.
He kissed her.

Carving at Khajuraho, India

Inanna spoke:
   'What I tell you
   Let the singer weave into song.
   What I tell you,
   Let it flow from ear to mouth,
   Let it pass from old to young:

   My vulva, the horn,
   The Boat of Heaven,
   Is full of eagerness like the young moon.
   My untilled land lies fallow.

   As for me, Inanna,
   Who will plough my vulva?
   Who will plough my high field?
   Who will plough my wet ground?

   As for me, the young woman,
   Who will plough my vulva?
   Who will station the ox there?
   Who will plough my vulva?'

Dumuzi replied:
   'Great Lady, the king will plough your vulva.
   I, Dumuzi the King, will plough your vulva.'

Inanna:
   'Then plough my vulva, man of my heart!
   Plough my vulva!'

At the king's lap stood the rising cedar.
Plants grew high by their side.

Inanna sang:
   'He has sprouted; he has burgeoned;
   He is lettuce planted by the water.
   He is the one my womb loves best.

   My well-stocked garden of the plain,
   My barley growing high in its furrow,
   My apple tree which bears fruit up to its crown,
   He is lettuce planted by the water.

   My honey-man, my honey-man sweetens me always.
   My lord, the honey-man of the gods,
   He is the one my womb loves best.
   His hand is honey, his foot is honey,
   He sweetens me always.

My eager impetuous caresser of the navel,
My caresser of the soft thighs,
He is the one my womb loves best,
He is lettuce planted by the water.'

Dumuzi sang:
'O Lady, your breast is your field.
Inanna, your breast is your field.
Your broad field pours out plants.
Your broad field pours out grain.
Water flows from on high for your servant.
Bread flows from on high for your servant.
Pour it out for me, Inanna.
I will drink all you offer.'

Inanna sang:
'Make your milk sweet and thick, my bridegroom.
My shepherd, I will drink your fresh milk.
Wild bull, Dumuzi, make your milk sweet and thick.
I will drink your fresh milk.

Let the milk of the goat flow in my sheepfold.
Fill my holy churn with honey cheese.
Lord Dumuzi, I will drink your fresh milk.

My husband, I will guard my sheepfold for you.
I will watch over your house of life, the storehouse,
The shining quivering place which delights Sumer –
The house which decides the fates of the land,
The house which gives the breath of life to the people.
I, the queen of the palace, will watch over your house.'

Dumuzi spoke:
'My sister, I would go with you to my garden.
Inanna, I would go with you to my garden.
I would go with you to my orchard.
I would go with you to my apple tree.
There I would plant the sweet, honey-covered seed.'

Inanna spoke:
'He brought me into his garden.
My brother, Dumuzi, brought me into his garden.
I strolled with him among the standing trees,
I stood with him among the fallen trees,
By an apple tree I knelt as is proper.

Before my brother coming in song,
Who rose to me out of the poplar leaves,
Who came to me in the midday heat,
Before my lord Dumuzi,
I poured out plants from my womb.
I placed plants before him,
I poured out plants before him.
I placed grain before him,
I poured out grain before him.
I poured out grain from my womb.'

Inanna sang:
'Last night as I, the queen, was shining bright,
Last night as I, the Queen of Heaven, was shining bright,
As I was shining bright and dancing,
Singing praises at the coming of the night –

He met me – he met me!
My lord Dumuzi met me.
He put his hand into my hand.
He pressed his neck close against mine.

My high priest is ready for the holy loins.
My lord Dumuzi is ready for the holy loins.
The plants and herbs in his field are ripe.
O Dumuzi! Your fullness is my delight!'

She called for it, she called for it, she called for the bed!
She called for the bed that rejoices the heart.
She called for the bed that sweetens the loins.
She called for the bed of kingship.
She called for the bed of queenship.
Inanna called for the bed:
'Let the bed that rejoices the heart be prepared!
Let the bed that sweetens the loins be prepared!
Let the bed of kingship be prepared!
Let the bed of queenship be prepared!
Let the royal bed be prepared!'

Inanna spread the bridal sheet across the bed.
She called to the king:
'The bed is ready!'
She called to her bridegroom:
'The bed is waiting!'

He put his hand in her hand.
He put his hand to her heart.
Sweet is the sleep of hand-to-hand.
Sweeter still the sleep of heart-to-heart.

Inanna spoke:
  'I bathed for the wild bull,
  I bathed for the shepherd Dumuzi,
  I perfumed my sides with ointment,
  I coated my mouth with sweet-smelling amber,
  I painted my eyes with kohl.

  He shaped my loins with his fair hands,
  The shepherd Dumuzi filled my lap with cream and milk,
  He stroked my pubic hair,
  He watered my womb.
  He laid his hands on my holy vulva,
  He smoothed my black boat with cream,
  He quickened my narrow boat with milk,
  He caressed me on the bed.

  Now I will caress my high priest on the bed,
  I will caress the faithful shepherd Dumuzi,
  I will caress his loins, the shepherdship of the land,
  I will decree a sweet fate for him.'

Anon. (Egypt)

From an Ancient Egyptian love lyric (c. 570–c. 1085 BC).
Trans. Joseph Kaster

I

Is there anything sweeter than this hour?
  for I am with you, and you lift up my heart –
  for is there not embracing and fondling when you visit me
  and we give ourselves up to delights?
  If you wish to caress my thigh,
  then I will offer you my breast also – it won't thrust you away!

Would you leave because you are hungry?
  – are you such a man of your belly?
Would you leave because you need something to wear?
  – I have a chestful of fine linen!

Would you leave because you wish something to drink?
  Here, take my breasts! They are full to overflowing, and
    all for you!

Glorious is the day of our embracings;
I treasure it a hundred thousand millions!

II

Your love has gone all through my body
   like honey in water,
   as a drug is mixed into spices,
   as water is mingled with wine.
Oh that you would speed to see your sister
   like a charger on the battlefield, like a bull to his pasture!
For the heavens are sending us love like a flame spreading through straw
   and desire like the swoop of the falcon!

Homer (Greece)

c. 850–c. 800 BC

Very little is known about the life of Homer, one of the finest of the Greek epic poets. Seven cities have claimed to be his birthplace, and there is some uncertainty about his biographical dates. By tradition he was a blind wandering minstrel and achieved legendary status as the supposed author of the Iliad *and* Odyssey. *Although the origins of these poems are now disputed (they are now generally believed to be the work of a number of oral poets of the time), their influence on Western literature remains profound.*

From the **Iliad**, Book XIV (*c.* 700 BC). *Trans. E.V. Rieu*

Now Here of the Golden Throne, looking out from where she stood on the summit of Olympus, was quick to observe two things. She saw how Poseidon, who was both her Brother and her Brother-in-law, was bustling about on the field of battle, and she rejoiced. But she also saw Zeus sitting on the topmost peak of Ida of the many springs; and this sight filled the ox-eyed Lady Here with disgust. She began to wonder how she could bemuse the wits of aegis-bearing Zeus; and she decided that the best way to go about the business was this. She would deck herself out to full advantage and visit him on the mountain. If he succumbed to her beauty, as well might be, and wished to fold her in his arms, she would benumb his busy brain and close his eyes in a soothing and forgetful sleep. Accordingly, she made her way to the bedroom that had been built for her by her own Son Hephaestus, who had fitted the stout doors, when he hung them on their posts, with a secret lock which no other god could open. Here went in and closed the polished doors behind her. She began by removing every stain from her comely body with ambrosia, and anointing herself with the delicious and imperishable olive-oil she used. It was perfumed and had only to be stirred in the Palace of the Bronze Floor for its scent to spread through heaven and earth. With this she rubbed her lovely skin; then she combed her hair, and with her own hands plaited her shining locks and let them fall in their divine beauty from her immortal head. Next she put on a fragrant robe of delicate material that Athene with her skilful hands had made for her and lavishly embroidered. She fastened it over her breast with golden clasps and, at her waist, with a girdle from which a hundred tassels hung. In the pierced lobes of her ears she fixed two earrings, each a thing of lambent beauty with its cluster of three drops. She covered her head with a beautiful new headdress, which was as bright as the sun; and last of all, the Lady goddess bound a fine pair of sandals on her shimmering feet.

.   .   .

'Here,' said the Cloud-gatherer Zeus, 'that is a journey you may well postpone. Today, let us enjoy the delights of love. Never has such desire, for goddess or woman, flooded and overwhelmed my heart; not even when I loved Ixion's wife, who bore Peirithous to rival the gods in wisdom; or Danaë of the slim ankles, the daughter of Acrisius, who gave birth to Perseus, the greatest hero of his time; or the far-famed daughter of Phoenix, who bore me Minos and the godlike Rhadamanthus; or Semele, or Alcmene in Thebes, whose son was the lion-hearted Heracles, while Semele bore Dionysus to give pleasure to mankind; or Demeter Queen of the Lovely Locks, or the incomparable Leto; or when I fell in love with you yourself – never have I felt such love, such sweet desire, as fills me now for you.'

'Dread Son of Cronos, you amaze me,' said the Lady Here, still dissembling. 'Suppose we do as you wish and lie down in each other's arms on the heights of Ida where there is no privacy whatever, what will happen if one of the eternal gods sees us asleep together and runs off to tell the rest? I certainly do not relish the idea of rising from such a bed and going back to your palace. Think of the scandal there would be. No, if it is really your pleasure to do this thing, you have a bedroom that your own Son Hephaestus built for you, and the doors he made for it are solid. Let us go and lie down there, if that is what you wish to do.'

'Here,' said Zeus the Cloud-compeller, 'you need not be afraid that any god or man will see us. I shall hide you in a golden cloud too thick for that. Even the Sun, whose rays provide him with the keenest sight in all the world, will not see us through the mist.'

As he spoke, the Son of Cronos took his Wife in his arms; and the gracious earth sent up fresh grass beneath them, dewy lotus and crocuses, and a soft and crowded bed of hyacinths, to lift them off the ground. In this they lay, covered by a beautiful golden cloud, from which a rain of glistening dewdrops fell.

Archilochus (Greece)

c. 680–*c.* 640 BC

Born in Paros, the illegitimate son of a slave woman and an aristocrat, Archilochus is regarded by many as the first poet of the Greek lyric age. He became famous among the Greeks for his vituperative satires and anti-heroic opinions and, although only a few fragments of his work survive, is generally hailed as a genius. A mercenary soldier, he died in battle.

From **'The Seduction'**. *Trans. Kenneth McLeish*

I said, 'Be mine.'
She said, 'In mourning?
But can't you wait? Heart pounds?
There's someone else at home.
Longs for it, pretty, shy. Try her.'
I said, 'Daughter of noble Amphimedo

Who sleeps in the deeps of Earth,
God gives us pleasures, delights of youth,
Quite apart from the One Great Thing.
God willing, we'll marry, let's plan it,
No hurry, as soon as your mourning's done.
Tell me what you'd like. Here, in your garden,

Long grass beside the wall. Neoboule?
She's not for me. Her blooms have faded,
Grace gone, no self-control,
She's mad for it. Me, marry her?
He'd like that, him next door.
She's far too hot, too fond of men,
She'd puppy me weeks before their time.
To Hell with her! But you!
Pure, honest, chaste – it's you I want.'

That's what I said. Then I picked her up
And laid her gently down among the
        flowers.
I covered her, my cloak. I cupped her face.
No more tears. The frightened fawn lay still.
I stroked her breast, gently,
She showed me her sanctuary, untrodden.
I stroked her hair; I held her loveliness,
I gave her my brightness, my manhood.

Alcman (Greece)

fl. 620 BC

Alcman is regarded as the earliest known Greek lyric choral poet. Little is known of his life, except that he may have come from Sardis in Lydia, and that he lived in Sparta. His best-known work is the Parthenion – *a song to be sung by two choirs of women. Otherwise, only fragments survive.*

Fragment. Trans. David A. Campbell

. . . with limb-loosening desire; and her glances are more melting than sleep or death.

Sappho (Greece)

b. 612 BC

Sappho, one of the few female Greek lyric poets, was born in Lesbos of an aristocratic family. She wrote seven books of poetry, consisting mainly of love-songs and love poems, but little else is known of her life – the famous legend of her unrequited love for Phaon and subsequent suicide has never been verified. Her expressed affection for, and leading contribution to, a group of young women dedicated to the cult of the goddess Aphrodite is the origin of the word 'Sapphic'.

Fragments

Once again Love [Eros], the loosener of limbs, shakes me,
        that bitter-sweet, irresistible creature.

Trans. Josephine Balmer

That one seems to me to be like the gods, the man whosoever sits facing you and listens nearby to your sweet speech and desirable laughter – which surely terrifies the heart in my chest; for as I look briefly at you, so can I no longer speak at all, my tongue is silent, broken, a silken fire suddenly has spread beneath my skin, with my eyes I see nothing, my hearing hums, a cold sweat grips me, a trembling seizes me entire, more pale than grass am I, I seem to myself to be little short of dead. But everything is to be endured, since even a pauper . . .

Trans. John D. Winkler

. . . like the sweet-apple
turning red at the top of the highest branch
forgotten by the apple-gatherers – no,
not quite forgotten, for they could not reach so far . . .

Trans. Josephine Balmer

Asklepiades

fl. 270 BC

Born on Samos, Asklepiades was the leader of a group of contemporary epigrammatists. He was much admired for his expression and treatment of love elegies and drinking songs, and for transforming the epigram into an accessible form of poetry. About 40 epigrams survive although the authenticity of some is doubtful.

From **The Greek Anthology**, Books V and XII (compiled 10th century AD).
Trans. Kenneth McLeish

We were having fun, that devil Hermione
   and I.
Her belt! Embroidered with flowers;
Writing, all the way round, gold letters:
'Kiss me quick. No offence, but there's a
   queue.

(Book V)

Dorkion, sweet little tomboy,
Knows Cupid's every trick:
Arrows of desire – those eyes! –
Tiptilted cap, short shirt, no knickers . . .

(Book XII)

Sophocles (Greece)

c. 496–*c.* 405 BC

Sophocles is today acknowledged as one of the finest of Greek tragedians. Born at Colonnus, just outside Athens, he won distinction for writing dramas at an early age, first winning a prize for tragedy in 468 BC, when he defeated the then venerated Aeschylus. Although he wrote over 100 plays, only seven tragedies survive, the best-known of which is Oedipus the King. *An innovator in his art, Sophocles transformed tragedy by introducing a third actor on stage, thus increasing the complexity and importance of dialogue.*

From **'The Lovers of Achilles'**. *Trans. Anne Carson*

This disease is an evil bound upon the day.
Here's a comparison – not bad, I think:
when ice gleams in the open air,
children grab.
Ice-crystal in the hands is
at first a pleasure quite novel.

But there comes a point –
you can't put the melting mass down,
you can't keep holding it.
Desire is like that.
Pulling the lover to act and not to act,
again and again, pulling.

The Bible

From 'The Song of Solomon' ('Song of Songs'). (King James version, 1611)

CHAPTER 5

1 I am come into my garden, my sister, my spouse: I have gathered my myrrh with my spice; I have eaten my honeycomb with my honey; I have drunk my wine with my milk: eat, O friends; drink, yea, drink abundantly O beloved.

2 I sleep, but my heart waketh: it is the voice of my beloved that knocketh, saying, Open to me, my sister, my love, my dove, my undefiled: for my head is filled with dew, and my locks with the drops of the night.

3 I have put off my coat; how shall I put it on? I have washed my feet; how shall I defile them?

4 My beloved put in his hand by the hole of the door, and my bowels were moved for him.

5 I rose up to open to my beloved; and my hands dropped with myrrh, and my fingers with sweet smelling myrrh, upon the handles of the lock.

6 I opened to my beloved; but my beloved had withdrawn himself, and was gone: my soul failed when he spake: I sought him, but I could not find him; I called him, but he gave me no answer.

7 The watchmen that went about the city found me, they smote me, they wounded me: the keepers of the walls took away my veil from me.

8 I charge you, O daughters of Jerusalem, if ye find my beloved, that ye tell him, that I am sick of love.

9 What is thy beloved more than another beloved, O thou fairest among women? what is thy beloved more than another beloved, that thou dost so charge us?

10 My beloved is white and ruddy, the chiefest among ten thousand.

11 His head is as the most fine gold, his locks are bushy, and black as a raven.

12 His eyes are as the eyes of doves by the rivers of waters, washed with milk, and fitly set.

13 His cheeks are as a bed of spices, as sweet flowers: his lips like lilies, dropping sweet smelling myrrh.

14 His hands are as gold rings set with the beryl: his belly is as bright ivory overlaid with sapphires.

15 His legs are as pillars of marble, set upon sockets of fine gold: his countenance is as Lĕb'-ă-non, excellent as the cedars.

16 His mouth is most sweet: yea, he is altogether lovely. This is my beloved, and this is my friend, O daughters of Jerusalem.

CHAPTER 7

How beautiful are thy feet with shoes, O prince's daughter! the joints of thy thighs are like jewels, the work of the hands of a cunning workman.

2 Thy navel is like a round goblet, which wanteth not liquor: thy belly is like an heap of wheat se: about with lilies.

3 Thy two breasts are like two young roes that are twins.

4 Thy neck is as a tower of ivory; thine eyes like the fishpools in Hĕsh'-bŏn, by the gate of Băth-rĕb'-bim: thy nose is as the tower of Lĕb'-ă-non which looketh toward Damascus.

5 Thine head upon thee is like Carmel, and the hair of thine head like purple; the king is held in the galleries.

6 How fair and how pleasant art thou, O love, for delights!

7 This thy stature is like to a palm tree, and thy breasts to clusters of grapes.

8 I said, I will go up to the palm tree, I will take hold of the boughs thereof: now also thy breasts shall be as clusters of the vine, and the smell of thy nose like apples;

9 And the roof of thy mouth like the best wine for my beloved, that goeth down sweetly, causing the lips of those that are asleep to speak.

10 I am my beloved's, and his desire is toward me.

11 Come, my beloved, let us go forth into the field; let us lodge in the villages.

12 Let us get up early to the vineyards; let us see if the vine flourish, whether the tender grape appear, and the pomegranates bud forth: there will I give thee my loves.

13 The mandrakes give a smell, and at our gates are all manner of pleasant fruits, new and old, which I have laid up for thee, O my beloved.

Lucretius (Rome)

c. 99–*c.* 55 BC

A Roman philosopher and poet, Lucretius is best remembered for his only work, De Rerum Natura – *written in six books and probably not completed. A great follower of the Greek materialist philosopher, Epicurus, Lucretius's intention was to explain the world in physical terms, and so to free people from their superstitious belief in the gods. Nothing is known of his life, and the allegation by St Jerome that he committed suicide has never been confirmed.*

From **De Rerum Natura**, Book IV. *Trans. John Dryden*

Thus, therefore, he who feels the fiery dart
Of strong desire transfix his amorous heart,
Whether some beauteous boy's alluring face
Or lovelier maid with unresisted grace
From her each part the winged arrow sends,
From whence he first was struck, he thither
    tends.
Restless he roams, impatient to be freed
And eager to inject the sprightly seed.
For fierce desire does all his mind employ,
And ardent love assures approaching joy.
Such is the nature of that pleasing smart
Whose burning drops distil upon the heart
The fever of the soul shot from the fair
And the cold ague of succeeding care.
If absent, her idea still appears,
And her sweet name is chiming in your ears;
But strive those pleasing phantoms to
    remove,

And shun th'aerial images of love
That feed the flame; when one molests thy
    mind
Discharge thy loins on all the leaky kind –
For that's a wiser way than to restrain
Within thy swelling nerves that hoard of
    pain;
For every hour some deadlier symptom
    shows,
And by delay the gathering venom grows
When kindly applications are not used.
The scorpion, love, must on the wound be
    bruised.
On that one object 'tis not safe to stay,
But force the tide of thought some other way:
The squandered spirits prodigally throw
And in the common glebe of nature sow.
Nor wants he all the bliss that lovers feign
Who takes the pleasure and avoids the pain;

For purer joys in purer health abound,
And less affect the sickly than the sound.
When love its utmost vigour does employ,
Even then, 'tis but a restless wandering joy;
Nor knows the lover, in that wild excess,
With hands or eyes what first he would
    possess,
But strains at all, and fastening where he
    strains
Too closely presses with his frantic pains –
With biting kisses hurts the twining fair,
Which shows his joys imperfect, insincere,
For stung with inward rage, he flings around
And strives t'avenge the smart on that which
    gave the wound.
But love those eager bitings does restrain,
And mingling pleasure mollifies the pain.
For ardent hope still flatters anxious grief,
And sends him to his foe to seek relief
Which yet the nature of the thing denies,
For love, and love alone of all our joys
By full possession does but fan the fire,
The more we still enjoy, the more we still
    desire.
Nature for meat and drink provides a space,
And when received they fill their certain
    place;
Hence thirst and hunger may be satisfied.
But this repletion is to love denied.
Form, feature, colour, whatsoe'er delight
Provokes the lover's endless appetite,
These fill no space, nor can we thence
    remove
With lips or hands or all our instruments of
    love:
In our deluded grasp we nothing find
But thin aerial shapes that fleet before the
    mind.
As he who in a dream with drought is cursed

And finds no real drink to quench his thirst
Runs to imagined lakes his heat to steep,
So love with phantoms cheats our longing
    eyes,
Which hourly seeing never satisfies.
Our hands pull nothing from the parts they
    strain
But wander o'er the lovely limbs in vain,
Nor when the youthful pair more closely
    join,
When hands in hands they lock, and thighs
    in thighs they twine,
Just in the raging foam of full desire
When both press on, both murmur, both
    expire,
They gripe, they squeeze, their humid
    tongues they dart,
As each would force their way to t'other's
    heart –
In vain: they only cruise about the coast,
For bodies cannot pierce, nor be in bodies
    lost,
As sure they strive to be when both engage
In that tumultuous momentary rage.
So tangled in the nets of love they lie,
Till man dissolves in that excess of joy.
Then when the gathered bag has burst its
    way
And ebbing tides the slackened nerves
    betray,
A pause ensues, and Nature nods a while,
Till with recruited rage new spirits boil;
And then the same vain violence returns,
With flames renewed th'erected furnace
    burns.
Again they in each other would be lost,
But still by adamantine bars are crossed.
All ways they try, successless all they prove
To cure the secret sore of lingering love.

Automedon (Greece)

c. 90–50 BC

Nothing is known of this Greek poet of the Roman period. He is survived by a dozen humorous and satirical poems.

From **The Greek Anthology**, Book V (compiled 10th century AD).
Trans. Kenneth McLeish

> Turkish. Belly-dancer. Sexy tricks.
> (That quivering! Those fingernails!)
> What do I like best? Hands here, here,
> Soft, soft, stroking – or better,
> Piping that little old man of mine,
> Fondling each foldlet, tonguing,
> Tickling, easing, teasing,
> Then slipping on top, and . . .
> I tell you, she could raise the dead.

Meleager (Greece)

fl. 80 BC

A Greek poet born in Gadara of Syrian parentage, Meleager is best remembered as the compiler of the Garland, *a volume of short epigrammatic poems which appears in the famous* Greek Anthology. *His work is said to have influenced many of the early Roman erotic poets.*

From **The Greek Anthology**, Book XII (compiled 10th century AD).
Trans. Kenneth McLeish

> Hot day. Dying of thirst. Slake myself
> Kissing Antiochos. White . . . white . . . soft . . .
> Thirst gone. 'Great Zeus above,
> Does it work for you too, kissing Ganymede,
> Sipping his nectar, draining his droplets?
> I know what you mean. Antiochos!
> I've just sipped Antiochos, honey of the soul.'

Priapeia (Rome)

c. 1st century BC

A collection of short Latin poems in the shape of jocose epigrams affixed to the statues of the god Priapus. They were written by, among others, Martial and Petronius, and possibly Catullus, Tibullus, Cinna and Anser.

Let the first syllable of PEnelope be followed by the first of DIdo, the first of CAnus by that of REmus. What is made from these thou to me, when caught in my garden, O thief, shalt give; by this punishment thy fault is atoned for. [PE-DI-CA-RE = to sodomize]

Catullus (Rome)

c. 84–*c.* 54 BC

A Latin poet, Catullus was born in Verona, but went to Rome as a wealthy young man, where he soon became accepted by members of the fashionable set. It was in Rome that he had an unrequited affair with Clodia – the 'Lesbia' to whom he wrote the passionate and, on occasion, hate-filled erotic verse for which he is best known. A great innovator, he was the leader of the neoterici, *or New Poets of the late Republic – breaking with the tradition of Rome's past and finding models in Greek poetry.*

Fragments. Trans. Peter Whigham

Lesbia
live with me
& love me so
we'll laugh at all
the sour-faced strict-
ures of the wise.
This sun once set
will rise again,
when our sun sets
follows night &
an endless sleep.
Kiss me now a
thousand times &
now a hundred
more & then a
hundred & a
thousand more again
till with so many
hundred thousand
kisses you & I
shall both lose count
nor any can
from envy of

so much of kissing
put his finger
on the number
of sweet kisses
you of me &
I of you,
darling, have had.

~

Lesbia's sparrow!
Lesbia's plaything!
in her lap or at her breast
when Catullus's desire gleams
and fancies playing at something,
perhaps precious,
a little solace for satiety
when love has ebbed,
you are invited to nip her finger
you are coaxed into pecking sharply,
if I could play with you
her sparrow
lifting like that my sorrow
I should be eased

as the girl was of her virginity
when the miniature apple,
gold/undid
her girl's girdle
– too long tied.

~

Just now I found a young boy
stuffing his girl,
I rose, naturally, and
(with a nod to Venus)
fell and transfixed him there
with a good stiff prick,
like his own.

Virgil (Rome)

70–19 BC

Generally considered the greatest of all Latin poets, Virgil was born near Mantua, and lived variously in Cremona, Milan and Naples (where he was buried). His background as a farmer's son was reflected in his pastoral poems, the Eclogues *and Georgics. It is, however, for his great epic poem about the fall of Troy, the* Aeneid, *that he is best remembered. A great influence on other, later writers, Virgil was chosen by Dante as the guide through Purgatory and Hell in* The Divine Comedy.

From the **Aeneid**, Book IV (*c.*29–*c.*19 BC). *Trans. Kenneth McLeish*

Priests, prophets, helpless. She's beside
  herself –
What use are prayers or altars? Passion
  gnaws
Her very marrow; love eats her heart.
Raging, on fire, she roams the town.
She's a doe, a doe in Cretan woods,
Grazing, wounded by some lucky shot
By a shepherd who passes on his way,
Not knowing, leaving his dart
Full in her flank. It hangs; she burns; she
  runs.
So Dido. She shows her prince her town:
'Aeneas, look! All Carthage at your feet!'
She speaks, interrupts herself, falls dumb.
Each night, another banquet: 'Tell me
  again,
The Fall of Troy, again!' She's mad for it,
Hangs on his lips as he tells the tale.
The guests go home, Moon dims her lamps,
Setting stars say 'Sleep' –
And Dido frets in empty rooms,
Tosses and turns on empty bed. He's there,

He's not there, she sees him, hears him;
She snatches little Iulus, dandles him –
So like his father! – kisses him, kisses him
To soothe the longing she dare not speak.

.   .   .

In Heaven, Queen Juno saw. 'She's trapped.
Honour, reputation? Sick beyond cure.'
Her Heavenly Majesty went straight to
  Venus.
'Fine victory! Such noble spoils
For you and that boy of yours!
Two tricksy gods, one mortal – what a
  fight!
D'you think I don't know what you really
  fear –
My Carthage, its battlements, its towers?
Enough! Our rivalry must end.
Let's work together, bring them together,
Make eternal union. You've got your heart's
  desire:
Queen Dido, bone-sick with passion, blazing.
Are you listening? I'll explain my plan.

They're going hunting, Aeneas and poor
      Dido,
In the woods, as soon as tomorrow's Sun
Leaps from his bed and unveils the sky.
Beaters, shaking the branches, setting their
      nets,
Ringing the coverts. I'll take those two,
Blanket them: clouds, rain, I'll shake the sky.
They'll scatter, the hunters, run for shelter –
And in the dark those two will come to the
      same deep cave,
Her Majesty; the Trojan. I'll wait for them
      there,
And there – with your approval, divine assent
I'll unite the pair of them, I'll make her his.
A kind of wedding.' 'Yes!' said Venus,
'Yes!' – and giggled at the plan.

          .   .   .

Dawn leaves the bed of Dark and climbs the
      sky.
Light's kindled. Up they get, my lords of
      Carthage.
Nets, snares, broad hunting spears,
Horses, riders, a sniff of hounds.
She's late, Her Majesty. There at her door
Their lordships wait; her horse, its purple,
      gold,
Curvetting champing at foam-flecked bit.
At last she's here. Her courtiers throng.
Embroidered dress, in local style,

Gold quiver, braids of gold, gold catch
In the belt that waists that dress.
Now the Trojans. Iulus – look! –
Dancing with excitement. And at their head
Aeneas, handsomest of all, rides by her side;
His followers, and hers, line up behind.
Off to the hills, the tangled woods, the
      game!
Goats scatter, clatter, rock to rock;
Deer swirl, a herd, down to open plain,
A dust-cloud. Young Iulus, high on great big
      horse,
Out-trots each man in turn. Goats! Deer!
Tame prey! Please, gods, send frothing boar
Or yellow lion – I'll know just what to do!

          .   .   .

Sky rumbles. Gathers. Rain.
Trojans, Carthaginians, scatter. Iulus, their
      lordships,
Shelter. Torrents, streaming. And those two,
Dido, Aeneas of Troy, find the self-same
      cave.
Mother Earth, Juno Lady of Union, give the
      sign.
Fires flare, the sky's on fire, Nymphs howl,
Howl on high peaks. Death's birthday,
      disaster-day.
Dido's reputation, her honour – put away.
Her love's not secret now.
She calls this marriage, to veil her sin.

Horace (Rome)

65–8 BC

The Roman poet and satirist Horace was born in Apulia and educated in Athens and Rome. In 44 BC he fought with Brutus at the Battle of Philippi, returned penniless, and, as he later described, was driven to write poetry through poverty. His writings soon brought him into contact with Virgil, and he was eventually recommended to the patronage of the Emperor Augustus. Apart from the Epodes, *which deal mainly with love and politics, he is best known for his* Odes *and* Satires, *and for an influential critical work,* Ars poetica.

'To A Randy Old Woman' (**Epodes**, *c.* 30 BC). *Trans. anon.*

'Why so droopy?' did I hear you say?
You're half as old as time. You stink.
That single fang! That furrowed brow –
Not from thinking, a century of ploughing!
Spindle shanks, arsehole
Drooling like the incontinent cow you are.
'No, but what turns you on?' You're joking –
Those saggy tits, that shopping-bag
You call a belly, that bony bum, those piano
    legs?
I've had them to here. Go, stagger to your
    grave
Past legions of dead admirers, in line
    erect.
What's that? Pearls? You've piles of pearls?
Pray god no other bride piles pearls like
    those!
Philosophy books, dust-jacketed in silk?
I'm sorry, not even reading will get me
    going.
If it's uplift you're after, if that's your
    thrust,
Stop talking, put lips and tongue to other
    use.

Propertius (Rome)

c. 48–*c.*15 BC

The Roman poet Sextus Propertius was born in Assisi and educated for the law in Rome, but like his friend Ovid turned instead to poetry. His four books of elegant and impassioned elegies largely record the vicissitudes of the poet's relationship with his mistress 'Cynthia'.

From **Elegies**, Book II. *Trans. Kenneth McLeish*

Night's best of all. Night brings delight.
Night and that bed, that narrow bed
We chat in as the candle glows,
And when it's out play other games.
She nestles naked in my arms,
Slips nightie on, plays peekaboo;
She kisses drowsy eyes awake –
'Poor darling! *What* a sleepy-head!'
We make a maze of loving arms;
We kiss, and kiss, and kiss, and kiss . . .
Eyes open – kissing blind's no fun –
Love feasts eyes first, then lips and tongue.
Prince Paris of Troy, they say, was lost
When Helen, nude, left hubby's bed.
When Diana glimpsed Endymion nude,
She stripped and took the lad to bed.
Remember them, take off that dress –
So pretty . . . hate to get it torn . . .
Love-wrestling . . . wrestling . . . carried
    away . . .
You're bruised, please don't let Mummy
    see.
Tip-tilted breasts, not born to blush
Unseen, at least not yet. We've time;
We're young; fate's on our side; let's
    live
And love; death's dark comes soon
    enough.
Let's hug so close that when we die
They'll never part us, think us one –
Love-birds, my darling, cock and hen,
Paired souls; a union; unity.

Ovid (Rome)

43 BC–AD 17

A Latin poet, born in Sulmo (now Solmona, in the Abruzzi), Ovid studied rhetoric in Rome, but chose not to follow a career in the law. In AD 8 he was banished by Augustus to Tomi, on the Black Sea, perhaps because his playful treatise on love, the Ars Amatoria, *had offended the moralistic emperor. His witty and exuberant collection of myth and legend,* Metamorphoses, *has proved one of the most influential texts in Western literature, providing fodder for writers from Boccaccio through Shakespeare to Shelley and beyond.*

From **Amores**, Book III (*c.* 16 BC). *Trans. Kenneth McLeish*

She'd looks, she'd style,
I'd been after her for weeks.
There we were, lying there,
Cosying up – and nothing.
I wanted it, she wanted it –
And *could* I get it up?
She held me in her arms –
White snow they were, ivory –
We tongue-kissed, snuggled,
She called me 'Rambo',
'Hammerdrill', you name it –
Nothing. I sagged: an icicle
(Except that icicles are stiff);
A deadweight, a dodo,
A pricked balloon.
At my age! Embarrassing.
And think of the future –
If I *have* a future. No joy.
Might as well take nuns to bed,
Baby sisters – no risk, no problem.
And this from me – *me*!
Twice with Chlide, the other day;
Pitho three times; Libas three;
Not to mention Corinna,
Same night, nine times, a record.
There's only one explanation –
Witchcraft. A droopy spell.
Chanting, potions,
Little wax image, pins in the –
Paranoid?
Spells turn wheat to weed,
Fountains to dust-holes,
Curdle chestnuts, wizen grapes –

Boneless willy? Right along.
Witchcraft, then, and nerves:
The only explanation.
I mean, there she was, there I was,
Breathing each other, wet-teeshirt close.
She stroked me. Father Time
Would have twitched. The Mummy
Would have risen in his tomb –
And what did I do? Guess.
Oh god, I had it all –
Except I never had it.
'Let her like me – granted.
'Let her kiss me – granted.
'Alone together – granted.
Prayers answered, all but one.
Cash in the bank: no problem
Unless you try to spend it – the miser's
    dream.
I was Tantalus in Hades
gaping at goodies
Marked 'Look but don't touch';
Who lies there all night with his darling
And gets up still ready for church?
When I think of those kisses –
Oaks would have danced for them,
Stones would have swooned for them,
Steel would have, flesh would've –
Forget it. I must have been dead.
Lifeless, departed, defunct.
She was painting for the blind,
Singing for the deaf. I just lay there.
I did what I could. I *imagined*:
'Do *this*, put that *there*,

The dying slave Michelangelo

Now perhaps if we . . . ' Nothing.
Limp. Yesterday's rose.
Whereas *now*! Thrusting, eager,
Bright-eyed and bushy-tailed and – late!
Stop *doing* that! Bastard!
Where were you when I needed you?
The things I do for you! The cash I spend!
She does her damnedest, takes you in
    hand,
Softly, softly, a million tricks –
And all you do is sulk. Gods, *was* she cross!

'You're weird,' she told me. 'Sick.
Who sent you? Who told you
You could flop out here? You're
    hypnotized?
Worn out, with someone else –?'
Next minute, gone. Bare feet on the
    floor,
Flash of nightie. Water, splashing.
(Clever, that: confuse the maids, save
    face –
She always splashes, afterwards.)

~

From **Metamorphoses**, Book III: 'Echo and Narcissus' (AD 2–8).
Trans. Mary M. Innes

So, when she saw Narcissus wandering through the lonely countryside, Echo fell in love with him, and followed secretly in his steps. The more closely she followed, the nearer was the fire which scorched her: just as sulphur, smeared round the tops of torches, is quickly kindled when a flame is brought near it. How often she wished to make flattering overtures to him, to approach him with tender pleas! But her handicap prevented this, and would not allow her to speak first; she was ready to do what it would allow, to wait for sounds which she might re-echo with her own voice.

The boy, by chance, had wandered away from his faithful band of comrades, and he called out: 'Is there anybody here?' Echo answered: 'Here!' Narcissus stood still in astonishment, looking round in every direction, and cried at the pitch of his voice: 'Come!' As he called, she called in reply. He looked behind him, and when no one appeared, cried again: 'Why are you avoiding me?' But all he heard were his own words echoed back. Still he persisted, deceived by what he took to be another's voice, and said, 'Come here, and let us meet!' Echo answered: 'Let us meet!' Never again would she reply more willingly to any sound. To make good her words she came out of the wood, and made to throw her arms round the neck she loved: but he fled from her, crying as he did so, 'Away with these embraces! I would die before I would have you touch me!' Her only answer was: 'I would have you touch me!' Thus scorned, she concealed herself in the woods, hiding her shamed face in the shelter of the leaves, and ever since that day, she dwells in lonely caves. Yet still her love remained firmly rooted in her heart, and was increased by the pain of having been rejected. Her anxious thoughts kept her awake, and made her pitifully thin. She became wrinkled and wasted; all the freshness of her beauty withered into the air. Only her voice and her bones were left, till finally her voice alone remained; for her bones, they say, were turned to stone. Since then, she hides in the woods, and, though never seen on the mountains, is heard there by all: for her voice is the only part of her that still lives.

Narcissus had played with her affections, treating her as he had previously treated other spirits of the waters and the woods, and his male admirers too. Then one of those he had scorned raised up his hands to heaven and prayed: 'May he himself fall in love with another, as we have done with him! May he too be unable to gain his loved one!' Nemesis heard and granted this righteous prayer.

There was a clear pool, with shining silvery waters, where shepherds had never made their way; no goats that pasture on the mountains, no cattle had ever come there. Its peace was undisturbed by bird or beast or falling branches. Around it was a grassy sward, kept ever green by the nearby waters; encircling woods sheltered the spot from the fierce sun, and made it always cool.

Narcissus, wearied with hunting in the heat of the day, lay down here: for he was attracted by the beauty of the place, and by the spring. While he sought to quench his thirst, another thirst grew in him, and as he drank, he was enchanted by the beautiful reflection that he saw. He fell in love with an insubstantial hope, mistaking a mere shadow for a real body. Spellbound by his own self, he remained there motionless, with fixed gaze, like a statue carved from Parian marble. As he lay on the bank, he gazed at the twin stars that were his eyes, at his flowing locks, worthy of Bacchus or Apollo, his smooth cheeks, his ivory neck, his lovely face where a rosy flush stained the snowy whiteness of his complexion, admiring all the features for which he was himself admired. Unwittingly, he desired himself, and was himself the object of his own approval, at once seeking and sought, himself kindling the flame with which he burned. How often did he vainly kiss the treacherous pool, how often plunge his arms deep in the waters, as he tried to clasp the neck he saw! But he could not lay hold upon himself. He did not know what he was looking at, but was fired by the sight, and excited by the very illusion that deceived his eyes. Poor foolish boy, why vainly grasp at the fleeting image that eludes you? The thing you are seeking does not exist: only turn aside and you will lose what you love. What you see is but the shadow cast by your reflection; in itself it is nothing. It comes with you, and lasts while you are there; it will go when you go, if go you can.

No thought of food or sleep could draw him from the spot. Stretched on the shady grass, he gazed at the shape that was no true shape with eyes that could never have their fill, and by his own eyes he was undone. Finally he raised himself a little. Holding out his arms to the surrounding woods: 'Oh you woods,' he cried, 'has anyone ever felt a love more cruel? You surely know, for many lovers have found you an ideal haunt for secret meetings. You who have lived so many centuries, do you remember anyone, in all your long years, who has pined away as I do? I am in love, and see my loved one, but that form which I see and love I cannot reach: so far am I deluded by my love. My distress is all the greater because it is not a mighty ocean that separates us, nor yet highways or mountains, or city walls with close-barred gates. Only a little water keeps us apart. My love himself desires to be embraced: for whenever I lean forward to kiss the clear waters he lifts up his face to mine and strives to reach me. You would think he could be reached – it is such a small thing that hinders our love. Whoever you are, come out to me! Oh boy beyond compare, why do you elude me? Where do you go, when I try to reach you? Certainly it is not my looks or my years which you shun, for I am one of those the nymphs have loved. With friendly looks you proffer me some hope. When I stretch out my arms to you, you stretch yours towards me in return: you laugh when I do, and often I have marked your tears, when I was weeping. You answer my signs with nods, and, as far as I can guess from the movement of your lovely lips, reply to me in words that never reach my ears. Alas! I am myself the boy I see. I know it: my own reflection does not deceive me. I am on fire with love for my own self. It is I who kindle the flames which I must endure. What should I do? Woo or be wooed? But what then shall I seek by my wooing? What I desire, I have. My very plenty makes me poor. How I wish I could separate myself from my body! A new prayer this, for a lover, to wish the thing he loves away! Now grief is sapping my strength; little of life remains for me – I am cut off in the flower of my youth. I have no quarrel with death, for in death I shall forget my pain: but I could wish that the object of my love might outlive me: as it is, both of us will perish together, when this one life is destroyed.'

When he had finished speaking, he returned to gazing distractedly at that same face. His tears disturbed the water, so that the pool rippled, and the image grew dim. He saw it disappearing, and cried aloud: 'Where are you fleeing? Cruel creature, stay, do not desert one who loves you! Let me look upon you, if I cannot touch you. Let me, by looking, feed my ill-starred love.' In his grief, he tore away the upper portion of his tunic, and beat his bared breast with hands as white as marble. His breast flushed rosily where he struck it, just as apples often shine red in part, while part gleams whitely, or as grapes, ripening in variegated clusters, are tinged with purple. When Narcissus saw this reflected in the water – for the pool had returned to its former calm – he could bear it no longer. As golden wax melts with gentle heat, as morning frosts are thawed by the warmth of the sun, so he was worn and wasted away with love, and slowly consumed by its hidden fire. His fair complexion with its rosy flush faded away, gone was his youthful strength, and all the beauties which lately charmed his eyes. Nothing remained of that body which Echo once had loved.

The nymph saw what had happened, and although she remembered her own treatment, and was angry at it, still she grieved for him. As often as the unhappy boy sighed 'Alas,' she took up his sigh, and repeated 'Alas!' When he beat his hands against his shoulders she too gave back the same sound of mourning. His last words as he gazed into the familiar waters were: 'Woe is me for the boy I loved in vain!' and the spot re-echoed the same words. When he said his last farewell, 'Farewell!' said Echo too. He laid down his weary head on the green grass, and death closed the eyes which so admired their owner's beauty. Even then, when he was received into the abode of the dead, he kept looking at himself in the waters of the Styx. His sisters, the nymphs of the spring, mourned for him, and cut off their hair in tribute to their brother. The wood nymphs mourned him too, and Echo sang her refrain to their lament.

The pyre, the tossing torches, and the bier, were now being prepared, but his body was nowhere to be found. Instead of his corpse, they discovered a flower with a circle of white petals round a yellow centre.

Petronius (Rome)

d.c. AD 65

A Latin satirical writer, usually identified as the Gaius Petronius Arbiter mentioned by Tacitus as one of Nero's courtiers, a former governor and consul who was condemned to suicide after being implicated in conspiracy. Only fragments of his long prose narrative The Satyricon *survive, and these relate the bawdy low-life travels of two friends.*

From **The Satyricon**. *Trans. J.P. Sullivan*

However, Eumolpus, our champion in time of trouble and the author of the present harmony, to prevent the general merriment lapsing into silence without a few stories, began a succession of gibes about feminine fickleness – how easily they fell in love, how quickly they forgot even their children. There was no woman so pure that she could not be driven crazy by some stranger's physical attractions. He wasn't thinking of old tragedies or famous historical names but of something that happened within his own living memory, and he would tell us about it if we wanted to hear it. So when everyone's eyes and ears were turned to him, he began the following story.

'There was once a lady of Ephesus so famous for her fidelity to her husband that she even attracted women from neighbouring countries to come just to see her. So when she buried her husband, she was not satisfied with following him to his grave with the usual uncombed hair or beating her breast in front of the crowd, but she even accompanied the dead man into the tomb, and when the corpse was placed in the underground vault, she began watching over it from then on, weeping day and night. Neither her parents nor her relations could induce her to stop torturing herself and seeking death by starvation. Finally the magistrates were repulsed and left her, and this extraordinary example to womankind, mourned by everyone, was now spending her fifth day without food. A devoted servant sat with the ailing woman, added her tears to the lady's grief, and refilled the lamp in the tomb whenever it began to go out. Naturally there was only one subject of conversation in the whole town: every class of people admitted there had never been such a shining example of true fidelity and love.

'In the meantime the governor of the province ordered the crucifixion of some thieves to be carried out near the humble abode where the wife was crying over the corpse of the lately deceased. Next night the soldier who was guarding the crosses to prevent anyone removing one of the bodies for burial noticed a light shining clearly among the tombs and, hearing the sounds of someone mourning, he was eager to know – a general human failing – who it was and what was going on. Naturally he went down into the vault and, seeing a beautiful woman, at first stood rooted to the spot as though terrified by some strange sight or a vision from hell. When he observed the dead man's body and noted the woman's tears and scratched face, surmising rightly that here was a woman who could not bear her intense longing for the dead man, he brought her his bit of supper and began pleading with the weeping woman not to prolong her hopeless grief and break her heart with useless lamentation. The same end, the same resting-place awaited everyone, he told her – along with all the other things that restore grief-stricken minds to sanity. But in spite of the stranger's consoling words, the woman only tore at her breast more violently and draped her mangled hair over the body of the dead man.

The soldier still refused to withdraw; instead, using the same arguments, he tried to press food on her servant until the girl, seduced by the smell of the wine, first gave in herself, stretched out her hand to his tempting charity, and then, refreshed by the food and drink, began to lay siege to her mistress's resolution.

' "What good is it," she said to her, "for you to drop dead of starvation, or bury yourself alive or breathe your last innocent breath before fate demands it?

Believe you that ashes or the buried ghosts can know?

Won't you come back to life? Won't you give up your womanly error and enjoy the comforts of life as long as you can? That very corpse lying there should be your encouragement to live."

'No one is ever reluctant to listen when pressed to eat or stay alive. Parched from taking nothing day after day, the woman allowed her resolution to be sapped and filled herself with food no less avidly than the girl who had given in first.

'But you know what temptations follow on a full stomach. The inducements the soldier had used to persuade the lady into a desire to live became part also of an attempt on her virtue. For all her chastity the man appealed to her: he was neither unpleasing nor ill-spoken, she thought. Moreover, her maid spoke on his behalf and quoted the line:

Would you fight even a pleasing passion?

'Need I say more? The woman couldn't refuse even this gratification of the flesh and the triumphant soldier talked her into both. They then slept together, not just the night they first performed the ceremony but the next night too, and then a third. The doors of the vault were of course closed, so if a friend or a stranger came to the tomb, he thought that the blameless widow had expired over her husband's body.

'Actually the soldier, delighted with the lady's beauty and the whole secret liaison, had bought whatever luxuries he could afford and carried them to the tomb on the very first night. As a result, the parents of one of the crucified men, seeing the watch had been relaxed, took down the hanging body in the dark and gave it the final rites. The soldier, tricked while he lay enjoying himself and seeing next day one of the crosses without a corpse, in terror of punishment, explained to the woman what had happened. He would not wait for the judge's verdict, he said – his own sword would carry out sentence for his dereliction of duty. Only let her provide a place for him in death and let the tomb be the last resting-place for both her lover and her husband. The woman's pity was equal to her fidelity:

' "Heaven forbid," she said, 'that I should see simultaneously two funerals, for the two men I hold dearest. I'd rather hang the dead than kill the living.'

'Suiting the deed to the word, she told him to take the body of her husband from the coffin and fix it to the empty cross. The soldier followed the sensible woman's plan, and next day people wondered how on earth the dead man had managed to get up on the cross.'

The sailors greeted the story with roars of laughter.

Martial (Rome)

(*c.* AD 40–*c.* AD 104)

Martial moved from his native Spain to Rome in AD *64 to take up a career as a professional poet. A friend of the Younger Pliny and Juvenal, his major work consists of the twelve volumes of* Epigrams *(*AD *86–101), over 1,500 short and pithy poems vividly satirizing the vices of Imperial Rome, though with an amused tolerance and much salacity.*

From **Epigrams**. *Trans. James Michie*

When you say, 'Quick, I'm going to come,'
Hedylus, I go limp and numb.
But ask me to hold back my fire,
And the brake accelerates desire.
Dear boy, if you're in such a hurry,
Tell me to slow up, not to worry.

~

People have the oddest kinks.
My friend Flaccus fancies, ears and all, a lynx;
In Canius's opinion
You can't beat a coal-black Abyssinian;
Publius gets the itch
With a little terrier bitch;
Cronius is in love with a monkey that looks like him – almost human;
Marius cuddles a deadly ichneumon;
Lausaus likes his talking magpie; Glaucilla, more reckless,
Coils her pet snake into a shivery necklace;
Telesilla,
When her nightingale died, erected a commemorative pillar.
Since it's every master to his own monstrous taste,
Why, sweet, Cupid-faced
Labycas, shouldn't you too be embraced?

Pan Chieh-Yu (China)

fl. 1st century BC

Pan Chieh-Yu is the title of honour given to an imperial concubine; the author's real name is unknown. The only facts available are that she was initially the favourite of Emperor Ch'eng of the Han dynasty, who reigned c. *32* BC, *but was later usurped and became an attendant in the Imperial Tombs.*

'A Song of Grief'. *Trans. Kenneth Rexroth and Ling Chung*

> I took a piece of the fine cloth of Ch'i,
> White silk glowing and pure like frosted snow,
> And made you a doubled fan of union and joy,
> As flawlessly round as the bright moon.
> It comes and goes in my Lord's sleeves.
> You can wave it and start a cooling breeze.
> But I am always afraid that when Autumn comes,
> And the cold blasts drive away the heat,
> You will store it away in a bamboo case,
> And your love of it will stop midway.

Strato (Greece)

fl. AD 125

Strato was a Greek poet, whose work is found in The Greek Anthology, *a collection of the disparate surviving poems largely from the Hellenistic period. Strato's hundred-odd witty and titillating verses come from the collection* Mousa Paidike *(pederastic poems) from* The Palatine Anthology, *a tenth-century manuscript rediscovered in the Count Palatine's Heidelberg library in 1606.*

From **The Greek Anthology**, Book XII (compiled 10th century AD). *Trans. Kenneth McLeish*

> Don't hitch your dear little cunt against that wall,
> Cyris darling. It's stone – it'll never get it up.

~

> Fitness expert. Big gym-man.
> Training this peachy little boy.
> Bends him over, the whole routine,
> Press-ups, ball-play. Working up a sweat
> When out of nowhere, Dad appears.
> Looking for Sonny. Whoops!
> Up and over. Back-flip. 'Submit, submit!'
> Dad's a wrestling fan, seen it all before.
> 'Don't try so hard next time, you'll pull it off.'

Apuleius (Rome)

c. AD 125–160

A Latin satirist, Apuleius was born in North Africa and studied at Carthage and Athens, where he became attracted to religious mysteries – so much so that upon marrying a wealthy middle-aged woman older than himself, he was accused of having used magic to gain her affections. His best-known work is the Metamorphoses *or* The Golden Ass *– a satire on corrupt priests and the vices of his day – regarded as a forerunner of the picaresque tradition that culminated in Fielding's* Tom Jones. *Hugely popular in the high Middle Ages, stories from* The Golden Ass *appear in Boccaccio's* Decameron *and in the 15th-century* Les Cent nouvelles nouvelles, *among other works.*

From **Metamorphoses** (**The Golden Ass**): 'Cupid and Psyche'.
Trans. Robert Graves

Psyche was left alone, in so far as a woman haunted by hostile Furies can be called alone. Her mind was as restless as a stormy sea. When she first began making preparations for her crime, her resolve was firm; but presently she wavered and started worrying about all the different aspects of her calamity. She hurried, then she dawdled; at one moment she was bold and at another frightened; she felt nervous and then she got angry again. For, although she loathed the animal, she loved the husband it seemed to be. However, as evening drew on, she finally acted rapidly and prepared what was needed to do the dreadful deed.

'Night fell, and her husband came to bed, and after preliminary amorous skirmishes he fell fast asleep. Psyche was not naturally either very strong or very brave, but the cruel power of fate made a man of her. Holding the knife in a murderous grip, she uncovered the lamp and let its light shine on the bed.

'There lay the gentlest and sweetest of all wild creatures, Cupid himself, lying in all his beauty, and at the sight of him the flame of the lamp spurted joyfully up and the knife turned its edge for shame.

'When Psyche saw this wonderful sight she was terrified. She lost all control of her senses and, pale as death, fell trembling to her knees, where she tried to hide the knife by plunging it in her own heart. She would have succeeded, too, had the knife not shrunk from the crime and twisted itself out of her foolhardy hands. Faint and unnerved though she was, she began to feel better as she stared at Cupid's divine beauty: his golden hair, washed in ambrosia and still scented with it, curls straying over white neck and flushed cheeks and falling prettily entangled on either side of his head – hair so bright that it darkened the flame of the lamp. At his shoulders grew soft wings of the purest white and, though they were at rest, the tender down fringing the feathers quivered attractively all the time. The rest of his body was so smooth and beautiful that Venus could never have been ashamed to acknowledge him as her son. At the foot of the bed lay this great god's gracious weapons, his bow, quiver and arrows.

'Psyche's curiosity could be satisfied only by a close examination of her husband's weapons. She pulled an arrow out of the quiver and touched the point with the tip of her thumb to try its sharpness; but her hand was trembling and she pressed too hard. The skin was pierced and out came a drop or two of blood. So Psyche accidentally fell in love with Love. Burning with greater passion for Cupid even than before, she flung herself panting upon him, desperate with desire, and smothered him with sensual, open-mouthed kisses; her one fear now being that he would wake too soon.

'While she clung to him, utterly bewildered with delight, the lamp which she was still holding, whether from horrid treachery or destructive envy, or because it too longed to touch and kiss such a body, spurted a drop of scalding oil on the god's right shoulder. What a bold and impudent lamp, what a worthless servant of Love – for the first lamp was surely invented by some lover who wished to prolong the pleasures of the night – so to scorch the god of all fire! Cupid sprang up in pain and, seeing that the bonds of faith were shattered and in ruins, spread his wings and flew away from the kisses and embraces of his unhappy wife without a word; but not before Psyche had seized his right leg with both hands and clung to it. She looked very queer, carried up like that through the cloudy sky; but soon her strength failed her and she tumbled down to earth again.'

FROM THE FALL OF ROME TO THE RENAISSANCE

From *Commentaries on St Paul's Epistle to the Romans* Giulio Clovio

The Middle Ages or medieval period began in the year 476, with the fall of the Roman Empire, and ended in the fourteenth century when it was superseded by a period of renewed interest in classical culture that came to be called the Renaissance. Such designations are little more than conveniences for historians; history itself is never that tidy. Nor can these terms be applied meaningfully to cultures outside the Western Christian tradition.

Much of the Oriental erotic literature of this period differed from its European counterpart in its intensely personal nature and in its greater awareness of the pleasurable rather than the procreative aspect of sex which dominated Christian thought. In Oriental culture the physical and the metaphysical were inseparable.

India

The equation of sex with guilt, which was to play such a large part in Christian culture, had no role in the early erotic literature of India, which expresses the Hindu belief in the libido as the basic driving energy of humankind and in the sexual act as something both divine and pleasurable. The *Kama Sutra* (see page 75), written some time between the first and the fourth centuries by an author named Mallanaga, a member of the Vatsyayana sect, makes the connection between divinity and pleasure transparent. Originally a collection of aphorisms later linked by a commentator, it reveals an intention of reconciling *kama* (erotic love and artistic pleasure) with *dharma* (religious obligation) and *artha* (social well-being).

At one level the *Kama Sutra* is a manual of sexual conduct. Indeed, it has been dismissed as possessing no more literary or erotic merit than a list of recipes in a cookery book. But this criticism ignores not only the beauty of its language, but also its belief in the centrality of sex to human life, with its insistence upon the importance of foreplay and equal pleasure for both women and men. This, as well as the racist allure of the exotic, is surely what has made the book so erotically appealing, certainly to English readers, ever since it was translated by the nineteenth-century orientalist, Sir Richard Burton.

At the heart of Sanskrit lyric poetry of this period is the notion of *rasa*, the juice or essential pervading flavour of an emotional situation and, by extension, it also comes to mean erotic feeling. This notion of sexual energy is captured in the poetry of Bhartrihari (see page 79), a fifth-century Buddhist who vacillated between a life of sexual indulgence and monkhood, as he explored what proved to be the equally unsatisfying tugs of worldly concerns and erotic desires with those of the ascetic ideal. In *Passionate Encounters* woman is passion's object and a magical enigma enticing men into inescapable bondage. But Bhartrihari does not sink to the misogynistic depths of the early Christian ascetics. In Hindu erotic literature woman is cursed not because she becomes repugnant to man, but because her beauty continues to lure him.

The poetry of Bilhana (see page 84), an eleventh-century travelling court poet, captures in part an intensity of erotic love by the poems' formal style, and also by the rich web of sensuously descriptive, sonorous language with which he captures his former lover's emotions, movements and physical beauty. All is intended to stimulate the response of a cultivated audience.

The ritualistic and sacred nature of sexual intercourse and the guilt-free nature of sexual desire infuses Indian religious literature and art until the nineteenth century. Then, the strictly puritan Brahmin sect, encouraged by the English imperialists who imposed their prudish Victorian moral standards, led to a denial of past eroticism – an attitude from which India still suffers.

Islam

Despite its strict codes of moral behaviour, the Islamic Arab world has in the past produced a huge amount of erotic literature – from sex manuals to sensuous poetry and crude, bawdy farce. Religious taboos did not prevent male Arab writers and poets from exploring adultery, homosexuality (see 'Nizam the pederast', page 81) or female sexual desire. But the culture was more fiercely misogynistic than anywhere in the Oriental world; there is no erotic literature written by an Arab woman and it is unlikely that any ever existed. A medical book from this period offers the following advice: 'Breaking a maiden's seal is one of the best antidotes for one's ills; cudgelling her unceasingly, until she swoons away, is a mighty remedy for man's depression. It cures all impotence.' This is very different from the pleasurable pain recommended in the *Kama Sutra*.

None the less, Islamic culture in this period was less repressed than Christian culture of the period: sexual pleasure was accepted as a natural part of human activity, and human nature was not thought to be inherently evil. This is made abundantly clear in *Tales from the Thousand and One Nights*, also known as *Arabian Nights* (see page 102). It is impossible to date this collection of folk tales from Indian, Persian and Arabic sources accurately. Sir Richard Burton, who translated it into English in the nineteenth century, believed the earliest tales date from the eighth century and the latest from the sixteenth century.

The framework derives from a lost book of Persian fairy tales called *Hazar Afsanah* (*A Thousand Tales*), translated into Arabic *c.* 850. It involves a king who kills his wives the morning after consummating the union, until he marries the intelligent Scheherazade who saves her life by the tales she tells him. Like the writings of Boccaccio and Chaucer, the tales present social criticism, humour, satire, love, romance, bawdiness and farce. The cuckold, the sexually rapacious woman, and all the standard characters in Western erotic literature, are present, but *Arabian Nights* has more magic, joy and fun than any corresponding European collection. Some passages have an exquisite and exotic beauty comparable to 'The Song of Solomon' (see page 40), while others indulge in hilariously inventive sexy wordplay. And throughout, unlike so much of Western culture, sex is treated as a natural part of human behaviour; it is neither ignored nor allowed a disproportionate dominance.

The best-known Arab treatise on sexual technique is *The Perfumed Garden* (see page 141), compiled and written by the Tunisian, Umar ibn Muhammed al-Nefzawi in the sixteenth century. Like the *Kama Sutra*, its Sanskrit counterpart, it is much more than a sex manual, but it achieves far greater erotic poetic heights. It, too, has been compared to the 'The Song of Solomon', as well as to the erotica of the Greeks and Elizabethans, for its pure, free, non-obsessional, guilt-free eroticism.

As in India, the Islamic world came to adopt many Western sexual taboos which seriously affected the production of erotic literature and led to a repudiation of its richly erotic literary past.

China

Fifth-century China, which had been converted to Confucianism in the second century BC, strongly disapproved of chastity and made no connection between sex and guilt. This attitude, however, did not prevent subsequent waves of repressive censorship. The older tradition of Taoism (since the sixth century BC) further stressed the importance of acting in conformity with nature rather than striving against it.

Symbolism is an essential element of Chinese erotica. Jade, the most precious stone to the Chinese, is interpreted as the petrified semen of the celestial dragon. The popular expression for sexual intercourse is 'drinking at the fountain of jade'; female genitalia are the 'gateway of jade', and the penis is the 'flute of jade' which a woman can play on with her fingers as well as her lips. Once you know that 'wine from the grape' is *yin*, or female juice, that 'gateways of life' are the testes, that a stallion or a tree are both metaphors for the penis, that a deer, clouds, a lemon and, most commonly, a peach, are all metaphors for the vagina, and that clouds, wind and rain are images for sexual intercourse, the erotic content of Chinese poetry (and painting) becomes clear.

Much Chinese erotic poetry during this period was written by women; in fact, the earliest is by Pan Chieh-yu (see page 56) in the first century BC. When compared with the relative absence of the female voice in European erotic literature during the same period her work appears all the more remarkable. The songs attributed to a young woman named Tzu Yeh (see page 76), are popular folk songs of Wu, today's Kiangsu and Chekiang provinces. Chao Luan-Luan (see page 81), possibly from the T'ang dynasty (618–907), was an elegant prostitute whose poems are described by her translator, perhaps a little unfairly, as 'a sort of advertising copy in praise of the parts of a woman's body, written for courtesans and prostitutes'.

During the early sixteenth century the attitude of the Ming dynasty (1368–1644) towards erotic literature was unusually permissive. Bawdy comedies were commonplace in the theatre, and the erotic novel *Chin P'ing Mei* (see page 126) was written and published during this period. Even so, overtly erotic poetry was not considered the province of women writers who were not courtesans. This makes the writings (see page 122) of the poet Huang O, daughter of a senior court official, unique.

According to legend, the eroticism of *Chin P'ing Mei*, which translates directly as 'Metal Vase Plum-Blossom', but is otherwise known as *The Golden Lotus*, was a deliberate ploy on the part of the writer to bring about the death of an enemy who, unable to put it down and intent on turning over the pages as rapidly as possible, licked his fingers and so came into contact with the deadly poison which had been rubbed on to the thin paper. It may have been written by Wang Shih-cheng, a notable scholar, or perhaps by a student of his named Hsu Wei during this period of the Ming dynasty. Telling at great length of the adventures of Hsi-men Ch'ing, his six wives and many concubines, this novel is extraordinary on many counts, not least for challenging Confucianism. Since the Sung dynasty (960–1279) this had become a puritanical and ascetic creed, which taught that man's only spiritual concern should be the restoration of his natural state to its primal beauty, unmarred by the stirrings of appetites and emotions.

That there were no injunctions against erotic literature in the Ming code may simply mean that the development of the popular novel was too new a thing to attract the attention of the rulers; early in the succeeding Ch'ing, or Manchu, dynasty (1644–1911) an edict was issued suppressing immoral novels on the grounds that 'It is certain that licentious novels are likely to have a bad effect on my people, depraving their morals and poisoning their minds'.

Japan

Japanese literature has from earliest times been concerned with the pleasures of love-making. Shinto, the original phallic-worshipping religion of Japan since the tenth century BC, viewed love and sexuality as a good, devoid of sin. The Shinto legend of Creation was a sexual act, and much of Japanese literature dating from the ninth century reveals an erotic reaction to religion. Human sexuality as a part of Nature in all its aspects was celebrated rather than denied. 'Pillow books', originally scrolls of erotic prints specifically designed as sex manuals, were produced at least as early as the eighth century. These later became illustrated literary jottings and aphorisms intended to amuse, delight and perhaps mildly titillate. The most famous is that of Sei Shonagon, an eleventh-century courtesan.

According to Peter Webb, author of *The Erotic Arts* (1975), 'A noticeable feature of Japanese erotic art is the absence of nudity . . . [This fact] is not, however, due to any Victorian concept of shame relating to the human body . . . clothes can be sexually stimulating, and beautiful garments . . . when lovingly depicted . . . conjure up a voluptuousness that nudity could never inspire.' The importance of clothes and sensuous cloth in the Japanese notion of erotica is wonderfully illustrated in *The Confessions of Lady Nijō* (see page 101). Written by a concubine in the fourteenth century, this is a sophisticated autobiographical 'novel' unlike anything produced in Europe at that time.

Japanese culture both during this period and after was relatively unaffected by religious or moralizing censoriousness, and erotic literature has formed a significant genre within the literary tradition of Japan.

Early Medieval Europe

After the fall of Rome in the fifth century, although pockets of pagan resistance continued for centuries, the spread of Christian monotheism rather than the barbarian victory represented the greater disruptive challenge to social customs, morals and beliefs, and had an enormous effect on literature. In Greek and Roman civilization Eros and his Roman counterpart Amor or Cupid had stood at the head of hedonistic cultures in which neither sexuality nor its representation by artists were associated with sin or shame. Christianity, however, placed carnal love as the polar opposite to spiritual love. A preoccupation with human motive as the source of moral value became a major interest, and the values of asceticism, dating from a monastic movement in the fourth century and embodying the notion of human beings prised loose from the physical world, gained ascendancy. A preoccupation with the human body in the literature of the ancient world was replaced by concern for the frail workings of the human will.

When St Augustine converted to Christianity in 387, he renounced fleshly pleasures and bundled his concubine and son off to Africa. In his *Confessions*, while admitting to the compulsive force of sexual habit which caused his wet dreams, he expressed a wish for a state in which the will could control sexual desire, and a time when spiritual desire would be satisfied but 'not devoured by satiety' (see page 78). St Jerome, a fourth-century Dalmatian priest of even more vigorous ascetic views, apparently wrote deliberately to heighten sexual anxiety among the faithful. He communicated an acute awareness of the sexual dangers of the flesh (see page 78), which could be controlled only by rigid codes of diet and by the strict avoidance of situations of sexual attraction. His erotic fantasies about women were extreme. One devout, educated young woman who came to him for spiritual guidance was vehemently condemned by this clearly troubled saint as an evil harlot. Jerome was incapable of accepting that female and male could become one in Jesus Christ.

Given the Biblical prescriptions, it may seem surprising that so many poets of the early Middle Ages penned elegant erotic Latin verse in praise of homosexuality. Influenced by views of asceticism, however, there was widespread acceptance of *amicita* or 'passionate friendship' based on the model of the relationship between David and Jonathan: 'I am distressed for thee, my brother Jonathan; very pleasant hast thou been unto me. Thy love was wonderful, passing the love of women.' (2 Samuel 1:26.)

But belief in mere friendship between the eighth-century cleric Alcuin and some of his pupils, however, is stretched. His poetry contains many allusions to classical literature, especially Virgil's often blatantly homosexual *Eclogues*, and he named a favourite student after one of a pair of lovers – Alexis and Corydon – from the second eclogue. Alcuin's passionate poem and equally passionate letter (see page 80) may have been written to the same person, a friend and church superior.

Three centuries later homoeroticism is also strongly present in the personal correspondence of St Anselm (see page 82). He may have been a believer in the ascetic teachings of Augustine, but when appointed Archbishop of Canterbury in 1093, Anselm prevented the promulgation of the first proposed anti-homosexual legislation in England.

In his youth, even the prominent theologian Peter Abelard wrote verses of homoerotic love (see page 84), although it is for his passionate love affair with Heloise that he is now best remembered. Abelard's somewhat bald description of their love-making compared to Heloise's torment of frustrated sexual desire suggests she was right in accusing him of feeling lust rather than love, but their story of sexual passion and pain captured the imaginations of lovers of romance ever after. Alexander Pope was inspired by their letters to write his famous poem on the passion of love, 'Eloise to Abelard' (1716), and allusion to their erotic torment can be found in countless romantic novels, including Charlotte Brontë's *Jane Eyre* (1847) and Thomas Hardy's *Tess of the D'Urbervilles* (1891).

The twelfth century witnessed what one historian has called 'The Triumph of Ganymede' – something approaching a male homosexual subculture as manifested by countless poems throughout Europe at that time. Medieval authors were familiar with the story of Ganymede's ravishment and abduction by Zeus and subsequent career as cup-bearer to the gods through Virgil's *Aeneid* and Ovid's *Metamorphoses*. Indeed, his name became synonymous with what the ancient world called 'the beloved' in a homosexual relationship, and for a while the term 'ganymed' replaced the pejorative 'sodomita'. What is remarkable about the homoerotic poems by the churchmen of the time, including Marbod, Bishop of Rennes (see page 87), Hilary the Englishman, a student of Abelard's (see page 88), and the uniquely surviving poem by an anonymous, apparently lesbian, nun (see page 88), is the complete absence of any concept of sin.

The High Middle Ages

The period of the twelfth and thirteenth centuries, known as the High Middle Ages due to an awakened interest in classical literature, is notable for its relatively large number of women writers. The sometimes sexually explicit women troubadours of France, the exquisite *lais* of Marie de France (see page 93), and the body of work which includes some graphically erotic Welsh verse by Gwerful Mechain (see page 114) attest to a growing number of women with the confidence to express their ideas and fully competent in a literary language. Exposed to an orally delivered (if not composed) literature of the love lyric and the romance, aristocratic and educated women found poetic voices to articulate their own, often quite different, perceptions of the experience of love.

The visionary literature of medieval women mystics of this period, who include Angela of Foligno, Margery Kempe, St Gertrude and Hadewijch (see pages 99–101) often surpassed that of men in their erotic or unitive images. Based on meditations of the Crucifixion, on the dialectics of desire and the interplay of aggression and surrender, their imagery of penetration is explicitly erotic and divine, as well as intensely feminine. In this tradition the ecstasies of St Teresa of Avila in the sixteenth century were to inspire both the English Catholic poet Richard Crashaw (see page 160) and the great Italian baroque sculptor Giovanni Bernini (1698–1680) (see page 83). The luminous sensuality of Bernini's sculpture with its profane, theatre-like decor in the church of Santa Maria della Vittoria in Rome is so startling that a current guidebook is compelled to explain: 'This presentation of divine love must be appreciated in conjunction with St Teresa's own description of her ecstasy when God sent his seraph to pierce her heart with an arrow: "The pain was so sharp that I cried aloud but at the same time I experienced such delight that I wished it would last forever."'

The High Middle Ages is also notable for the flowering of vernacular literature. The songs of the Goliards, wandering students who wrote and performed lusty and earthy entertainments, formed a bridge between Latin, previously the language of writing, and the vernacular, and between the religious and the secular. Many of their songs exuberantly celebrated carnality and lewdness with sharp sensuousness, and many implicitly acknowledged female sexuality. The *Carmina Burana*, Carl Orff's popular cantata, is probably the best-known collection of Goliard songs (see page 90). But perhaps the greatest of them all is 'The Confession' by a Bohemian scholar known simply as the 'Archpoet' (see page 91). It is one of the first articulate rebellions against the asceticism of the early Christian fathers.

The vernacular love songs of the Provençal troubadours written between 1095 and 1295 were infinitely more delicate than anything produced by the Goliards, expressing in lyric form a love first encoded by the monk Andreas Capellanus (*fl.* 1180s) in *The Art of Courtly Love*. Recent scholars suggest that Cappellanus's view of courtly love may have been tongue in cheek. Certainly he was influenced by Ovid, whose own erotic writing was openly mischievous. The essential ingredients of the mixture of behaviours and emotions which the troubadours themselves called *fins d'amors*, are humility, courtesy, the idealized lady and something approaching a religion of love. These Provençal songs were predominantly adulterous love songs, the eroticism of which lay in the tension between desire and unrequited love, an emotion entirely new in Western society. This love, however, was not necessarily platonic, as the implicit sexuality of the songs of the Comtessa de Dia (see page 92) and Arnaut Daniel (see page 96) reveal. Daniel was much admired later by Petrarch (1304–74), and also by Dante, who wrote: 'In verses of love and tales of romance he surpassed them all.'

The earliest examples of German vernacular verse, called *Minnesang*, which first appeared in the mid twelfth century, were strongly influenced by the Provençal courtly love lyric. Their main exponent, Walther von der Vogelweide, however, turned the courtly ideals on their head. In one of his songs, reversing the traditional courtly power structure, he insists that courtly joy and praise of the lady depends entirely on the poet. By employing farce, he also shattered the image of the unattainable, eternally beautiful lady (see page 95).

The adventure romances of Chrétien de Troyes were yet another product of the twelfth-century French cultural renaissance that was to have such a long and powerful influence on Western erotic literature and, indeed, on literature in general. Although he was out of sympathy with *fins d'amors* and critical of their non-conjugal, anti-social nature, it is to Chrétien that we owe the European genre of the Arthurian courtly romance with its central, consummated, adulterous love affair between Lancelot and Guinevere. Chrétien achieves erotic effect by a deliberate lack of explicitness: ' . . . he held her in his arms and she held him in hers . . . the two of them felt a joy and wonder the equal of which has never been heard or known. But I shall let it remain a secret for ever, since it should not be written of: the most delightful and choicest pleasure is that which is hinted at, but never told.' Eros had seldom played so coy. Yet it took little more than the addition of a smile on the lover's face in *Lancelot du Lac*, the early thirteenth-century French prose 'vulgate' version, to make the lustful

Francesca da Rimini in Dante's *Inferno* cite this story as the cause of her downfall. This must be one of the earliest cases of attributing corrupting power to the written word.

It seems reasonable to suppose that the immoral nature of their subject matter is what contributed to the success of these medieval romances. Much older than the tale of Lancelot and Guinevere is the hugely popular story of Tristan and Isolde, which aroused moral censure at the time for lasciviously depicting the consummation of adulterous love. The *Tristran* of Thomas of Britain or Brittany (see page 93) captures the orgasmic moment of death, which Richard Wagner was to celebrate in his opera 700 years later (see page 267).

The Romance of the Rose (see page 97) was another medieval bestseller. It survives in just under 300 manuscripts, and with the invention of printing it went almost immediately into fourteen editions. The first 4,058 lines of this allegorical romance were written by Guillaume de Lorris around 1237 and the remaining 17,622 lines by Jean de Meun some 40 years later. The narrative takes the form of a lover's desire and eventual possession of a rose. Not all readers admired it, and it is possible that not all critics appreciated – or perhaps even apprehended – the irony employed by the writers or the symbolism of the rose-sanctuary-cunt. Christine de Pisan (1364–*c.* 1430), the French author who, as an admirer of Petrarch and Boccaccio, was clearly no prude, was outraged by Meun's misogyny and thought it vulgar: 'I daresay even the Goliards would be shocked to read or hear it in public. . . . ' It seems likely that part of *The Romance of the Rose* was translated into English by Chaucer in the fourteenth century.

The finest English example of the romance genre, *Sir Gawain and the Green Knight* (late fourteenth century), is distinctly more low key than any of its European counterparts. Yet the way in which this unknown contemporary of Chaucer who, writing in a northwestern dialect, interlaces fast-moving scenes of the hunt with slow-moving, slyly perilous seduction scenes makes it impossible to deny the erotic content of the attempts on Gawain's chastity – perhaps because of its very subtlety (see page 107).

The English contribution to erotic literature during the Middle Ages when compared to that of Europe and the rest of the world was small. The earliest English secular poetry of a sexual nature is found among the famous collection of riddles in what is known as *The Exeter Book* (see page 80), a manuscript of Old English poetry copied *c.* 940 and given by Bishop Leofric (*d.* 1072) to Exeter Cathedral. Possibly dating back to the second century, the poems are scatological, perhaps even childish, yet they possess a certain disarming innocence and seductive charm. To the monks who copied them out and presumably read them to each other they may well have given some light erotic relief.

The riddle played a part in the development of Welsh erotic poetry, which was also influenced by French verse of this period (the *pastourelle* and the *fabliaux*) in their stress upon female sexual insatiability. Much of this poetry, especially the *fabliaux*, may have been deliberately anti-erotic in its desire to shock, rather than erotic in the sense of stimulating sexual excitement in its intended audience. Gwerful Mechain is the only female poet of medieval Wales survived by a substantial body of work. Her erotic poems offer an image of a sexually empowered woman very different from the passivity of the courtly love ideal. Her poem 'The Female Genitals' (see page 114) differs from Dafydd ap Gwilym's 'The Penis' (see page 109), for which it forms a natural partner, in that it contains no element of personal boasting. Dafydd's poem is cast in the form of a complaint addressed to the unruly penis, a subject which preoccupied so many ancient Roman poets (but not one that bothered the unrequited troubadours). But it is, in fact, an elaborate means of boasting the poet's sexual prowess. Phallocentricity was not confined to Celtic or European culture, as the poem by the Arabian Ibn Kamal attests (see page 128).

In Celtic-speaking lands the normal medium for narrative literature was prose; verse was the medium for personal expression and the public arts of panegyric, elegy and satire. In England the situation was the reverse, as Chaucer's poetry exemplifies. Chaucer turned his hand to many different types of erotica: in *The Retraction* he refers to having written 'many a lecherous lay', and he was adept at anglicizing the French *fabliaux*, which expressed an approach to life and sex that frequently overlapped the Goliardic songs.

Chaucer did not, however, imitate the pronounced scorn and hatred of women expressed in the *fabliaux*. His Wife of Bath is casually promiscuous, but to be gently laughed at and appreciated rather than morally condemned. Widely celebrated for his comic-erotic skills, it is his tragic love story 'Troilus and Creseyde' (see page 105) that the twentieth-century English critic C.S. Lewis considered the greatest erotic poetry in the world: 'It is a lesson worth learning how Chaucer can so triumphantly celebrate the flesh without becoming either delirious like Rossetti or pornographic like Ovid.'

There are many parallels between Chaucer and his contemporary Boccaccio, who was the Italian master of medieval erotic literature. Both, for example, used the Troilus and Cressida story, but unlike Chaucer, who understood well the bitter-sweetness of Eros, Boccaccio turned his version, *Il Filostrato*, into a bitter attack on women. Misogyny, mostly in the form of castrating female sexual incontinence, is also present in his *Decameron* (see page 104), a collection of stories from chivalry, romance, saga, fable, legend, myth, *fabliau* and *conte*. The stories are tied together in a loose framework in which a group of ten nobles leaves Florence to escape the plague. They spend ten days (hence the title) in telling stories, each of them telling one tale per day, making 100 in all.

The *Decameron* was heavily influenced by classical erotic literature, by the medieval French tradition of chivalric romance, and by the Italian tradition of love literature, which supremely, in *The Divine Comedy* by Dante (1265–1321), had surpassed its French and Provençal progenitors. The *Decameron* nevertheless reflects a period of cultural transition. looking forward to the Renaissance. Whereas Chaucer displays a concern with the inward psychology and differentiation of individuals, Boccaccio is pre-eminently interested in the moment of action when, by word or deed, the mind and the outer world coincide. Not for him the situation of unrequited love with the idealistic, untouchable lady; the misogyny notwithstanding, the heroines of the *Decameron* are, on the whole, creatures of flesh and blood with their own desires, strong opinions and determination to act.

If Dante's comedy was divine, Boccaccio's was human. Illicit love, adultery, homosexuality, animal lust and sexual pleasure are all depicted. For this early humanist, sex is omnipresent; it is a natural part of human nature and infinitely more interesting than reason. The overwhelming response demanded – and achieved – is that of laughter although the actual descriptions of love-making are on the whole stylized and almost mechanical. Some of the more sexually explicit tales (especially those told by Dioneo, whose name was derived from 'Dionysus', god of wine-drinking and ecstatic fervour) were constantly censured by the puritanical, but it was mainly the blasphemy and profanity that caused many translated editions to be cut or bowdlerized. The Council of Trent removed it from the Index of forbidden books in 1537 only when the clerical sinners and erring nuns were metamorphosed into lay folk.

The literary device of a group of storytellers taking it in turns to tell a tale, which forms part of the early development of the novel, is also used in the *Les Cent nouvelles nouvelles* (*The Hundred Tales*), which is set in the Burgundian court in the mid-fifteenth century and attributed to the Provençal writer Antoine de la Sale. The same device was also used in the *Heptameron* written, or at least compiled, by Marguerite de Navarre. From a twentieth-century perspective such tales may seem little more than mildly titillating, licentious, comic diversions. Although sex is rarely pleasurable for the characters in the *Heptameron*, the story on page 119 is something of an exception. But humour and eroticism are not necessarily antithetical.

Like the pander, or 'go-between' present in the Troilus and Cressida tale, the role of the voyeur in sexual intrigue was much loved in medieval erotic literature. It is somewhat artificially incorporated into a story from *The Hundred Tales* entitled 'The Calf' (see page 111), but it still adds an element of excitement, a titillating fear of discovery, as well as appealing to the desire for illicit or vicarious sex in the reader or listener. He (it's usually a he, Lady Nijō (see page 101) is a rarity) acts the part of pander between the writer and reader. Joannot Martorell who, with Marti Joan de Galba, wrote the little-known Catalan masterpiece *Tirant lo Blanc*, plays a novel joke on the erotic sensibilities of his readers in the description of the voyeuristic role played by his knightly hero (see page 115). This was a book that appealed to Cervantes (1547–1616), as the following reaction of one of his lustful characters in *Don Quixote* reveals: ' "God help me!" shouted the priest. "Here's *Tirant lo Blanc!* Give it here, friend, for I promise you I've found a wealth of pleasure and a gold mine of enjoyment in it." ' Later treatments of voyeurism include *Five Women Who Loved Love* (see page 165) by the seventeenth-century Japanese author Ihara Saikaku, and 'The Eve of St Agnes' (see page 222) by John Keats who achieves the acme of erotic voyeuristic effect.)

The Later Middle Ages

Anti-clericalism and erotica became almost natural bedfellows during the mid to late Middle Ages. It was a subject much loved by the often priapic or scatological, always funny and sometimes voluptuous, French *fabliaux*. These comprised eight-syllable rhymed verses, rarely more than 400 lines long. The were written in the vernacular and, unlike the *fins d'amors* of the troubadours, were intended to stimulate laughter. The use of the vernacular, a rejection of medieval asceticism and of courtly *fins d'amors*, the humanism of Renaissance thinking, and eventually Protestantism, all provided fresh stimuli to this genre. Doubtless the illicit sexual proclivities of the women and men of God provided justification for satirical sketches, but there is something almost childishly gleeful in the works of writers like Marguerite de Navarre (see page 119), François Rabelais (see page 123) and the Italian Pietro Aretino (see page 117), as they break the rules of decorum while describing how nuns and priests break the rules of the Church. Sometime adviser to the Pope, Aretino was one of the earliest defenders of the erotic arts; he condemned the 'miserable propriety which forbids our eyes to see what pleases us most. What harm is there in seeing a man mount a woman? Should animals enjoy more freedom than we do?' Aretino is widely acclaimed as the 'inventor' of pornography.

Crammed full of allusion, pun and sexual innuendo, there is nothing veiled about the erotic ballades of François Villon (see page 113); indeed, many of them may be accurately described as pornographic in the sense that he takes his readers into the brothels of fifteenth-century France. The stark realism of this undeniably phallocentric poet, who has been described as a true descendant of the Goliardic 'Archpoet', is a far cry from the erotic spirituality of the *Rymes* of Pernette du Guillet (see page 122), which challenged the conventional misogynistic view of female sexuality in most of the erotic literature produced by men of this period.

So, too, do the frankly sensuous sonnets of Louise Labé (see page 123), published in 1555 but probably written in her youth. Called '*la belle rebelle*' by one of her admirers, Labé's unconventional lifestyle was described by a contemporary: 'She graciously received in her house nobles, gentlemen and other worthy persons with amusements and conversation ... and exquisite meals, after which she revealed her most private charms. In a word, she gave her body to those who paid, nevertheless not to everyone and never to dull or low-born people ... which is contrary to the custom of those of her profession and quality.' To an outraged Puritan, John Calvin (1509–1604), however, she was '*plebeia meretrix*'.

Predictably, Calvin not only attacked Labé but also condemned the fiction of Rabelais with its vigorously oral, anal and genital humour (see page 123). Strangely, in the eighteenth century, Voltaire was also fiercely critical of Rabelais, accusing this brilliantly licentious satirist of being filthy, boring, extravagant and unintelligible. He was appreciated, however, by many including Montaigne, La Fontaine, Nashe and Swift, and his influence is clearly discernible in Lawrence Sterne's *Tristram Shandy* (see page 198) and Joyce's *Ulysses* (see page 299). It is not easy to fix Rabelais in either the medieval or Renaissance tradition. Despite his classical learning and his opposition to medieval university 'scholasticism', the writing of this friar remains ambiguous in its parody of humanism. His women could be as sexually rapacious as any found in medieval texts; indeed, one of his characters advises building city walls out of women's vulvas because they are more resistant to wear and tear than bricks. Rabelais was a Renaissance figure, a supporter of church reform, and yet remained a product of the Middle Ages. *Pantagruel* (1533) has been described as one of those great books which makes the distinction between medieval and Renaissance meaningless, except as a notation of the passage of time.

Pierre de Ronsard, an indisputable master of French Renaissance erotic literature, made a significant contribution to the enrichment of the poetic language of love. In his collection of poems, *Amours* (1552), and his ribald '*gaillardises*' he eschewed the euphemistic Old French use of Latinate terms for the genitals and love-making, and following in the tradition of Rabelais, made it almost a humanistic principle to use the vulgar tongue (see page 129). He and his followers became known as the poets of the *Pléiade*. Ronsard's *La Bouquinade*, a tale of the war between Amor and Pan (the latter was known for the sexual energy with which he pursued both nymphs and shepherds, but would settle for solitary erotic satisfaction were his amorous ambitions frustrated), is notable for its merging of the meanings of 'satyr' and 'satire'. This was to influence the style and content of erotic literature for at least two centuries.

Pierre de Bourdeille, Seigneur de Brantôme, was another star in the constellation of French erotic writers of this period. The son of a lady-in-waiting to Queen Marguerite of Navarre, his 'memoirs' revel in the nefarious sexual adventures of the French court. *The Lives of Gallant Ladies* (see page 130) is a mine of erotic detail about such sexual practices as the use of the *godemiche* (dildo), the pleasures of oral sex and the delights of lesbian sex. He viewed this as some sort of harmless sexual training for young women prior to marriage which was infinitely preferable to risking pregnancy: 'There is a great difference betwixt throwing water in a vessel and merely watering about it and around the rim.' This phallocentric attitude towards lesbianism was to be a regular standby for pornographers ever after; it appears, for example, in a quasi-educational 'adult' movie made by the American Candida Royalle in 1991. Brantôme was very aware of the power of erotic literature to excite. He records how one particular 'Gallant Lady', who kept a statue of Aretino in her room, confessed to her lover that 'books and other devices had served her well'. Another, on looking at a book of postures (this may be another reference to Aretino) 'fell into such an ecstasy of amorous desire ... that she saw no further than the fourth page, fainting right away at the fifth'. 'Fainting', like 'dying', was what ladies tended to experience when they reached sexual climax, as Samuel Richardson's *Pamela* (see page 185) was to discover.

In much English erotic poetry of the sixteenth century, culminating in the 'High Renaissance' of the late Elizabethans, there is far greater spiritualization in writing about love, and at the same time a growth in sensuousness. Petrarch (1304–72), widely regarded as 'the father' of Italian humanism, was an important influence; his love sonnets were translated and imitated by Sir Thomas Wyatt (1503–42), whose own love poetry, some of which was also influenced by Aretino, heralded the Elizabethan literary renaissance.

Ovid was probably the biggest single influence on Elizabethan erotic poets, who include Spenser, Marlowe, Sidney, Barnes, Nashe and Shakespeare. All were indebted to Ovid's erotic mythological narrative poetry, and especially to his awareness of sexual love as something that could be humourous and grotesquely savage, as well as beautiful, emotionally compelling and an essential part of what it is to be human.

Christopher Marlowe translated Ovid's elegies and his debt to the Roman is nowhere more strongly apparent than in 'Hero and Leander' (see page 136) in which he reveals an awareness of the deep-lying psycho-cultural connection with sexuality that exists in the ambiguous notion of metamorphosis. Shakespeare was also attracted to the Ovidian mythological erotic narrative. *Venus and Adonis* (see page 137), thought to be his first publication, describes the passionately sensuous love of the goddess for the beautiful youth who resists, preferring to join the hunt for the boar, where he is killed. The interlacing of love and war (a technique previously put to erotic effect in the fourteenth-century *Sir Gawain and the Green Knight*) imbues the poem with a powerful eroticism which brilliantly exploits the common sixteenth-century use of 'dying' as a metaphor for orgasm.

The Faerie Queene (see page 132) by Edmund Spenser shows influences in addition to those from Ovid. He based the poem on the chivalrous romance epic popularized by the Italian Ludovico Ariosto (1474–1533) whose *Orlando Furioso* (1532) had given this medieval genre an innovative erotic charge. Spenser's fairyland was a romantic world which was to appeal to the eighteenth-century romantic medievalists, and an erotic world to which Keats, especially, was drawn in 'The Eve of St Agnes' (see page 222).

It has been said that Elizabethan poetry deserves the name erotic and is rarely coarse, while Elizabethan drama is frequently coarse but rarely erotic. At times, of course, a dramatist such as Shakespeare could reach sublime erotic heights, most notably in *Antony and Cleopatra* and *Troilus and Cressida*, but there is some truth in this aphorism. Certainly, much of the popular drama of the time is bawdy and scatological, appealing to a sense of humour which can be shared by a large and often disparate audience, rather than to the senses of touch, sight, hearing, smell and taste, which fuel a more privately experienced imaginative erotic response.

Doubtless the rise of Puritanism played a part in this. The *double entendres* of so much of Elizabethan drama may have been the result of the need for writers to wrap up meaning to evade the censoriousness of the Puritan mind, and humorous wordplay provided a means of doing this. Prose and poetry, largely the preserve of the educated, upper-class male, could get away with appealing more directly, and intimately, to the individual prepared to accept, enjoy and risk any danger that might lie in a private erotic response. Poetry was not, however, always immune. In 1599 the Archbishop of Canterbury ordered Christopher Marlowe's translation of Ovid's *Amores* to be burned on the grounds that it was 'scurrilous and offensive', a judgement that Ovid might well have enjoyed.

Mallanaga

c. 1st–*c.* 4th century

The Kama Sutra *was written by an Indian monk named Mallanaga who belonged to the Vatsyayana sect. Originally a collection of aphorisms, it was later linked and explained by a narrator intent on reconciling* kama *(life of the senses) with* dharma *(religious obligation) and* artha *(social well-being). Translated into English by two Victorian erotophiles, Sir Richard Burton and F.F. Arbuthnot, the work was published by the Kama Shastra Society which they founded in order to publish Oriental erotic classics.*

From the **Kama Sutra**, Chapter VII: 'Of the Various Modes of Striking, and of the Sounds Appropriate to them'. *Trans. Sir Richard Burton and F.F. Arbuthnot*

Sexual intercourse can be compared to a quarrel, on account of the contrarieties of love and its tendency to dispute. The place of striking with passion is the body, and on the body the special places are:

> The shoulders.
> The head.
> The space between the breasts.
> The back.
> The jaghana, or middle part of the body.
> The sides.

Striking is of four kinds, viz.:

> Striking with back of the hand.
> Striking with the fingers a little contracted.
> Striking with the fist.
> Striking with the open palm of the hand.

On account of its causing pain, striking gives rise to the hissing sound, which is of various kinds, and to the eight kinds of crying, viz.:

The sound of Hin.
The thundering sound.
The cooing sound.
The weeping sound.
The sound Phut.
The sound Phât.
The sound Sût.
The sound Plât.

Besides these, there are also words having a meaning, such as 'mother', and those that are expressive of prohibition, sufficiency, desire of liberation, pain or praise, and to which may be added sounds like those of the dove, the cuckoo, the green pigeon, the parrot, the bee, the sparrow, the flamingo, the duck, and the quail, which are all occasionally made use of.

Blows with the fist should be given on the back of the woman, while she is sitting on the lap of the man, and she should give blows in return, abusing the man as if she were angry, and making the cooing and the weeping sounds. While the woman is engaged in congress the space between the breasts should be struck with the back of the hand, slowly at first, and then proportionately to the increasing excitement, until the end.

At this time the sounds Hin and others may be made, alternately or optionally, according to habit. When the man, making the sound Phât, strikes the woman on the head, with the fingers of his hand a little contracted, it is called Prasritaka, which means striking with the fingers of the hand a little contracted. In this case the appropriate sounds are the cooing sound, the sound Phât, and the sound Phut in the interior of the mouth, and at the end of congress the sighing and weeping sounds. The sound Phât is an imitation of the sound of a bamboo being split, while the sound Phut is like the sound made by something falling into water. At all times when kissing and such like things are begun, the woman should give a reply with a hissing sound. During the excitement when the woman is not accustomed to striking, she continually utters words expressive of prohibition, sufficiently, or desire of liberation, as well as the words 'father', 'mother', intermingled with the sighing, weeping and thundering sounds. Towards the conclusion of the congress, the breasts, the jaghana, and the sides of the woman should be pressed with the open palms of the hand, with some force, until the end of it, and then sounds like those of the quail, or the goose should be made.

Tzu Yeh

c. 3rd–*c.* 4th century

Forty two poems are attributed to a young woman known by the name of Tzu Yeh. The Tzu Yeh poems are popular folk songs of Wu, the Kiangsu and Chekiang provinces of modern China, which were widely imitated from the 4th–9th centuries.

Songs. *Trans. Kenneth Rexroth and Ling Chung*

It is night again
I let down my silken hair

Classic Kama Sutra (Indian – late 18th century)

Over my shoulders
And open my thighs
Over my lover.
'Tell me, is there any part of me
That is not lovable?'

~

I had not fastened my sash over my gown,
When you asked me to look out the window.
If my skirt fluttered open,
Blame the Spring wind.

St Augustine

354–430

Born at Tagaste, Numidia, Aurelius Augustinus – as he was born – was of Roman descent, but studied rherotic in Carthage, where he fathered a son by his concubine. He lectured at Tagaste and Carthage and for ten years was a Manichean, though he later went to Rome and was converted to Christianity. In 391, while visiting Hippo, he was ordained priest, and in 396 became bishop. He was canonized after his death. St Augustine's central tenet of the corruption of human nature through the fall of man and the consequent slavery of the human will moulded Christian doctrine.

From **Confessions** (*c.* 397). *Trans. anon.*

When I love thee, what kind of thing is it that I love? Not the beauty of bodyes, not the order of tyme; not the cleerness of this light which our eyes are so glad to see; not the harmony of sweet tongues in Musique; not the fragrancy of flowres, and other unctuous and aromatical odours; not Manna, nor any thing of sweet and curious tast; not carnall creatures which may delightfully be imbraced by flesh and blood: They are not these thinges which I love in loving God. And yet I love a kind of *Light,* a kind of *voyce,* a kind of *odour,* a kind of *food,* and a kind of *imbracing,* when I love my God: the *light,* the *voyce,* the *odour,* the *food,* and the *imbracing* of my inward man, where that shines to my soule which is not circumscribed by any place; that sounds to myne eare which is not stolne and snatched away by tyme; that yieldeth smell which is not scattered by ayre; that savours in tast which is not consumed by eating; that remayns enjoyed which is not devoured by satiety; this is that which I love when I love my God.

St Jerome

c. 341–420

A Dalmatian-born Roman monk, Jerome (Eusebius Sophronius Hieronymous) dedicated his considerable scholarship to the Scriptures after suffering a terrifying vision of damnation during a journey to the Holy Land in 374. His work includes the Vulgate (Latin) Bible, and much fiery invective against targets ranging from women to St Augustine.

From **Letters, Patrologia Latina (Migne)**. *Trans. Peter Brown*

O how often, when I was living in the desert, in that lonely waste, scorched by the burning sun, that affords to hermits their primitive dwelling place, how often did I fancy myself surrounded by the pleasures of Rome . . . though in my fear of Hell, I had condemned myself to this prison house, where my only companions were scorpions and wild beasts, I often found myself surrounded by bands of dancing girls. My face pale with fasting; but though my limbs were cold as ice, my mind was burning with desire, and the fires of lust kept bubbling up before me while my flesh was as good as dead.

Bhatrihari

c. 570–c. 651

An Indian philosopher and poet of noble birth, attached to the court at Valabhi (in modern Gujarat), Bhatrihari is remembered for his three satakas *(collections of poems) concerning, respectively, erotic love, ethics and renunciation. He is also thought to have been the author of key works on the Sanskrit language.*

From **Passionate Encounters**. *Trans. Barbara Stoller Miller*

Bearing the lustre of a full moon
at its loftiest phase,
the lotus-face of a slender girl
locks honey in her lips.
What is tart now like unripe fruit
on vines of gourd,
when time has run its course
will be an acrid poison.

How could men of wisdom
let their mind's vigour be sapped,
be distracted by the ignominies of courting
at the gates of an evil king's palace,
were it not for girls' flashing lotus eyes,
splendid as the newly risen moon,
girls with belts of bells playing
on fine waists bent by heavy breasts.

Women bathed in sandalwood scents,
flashing antelope-eyes,
arbours of fountains, flowers,
and moonlight,
a terrace swept with breezes
of flowering jasmine –
in summer they stimulate
love and the love-god himself.

Winds laden with perfumes,
branches tipped with tender shoots;
mates of cuckoos whose drunken cries
express their longing;
moonlike faces of women
with drops of moisture from sports of love –
how do nature's riches spread
to make such opulence in summer?

Alcuin (or Ealwhine)

735–804

A scholar, theologian and poet, Alcuin was born in York, but is best remembered for his influences in Europe. After studying in England he visited Rome, and it was on his return from there, in 781, that he met the Emperor Charlemagne, and became his adviser and friend. Apart from a two-year visit to England, he remained in France, becoming Archbishop of Tours. The author of several theological and philosophical works, Alcuin was a central figure in the Carolingian Renaissance.

[From poem to a friend]. Trans. John Boswell

> Love has pierced my heart with its flame . . . ,
> And love always burns with fresh fire.
> Neither land nor sea, hills nor woods nor mountains
> Can impede or block the path to him,
> Loving father, who ever licks your breast
> And who washes, beloved, your chest with his tears.
> . . . All joys are changed into sad mournings,
> Nothing is permanent, everything will pass.
> Let me therefore flee to you with my whole heart,
> And do you flee to me from the vanishing world. . . .

[From letter written to a friend – a bishop and possibly the recipient of the above poem].
Trans. John Boswell

I think of your love and friendship with such sweet memories, reverend bishop, that I long for that lovely time when I may be able to clutch the neck of your sweetness with the fingers of my desires. Alas, if only it were granted to me, as it was to Habakkuk, to be transported to you, how would I sink into your embraces, . . . how would I cover, with tightly pressed lips, not only your eyes, ears, and mouth but also your very finger and toes your, not once but many a time.

Anon.

From **Anglo-Saxon riddles** (**The Exeter Book,** 7th century).
Trans. Michael Alexander

> This knave came in where he knew she'd be,
> Standing in a corner. He stepped across to her
> With the briskness of youth, and, yanking up his own
> Robe with his hands, rammed something stiff
> Under her girdle as she stood there,
> Did what he wanted; they wobbled about.
> The serving-man hurried. His servant was capable,
> Useful at times; but at every bout
> His strength grew tired sooner than hers did.
> Weary of the grind. Gradually there were signs
> That there grew beneath her girdle what good men often
> Long for in their hearts and lay out good money for.

[Answer: A poker]

Chao Luan-Luan

c. 8th century

Little is known of this author other than that she was a sophisticated prostitute in the city of Ch'ang An, the capital of the T'ang dynasty.

'**Creamy Breasts**'. *Trans. Kenneth Rexroth and Ling Chung*

> Fragrant with powder, moist with perspiration,
> They are the pegs of a jade inlaid harp.
> Aroused by spring, they are soft as cream
> Under the fertilizing mist.
> After my bath my perfumed lover
> Holds them and plays with them
> And they are cool as peonies and purple grapes.

Anon. (Arabia)

'**Nizam the pederast**' (9th century).

> Nizam the pederast, whose delight in boys
> Was known throughout Bagdad, one afternoon
> In a secluded place saw in a clearing
> The flash of limbs behind a nearby bush,
> And looking closer came upon a youth
> Who seemed more lovely than his dreams had promised,
> Lying asleep in shade, his head pressed deep
>
> Into crossed arms, his long slim body
> Quite naked, the firm buttocks firmly offered.
> Quick as a jackal pouncing, Nizam jumped
> Upon the lad, his robe about his waist,
> The startled boy pierced by his lusty cock
> Before you could say knife. Not until later,
> When boy lay panting on the flattened grass,
> Did Nizam, pausing to embrace his love,
> Discover him a her, surprised but pleased
> At being given such pleasure at a source
> No previous lover seemed to know about.
>
> Nizam converted? Never. But the girl
> Now gives her lovers strange instruction.

Abu Sa'id

978–1066

Abu Sa'id was a Persian poet exemplifying the guilt-free nature of Eastern erotic poetry and art in which love transcends the pleasures of the flesh.

'I Asked My Love'.

> I asked my love: 'Why do you make yourself so beautiful?'
>   'To please myself.
> I am the eye, the mirror, and the loveliness;
> The loved one and the lover and the love.'

St Anselm

1033–1109

The Italian-born cleric Anselm was born into a noble family and entered the Benedictine monastery at Bec, Normandy in 1057, where his reputation as a formidable theologian – he laid the foundations of medieval Scholasticism and originated the 'Ontological Argument' for the existence of God – led to his appointment in 1093 as Archbishop of Canterbury. Anselm's scathing intellect led him into disputes with fellow clergy and successive English kings. He died and is buried at Canterbury and was canonized in 1494.

[From letter to Dom. Gilbert.] Trans. John Boswell

Brother Anselm to Dom Gilbert, brother, friend, beloved lover . . . sweet to me, sweetest friend, are the gifts of your sweetness, but they cannot begin to console my desolate heart for its want of your love. Even if you sent every scent of perfume, every glitter of metal, every precious gem, every texture of cloth, still it could not make up to my soul for this separation unless it returned the separated other half.

The anguish of my heart just thinking about this bears witness, as do the tears dimming my eyes and wetting my face and the fingers writing this.

You recognized, as I do now, my love for you, but I did not. Our separation from each other has shown me how much I loved you; a man does not in fact have knowledge of good and evil unless he has experienced both. Not having experienced your absence, I did not realize how sweet it was to be with you and how bitter to be without you.

But you have gained from our very separation the company of someone else, whom you love no less – or even more – than me; while I have lost you, and there is no one to take your place. You are thus enjoying your consolation, while nothing is left to me but heartbreak.

The Ecstasy of Saint Teresa Bernini

Bilhana

11th century

Bilhana was an Indian court poet who, according to legend, had a secret affair with his pupil, the beautiful daughter of a king. When this was discovered he was sentenced to death but was pardoned by the goddess Kali when she read the fifty beautiful love poems he had writen to his mistress.

From 'Fantasies of a Love-Thief'. *Trans. Barbara Stoller Miller*

Even now,
if I see her again,
her full moon face, lush new youth,
swollen breasts, passion's glow,
body burned by fire from love's arrows –
I'll quickly cool her limbs!

Even now,
if I see her again,
a lotus-eyed girl
weary from bearing her own heavy breasts –
I'll crush her in my arms
and drink her mouth like a madman,
a bee insatiably drinking a lotus!

Even now,
I remember her in love –
her body weak with fatigue,
swarms of curling hair
falling on pale cheeks,
trying to hide

the secret of her guilt.
Her soft arms
clung
like vines on my neck.

Even now,
I remember her:
deep eyes' glittering pupils
dancing wildly in love's vigil,
a wild goose
in our lotus bed of passion –
her face bowed low with shame
at dawn.

Even now,
if I see her again,
wide-eyed,
fevered from long parting –
I'll lock her tight in my limbs,
close my eyes, and never leave her!

Peter Abelard

1079–1142

A highly regarded French scholar and theologian, Peter Abelard was born in Brittany, and studied at Paris, where his brilliance gained him an academic chair and worldwide renown. His famous affair with one of his pupils, Heloise, led to his castration by her avenging uncle and his withdrawal from teaching into an abbey, though the popularity of his lectures soon brought about his return. Eventually condemned by various church councils for the unorthodoxy of his teachings, he withdrew from public life and died in a priory.

'More than a brother to me'. *Trans. John Boswell*

More than a brother to me, Jonathan,
One in soul with me . . .
How could I have taken such evil advice
And not stood by your side in battle?
How gladly would I die
And be buried with you!
Since love may do nothing greater than this,
And since to live after you
Is to die forever:
Half a soul
Is not enough for life.
Then – at the moment
of final agony –
I should have rendered
Either of friendship's dues:

To share the triumph
Or suffer the defeat;
Either to rescue you
Or to fall with you,
Shedding for you that life
Which you so often saved,
So that even death would join

Rather than part us.

I can still my lute,
But not my sobs and tears:
A heart too is shattered
By the plucking of stricken hands,
The hoarse sobbing of voices.

~

From **Historia calamitatum** (*c.* 1132). *Trans. Betty Radice*

There was in Paris at the time a young girl named Heloise, the niece of Fulbert, one of the canons, and so much loved by him that he had done everything in his power to advance her education in letters. In looks she did not rank lowest, while in the extent of her learning she stood supreme. A gift for letters is so rare in women that it added greatly to her charm and had won her renown throughout the realm. I considered all the usual attractions for a lover and decided she was the one to bring to my bed, confident that I should have an easy success; for at that time I had youth and exceptional good looks as well as my great reputation to recommend me, and feared no rebuff from any woman I might choose to honour with my love. Knowing the girl's knowledge and love of letters I thought she would be all the more ready to consent, and that even when separated we could enjoy each other's presence by exchange of written messages in which we could speak more openly than in person, and so need never lack the pleasures of conversation.

All on fire with desire for this girl I sought an opportunity of getting to know her through private daily meetings and so more easily winning her over; and with this end in view I came to an arrangement with her uncle, with the help of some of his friends, whereby he should take me into his house, which was very near my school, for whatever sum he liked to ask. As a pretext I said that my household cares were hindering my studies and the expense was more than I could afford. Fulbert dearly loved money, and was moreover always ambitious to further his niece's education in letters, two weaknesses which made it easy for me to gain his consent and obtain my desire: he was all eagerness for my money and confident that his niece would profit from my teaching. This led him to make an urgent request which furthered my love and fell in with my wishes more than I had dared to hope; he gave me complete charge over the girl, so that I could devote all the leisure time left me by my school to teaching her by day and night, and if I found her idle I was to punish her severely. I was amazed by his simplicity – if he had entrusted a tender lamb to a ravening wolf it would not have surprised me more. In handing her over to me to punish as well as to teach, what else was he doing but giving me complete freedom to realize my desires, and providing an opportunity, even if I did not make use of it, for me to bend her to my will by threats and blows if persuasion failed? But there were two special reasons for his freedom from base suspicion: his love for his niece and my previous reputation for continence.

Need I say more? We were united, first under one roof, then in heart; and so with our lessons as a pretext we abandoned ourselves entirely to love. Her studies allowed us to withdraw in private, as love desired, and then with our books open before us, more words of love than of our reading passed between us, and more kissing than teaching. My hands strayed oftener to her bosom than to the pages; love drew our eyes to look on each other more than reading kept them on our texts. To avert suspicion I sometimes struck her, but these blows were prompted by love and tender feeling rather than anger and irritation, and were sweeter than any balm could be. In short, our desires left no stage of love-making untried, and if love could devise something new, we welcomed it. We entered on each joy the more eagerly for our previous inexperience, and were the less easily sated.

Heloise

c. 1100–c. 1163

Heloise was educated in a convent at Argenteuil, and bore a son by Peter Abelard whom she refused to marry because of her philosophical opposition to marriage. When Peter Abelard was castrated by her avenging uncle, Heloise displayed her love for him by becoming a prioress.

[*From a letter to Peter Abelard addressed 'To her only one after Christ, she who is his alone in Christ'*] (*c. 1132*). *Trans. Betty Radice*

In my case, the pleasures of lovers which we shared have been too sweet – they can never displease me, and can scarcely be banished from my thoughts. Wherever I turn they are always there before my eyes, bringing with them awakened longings and fantasies which will not even let me sleep. Even during the celebration of the Mass, when our prayers should be purer, lewd visions of those pleasures take such a hold upon my unhappy soul that my thoughts are on their wantonness instead of on prayers. I should be groaning over the sins I have committed, but I can only sigh for what I have lost. Everything we did and also the times and places are stamped on my heart along with your image, so that I live through it all again with you. Even in sleep I know no respite. Sometimes my thoughts are betrayed in a movement of my body, or they break out in an unguarded word. In my utter wretchedness, that cry from a suffering soul could well be mine: 'Miserable creature that I am, who is there to rescue me out of the body doomed to this death?' Would that in truth I could go on: 'The grace of God through Jesus Christ our Lord.' This grace, my dearest, came upon you unsought – a single wound of the body by freeing you from these torments has healed many wounds in your soul. Where God may seem to you an adversary he has in fact proved himself kind: like an honest doctor who does not shrink from giving pain if it will bring about a cure. But for me, youth and passion and experience of pleasures which were so delightful intensify the torments of the flesh and longings of desire, and the assault is the more overwhelming as the nature they attack is the weaker.

Marbod, Bishop of Rennes

1035–1123

Marbod, French Bishop of Rennes, is best known as the author of a Latin 'Lapidaire', an allegorical poem in praise of precious stones, which was translated into French in the 12th and 13th centuries, and which is unusually sympathetic to women.

From **'The Unyielding Youth'**. *Trans. John Boswell*

Horace composed an ode about a certain boy
Whose face was so lovely he could easily have been a girl,
Whose hair fell in waves against his ivory neck,
Whose forehead was white as snow and his eyes as black as pitch,
Whose soft cheeks were full of delicious sweetness
When they bloomed in the brightness of a blush of beauty.
His nose was perfect, his lips flame red, lovely his teeth –
An exterior formed in measure to match his mind.

. . .

This vision of a face, radiant and full of beauty,
Kindled with the torch of love the heart of whoever beheld him.
But this boy, so lovely and appealing,
A torment to all who looked upon him,
Was made by nature so cruel and unyielding
That he would die rather than yield to love.
Harsh and ungrateful, as if born of a tiger,
He only laughed at the soft words of admirers,
Laughed at their vain efforts,
Laughed at the tears of a sighing lover.
He laughed at those whom he himself was causing to perish.
Surely he is wicked, cruel and wicked,
Who by the viciousness of his character denies the beauty of his body.
A fair face should have a wholesome mind,
Patient and not proud but yielding in this or that.
The little flower of age is swift, of surpassing brevity;
Soon it wastes away, vanishes, and cannot be revived.
This flesh so fair, so milky, so flawless,
So healthy, so lovely, so glowing, so soft –
The time will come when it is ugly and rough,
When this youthful skin will become repulsive.
So while you bloom, adopt a more becoming demeanour.

Hilary

12th century

Known as Hilary the Englishman, the poet Hilary lived in Paris where he was a pupil of Peter Abelard. He is renowned for his love poems which explored at length the theme of unyielding youth.

'To an English Boy'. *Trans. John Boswell*

Beautiful boy, flower fair,
Glittering jewel, if only you knew
That the loveliness of your face
Was the torch of my love.

The moment I saw you,
Cupid struck me; but I hesitate,
For my Dido holds me,
And I fear her wrath.

Oh, how happy would I be
If for a new favourite
I could abandon this love
In the ordinary way.

I will win, as I believe,
For I will yield to you in the hunt:
I am the hunted, you are the hunter,
And I yield to any hunter like you.

Even the ruler of heaven,
Once the ravisher of boys,
If he were here now would carry off
Such beauty to his heavenly bower.

Then, in the chambers of heaven,
You would be equally ready for either task:
Sometimes in bed, other times as cupbearer –
And Jove's delight as both.

Anon. (a lesbian nun – Germany)

c. 12th century

'To G' (*c.* 12th century). *Trans. John Boswell*

To G., her singular rose,
From A. – the bonds of precious love.
What is my strength, that I should bear it,
That I should have patience in your absence?
Is my strength the strength of stones,
That I should await your return?
I, who grieve ceaselessly day and night
Like someone who has lost a hand or a foot?
Everything pleasant and delightful
Without you seems like mud underfoot.
I shed tears as I used to smile,
And my heart is never glad.
When I recall the kisses you gave me,
And how with tender words you caressed my little breasts,
I want to die

La Maddalena Titian

Because I cannot see you.

What can I, so wretched, do?

Where can I, so miserable, turn?

If only my body could be entrusted to the earth

Until your longed-for return;

Or if passage could be granted me as it was to Habakkuk,

So that I might come there just once

To gaze on my beloved's face –

Then I should not care if it were the hour of death itself.

For no one has been born into the world

So lovely and full of grace,

Or who so honestly

And with such deep affection loves me.

I shall therefore not cease to grieve

Until I deserve to see you again.

Well has a wise man said that it is a great sorrow for a man to be without that

Without which he cannot live.

As long as the world stands

You shall never be removed from the core of my being.

What more can I say?

Come home, sweet love!

Prolong your trip no longer;

Know that I can bear your absence no longer.

Farewell.

Remember me.

Anon.

'Under the Linden Tree' (Carmina Burana, 12th century).
Trans. David Parlett

Ich was ein chint so wolgetan
  virgo dum florebam . . .

Oh, what a lovely girl I was
  when I was young and pure!
Everyone thought the world of me –
  I charmed them, to be sure!

  Alas and lack-a-day!
Thrice cursèd be the linden tree
  that grows along the way!

One day I went off to the fields
  to pluck me a bouquet:
but a vagabond lay there, with plans
  to pluck ME, so to say!

  Alas . . .

He took me by the fair white hand –
  not without hesitation –
and led me to the field himself –
  with some prevarication.

Alas . . .

He then grabbed at my nice white dress
  very indecently,
and gripped me harder by the hand –
  excruciatingly.

  Alas . . .

He murmured 'Come along, my girl:
  these woods look good enough.'
'But as for me, I hate this route!'
  I cried, and all that stuff.

  Alas . . .

'Under a tallish linden tree,
  not very far from hence,
you'll find I've left a lovely lute –
  and suchlike instruments.'

  Alas . . .

But when we reached that linden tree
  he said 'Here's where we'll sit –'

(He was a-quiver with desire!) –
  'Let's play around a bit.'

  Alas . . .

With that, he seized me bodily –
  not without nervousness –
and said 'I'd like to marry you –
  you've got a pretty face!'

  Alas . . .

Then tearing off my little gown
  he bared me pink as ham
and battered down my last defence
  with a rampant battering-ram!

  Alas . . .

Up with his bow and arrows then –
  how well his hunt did go!
For he had played me false, and won.
  'Thanks, darling. Cheerio!'

  Alas . . .

The 'Archpoet'

c. 1130–*c.* 1165

Little is known about the life of this German secular Latin poet, but he is believed to have been an itinerant poet from German Bohemia who attached himself to Reginald von Dassell, Archbishop of Cologne and Arch-Chancellor to the Emperor Frederick Barbarossa.

From **'The Confession'**. *Trans. Helen Waddell*

Never yet could I endure
Soberness and sadness,
Jests I love and sweeter than
Honey find I gladness.
Whatsoever Venus bids
Is a joy excelling,
Never in an evil heart
Did she make her dwelling.

Down the broad way do I go,
Young and unregretting,
Wrap me in my vices up,
Virtue all forgetting,
Greedier for all delight
Than heaven to enter in:
Since the soul in me is dead,
Better save the skin.

Pardon, pray you, good my lord,
Master of discretion,
But this death I die is sweet,
Most delicious poison.
Wounded to the quick am I
By a young girl's beauty:
She's beyond my touching?   Well,
Can't the mind do duty?

Hard beyond all hardness, this
Mastering of Nature:
Who shall say his heart is clean,
Near so fair a creature?
Young are we, so hard a law,
How should we obey it?
And our bodies, they are young,
Shall they have no say in't?

Sit you down amid the fire,
Will the fire not burn you?
To Pavia come, will you
Just as chaste return you?
Pavia, where Beauty draws
Youth with finger-tips,
Youth entangled in her eyes,
Ravished with her lips.

Let you bring Hippolytus,
In Pavia dine him,
Never more Hippolytus
Will the morning find him.
In Pavia not a road
But leads to venery,
Nor among its crowding towers
One to chastity.

Comtessa (Beatriz) de Dia

12th century

Possibly one of twin daughters of Marguerite de Bourgogne Comte (d. 1163) and of Guigues IV, dauphin of the Viennois and Count of Albon (d. 1142), the Comtessa de Dia may have married Guillem of Poitiers and have taken a famous troubadour, Raimbaut d'Orange, as her lover.

'I have been in great distress'. *Trans. Peter Dronke*

I have been in great distress
for a knight for whom I longed;
I want all future times to know
how I loved him to excess.
    Now I see I am betrayed –
he claims I did not give him love –
such was the mistake I made,
naked in bed, and dressed.

How I'd long to hold him pressed
naked in my arms one night –
if I could be his pillow once,
would he not know the height of bliss?

Floris was all to Blanchefleur,
yet not so much as I am his:
I am giving my heart, my love,
my mind, my life, my eyes.

Fair, gentle lover, gracious knight,
if once I held you as my prize
and lay with you a single night
and gave you a love-laden kiss –
    my greatest longing is for you
to lie there in my husband's place,
but only if you promise this:
to do all I'd want to do.

Thomas (of Britain or Brittany)

fl. 1160–1170

Thomas was the Anglo-Norman author of the earliest extant poem about Tristan (here 'Tristran'), the Celtic hero of medieval romance. This version is thought to have been written to please the Angevin court of Henry II of England and Queen Eleanor, as it contains a euology of London.

From **Tristran** (*c.* 1152). *Trans. A.T. Hatto*

[Tristran has just died.]

As soon as Ysolt heard this news she was struck dumb with grief. So afflicted is she that she goes up the street to the Palace in advance of the others, without her cloak. The Bretons have never seen a woman of her beauty; in the city they wonder whence she comes and who she may be. Ysolt goes to where she sees his body lying, and, turning towards the east, she prays for him piteously. 'Tristran, my love, now that I see you dead, it is against reason for me to live longer. You died for my love, and I, love, die of grief, for I could not come in time to heal you and your wound. My love, my love, nothing shall ever console me for your death, neither joy nor pleasure nor any delight. May this storm be accursed that so delayed me on the sea, my sweetheart, so that I could not come! Had I arrived in time, I would have given you back your life and spoken gently to you of the love there was between us. I should have bewailed our fate, our joy, our rapture, and the great sorrow and pain that have been in our loving. I should have reminded you of this and kissed you and embraced you. If I had failed to cure you, then we could have died together. But since I could not come in time and did not hear what had happened and have come and found you dead, I shall console myself by drinking of the same cup. You have forfeited your life on my account, and I shall do as a true lover: I will die for you in return!'

She takes him in her arms and then, lying at full length, she kisses his face and lips and clasps him tightly to her. Then straining body to body, mouth to mouth, she at once renders up her spirit and of sorrow for her lover dies thus at his side.

Tristran died of his longing, Ysolt because she could not come in time. Tristran died for his love; fair Ysolt because of tender pity.

Marie de France

fl. late 12th century

Marie de France is the name given to the author of a book of short narrative poems intended to be sung, known as The Lais of Marie de France. Whoever wrote these exquisite courtly lais was clearly well educated and possibly of noble birth. Suggestions as to her true identity include Mary, Abbess of Reading, Marie de Meulan, or Marie, Countess of Boulogne.

From **Rossignol**. *Trans. Glyn S. Burgess and Keith Busby*

I shall relate an adventure to you from which the Bretons composed a lay. *Laüstic* is its name,
I believe, and that is what the Bretons call it in their land. In French the title is *Rossignol*, and
Nightingale is the correct English word.

In the region of St Malo was a famous town and two knights dwelt there, each with a fortified
house. Because of the fine qualities of the two men the town acquired a good reputation. One
of the knights had taken a wise, courtly and elegant wife who conducted herself, as custom
dictated, with admirable propriety. The other knight was a young man who was well known
amongst his peers for his prowess and great valour. He performed honourable deeds gladly
and attended many tournaments, spending freely and giving generously whatever he had. He
loved his neighbour's wife and so persistently did he request her love, so frequent were his
entreaties and so many qualities did he possess that she loved him above all things, both for
the good she had heard about him and because he lived close by. They loved each other
prudently and well, concealing their love carefully to ensure that they were not seen, disturbed
or suspected. This they could do because their dwellings were adjoining. Their houses, halls
and keeps were close by each other and there was no barrier or division, apart from a high wall
of dark-hued stone. When she stood at her bedroom window, the lady could talk to her
beloved in the other house and he to her, and they could toss gifts to each other. There was
scarcely anything to displease them and they were both very content except for the fact that
they could not meet and take their pleasure with each other, for the lady was closely guarded
when her husband was in the region. But they were so resourceful that day or night they
managed to speak to each other and no one could prevent their coming to the window and
seeing each other there. For a long time they loved each other, until one summer when the
copses and meadows were green and the gardens in full bloom. On the flower-tops the birds
sang joyfully and sweetly. If love is on anyone's mind, no wonder he turns his attention towards
it. I shall tell you the truth about the knight. Both he and the lady made the greatest possible
effort with their words and with their eyes. At night, when the moon was shining and her
husband was asleep, she often rose from beside him and put on her mantle. Knowing
her beloved would be doing the same, she would go and stand at the window and stay awake
most of the night. They took delight in seeing each other, since they were denied anything
more. But so frequently did she stand there and so frequently leave her bed that her husband
became angry and asked her repeatedly why she got up and where she went. 'Lord,' replied
the lady, 'anyone who does not hear the song of the nightingale knows none of the joys of this
world. This is why I come and stand here. So sweet is the song I hear by night that it brings me
great pleasure. I take such delight in it and desire it so much that I can get no sleep at all.'
When the lord heard what she said, he gave a spiteful, angry laugh and devised a plan to
ensnare the nightingale. Every single servant in his household constructed some trap, net or
snare and then arranged them throughout the garden. There was no hazel tree or chestnut
tree on which they did not place a snare or bird-lime, until they had captured and retained it.
When they had taken the nightingale, it was handed over, still alive, to the lord, who was overjoyed to hold it in his hands. He entered the lady's chamber. 'Lady,' he said, 'where are you?
Come forward and speak to us. With bird-lime I have trapped the nightingale which has kept

you awake so much. Now you can sleep in peace, for it will never awaken you again.' When the lady heard him she was grief-stricken and distressed. She asked her husband for the bird, but he killed it out of spite, breaking its neck wickedly with his two hands. He threw the body at the lady, so that the front of her tunic was bespattered with blood, just on her breast. Thereupon he left the chamber. The lady took the tiny corpse, wept profusely and cursed those who had betrayed the nightingale by constructing the traps and snares, for they had taken so much joy from her. 'Alas,' she said, 'misfortune is upon me. Never again can I get up at night or go to stand at the window where I used to see my beloved. I know one thing for certain. He will think I am faint-hearted, so I must take action. I shall send him the nightingale and let him know what has happened.' She wrapped the little bird in a piece of samite, embroidered in gold and covered in designs. She called one of her servants, entrusted him with her message and sent him to her beloved. He went to the knight, greeted him on behalf of his lady, related the whole message to him and presented him with the nightingale. When the messenger had finished speaking, the knight, who had listened attentively, was distressed by what had happened. But he was not uncourtly or tardy. He had a small vessel prepared, not of iron or steel, but of pure gold with fine stones, very precious and valuable. On it he carefully placed a lid and put the night-ingale in it. Then he had the casket sealed and carried it with him at all times.

This adventure was related and could not long be concealed. The Bretons composed a lay about it which is called *Laüstic*.

Walther von der Vogelweide

c. 1170–*c.* 1230

The greatest German lyric poet of his age, though probably Austrian by birth, Walther von der Vogelweide was attached to courts in Vienna and around Germany, and is thought to be buried in Würzburg. His innovative work transcended the strict formal conventions of courtly poems.

'Under the linden'. *Trans. Alan Bold*

Under the linden
Near the common
Where both of us had shared a bed;
There, lying where we'd lain,
You'll come upon
Some grass and flowers neatly spread.
Outside the forest in the dell
tarantara!
    sweetly sang the nightingale.

I came there only
To discover
My darling was already there;
That was when he called me
'Divine creature':

I'll always hold that greeting dear.
Some kisses! More than ten hundred!
tarantara!
    that's what made my lips so red.

I saw he'd made us
From the flowers
A beautifully luxuriant bed;
Some stranger who might pass
This bed of ours
Will smile, knowing why it was made.
The roses give the game away,
tarantara!
    they reveal where my head lay.

If anyone knew
He'd slept with me
(Which God forbid!) I'd die of shame;
What our bodies did and how
No one will know

Except, that is, for me and him.
And of course the little bird,
tarantara!
    who's not going to say a word.

Arnaut Daniel

fl. 1180–1210

A Provençal poet born at the Castle of Rebeyrac in Périgord to a poor but noble family, Daniel was the most highly regarded troubadour at the court of Richard Coeur-de-Lion. He introduced the sestina *later adapted by Dante and Petrarch.*

'The firm desire'. *Trans. Anthony Bonner*

The firm desire which enters
my heart cannot be taken from me by the beak or nail
of that talebearer whose evil words cost him his soul,
and since I dare not beat him with a branch or rod,
I shall at least, in secret, free from any spying uncle,
rejoice in love's joy, in an orchard or in a chamber.

But when I think of that chamber
which, to my misfortune, no man enters
and is guarded as if by brother or by uncle,
my entire body, even to my fingernail,
trembles like a child before a rod,
such fear I have of not being hers with all my soul.

Would that I were hers, if not in soul
at least in body, hidden within her chamber;
for it wounds my heart more than blows of rod
that I, her serf, can never therein enter.
No, I shall be with her as flesh and nail
and heed no warnings of friend or uncle.

Even the sister of my uncle
I never loved like this with all my soul!
As near as is the finger to the nail,
if it please her, would I be to her chamber.
It can bend me to its will, that love which enters
my heart, better than a strong man with a sharp rod.

Since flowered the dry rod,
or from Adam came forth nephew and uncle,
there never was a love so true as that which enters
my heart, neither in body nor in soul.
And wherever she may be, outside or in her chamber,
I shall be no further than the length of my nail.

As if with tooth and nail
my heart grips her, or as the bark the rod;
for to me she is tower, palace and chamber
of joy, and neither brother, parent or uncle
I love so much; and in paradise my soul
will find redoubled joy, if lovers therein enter.

Arnaut sends his song of nail and uncle
(by leave of her who has, of his rod, the soul)
to his Desirat, whose fame all chambers enters.

Jean de Meun

c. 1250–c. 1305

Jean de Meun was born near Orléans and educated at the University of Paris. He became a noted rhetorician and was the author of the second part of The Romance of the Rose. *The poem as a whole lies at the heart of the medieval love debate and was begun by Guillaume de Lorris (c. 1212–1237) some forty years earlier. De Lorris's contribution consists of an elaborate allegorical dream vision while de Meun's continuation provides wide-ranging and often satirical digressions. De Meun's anti-feminist satire drew the wrath of the Italian-born writer Christine de Pizan, initiating the literary battle known as the* 'Querelle de la Rose'.

From **The Romance of the Rose** (*c.* 1230). *Trans. Kenneth McLeish*

'My son, Love rules everything; his key holds everything. As Virgil himself says, in a fine, strong phrase in the *Bucolics*: "Love conquers all; let's welcome it." That line says it all, with grace and truth; it couldn't be better put. My son, be generous to this lover so that God may be generous to you both. Grant him the gift of the rose.'

'Willingly, Lady,' replied Fair Welcome. 'But he must pluck it while only the two of us are there. I see that he loves sincerely; I should have received him long ago.'

I thanked him a thousand times for his gift, and at once set out, an eager pilgrim, a full-hearted suitor, towards the opening which was the goal of my pilgrimage. I carried with me – no light weight – the sack and the stout, strong rod which needed no iron tip for travelling. The sack was well-made, of supple, seamless skin. And it was by no means empty: When Nature, who gave it me, designed it, she filled it with two large hammers – so cleverly made that not even Daedalus himself could have devised them with greater skill or craft. She made them knowing that I'd have horses to shoe on my journey – and indeed I do whenever I get the chance, skilled as I am at blacksmith-work. I tell you, my hammers and rod are dearer to me even than my lute or harp.

By providing these implements and teaching me how to use them, Nature did me a great honour. She gave me the rod herself, and wanted it polished before I learned to read. There was no need whatever to tip it: it was as serviceable without. Ever since she gave it to me, I've kept it safe, kept it always to hand. I'll do my best never to lose it, for I value it more than a million gold pieces. It delights me to look at it, and when I feel it fulfilled and happy, I thank her with all my heart. How often it's comforted me in my travels! It's invaluable. How? If I'm in strange parts, I test channels where I can see nothing, to find out if they can be forded. It probes the way for me, and with its help I cross the channels, trust the banks and the stream between. (Some channels are deep, with banks so far apart that it would be easier and less tiring to swim two leagues in open sea; I've tried them, and know their dangers. But I've never come to harm, because each time, as soon as I was ready to enter, I probed them – and if they were too deep for me to touch bottom with rod or oar, I kept to the edges, kept to the banks, till I reached the other side. If I hadn't had Nature's weapons, I'd have been lost. But let's leave these wide roads to those who enjoy travelling them; those of us who take life as it comes will keep to seductive bypaths, alleyways rather than major roads.)

My intention, if I could haul my tackle to the harbour, was to bring it close enough to the holy objects to touch them. I'd been through so much and come so far, untipped rod or no! I knelt, eagerly, zestfully, between the two lovely pillars, consumed with eagerness to worship the beautiful, sacred sanctuary with a devoted and pious heart. Everything had been singed away by fire (which no power on Earth can withstand); nothing could be seen but the sanctuary, immaculate. I moved aside the curtain which covered the holy objects, and moved to explore the sacred place more intimately. I kissed the holy spot devotedly, and then tried to put my rod into the aperture, with the sack hanging behind. My intention was to pass safely into the passage, and I hoped to shoot the rod in at the first attempt. But it slipped out. I put it in again, to no avail: out it came again. Its way was blocked, I discovered, by a screen which I could feel but not see – a screen at the very entrance to the passage, which had given it extra strength and security from the moment it was made.

I pushed hard, time and again, but to no avail. Then, I discovered a narrow slit through which I could pass beyond if I tore the screen. Using my rod, I did so, and found myself in the opening. To my annoyance I was still only halfway in, and I was exhausted. But to relax would have been to lose everything, so I pressed on till the entire rod was inside. The sack, with its pounding hammers, still hung outside; the passage was so narrow that I was in great discomfort, not having yet made a wide enough space. Indeed, if I was any judge, no one had ever been there before me: the place was still too little known to be able to charge tolls. Perhaps, since then, it's done for others what it did for me. But to tell the truth, I loved it so much that I'm loath to believe that the same favours have been given to others. We don't like to distrust the things we love, because it dishonours them; and yet I find it hard to trust. All I can say is that when I entered it was by no means a well-worn, well-trodden path. But since there was nowhere else to get in to pluck the bud, I pressed on with all my strength.

I must explain how I carried on till I was able to pluck the bud. You young gentlemen must know what's done and how it's done, so that when the sweet season returns and you feel the urge to pluck roses (closed or open), you'll know exactly how to find success. If you know no other way to reach your goal, do as I did; but if, when you've heard my way you know an easier or better way to negotiate the passage, use it. I'm explaining my method free of charge, and for that you should be grateful.

Cramped as I was, I'd now come so close to the bush that I could reach out to pluck the bud whenever I chose. Fair Welcome had begged me, in God's name, to commit no outrage, and I'd guaranteed to do no more than we both desired. I took hold of the bush – it was as sappy as a willow – and as soon as I had it in both hands without pricking myself, I began shaking the bud gently: I wanted to damage it as little as possible. Some of the branches shook and quivered, but I was careful not to break any of them. Even though I'd had to cut slightly into the bark, and for all my eagerness to possess the bud, I didn't want to harm the bush.

At last, as I shook the bud, probing it gently open to explore the petals – it was so beautiful that I wanted to know it right to the root – I scattered a little seed on it. The seeds mixed inseparably, and the whole soft bush began to stretch and widen. I shouldn't have done that, but I was sure that dear, open-hearted Fair Welcome would hardly be angry, and would let me do anything he knew might please me. He did remind me of our agreement, and said that I was rough, was doing harm; but he didn't forbid me to uncover and hold every part of bush, branches, flower or leaf.

When I realized the position I'd attained – attained honourably and without cheating, but by openness and fairness to all my benefactors, as befits an honest debtor (and I was certainly their debtor, since thanks to them I'd won riches beyond imagining) – when I realized this, I gave thanks, between delicious kisses, ten or twenty times to the god of Love, to Venus (who'd helped me more than anyone), and to all the barons of the host (whose help I beg God grant to all true lovers). I spurned only Common Sense, who'd given me a good deal of trouble for nothing, and Riches, the hag who'd pitilessly barred me from the path she guarded, and who'd made no effort to protect the secret path by which I'd entered this place. I cursed the deadly enemies who'd held me back so long – and especially Jealousy, with her marigold-crown of concern, who withholds roses from lovers, and does so still.

Before I left that place – and I'd have liked to stay for ever – I plucked, with great delight, the flower from the leafy bush. So I have my red rose. And then it was dawn, and I woke up.

Angela of Foligno

c. 1248–1309

From Foligno near Assisi, Angela joined a Franciscan order of tertiaries and entered the order upon the death of her husband and children. Aged 43 she had a vision of God's love which she dictated to her brother/secretary, Brother Arnaldo.

From **Vitae**. *Trans. Elizabeth Alvida Petroff*

And then the eyes of her soul were opened, and she saw Love, which was coming gently towards her, and she saw its head and not the end, but only its continuation. She didn't know how to give any comparison with its colour. And suddenly, when love came to her, it seemed that she saw with the eyes of her soul open, more clearly than anything could be seen with the eyes of the body; and love made toward her as if in the likeness of a sickle. This is not to say that there is to be understood any measurable similarity, for in the beginning love retracted itself, not giving its self as much as it gave her to understand and as much as she then understood him. On account of this it made her very faint, and now there is no measurable or sensible similarity, for the understanding is ineffable according to the operation of divine grace.

Hadewijch

Early 13th century

There are few biographical details of the life of this Flemish mystic and poet, although she is believed to have come from an aristocratic family and lived in Brabant. She was also a member of the Beguines – women who dedicated themselves to a life of spirituality without taking the veil. By the middle of the 16th century her name and all she had written had fallen into oblivion, but her work was rediscovered in 1838. Today she is regarded as an important exponent of love mysticism.

From **Visions**. *Trans. Mother Columba Hart*

I desired to have full fruition of my Beloved, and to understand and taste him to the full . . . I wished that he might content me interiorly with his Godhead, in one spirit, and that for me he should be all that he is, without withholding anything from me. For above all the gifts that I ever longed for, I chose this gift: that I should give satisfaction in all great sufferings. For that is the most perfect satisfaction: to grow up in order to be God with God.

[Christ first sends an eagle to her as a messenger of his coming and then appears in several forms himself.]

With that he came in the form and clothing of a Man, as he was on the day when he gave us his Body for the first time, looking like a Human Being and a Man, wonderful, and beautiful, and with glorious face, he came to me as humbly as anyone who wholly belongs to another. Then he gave himself to me in the shape of the Sacrament, in its outward form, as the custom is; and then he gave me to drink from the chalice, in form and taste, as the custom is. After that he came himself to me, took me entirely in his arms, and pressed me to him; and all my members felt his in full felicity, in accordance with the desire of my heart and my humanity. So I was outwardly satisfied and fully transported. Also then, for a short while, I had the strength to bear this; but soon, after a short time, I lost that manly beauty outwardly in the sight of his form. I saw him completely come to nought and so fade and all at once dissolve that I could no longer perceive him outside me, and I could no longer distinguish him within me. Then it was to me as if we were one without difference. . . . After that I remained in a passing away in my Beloved, so that I wholly melted away in him and nothing any longer remained to me of myself; and I was changed and taken up in the spirit.

St Gertrude

c. 1257–1302

A German mystic and Benedictine based at the nunnery of Helfta in Thuringia, Gertrude underwent a profound conversion at the age of 25, recording and dictating her visions (and those of her friend Mechthild of Hackeborn). The publication of these Latin Revelations *in 1536 caused a sensation and secured her reputation as one of the most important medieval mystics. Although she was never formally canonized, 16 November was set aside as her feast day.*

From **The Life and Revelations of Saint Gertrude** (1536).
Modernized M. Westminster

'I beseech thee, by the merits and prayers of all here present, to pierce my heart with the arrow of thy love.' I soon perceived that my words had reached Thy Divine Heart, both by an interior effusion of grace, and by a remarkable prodigy which Thou didst show me in the image of Thy crucifixion.

After I had received the Sacrament of life, and had retired to the place where I pray, it seemed to me that I saw a ray of light like an arrow coming forth from the wound of the right side of the crucifix, which was in an elevated place, and it continued, as it were, to advance and retire for some time, sweetly attracting my cold affections.'

Lady Nijō

fl. 1307

A Japanese courtier from the age of 14, Lady Nijō was in the service of a retired Emperor in Kyoto. Her autobiographical narrative records her experiences as well as several love affairs, and ends with an account of her life as an itinerant Buddhist nun.

From **The Confessions of Lady Nijō** (*c.* 1307). *Trans. Karen Brazell*

Upon my return to the palace at that time GoFukakusa observed that the style of painting on the fan differed from anything else I had and asked who had given it to me, questioning me with such persistence that I finally told him quite plainly what had happened. It came as no surprise that the beauty of the fan led him to become enamoured of the artist, and on several occasions after that I conveyed messages for them. Finally it was somehow arranged for the girl to come to the palace on the tenth day of the tenth month.

That evening His Majesty was tense and nervous. He was still fussing over his costume when Middle Commander Sukeyuki arrived to announce that he had escorted the young lady to the palace. 'Then have her carriage pulled up near the Fishing Pavilion at the south end of Kyōgoku Street,' His Majesty ordered. 'Tell her to wait there a moment.'

The bells were striking eight at the arrival of the young woman who had remained unseen for three years. For the occasion I had selected a red formal jacket to go over a deep crimson gown and a two-layered green and orange undergarment with an ivy design embroidered in purple thread. Since GoFukakusa had instructed me to escort her in, I went to the place where her carriage was waiting. As she descended from her carriage the rustling of her gowns was unusually loud and coarse. I led her to a small room, carefully decorated and elaborately scented, beside His Majesty's living quarters. She appeared uncomfortable in her stiff costume, which consisted of a gown embroidered with huge fans, two undergowns lined in green, and crimson pleated trousers. From the back she looked bulky, her collar drawn up as high as a priest's. But she was without question a beautiful woman – her face delicate, her nose finely moulded, her eyes vivid – despite the fact that she was obviously not of aristocratic birth. She was a well-developed girl with a fair complexion and had the advantage of being both tall and plump; had she been a member of the court, in fact, she would have been perfect in the principal female role at a formal ceremony of state, carrying the sword, with her hair done up formally.

When he learned that she had entered the room, Gofukakusa made his apperance, attired in a pale violet robe decorated with woven chrysanthemums, and wearing wide-legged trousers. His clothes were so heavily scented that the fragrance preceded him; it was even wafted to my side of the screens. They talked together, and her reponses were so glib and wordy that I suspected his displeasure and was amused. After they retired I went to my customary place near the bedroom. Saionji Sanekane stood guard on the lower veranda on the other side of a paper screen.

Before long – indeed, before it seemed possible that anything could have happened – it was all over. To everyone's astonishment, His Majesty hurriedly left the room and summoned me to his quarters. 'That was as sad as Tamagawa Village,' he muttered, and even I felt sorry for her.

Anon. (Arabia)

From **Tales from the Thousand and One Nights** (**Arabian Nights**):
'The Porter and the Three Girls of Baghdad' (c. 14th century). *Trans. N.J. Dawood*

The porter quickly drained his cup. He kissed his hostesses' hands and recited verses in their praise, his head swaying from side to side. The three girls again filled their cups, and so did the porter.

'My lady,' he said, bowing low before the eldest, 'I am your servant, your bondsman.'
'Drink,' she cried, 'and may your wine be sweet and wholesome!'

When they had drained their cups a second time, they rose and danced round the fountain, singing and clapping their hands in unison. They went on drinking until the wine took possession of their senses and overcame their reason, and, when its sovereignty was fully established, the first girl got up and cast off all her clothes, letting down her long hair to cover her nakedness. She jumped into the fountain, frolicking and washing her body, filling her mouth with water and squirting it at the porter. At length she came out of the pool and threw herself into the porter's lap. Then she pointed down to that which was between her thighs and said: 'Darling master, what do you call that?'

'The gateway to heaven,' the porter answered.

'Are you not ashamed?' cried the girl, and, taking him by the neck, began to beat him.

'Then it is your crack.'

'Villain!' cried the girl, and slapped him on his thigh.

'It is your thing!'

'No, no,' she cried, shaking her head.

'Then it is your hornets' nest,' said the porter.

All three slapped him, laughing, until his flesh was red.

'Then tell me what *you* call it!' he shouted.

'The Buttercup,' the girl replied.

'At last,' cried the porter. 'Allah keep you safe and sound O Buttercup.'

They passed the wine round and round again. Presently the second girl took off her clothes and threw herself onto the porter's lap. Pointing to that which was between her thighs, she said: 'Light of my eyes, what is the name of this?'

'The thing!' he answered.

'A naughty word,' she cried. 'Have you no shame?' And she slapped him so hard that the hall echoed to the sound.

'Then it must be the Buttercup.'

'No, no,' she cried, and slapped him on the neck.

'Well, what do you call it, my sister?'

'Sesame,' the second girl replied.

After the wine had gone round once more, and the porter had somewhat recovered from his beatings, the last girl, the fairest of the three, got up and threw off her clothes. The porter began to stroke his neck, saying, 'Allah save me from yet another beating!' as he watched her descend, utterly naked, into the fountain. She washed her limbs, and sported in the water. He marvelled at the beauty of her face, which resembled the full moon rising in the night sky, at the roundness of her breasts, and her graceful, quivering thighs. Then she came out of the water and laid herself across his lap.

'Tell me the name of this,' she said, pointing to her delicate parts.

The porter tried this name and that, and finally begged her to tell him and stop beating him.

'The Inn of Abu Mansoor,' the girl replied.

'Allah preserve you,' cried the porter, 'O Inn of Abu Mansoor.'

The girls dressed themselves and resumed their seats. Now the porter got up, undressed, and went down into the fountain. The girls watched him as he sported in the water and washed as they had done. Eventually he came out of the fountain, threw himself into the lap of the first girl, and rested his feet on the knees of the second. Pointing to his rising organ, he demanded of the first girl, 'And what do you call this, my queen?'

The girls laughed till they fell over on their backs. To every guess they hazarded he answered

'No', biting each one in turn, and kissing, pinching, and hugging them, which made them laugh all the more. Finally they cried, 'Brother, what is its name, then?'

'Know that this,' the porter replied, 'is my sturdy mule which feeds on buttercups, delights in sesame, and spends the night in the Inn of Abu Mansoor.'

Giovanni Boccaccio

1313–1375

An Italian story-writer and poet, Boccaccio is believed to have been born in Tuscany. He was the author of hugely influential works including the Decameron, Fiammetta, *a prose psychological romance, and 'Filostrato', a poem on the story of Troilus and Cressida. He inspired many British and European writers including Chaucer, Shakespeare, Dryden, Keats, Longfellow, Tennyson, Swinburne and George Eliot. He was dissuaded by Petrarch from entering holy orders when, in old age, he rued his early misspent youth.*

From the **Decameron** (1349–1351).

Nor had he long to wait before two female slaves made their appearance, bearing on their heads, the one a great and goodly mattress of wadding, and the other a huge and well-filled basket; and having laid the mattress on a bedstead in one of the rooms of the bagnio, they covered it with a pair of sheets of the finest fabric, bordered with silk, and a quilt of the whitest Cyprus buckram, with two daintily-embroidered pillows. The slaves then undressed and got into the bath, which they thoroughly washed and scrubbed: whither soon afterwards the lady, attended by two other female slaves, came, and made haste to greet Salabaetto with the heartiest of cheer; and when, after heaving many a mighty sigh, she had embraced and kissed him: – 'I know not', quoth she, 'who but thou could have brought me to this, such a fire hast thou kindled in my soul, little dog of a Tuscan!' Whereupon she was pleased that they should undress, and get into the bath, and two of the slaves with them; which, accordingly, they did; and she herself, suffering none other to lay a hand upon him, did with wondrous care wash Salabaetto from head to foot with soap perfumed with musk and cloves; after which she let the slaves wash and shampoo herself. The slaves then brought two spotless sheets of finest texture, which emitted such a scent of roses, that 'twas as if there was nought there but roses, in one of which having wrapped Salabaetto, and in the other the lady, they bore them both to bed, where, the sheets in which they were enfolded being withdrawn by the slaves as soon as they had done sweating, they remained stark naked in the others. The slaves then took from the basket cruets of silver most goodly, and full, this of rose-water, that of water of orange-blossom, a third of water of jasmine-blossom, and a fourth of nanfa water, wherewith they sprinkled them: after which, boxes of comfits and the finest wines being brought forth, they regaled them a while. To Salabaetto 'twas as if he were in Paradise; a thousand times he scanned the lady, who was indeed most beautiful; and he counted each hour as a hundred years until the slaves should get them gone, and he find himself in the lady's arms.

Geoffrey Chaucer

c. 1340–1400

The most influential of English medieval poets, Geoffrey Chaucer was the son of a London wine merchant and is believed to have been educated at the Inner Temple. In 1366 he married Philippa, a lady of the Queen's bedchamber, and in 1367 entered the royal household and held various official appointments which involved travelling in France and Italy (where he may have met Boccaccio and Petrarch). He is best known for his masterpiece The Canterbury Tales, *written c. 1387.*

From **Troilus and Criseyde** (1379–83).

This Troilus in armes gan hir streyne,
And seyde, 'O swete, as ever mote I goon,
Now be ye caught, now is ther but we tweyne;
Now yeldeth yow, for other boot is noon.'
To that Criseyde answered thus anoon,
'Ne hadde I er now, my swete herte dere,
Ben yolde, y-wis, I were now not here!'

O! sooth is seyd, that heled for to be
As of a fevre or othere greet syknesse,
Men moste drinke, as men may often see,
Ful bittre drink; and for to han gladnesse,
Men drinken often peyne and greet distresse;
I mene it here, as for this aventure,
That thourgh a peyne hath founden al his cure.

And now swetnesse semeth more swete,
That bitternesse assayed was biforn;
For out of wo in blisse now they flete.
Non swich they felten, sith they were born;
Now is this bet, than bothe two be lorn!
For love of god, take every womman hede
To werken thus, if it comth to the nede.

Criseyde, al quit from every drede and tene,
As she that juste cause hadde him to triste,
Made him swich feste, it joye was to sene,
Whan she his trouthe and clene entente wiste.
And as aboute a tree, with many a twiste,
Ditrent and wryth the sote wode-binde,
Gan eche of hem in armes other winde.

And as the newe abaysshed nightingale,
That stinteth first whan she biginneth singe,
Whan that she hereth any herde tale,

Or in the hegges any wight steringe,
And after siker dooth hir voys out-ringe;
Right so Criseyde, whan hir drede stente,
Opned hir herte, and tolde him hir entente.

And right as he that seeth his deeth y-shapen,
And deye moot, in ought that he may gesse,
And sodeynly rescous doth him escapen,
And from his deeth is brought in sikernesse,
For al this world, in swich present gladnesse,
Was Troilus, and hath his lady swete;
With worse hap god let us never mete!

Hir armes smale, hir streyghte bak and softe,
Hir sydes longe, fleshly, smothe, and whyte
He gan to stroke, and good thrift bad ful ofte
Hir snowish throte, hir brestes rounde and
     lyte;
Thus in this hevene he gan him to delyte,
And ther-with-al a thousand tyme hir kiste;
That, what to done, for joye unnethe he
     wiste.

Than seyde he thus, 'O, Love, O, Charitee,
Thy moder eek, Citherea the swete,
After thy-self next heried be she,
Venus mene I, the wel-willy planete;
And next that, Imeneüs, I thee grete;
For never man was to yow goddes holde
As I, which ye han brought fro cares colde.

Benigne Love, thou holy bond of thinges,
Who-so wol grace, and list thee nought
     honouren,

Lo, his desyr wol flee with-outen winges.
For, noldestow of bountee hem socouren
That serven best and most alwey labouren,
Yet were al lost, that dar I wel seyn, certes,
But-if thy grace passed our desertes.

And for thou me, that coude leest deserve
Of hem that nombred been un-to thy grace,
Hast holpen, ther I lykly was to sterve,
And me bistowed in so heygh a place
That thilke boundes may no blisse pace,
I can no more, but laude and reverence
Be to thy bounte and thyn excellence!'

And therewith-al Criseyde anoon he kiste,
Of which, certeyn, she felte no desese.
And thus seyde he, 'now wolde god I wiste,
Myn herte swete, how I you mighte plese!
What man,' quod he, 'was ever thus at ese
As I, on whiche the faireste and the beste
That ever I say, deyneth hir herte reste.

Here may men seen that mercy passeth right;
The experience of that is felt in me,
That am unworthy to so swete a wight.
But herte myn, of your benignitee,
So thenketh, though that I unworthy be,
Yet mot I nede amenden in som wyse,
Right thourgh the vertu of your heyghe
    servyse.

And for the love of god, my lady dere,
Sin god hath wrought me for I shal yow serve,
As thus I mene, that ye wol be my stere,
To do me live, if that yow liste, or sterve,
So techeth me how that I may deserve
Your thank, so that I, thurgh myn ignoraunce,
Ne do no-thing that yow be displesaunce.

For certes, fresshe wommanliche wyf,
This dar I seye, that trouthe and diligence,
That shal ye finden in me al my lyf,
Ne I wol not, certeyn, breken your defence;
And if I do, present or in absence,
For love of god, lat slee me with the dede,
If that it lyke un-to your womanhede.'

'Y-wis,' quod she, 'myn owne hertes list,
My ground of ese, and al myn herte dere,
Graunt mercy, for on that is al my trist;
But late us falle awey fro this matere;
For it suffyseth, this that seyd is here.
And at o word, with-outen repentaunce,
Wel-come, my knight, my pees, my suffisaunce!'

Of hir delyt, or joyes oon the leste
Were impossible to my wit to seye;
But juggeth, ye that han ben at the feste
Of swich gladnesse, if that hem liste pleye!
I can no more, but thus thise ilke tweye
That night, be-twixen dreed and sikernesse,
Felten in love the grete worthinesse.

O blisful night, of hem so longe y-sought,
How blithe un-to hem bothe two thou were!
Why ne hadde I swich on with my soule y-
    bought,
Ye, or the leeste joye that was there?
A-wey, thou foule daunger and thou fere,
And lat hem in this hevene blisse dwelle,
That is so heygh, that al ne can I telle!

But sooth is, though I can not tellen al,
As can myn auctor, of his excellence,
Yet have I seyd, and, god to-forn, I shal
In every thing al hoolly his sentence,
And if that I, at loves reverence,
Have any word in eched for the beste,
Doth tharwith-al right as your-selven leste.

For myne wordes, here and every part,
I speke hem alle under correccioun
Of yow, that feling han in loves art,
And putte it al in your discrecioun
T' encrese or maken diminucioun
Of my langage, and that I yow bi-seche;
But now to purpos of my rather speche.

Thise ilke two, that ben in armes laft,
So looth to hem a-sonder goon it were,
That ech from other wende been biraft,
Or elles, lo, this was hir moste fere,
That al this thing but nyce dremes were;

For which ful ofte ech of hem syde,
  'O swete,
Clippe ich yow thus, or elles I it mete?'

And, lord! so he gan goodly on hir see,
That never his look ne bleynte from hir face,

And seyde, 'O dere herte, may it be
That it be sooth, that ye ben in this place?'
'Ye, herte myn, god thank I of his grace!'
Quod tho Criseyde, and therwith-al him
  kiste,
That where his spirit was, for joye he niste.

Anon.

From **Sir Gawain and the Green Knight** (late 14th century).

69

But the lady's longing would not allow her to sleep,
Nor would she change the purpose pitched in her heart,
But rose up rapidly and ran to him
In a glorious robe that reached to the ground,
Trimmed with finest fur from pure pelts;
Not coifed as to custom, but with scores of costly jewels
Strung on her splendid hairnet.
Her fine-featured face and fair throat were unveiled,
Her breast was bare as was her back
She came in by the chamber door and closed it after her,
Cast open a casement and called on the knight,
And briskly thus rebuked him with rich words
    Of good cheer.
'Ah sir! What, sound asleep?
The morning's crisp and clear.'
He had been drowsing deep,
But now he had to hear.

70

The noble sighed ceaselessly in restless slumber
As threatening thoughts thronged in the early light
About fate, which the day after would deal him his destiny
At the Green Chapel where Gawain was to greet his man,
And be bound to bear his buffet unresisting.
But having recovered his wits properly,
He heaved himself out of dreams and answered hurriedly.
The lovely lady advanced, laughing sweetly
Swooped over his splendid face and kissed him softly.
He welcomed her worthily with noble cheer
And, gazing on her bright and glorious attire,

Her features so faultless her complexion so fine,
He felt a flush of rapture suffuse his heart.
Sweet and genial smiling slid them into joy
Till bliss burst forth between them, beaming happy
    And bright;
With joy the two contended
In talk of true delight,
Danger would have intervened
Had Mary not remembered her knight.

71

For that noble princess pressed him so hard,
So invited him to the very limit, that he felt forced
Either to accept her love or roughly refuse her.
He was concerned for his courtesy, lest he be called churlish,
But more especially for his evil plight if he should commit a sin,
And betray the honour of the owner of the house.
'God shield me! That shall not happen, for sure,' said the knight.
So with laughing affection he gently deflected
The words of love that dropped from her lips.
Said the lady to the knight, 'Blame will be yours
Unless you have a lover more beloved, who delights you more,
A maiden to whom you are committed, so fast bound
That you do not seek to break from her – which I see is so.
Tell me truly, I entreat you now:
By all the loves in the world, do not hide the truth
    With guile.'
Then gently, 'By Saint John,'
Said the knight with a smile,
'In faith I have no love,
Nor wish to yet a while.'

72

'Those words,' said the lady, 'are the worst there could be,
But I am truly answered, and it grieves me,
Give me now a gracious kiss, and I shall go from here
As a maid who is much in love, I have only sorrow.

Dafydd ap Gwilym

fl. Mid-14th century

Born in north Cardiganshire to an upper-class landed family of poets, Dafydd ap Gwilym is regarded as the first major exponent of the modern Welsh language. He was unequalled in his use of the short cywydd *metre (seven syllables) and the* dyfalu *(a long string of disparate metaphors).*

From 'The Penis' (*c.* 1330-1350). *Trans. Dafydd Johnston*

By God penis, you must be guarded
with eye and hand
because of this lawsuit, straight-headed pole,
more carefully for evermore;
net-quill of the cunt, because of
complaint a bridle must be put on your snout
to keep you in check so that you are not indicted
again, take heed you despair of minstrels.

I consider you the vilest of rolling-pins,
horn of the scrotum, do not rise up or wave about;
gift of the noble ladies of Christendom,
nut-pole of the lap's cavity,
snare shape, gander
sleeping in its yearling plumage,
neck with a wet head and milk-giving shaft,
tip of a growing shoot, stop your awkward jerking;
crooked blunt one, accursed pole,
the centre pillar of the two halves of a girl,
head of a stiff conger with a hole in it,
blunt barrier like a fresh hazel-pole.
You are longer than a big man's thigh,
a long night's roaming, chisel of a hundred nights;
auger like the shaft of the post,
leather-headed one who is called 'tail'.
You are a sceptre which causes lust,
the bolt of the lid of a girl's bare arse.

There is a pipe in your head,
a whistle for fucking every day.
There is an eye in your pate
which sees every woman as fair;
round pestle, expanding gun,
it is a searing fire to a small cunt;
roof-beam of girls' laps,
the swift growth is the clapper of a bell;

blunt pod, it dug a family,

snare of skin, nostril with a crop of two testicles.

You are a trouserful of wantonness,

your neck is leather, image of a goose's neckbone;

nature of complete falsity, pod of lewdness,

door-nail which causes a lawsuit and trouble.

Consider that there is a writ and an indictment,

lower your head, stick for planting children.

It is difficult to keep you under control,

cold thrust, woe to you indeed!

Often is your lord rebuked,

obvious is the rottenness through your head.

Margery Kempe

c. 1373–*c.* 1439

An English mystic, Kempe's father was mayor of King's Lynn, her husband (by whom she had 14 children) a wealthy brewer. Her dictated autobiography, The Book of Margery Kempe, *records her renunciations of worldliness, her pilgrimages, trial for heresy, and mystical visions and weepings.*

From **The Book of Margery Kempe** (*c.* 1432–1436). *Trans. S. W. Butler-Rowden*

Thus she had a very contemplation in the sight of her soul, as if Christ had hung before her bodily eye in his manhood. And when . . . it was granted to this creature to behold so verily his precious tender body, all rent and torn with scourges, fuller of wounds than ever was a dove-cote full of holes, hanging on the cross with the crown of thorns upon his head, his beautiful hands, his tender feet nailed to the hard tree, the rivers of blood flowing out plenteously from every member, the grisly and grievous wound in his precious side shedding blood and water for her love and salvation, then she fell down and cried with a loud voice, wonderfully turning and wresting her body on every side, spreading her arms abroad as if she would have died, and could not keep herself from crying, and from these bodily movements, for the fire of love that burnt so fervently in her soul with pure pity and compassion.

·   ·   ·

Then, as she lay still in the choir, weeping and mourning for her sins, suddenly she was in a kind of sleep. And anon, she saw with her ghostly eye, our Lord's body lying before her, and his head, so she thought, close by her, with his blessed face upwards, the seemliest man that ever might be seen or thought of.

And then came one with a dagger knife to her sight, and cut that precious body all along the breast. And anon she wept wondrous sore, having more memory, pity, and compassion of the passion of our Lord Jesus Christ than she had had before. . . .

And anon, in the sight of her soul, she saw our Lord standing right up over her, so near that she thought she took his toes in her hand and felt them, and to her feeling it was as if they had been very flesh and bone.

Anon.

'I have a noble cock' (early 15th century). *Trans. Russell Hope Robbins*

I have a gentle cock,
Croweth me day:
He doth me risen erly
My matins for to say.

I have a gentle cock,
Comen he is of gret:
His comb is of red coral,
His tail is of jet.

I have a gentle cock,
Comen he is of kinde:

His comb is of red coral,
His tail is of inde.

His legges ben of asor,
So gentle and so smale;
His spores arn of silver whit
Into the wortewale.

His eynen arn of cristal,
Loken all in aumber:
And every night he percheth him
In mine ladye's chaumber.

Antoine de la Sale

c.1386–c.1469

A French writer, born in Provence, de la Sale served in the house of Anjou first as a soldier then as a tutor. His works include accounts of his extensive travelling, a treatise on government and various prose romances, and he is a candidate for the authorship of the mid-15th-century Les Cent nouvelles nouvelles *(The Hundred Tales), a collection of bawdy tales based on Boccaccio's* Decameron *which were related at the court of Philip, Duke of Burgundy.*

From **The Hundred Tales:** 'The Calf' (*c.* 1456–1461).
Trans. Russell Hope Robbins

In the frontier marches of the country of Holland, some time ago a dashing young fellow made up his mind to do the worst thing he could – that is to say, get married! Although it was then mid-winter, as soon as he donned the sweet mantle of marriage, he got very hot. Nothing could temper him. The nights, which at this season last only nine or ten hours, were not sufficient or long-drawn-out enough for him to slake his most ardent desire for engendering issue. In fact, wherever he met his wife, whether she were in the bedroom or in the stable, he put her on her back; no matter where she was, there was always an encounter. Nor did this behaviour last for just a month or two; it went on for so very long that I would not care to describe it, on account of the difficulties which might ensue if many women came to know about the physical prowess of this great lover!

What more can I tell you?

He made love so passionately that the memory of his ability will always be fresh throughout that country. In truth, the wife in similar circumstances, who recently complained to the bailiff of Amiens about the tremendous overwork her husband gave her, had not such cause to bemoan as the wife in this story. Yet whatever was demanded, although now and then she could have dispensed with his pleasurable pain, she was never intractable to the spurs and obeyed her husband as she should.

One day after dinner, it happened that the weather was very lovely and the sun sent his beams and dispensed them over an earth painted and embroidered with beautiful flowers. Our pair conceived a desire to go and play in the wood, they two, all alone, and set off on their way.

Now, the key to this story must not be hidden from you. At the time our good couple had this whim, a farmer had lost his calf, which he had set out to pasture in a meadow bordering this wood. When he came to look for it, he didn't find it. This made him pretty angry. He set to searching for it in the meadows, the fields, and nearby places as well as in the wood, but he couldn't find out anything. Then it occurred to him that by chance it might have gone into some little copse, or to graze in some grassy gully, out of which it could easily jump when it had filled its belly. So that he could see better and more conveniently where his calf might have got, without having to run hither and yon, he chose what seemed to be the highest and most leafy tree in the wood and climbed up into it. When he reached the top of this tree, which revealed the terrain of the whole neighbourhood, he soon realized he was halfway toward finding his calf.

While this good farmer was peering on every side to spy out his calf, here come our man and his wife through the wood, talking, singing, frolicking, and disporting themselves as gay hearts do when they find themselves in pleasant surroundings. It's no wonder if desire stirred him and the urge swelled in him to make love to his wife in the wood, so charming and so heaven-sent. Looking all about, to right and left, for a suitable spot to carry out this intention as it best pleased him, he finally noticed the very noble tree at the top of which was the farmer, about whom of course he knew nothing. Under this tree, he proposed and decided to conduct his amorous incursions. When he got to the spot, it didn't take long – the stirrings of his passion taking the place of a marshal – before he set to work to woo his wife, for by then he was very eager and, for her part, his wife also.

He thought it would be nice to contemplate her front and rear, and thereupon undid her dress and pulled it off, leaving her in a little skirt. Then he lifted it way up high, in spite of her strong protestations. Not content with this, however, and to see and regard her beauty fully at his ease, he rolled her over and slapped her soundly three or four times on her plump behind. Then he turned her back again and, just as he had inspected her back, so he gazed at her front, although the good unsophisticated woman didn't wish to go along with this at all. She put up a great resistance and, God knows, didn't spare her tongue. She called him ill-mannered, crazy, overexcited with desire; again, immodest. It was a marvel what abuse she heaped on him. But nothing helped her. He was much stronger than she, and so he completed an inventory of every treasure she had. She was forced to endure it, preferring, like a sensible woman, the approbation of her husband rather than his displeasure if she refused. All her remonstrances were ignored, and this fine fellow passed the time meditating on her charms and, one can say this only with shame, he wasn't satisfied until his hands had assisted his eyes in revealing everything.

As he lay in this profound study, he said every now and then: 'I can see this! I can see that!'

And then he gloated on something else here, something else there. To anyone hearing him, he had the whole world in his vision – nay, very much more.

After a lengthy interval, still preoccupied in this pleasing contemplation, he exclaimed once again: 'Holy Mary, what things I do see!'

'All right, then,' interposed the farmer, perched up on the top of the tree, 'do you see my calf, good sir? It seems to me I can see its tail.'

Although he was much surprised, the husband quickly replied: 'The tail you see is not your calf's!'

With that, the husband turned and went off, and his wife followed him.

François Villon

1431–1485

The French poet François Villon was brought up and attended university in Paris. Charged with stealing gold and killing a priest, Villon took to a life on the road, writing verses in the jargon of criminals and 'ballades'. In 1462, he was arrested in Paris and sentenced to hang for his alleged part in the wounding of a papal notary, and although he was later reprieved, nothing is known of what happened to him. His major work is the autobiographical poem 'Grand Testament', melancholy and savagely humourous by turns.

From **'Grand Testament'** (*c.* 1461). *Trans. Peter Dale*

I love and serve my lady with a will,
but that's no reason you should call me mad.
For her, I'd hitch on sword and shield to kill.
She is the goods to please my every fad.
When customers arrive, I lightly pad
to bring in pots and wine. I serve them cheese
and fruit, and bread and water as they please
and say (depending on the tip I'm paid)
'Do call again and come here at your ease
in this whorehouse where we do a roaring
    trade.'

But then fine feelings end and turn to ill.
When she comes home without the cash, I'm
    had.
I cannot stand her, she has blood to spill.
I hate her, grab her belt, gown, shift and plaid
and swear I'll flog the lot and her to add
up for the loss of all the nightly fees.
But hands on hips she hollers if you please
how I am anti-Christ and won't get paid.
I grab a club and sign her, nose to knees,
in this whorehouse where we do a roaring trade.

We make peace then in bed. She takes my fill,
gorged like a dung-beetle, blows me a bad
and mighty poisonous fart. I fit her bill
she says, and laughing bangs my nob quite
    glad.
She thwacks my thigh and, after what we've
    had,
dead drunk we sleep like logs – and let the
    fleas.
Though when we stir her quim begins to tease.
She mounts; I groan beneath the weight – I'm
    splayed!
Her screwing soon will bring me to my knees
in this whorehouse where we do a roaring
    trade.

*V*ary the wind, come frost, I live in ease.
I am a fucker; she fucks as I please.
*L*ayman or laity – no matter of degrees!
*L*ayer on layer of onion overlaid,
*O*ur filth we love and filths upon us seize;
*N*ow we flee honour, honour from us flees
in this whorehouse where we do a roaring trade.

Gwerful Mechain

fl. 1480

Born in Powys, Gwerful Mechain is the only female poet of medieval Wales of whom any corpus of work survives. Her erotic poems form only a small proportion of her work.

'The Female Genitals'. *Trans. Dafydd Johnston*

Every foolish drunken poet,
boorish vanity without ceasing,
(never may I warrant it,
I of great noble stock),
has always declaimed fruitless praise
in song of the girls of the lands
all day long, certain gift,
most incompletely, by God the Father:
praising the hair, gown of fine love,
and every such living girl,
and lower down praising merrily
the brows above the eyes;
praising also, lovely shape,
the smoothness of the soft breasts,
and the beauty's arms, bright drape,
she deserved honour, and the girl's hands.
Then with his finest wizardry
before night he did sing,
he pays homage to God's greatness,
fruitless eulogy with his tongue:
leaving the middle without praise
and the place where children are con-
    ceived,
and the warm quim, clear excellence,
tender and fat, bright fervent broken
    circle,
where I loved, in perfect health,
the quim below the smock.

You are a body of boundless strength,
a faultless court of fat's plumage.
I declare, the quim is fair,
circle of broad-edged lips,
it is a valley longer than a spoon or a
    hand,
a ditch to hold a penis two hands long;
cunt there by the swelling arse,
song's table with its double in red.
And the bright saints, men of the church,
when they get the chance, perfect gift,
don't fail, highest blessing,
by Beuno, to give it a good feel.
For this reason, thorough rebuke,
all you proud poets,
let songs to the quim circulate
without fail to gain reward.
Sultan of an ode, it is silk,
little seam, curtain on a fine bright
    cunt,
flaps in a place of greeting,
the sour grove, it is full of love,
very proud forest, faultless gift,
tender frieze, fur of a fine pair of
    testicles,
a girl's thick grove circle of precious
    greeting,
lovely bush, God save it.

Joannot Martorell

b. 1413

and Marti Joan de Galba

fl. Mid-15th century

The picaresque Catalan medieval masterpiece Tirant lo Blanc *was jointly written by Joannot Martorell and Marti Joan de Galba. Martorell, a Catalan writer from Gandia, was son of the Chamberlain to King Martin the Humaine in Valencia; Marti Joan de Galba is thought to have contributed the episodes from North Africa and the final relief of Byzantium.*

From Tirant lo Blanc: 'How Pleasure-of-my-life placed Tirant in the Princess's Bed' (1490). *Trans. David H. Rosenthal*

'My desire to please you obliges me to do your bidding, for though my guilt will be great, I know you deserve such a prize, and now you shall see how much I wish to serve Your Lordship. When the emperor goes to supper, await me here, setting aside all sad thoughts, as I shall lead you to my lady's chamber. In the still of the night lovers find consolation, which fights with redoubled power against sombre misgivings.'

While they were talking, the emperor, who knew Tirant was in the duchess's room, sent for him and interrupted their conversation.

Then our knight took counsel with His Majesty for a long time about the war and the Greek army's provisions, since Tirant's men were now armed and ready to set out.

Once it was dark, Tirant went to the duchess's room and, while the emperor was eating with his noblewomen, Pleasure-of-my-life greeted our knight, who had donned a red satin cloak and doublet and held his naked sword aloft. She took his hand and led him to the princess's chamber, where there was a big chest with a hole cut in it to admit the air, in front of which stood Carmesina's bathtub.

After supper the ladies danced with the gallant knights, but as Tirant was absent, they soon stopped and the emperor retired. The damsels escorted Carmesina to her chambers, where they bade her goodnight, leaving her alone with her servants. Pleasure-of-my-life, with the excuse of taking out a fine linen wash cloth, opened the chest and left it slightly ajar. Then she put some clothes on top lest anyone notice, and while her mistress was disrobing, the damsel arranged things so that she was standing right in front of Tirant. Once she was naked, Pleasure-of-my-life picked up a candle, that he might enjoy himself still more, and looking the princess up and down, she said: 'On my faith, my lady, if Tirant were caressing you now in my stead, I believe he would be happier than if they had crowned him King of France.'

'Certainly not,' replied the princess, 'he would sooner be King of France.'

'Oh lord Tirant, where are you now? Why are you not touching what you prize most in this world? Look, Tirant: do you see my lady's hair? I kiss it in your name, you who are the best knight on earth. See her eyes and mouth? I kiss them for you. See her delicate breasts, one in each hand? I kiss them for you. Look how small, firm, white, and smooth they are. Look, Tirant, behold her belly, her thighs, and her sex. Ah, woe is me, if only I were a man! Oh

Tirant, where are you now? Why do you not come when I call you so piteously? Only Tirant's hands deserve to touch what mine are touching, as any man would happily gulp down such a morsel.'

Tirant, who saw everything, was delighted by these jests, while a great temptation crept over him to open the chest and get out.

After they had joked awhile, Carmesina got into her bath and asked Pleasure-of-my-life to undress and join her.

'I shall do so, but only on one condition.'

'What is that?' asked the princess.

'That you allow Tirant to lie in bed with you for an hour,' the damsel replied.

'Shut up; you must be mad!'

'My lady, grant me this favor: tell me what you would say if Tirant came one night un-beknownst to anyone and you found him beside you.'

'What would I say?' the princess replied. 'I would ask him to leave, but if he refused, I would sooner keep mum than risk disgrace.'

'Upon my faith, my lady,' said Pleasure-of-my-life, 'thus would I also behave.'

While they were talking, the Easygoing Widow entered, and the princess invited her into the tub. Then the widow stripped down to her red stockings and linen cap, and although she had a fair and well-proportioned figure, the stockings and cap suited her so ill that she looked like a devil, and certainly any lady or damsel you see so dressed will seem ugly, however genteel and noble she may be.

When the bath was finished, they brought the princess a pair of partridges cooked in malmsey and a dozen eggs with sugar and cinnamon. Then she got into bed.

The widow retired to her room, as did the other maidens except two who slept near the princess's chamber. Once they were asleep, Pleasure-of-my-life rose in her nightdress, helped Tirant out of the chest, and told him to undress, but his heart, hands, and feet were shaking.

'How now?' asked Pleasure-of-my-life. 'No man alive is brave in arms but afraid of women. In battle you are not daunted by all the knights in creation, and here you tremble at the sight of a mere damsel. Have no fear, for I shall remain by your side.'

'By the faith I owe to God, I would sooner enter the lists for a joust to the utterance with ten knights than commit such an act.'

Nonetheless, with her constant encouragement he finally roused his spirits, whereupon the damsel took his hand and he followed her, protesting: 'Dear maiden, as my fear derives from shame caused by the great love I bear my lady, I would sooner turn back now before she hears us. Upon beholding such presumption, she may very well change her mind, and I would rather die than live after offending Her Highness. I want to win her through love, not force, and when I see such impropriety caused by my devotion, my will ceases to accord with yours. For pity's sake, let us turn back lest I lose what I most cherish, as it seems a serious enough crime to have come here without erring further. For such a misdeed I ought to take my own life, and do not think, my lady, that I am stopping out of fear. When she learns I was so near her and yet refrained from doing harm, she will understand the depth of my chaste devotion.'

Pietro Aretino

1492–1557

The illegitimate son of a Tuscan nobleman, Pietro Aretino is widely regarded as the 'inventor of pornography'. He earned his living in Rome and Venice by publishing satirical pamphlets, and relied on his wit to gain the patronage of emperors and the Pope (which he lost after writing 16 erotically explicit Sonnetti Lussuriosi)*. His* Letters *(1537–1557) not only reflect his exuberant character, but are also a unique record of the events of his time. Aretino is said to have died by falling over backwards while laughing upon hearing of the illicit sexual adventures of his sister.*

From **The Lives of Nuns** (1527).

NANNA: I saw four Sisters, the Lord Abbot and three little white ruby Friars, in a cell, pulling off the Reverend Father's cassock, and putting a big velvet coat on him; they hid his tonsure under a small gold skull-cap, placed over it a velvet one, ornamented with crystal bobs, surmounted by a white plume, and, the sword at his side, the blissful Lord Abbott, be it said between us both, set apacing about like a Bartolomeo Coglioni. In the meanwhile, the Sisters had taken off their habits, the Novices their vestments; the latter put on the Sisters' attire, and these the Brothers', at least three of them; the fourth, rolled up in the Abbot's cassock, seated herself pontifically and began to imitate a Superior edicting laws for convents.

ANTONIA: What fine sport!

NANNA: It will be a great deal finer presently. His Reverend Paternity made a sign to the three Novices and leaning on the shoulder of one of them, a long thin fellow, formed before his age, ordered the others to pull the bird out of the nest, which was lying very quiet: then the sharpest and finest of the lot, took it on the palm of his hand and patted it on the back, as one pats the tail of a puss which sets asnorting, all in purring, and can in a little while no longer keep steady. The cock lifted its head, so that the stout Abbott, sticking his claws into the back of the most comely and youngest of the Nuns, and pulling her petticoats over her head, got her to prop her forehead against the bedstead; then, moving with his fingers the leaves of the Missal of the Arse, being wholly absorbed in his meditations, he set to musing over this breech, the mould of which was neither worn to the bones from leanness, nor too bloated with fat either, but plumpy; the cleft in the centre, being quivering, shone as living ivory. Those little dimples we behold on pretty women's chins and cheeks, lent themselves to view *ne le sue chiappettine* (to speak in the Florentine fashion), and their plump softness would have surpassed that of a mill-rat, born, bred and fattened in the flour. This Nun's skin was all so smooth, that a hand scarcely laid on the hollow of her loins would slip in one go to the bottom of her legs, quicker than one's foot upon ice; fancy whether the merest moss would have dared show itself there! no more than on an egg.

ANTONIA. Did the Father Abbot spend the whole day in contemplation, eh?

NANNA: Oh! no. While setting up his weapon in the Sister's target, after having previously wet it with spittle, he made her twist herself as women bringing forth or in the maternal throes. And that the spike might remain driven home more solidly, he gave a backward sign to his young calf, who, pulling down his breeches for him to his heels, administered the clyster to

His Reverence's *visibilium*; the latter kept his eyes rivetted on the other rakes. After having arranged two Sisters in the right way and at their ease upon the bed, they beat the sauce into their mortars, to the great vexation of the fourth, who, for being ever so slightly squint-eyed and dark skinned, spurned by all, had filled the glass pleasurer with warm water prepared for washing the Squire's hands, had seated herself upon a cushion on the ground, and, with the soles of her feet propped against the cell-wall, rushing on the huge crosier, buried it in her belly, as one thrusts a sword into a scabbard. At the odour of their pleasure, I wore myself more than clothes are worn by wearing, and I rubbed my little pussy with my hand, as cats rub their rumps on the roofs in January.

ANTONIA: Oh! oh! what was the upshot of the game?

NANNA: When they had tugged and sprawled half an hour: – 'All together, my lads!' cried the Lord Abbot; 'thou, kiss me, my little ducky; rub against me, come on, my dove!' and having one hand in the fair Angel's coynte, the other fondling the Cherubim's buttocks, now smacking one, now the other, he made the same wry-faces as that marble statue in the Belvidere makes at the serpents strangling him in the midst of his children. At length, the two Sisters stretched upon the bed, the two Novices, the Abbot, she whom he had under him, he whom he kept busy behind him, and the Nun with the Murano comforter, they all agreed to do it to measure, as Musicians or Blacksmiths agree in lifting the hammer, and, each attentive to the final, there was heard but: 'My darling! my darling! – Hug me! – Stretch me thy little tongue! – Yes! suck me there! – Give it me! – Take it! – Push harder! – Wait till I'm ready for it! – Have it now! – Squeeze me tight! – Help!' The one was muttering, the other caterwauling; you would have fancied a set of sol, fa, mi, re, do; and the topsy-turvy eyes, sighs, bouncings, convulsions were such that they caused chests, wooden beds, chairs, pots to rattle as houses shaken by an earth-quake.

ANTONIA: Or fire!

NANNA: Then eight sighs went off together, having slipped from the livers, lungs, hearts, of the Reverend *et cetera*, of the Sisters, Brothers; they occasioned such a wind, that it would have blown out eight torches. While blowing, they fell down from fatigue, as drunkards fall from wine. And I who had my nerves strung up, with the vexation of gazing on them, went away to sit down, and cast a glance over the glass comforter.

ANTONIA: Wait a moment. How couldst thou count the eight sighs?

NANNA: Thou art too captious; but listen.

ANTONIA: Say.

NANNA: On viewing the glass machine, I felt quite troubled, although what I had already witnessed would have sufficed to disturb the Solitude of the Camaldules, and by dint of gazing, I fell *in tentationem, et libera nos a malo*. Being then no longer able to hold out against the will of the flesh, which was goading my nature beastly, not having any warm water to pour into it, as the Sister had advised me when explaining for me the use of the crystal fruit, the spirit sharpened by necessity, I pissed into the handle.

ANTONIA: How?

NANNA: Through a hole wrought out on purpose, that it might be filled with lukewarm water. But what is the good of spinning out the plot for thee? I boldly pulled up my habit and, laying the knob of the stock upon a box, with the muzzle between my thighs, I began gently, very gently, to mortify my lust. The scalding was very keen, the head exceedingly big, and I endured at the same time martyrdom and enjoyment; but the enjoyment exceeded the martyrdom, and my soul gradually passed into the blistering. All bathed in sweat, riding like a true Knight-errant, I drove it so far in, that a little more and it had wholly disappeared; and while it was thus going into me, I fancied I was dying a milder death than is the life of the Blessed. After having held its beak in a good length of time, I felt all lathered over; quickly did I pull out the tool, and, once it was out, I remained with this smartening scald which eats away a scabby fellow the moment he removes his nails from his thighs. I glance at it, I behold it gory and am about to cry: Confession!

Marguerite de Navarre

1492–1549

Sister of Francis I of France, and wife first of the Duke of Alençon and then of Henry of Navarre, Marguerite presided over a highly educated and religiously tolerant court. Her chief work is the Heptameron, *modelled on Boccaccio's* Decameron, *consisting of stories and debates about love, and generally taking a moral and religious angle.*

From the **Heptameron** (1558). *Trans. P.A. Chilton*

In the country of Alès there was once a man by the name of Bornet, who had married a very decent and respectable woman. He held her honour and reputation very dear, as I am sure all husbands here hold the honour and reputation of *their* wives dear. He wanted her to be faithful to him, but was not so keen on having the rule applied to them both equally. He had become enamoured of his chambermaid, though the only benefit he got from transferring his affections in this way was the sort of pleasure one gets from varying one's diet. He had a neighbour called Sendras, who was of similar station and temperament to himself – he was a tailor and a drummer. These two were such close friends that, with the exception of the wife, there was nothing that they did not share between them. Naturally he told him that he had designs on the chambermaid.

Not only did his friend wholeheartedly approve of this, but did his best to help him, in the hope that he too might get a share in the spoils.

The chambermaid herself refused to have anything to do with him, although he was constantly pestering her, and in the end she went to tell her mistress about it. She told her that she could not stand being badgered by him any longer, and asked permission to go home to her parents. Now the good lady of the house, who was really very much in love with her husband, had often had occasion to suspect him, and was therefore rather pleased to be one up on him, and to be able to show him that she had found out what he was up to. So she said to her maid: 'Be nice to him, dear, encourage him a little bit, and then make a date to go to bed with him in my dressing-room. Don't forget to tell me which night he's supposed to be coming, and make sure you don't tell anyone else.'

The maid did exactly as her mistress had instructed. As for her master, he was so pleased with himself that he went off to tell his friend about his stroke of luck, whereupon the friend

insisted on taking his share afterwards, since he had been in on the business from the beginning. When the appointed time came, off went the master, as had been agreed, to get into bed,
as he thought, with his little chambermaid. But his wife, having abandoned her position of
authority in order to serve in a more pleasurable one, had taken her maid's place in the bed.
When he got in with her, she did not act like a wife, but like a bashful young girl, and he was
not in the slightest suspicious. It would be impossible to say which of them enjoyed themselves
more – the wife deceiving her husband, or the husband who thought he was deceiving his wife.
He stayed in bed with her for some time, not as long as he might have wished (many years of
marriage were beginning to tell on him), but as long as he could manage. Then he went out
to rejoin his accomplice, and tell him what a good time he had had. The lustiest piece of goods
he had ever come across, he declared. His friend, who was younger and more active than he
was, said: 'Remember what you promised?'

'Hurry up, then,' replied the master, 'in case she gets up, or my wife wants her for something.'

Off he went and climbed into bed with the supposed chambermaid his friend had just
failed to recognize as his wife. *She* thought it was her husband again, and did not refuse
anything he asked for (I say 'asked', but 'took' would be nearer the mark, because he did
not dare open his mouth). He made a much longer business of it than the husband, to the
surprise of the wife, who was not used to these long nights of pleasure. However, she did
not complain, and looked forward to what she was planning to say to him in the morning,
and the fun she would have teasing him. When dawn came, the man got up, and fondling
her as he got out of bed, pulled off a ring she wore on her finger, a ring that her husband
had given her at their marriage. Now the women in this part of the world are very superstitious
about such things. They have great respect for women who hang on to their wedding rings
till the day they die, and if a woman loses her ring, she is dishonoured, and is looked upon
as having given her faith to another man. But she did not mind him taking it, because
she thought it would be sure evidence against her husband of the way she had hoodwinked
him.

The husband was waiting outside for his friend, and asked him how he had got on. The man
said he shared the husband's opinion, and added that he would have stayed longer, had he not
been afraid of getting caught by the daylight. The pair of them then went off to get as much
sleep as they could. When morning came, and they were getting dressed together, the husband
noticed that his friend had on his finger a ring that was identical to the one he had given his
wife on their wedding day. He asked him where he had got it, and when he was told it had
come from the chambermaid the night before, he was aghast. He began banging his head
against the wall, and shouted: 'Oh my God! Have I gone and made myself a cuckold without
my wife even knowing about it?'

His friend tried to calm him down. 'Perhaps your wife had given the ring to the girl to look
after before going to bed?' he suggested. The husband made no reply, but marched straight
out and went back to his house.

There he found his wife looking unusually gay and attractive. Had she not saved her
chambermaid from staining her conscience, and had she not put her husband to the ultimate
test, without any more cost to herself than a night's sleep? Seeing her in such good spirits, the

husband thought to himself: 'She wouldn't be greeting me so cheerfully if she knew what I'd been up to.'

As they chatted, he took hold of her hand and saw that the ring, which normally never left her finger, had disappeared. Horrified, he stammered: 'What have you done with your ring?'

She was pleased that he was giving her the opportunity to say what she had to say.

'Oh! You're the most dreadful man I ever met! Who do you think you got it from? You think you got it from the chambermaid, don't you? You think you got it from that girl you're so much in love with, the girl who gets more out of you than I've ever had! The first time you got into bed you were so passionate that I thought you must be about as madly in love with her as it was possible for any man to be! But when you came back the *second* time, after getting up, you were an absolute devil! Completely uncontrolled you were, didn't know when to stop! You miserable man! You must have been blinded by desire to pay such tribute to my body – after all you've had me long enough without showing much appreciation for my figure. So it wasn't because that young girl is so pretty and so shapely that you were enjoying yourself so much. Oh no! You enjoyed it so much because you were seething with some depraved pent-up lust – in short the sin of concupiscence was raging within you, and your senses were dulled as a result. In fact you'd worked yourself up into such a state that I think any old nanny-goat would have done for you, pretty or otherwise! Well, my dear, it's time you mended your ways. It's high time you were content with me for what I am – your own wife and an honest woman, and it's high time that you found *that* just as satisfying as when you thought I was a poor little erring chambermaid. I did what I did in order to save you from your wicked ways, so that when you get old, we can live happily and peacefully together without anything on our consciences. Because if you go on the way you have been, I'd rather leave you altogether than see you destroying your soul day by day, and at the same time destroying your physical health and squandering everything you have before my very eyes! But if you will acknowledge that you've been in the wrong, and make up your mind to live according to the ways of God and His commandments, then I'll overlook all your past misbehaviour, even as I hope God will forgive me *my* ingratitude to Him, and failure to love Him as I ought.'

If there was ever a man who was dumbfounded and despairing, it was this poor husband. There was his wife, looking so pretty, and yet so sensible and so chaste, and he had gone and left her for a girl who did not love him. What was worse, he had had the misfortune to have gone and made her do something wicked without her even realizing what was happening. He had gone and let another man share pleasures which, rightly, were his alone to enjoy. He had gone and given himself cuckold's horns and made himself look ridiculous for evermore. But he could see she was already angry enough about the chambermaid, and he did not dare tell her about the other dirty trick he had played. So he promised that he would leave his wicked ways behind him, asked her to forgive him and gave her the ring back. He told his friend not to breathe a word to anybody, but secrets of this sort nearly always end up being proclaimed from the roof-tops, and it was not long before the facts became public knowledge. The husband was branded as a cuckold without his wife having done a single thing to disgrace herself.

Huang O

1498–1569

Huang O was the daughter of the President of the Board of Works in the Ming Court in China and is unique as a non-courtesan writer of erotic verse in her time.

To the tune **'Soaring Clouds'**. *Trans. Kenneth Rexroth and Ling Chung*

You held my lotus blossom
In your lips and played with the
Pistil. We took one piece of
Magic rhinoceros horn
And could not sleep all night long.
All night the cock's gorgeous crest
Stood erect. All night the bee
Clung trembling to the flower
Stamens. Oh my sweet perfumed
Jewel! I will allow only
My lord to possess my sacred
Lotus pond, and every night
You can make blossom in me
Flowers of fire.

Pernette du Guillet

c. 1520–1545

Pernette du Guillet was a French poet of aristocratic birth, closely associated with the Lyons school of poetry headed by Maurice de Scève, which took its lead from Petrarch and was characterized by an often obscure metaphysical symbolism. She is thought to have been de Scève's lover, and the subject of his 1544 love poem 'Délie'; he rewrote much of her poetry after her death.

From **'Élegie'** (*c.* 1545). *Trans. T. Anthony Perry*

But if he came straight for me,
I would let him boldly approach.
And if he wished to touch me ever so
    lightly,
I would, at the very least, throw a handful
Of the clear fountain's pure water
Right into his eyes or face.
Oh, if the water only had the power
To change him into Acteon:
Not to the extent of having him killed
And devoured by his dogs like a stag,
But so that he could feel himself into my
    slave
And servant transformed to such a degree
That Diana herself would envy
My having ravished his strength.
How great and happy I would be!
Indeed, I would think myself a goddess. . . .

François Rabelais

c. 1494–c. 1553

The French humanist and satirist François Rabelais was born in Chinon. Initially a member of the Franciscan order, he later transferred to the Benedictines, but in 1530 eventually left the cloisters to study medicine at Montpellier. A writer most often associated with bawdy humour, Rabelais is best remembered for his satirical allegories, Gargantua *and* Pantagruel. *Many of his books were banned by theologians of the day.*

From **Gargantua:** 'Of the Youthful Age of Gargantua' (1532).
Trans. Sir Robert Urquhart (d. 1651)

But hearken, good fellows, the spigot ill betake you, and whirl around your brains, if you do not give ear! this little lecher was always groping his nurses and governesses, upside down, arsiversy, topsiturvy, harri bourriquet, with a Yacco haick, hyck gio! handling them very rudely in jumbling and tumbling them to keep them going; for he had already begun to exercise the tools, and put his codpiece in practice. Which codpiece, or braguette, his governesses did every day deck up and adorn with fair nosegays, curious rubies, sweet flowers, and fine silken tufts, and very pleasantly would pass their time in taking you know what between their fingers, and dandling it, till it did revive and creep up to the bulk and stiffness of a suppository, or street magdaleon, which is a hard rolled up salve spread upon leather. Then did they burst out in laughing, when they saw it lift up its ears, as if the sport had liked them. One of them would call it her pillicock, her fiddle-diddle, her staff of love, her tickle-gizzard, her gentle titler. Another, her sugar-plum, her kingo, her old rowley, her touch-trap, her flap dowdle. Another again, her branch of coral, her placket-racket, her Cyprian sceptre, her tit-bit, her bob-lady. And some of the other women would give these names, my Roger, my cockatoo, my nimble-wimble, bush-beater, claw-buttok, eves-fropper, pick-lock, pioneer, bully-ruffin, smell-smock, trouble-gusset, my lusty live sausage, my crimson chitterlin, rump-splitter, shove-devil, down right to it, stiff and stout, in and to, at her again, my coney-borrow-ferret, wily-beguiley, my pretty rogue. It belongs to me, said one. It is mine, said another. What, quoth a third, shall I have no share in it? By my faith, I will cut it then. Ha, to cut it, said the other, would hurt him. Madam, do you cut little children's things? Were his cut off, he would be then Monsieur sans queue, the curtailed master. And that he might play and sport himself after the manner of the other little children of the country, they made him a fair weather whirl jack, of the wings of the windmill of Myrebalais.

Louise Labé

c. 1520–c. 1566

The French poet Louise Labé was born in Lyons and was attached to the Lyons school of humanist poetry led by Maurice de Scève. Her independence was the stuff of legend; she reputedly fought at the 1542 Siege of Perpignan disguised as a man. Her passionate lyric poems and Petrarchan Sonnets *(1555) are said to relate to her many love affairs, especially with the poet Olivier de Magny.*

Sonnet XVIII (1555). *Trans. Frances Webb*

Kiss me again, and kiss me still, and kiss.
Kiss me again, your kisses are like wine.
Kiss me again, seal me and countersign,
And I will give you this – and this – and this –

Three to your one. What! Am I still remiss?
Then take ten more, sweeter than muscardine.
O let me drink your kisses, and you mine,
And thus at ease savour each other's bliss.

So shall we each two lives in one discover,
Each living as beloved and as lover.
Eros, forgive this folly, love engendered:

Behind my soul's grim, fortified redoubt
I know no ease, till I have sallied out,
Taken the field, done battle and surrendered.

Johannes Secundus

1511–1536

A Dutch writer born in The Hague, Johannes Secundus, the pseudonym of Jean d'Everard, was born into a prosperous family. His father, Nicholaus, was a principal dignitary of the Netherlands who was appointed president of the Council of Holland by Charles V, and Secundus himself studied law and worked in Spain as a secretary to the Archoishop of Toledo. He is best known for Basia *– a posthumous collection of love poems strongly influenced by* Catullus.

'The kisses' (**Basia**, 1539). *Trans. Wayland Young*

A hundred hundred kisses,
A hundred thousand kisses,
A thousand thousand kisses,
And as many thousand thousand
As the drops in the Sicilian Sea
Or the stars in the sky.

At those rosy cheeks
At those swelling lips,
At those expressive eyes
I will go with continual energy
O lovely Neaera.

But while I am close attached
Against your rosy cheeks
Against your red lips
And your expressive eyes,
I cannot see your lips,
Nor your rosy cheeks
Nor your expressive eyes.
Alas, how has strife arisen

Between my eyes and my lips?
Could I bear even Jove
As a rival?
My eyes will not brook
My lips as rivals.

Witches Sabbath Parmigianino

Anon. (China)

From Chin P'ing Mei (The Golden Lotus, *c.* 1595)

'On the Magic Mountain she tastes of stolen Joys. In righteous Indignation Little Brother Yuen raises a Tempest in the Tea Room'

With an ingratiating smirk, Mother Wang turned to the young woman. 'I am just going to East Street, near the District Yamen; I know where I can get a first-rate wine. It will be some time before I return. Be so kind as to keep the gentleman company until then. There is still a little wine left in the jug there. Fill your cups from that when they are empty.'

'Please don't go on my account. I don't need any more wine'

'Oh, you two are no longer strangers. Why shouldn't you drink another cup together? Don't be so faint-hearted!'

'Don't go!' Gold Lotus protested once more, but she did not stir from her seat.

Mother Wang opened the door, and fastened it again from the outside, tying the latch string to the door post. She then sat down outside it and began quickly to spin yarn.

The lovers were now shut up together. Gold Lotus had pushed her seat back from the table, and from time to time she glanced surreptitiously at her companion. Hsi Men was gazing at her fixedly with brimming eyes.

At last he spoke. 'What did you say was your honourable family name?'

'Wu.'

'Oh, yes, Wu,' he repeated, absently. 'Not a very common name in this district – Wu. Might the pastry dealer, Wu Ta, the so-called Three-Inch Manikin, be any relation of yours?'

She flushed red for shame. 'My husband,' she breathed, drooping her head.

For a moment he was stricken dumb, and looked wildly around as though he had lost his senses. Then, in a pathetic tone of voice, he cried: 'What an outrage!'

'Why, what injury have you suffered?' she asked in amusement, eyeing him obliquely.

'An outrage to you, not to me!'

And now he began to pay court to her in long, flowery phrases, with many an 'Honoured Lady' and 'Gracious One'. Meanwhile, as she fingered her coat, and nibbled at the seam of her sleeve, she provided an accompaniment to his speech, without stopping her nibbling, in the shape of a spirited retort, or a mischievous sidelong glance. And now, on the pretext that the heat was oppressive, he suddenly drew off his thin, green silksurcoat.

'Would you oblige me by putting this on my adoptive mother's bed?' he begged her.

She turned away from him with a shrug.

'Why don't you do it yourself? Your hands are not paralyzed,' she replied, merrily nibbling her sleeve.

'Well, if you won't, you won't.'

With outstretched arm he reached over the table and threw the garment on to the stove on which the old woman slept. His sleeve caught on one of the chopsticks, and swept it to the floor, and – oh, how providentially! – the chopstick rolled under her dress! As he was about to fill her cup again, and to offer her more food, it was only natural that he should miss one of his chopsticks.

'Is this perhaps your chopstick?' she asked with a smile, pressing her little foot on it.

'Oh, there it is!' he said, in pretended surprise, and he stooped; but instead of picking up the chopstick he gently pressed his hand on her gayly embroidered slipper. She burst out laughing.

'What are you thinking of? I shall scream!'

He fell on his knees before her.

'Most gracious lady, take pity on a wretched man!' he sighed, while his hand crept upwards along her thigh.

Struggling and throwing up her hands, with outspread fingers, she cried: 'Why, you naughty, dissolute fellow! I'll give you such a box on the ears!'

'Ah, gracious lady, it would be bliss even to die at your hands!'

And without giving her time to reply, he took her in his arms and laid her down on Mother Wang's bed. There he loosened her girdle, and disrobed her. And now, sharing a pillow together, they also shared their delight.

Consider, worthy reader, that he who first possessed Gold Lotus was a feeble greybeard, the old moneybag, Chang. Now, this feeble greybeard, always with a drop on his nose, and his diet of beanflour gruel – what sort of pleasure could he afford her? Then came the Three-Inch Manikin. The extent of his powers may be left to the imagination. If now she encounters Hsi Men, one long familiar with the play of the moon and the winds, a strong and upstanding lover, must she not at last experience satisfaction?

Breast to breast – two mandarin ducks in love,
Tumbling merrily about in the water.
Head to head – a tender phoenix pair,
Busy and gay, building their nest of twigs.
She – fastening her red lips upon his cheek,
He – firmly clasping her upturned head.
Now the two golden clasps have fallen from her tresses,
And the black cloud of her hair lies outspread over the pillow.
His vows, deep as the sea and exalted as mountains,
And the thousand variations of his caress,
Banish the last lingering trace of reserve,
As a cloud is driven headlong by the wind.
Overcome by his tender violence
She utters a cry of bliss, like the song of the goldfinch.
The sweet saliva gathers in her mouth
And she thrusts out her tongue in voluptuous pleasure.
Through all the veins and arteries of her willow-lithe body
Heavily pulses the brimming, resistless tide of delight.
But now the panting breath of her cherry lips is more languid,
The dusk of twilight settles upon her eyes,
Her skin is agleam with a hundred fragrant pearls,
Her smooth bosom rises and falls like hurrying waves.

Now – all the sweetness of stolen love consumed –
Two lovers have completed their mating.

The cloud had poured forth its contents. The two lovers were just making themselves presentable again when old Mother Wang suddenly flung open the door and entered. She clapped hands as though in amazement, crying: 'Hi, hi, here's a pretty business!' And turning to Gold Lotus, where she stood in confusion:

'I asked you here to sew, not to go whoring! The best thing I can do is to go straight to your husband and tell him the truth, for he'll reproach me all the more if he discovers it behind my back!'

And she turned as if to go, but Gold Lotus, red with shame, held her fast by the coat.

'Adoptive mother, have pity!' she pleaded softly.

'On one condition only: from this day you must meet Master Hsi Men in secret whenever he wishes; whether I call you early in the morning or late at night, you must come. In that case I will be silent. Otherwise I shall tell your husband everything.'

Gold Lotus could not speak for shame.

'Well, what about it? Answer quickly, please!' the old woman insisted.

'I promise,' came the hardly audible reply.

Now the old woman turned to Hsi Men:

'Noble gentleman, you have had ten-tenths of your desire – now remember your promise! Otherwise . . . '

Ibn Kamal

d. 1573

Ibn Kamal was an Arab poet whose verse demonstrates the strong tradition within Muslim literature of erotic, misogynistic and 'medical' advice.

'How An Old Man Can Regain His Youth Through Sexual Potency'.
Trans. Mary Jo Lakeland

I prefer a young man for coition, and him only;
He is full of courage – he is my sole ambition,
His member is strong to deflower the virgin,
And richly proportioned in all its dimensions;
It has a head like to a brazier.
Enormous, and none like it in creation;
Strong it is and hard, with the head rounded off.
It is always ready for action and does not die down;
It never sleeps, owing to the violence of its love.
It sighs to enter my vulva, and sheds tears on my belly;
It asks not for help, not being in want of any;

It has no need of an ally, and stands alone the greatest fatigues,

And nobody can be sure of what will result from its efforts.

Full of vigour and life, it bores into my vagina,

And it works about there in action constant and splendid.

First from the front to the back, and then from the right to the left;

Now it is crammed hard in by vigorous pressure,

Now it rubs its head on the orifice of my vagina.

And he strokes my back, my stomach, my sides,

Kisses my cheeks, and anon begins to suck at my lips.

He embraces me close, and makes me roll on the bed,

And between his arms I am a corpse without life.

Every part of my body receives in turn his love-bites,

And he covers me with kisses of fire;

When he sees me in heat he quickly comes to me,

Then he opens my thighs and kisses my belly,

And puts his tool in my hand to make it knock at my door.

Soon he is in the cave, and I feel pleasure approaching.

He shakes me and thrills me, and hotly we both are working.

And he says, 'Receive my seed!' and I answer, 'Oh give it beloved one!

It shall be welcome to me, you light of my eyes!

Oh, you man of all men, who fillest me with pleasure.

For you must not yet withdraw it from me; leave it there,

And this day will then be free of all sorrow.'

He has sworn to God to have me for seventy nights,

And what he wished for he did, in the ways of kisses and embraces during all those nights.

Pierre de Ronsard

1524–1585

The son of a man of letters, the French lyric poet Pierre de Ronsard was born in Vendôme. He served the royal family as a page and later as a courtier, but was forced to retire because of increasing deafness. Withdrawing into his studies and writing, he became one of the founder members of the Pléiade *– a revolutionary group of poets which aimed to raise the status of the French language and literature, rejecting the formal classicism of the Middle Ages.*

From **Sonnets for Helen**

By looking too long on your perfect face

My heart caught fire, and such a heat dispersed

That my lips were swollen with thirst,

And speech itself was banished from its place.

You asked them bring well water of your grace

In a bejewelled vase, but, in my thirst,

I brushed the spot which, drinking, you brushed first
Still royal with your aromatic trace.
And well I knew the moment that I smudged it
With mine, the vase, impassioned with your kiss,
And to the flame subdued whose splendour touched it,
As in a furnace, was consumed with this.
How could I hope to rule my own desire,
When in an instant water changed to fire?

Giovanni Battista Guarini

1537–1612

An Italian poet and dramatist, Guarini served as a diplomat to Alfonso II, Duke of Ferrara, succeeding Tasso as court poet in 1577. His most famous work, the verse drama Il pastor fido *(The Faithful Shepherd), written in the 1580s, was widely translated and imitated in the subsequent vogue for the pastoral.*

'The shepherd Thirsis'. *Trans. Sir Robert Aytoun*

The shepherd Thirsis longed to die,
Gazing on the gracious eye
Of her whom he adored and loved,
When she whom no less passion moved
Thus said: 'O die not yet, I pray.
I'll die with thee if thou wilt stay.'
The shepherd then a while delays
The haste he had to end his days,
And while thus languishing he lies
Sucking sweet nectar from her eyes,

The lovely shepherdess, who found
The harvest of his love at hand,
With trembling eyes straight fell a-crying,
'Die, sweetheart, die, for I am dying.'
The shepherd then did straight reply,
'Behold, sweetheart, with thee I die.'
Thus did those lovers spend their breath
In such a sweet and deathless death
That they to life revived again,
Again to try death's pleasant pain.

Pierre de Bourdeille de Brantôme

c. 1540–1614

Pierre de Bourdeille was a French chronicler and satirist, who travelled widely in Europe as a soldier and courtier, meeting Mary Queen of Scots and Elizabeth I. In retirement, he wrote a set of lively and urbane memoirs (published in 1665 as Recueils d'aucuns discours*) which record the scandals and gossip of court life.*

From **The Lives of Gallant Ladies**: 'On the question as to what gives most satisfaction in love-making, The sense of touch, the sense of sight, or speech.' (*c.* 1594). *Trans. Alec Brown*

So it is that I have heard many lords and gallant nobles who have slept with great ladies say that they have found them a hundred times more lascivious and unrestrained in their speech than any common woman and others.

They know how to entertain a man delightfully with their talk, and this is the more pleasurable since it is out of the question, however vigorous a man be, for him to heave at the yoke in incessant ploughing, so that when the man comes to his orgasm and pause he finds it so very good, so appetizing, indeed, when his lady entertains him with lascivious talk and with spicy suggestions which even when Venus seems most sound asleep, can sometimes awaken her again immediately, and this goes to the point that when in conversation with their lovers in the presence of others, even in the presence of Queens and Princesses and so forth, many ladies can work the man up by utterance of words so lascivious and so delectable that both they and their lovers have an emission, just as if they were in bed, while others look on, imagining the talk to be anything than that.

This is why Mark Antony was so fond of Cleopatra and preferred her to his wife Octavia, who was a hundred times lovelier and more pleasing than Cleopatra. Cleopatra, you see, was one of those women with this sort of highly charged talk, and had such lascivious grace and manner and such a fine sense of words that Antony abandoned all else for love of her.

. . .

But in my time I knew one very lovely and estimable lady who was once discussing the events of the recent court wars with an estimable noble at court when she suddenly said 'I've heard the King has blown up all the c—s of such-and-such a country,' putting a 'c' instead of 'p', that is saying not *ponts*, c—s, that is to say not 'bridges',—blown up. As you may imagine, having just slept with her husband or else dreaming of her lover, she had that other little word on the tip of her tongue and the noble in question fell hotly in love with her for that very slip of the tongue.

Another lady whom I knew, entertaining another lady greater than she was, and praising and expatiating on her fine qualities, added: 'Lady So-and-so, I assure you, I am not saying this to be adulterous about you,' meaning to say adulatory about her. Now that was a clear sign that she was really thinking of adultery and committing it.

Anon. (England)

Elizabethan madrigal

My mistress in a hive of bees
In yonder flowery garden
They come to her with laden thighs
To ease them of their burden
As under the beehive lies the wax
And under the wax is honey
So under her waist her belly is placed
And under that, her cunny

Edmund Spenser

c. 1552–1599

The English poet Edmund Spenser was born in London but spent most of his adult life in Ireland as part of the colonial administration, returning to London after the destruction of his estates during the 1598 'Tyrone's Rebellion'. His major work is the long allegorical poetic romance The Faerie Queene *(first version published 1590), which explores humanist ideals and national identity through the adventures of six knights.*

From **The Faerie Queene**, Book II (1590)

And in the midst of all, a fountaine stood,
    Of richest substaunce, that on earth might bee,
    So pure and shiny, that the siluer flood
    Through euery channell running one might see;
    Most goodly it with curious imageree
    Was ouer-wrought, and shapes of naked boyes,
    Of which some seemd with liuely iollitee,
    To fly about, playing their wanton toyes,
Whilest others did them selues embay in liquid ioyes.

And ouer all, of purest gold was spred,
    A trayle of yuie in his natiue hew:
    For the rich mettall was so coloured,
    That wight, who did not well auis'd it vew,
    Would surely deeme it to be yuie trew:
    Low his lasciuious armes adown did creepe,
    That themselues dipping in the siluer dew,
    Their fleecy flowres they tenderly did steepe,
Which drops of Christall seemd for wantones to weepe.

Infinit streames continually did well
    Out of this fountaine, sweet and faire to see,
    The which into an ample lauer fell,
    And shortly grew to so great quantitie,
    That like a little lake it seemd to bee;
    Whose depth exceeded not three cubits hight,
    That through the waues one might the bottom see,
    All pau'd beneath with Iaspar shining bright,
That seemd the fountaine in that sea did sayle vpright.

And all the margent round about was set,
    With shady Laurell trees, thence to defend
    The sunny beames, which on the billowes bet,
    And those which therein bathed, mote offend.
    As *Guyon* hapned by the same to wend,

Two naked Damzelles he therein espyde,
   Which therein bathing, seemed to contend,
   And wrestle wantonly, ne car'd to hyde,
Their dainty parts from vew of any, which them eyde.

Sometimes the one would lift the other quight
   Aboue the waters, and then downe againe
   Her plong, as ouer maistered by might,
   Where both awhile would couered remaine,
   And each the other from to rise restraine;
   The whiles their snowy limbes, as through a vele,
   So through the Christall waues appeared plaine:
   Then suddeinly both would themselues vnhele,
And th'amarous sweet spoiles to greedy eyes reuele.

As that faire Starre, the messenger of morne,
   His deawy face out of the sea doth reare:
   Or as the *Cyprian* goddesse, newly borne
   Of th'Oceans fruitfull froth, did first appeare:
   Such seemed they, and so their yellow heare
   Christalline humour dropped downe apace.
   Whom such when *Guyon* saw, he drew him neare,
   And somewhat gan relent his earnest pace,
His stubborne brest gan secret pleasaunce to embrace,

The wanton Maidens him espying, stood
   Gazing a while at his vnwonted guise;
   Then th'one her selfe low ducked in the flood,
   Abasht, that her a straunger did avise:
   But th'other rather higher did arise,
   And her two lilly paps aloft displayd,
   And all, that might his melting hart entise
   To her delights, she vnto him bewrayd:
The rest hid vnderneath, him more desirous made.

With that, the other likewise vp arose,
   And her faire lockes, which formerly were bownd
   Vp in one knot, she low adowne did lose:
   Which flowing long and thick, her cloth'd arownd,
   And th'yuorie in golden mantle gownd:
   So that faire spectacle from him was reft,
   Yet that, which reft it, no lesse faire was fownd:
   So hid in lockes and waues from lookers theft,
Nought but her louely face she for his looking left.

Withall she laughed, and she blusht withall,
   That blushing to her laughter gaue more grace,
   And laughter to her blushing, as did fall:
   Now when they spide the knight to slacke his pace,
   Them to behold, and in his sparkling face
   The secret signes of kindled lust appeare,
   Their wanton meriments they did encreace,
   And to him beckned, to approch more neare,
And shewd him many sights, that courage cold could reare.

On which when gazing him the Palmer saw,
   He much rebukt those wandring eyes of his,
   And counseld well, him forward thence did draw.
   Now are they come nigh to the *Bowre of blis*
   Of her fond fauorites so nam'd a mis:
   When thus the Palmer; Now Sir, well auise;
   For here the end of all our trauell is:
   Here wonnes *Acrasia*, whom we must surprise,
Else she will slip away, and all our drift despise.

Eftsoones they heard a most melodious sound,
   Of all that mote delight a daintie eare,
   Such as attonce might not on liuing ground,
   Saue in this Paradise, be heard elswhere:
   Right hard it was, for wight, which did it heare,
   To read, what manner musicke that mote bee:
   For all that pleasing is to liuing eare,
   Was there consorted in one harmonee,
Birdes, voyces, instruments, windes, waters, all agree.

The ioyous birdes shrouded in chearefull shade,
   Their notes vnto the voyce attempted sweet;
   Th'Angelicall soft trembling voyces made
   To th'instruments diuine respondence meet:
   The siluer sounding instruments did meet
   With the base murmure of the waters fall:
   The waters fall with difference discreet,
   Now soft, now loud, vnto the wind did call:
The gentle warbling wind low answered to all.

There, whence that Musick seemed heard to bee,
   Was the faire Witch her selfe now solacing,
   With a new Louer, whom through sorceree
   And witchcraft, she from farre did thither bring:
   There she had him now layd a slombering,

In secret shade, after long wanton ioyes:
Whilst round about them pleasauntly did sing
Many faire Ladies, and lasciuious boyes,
That euer mixt their song with light licentious toyes.

And all that while, right ouer him she hong,
With her false eyes fast fixed in his sight,
As seeking medicine, whence she was stong,
Or greedily depasturing delight:
And oft inclining downe with kisses light,
For feare of waking him, his lips bedewd,
And through his humid eyes did sucke his spright,
Quite molten into lust and pleasure lewd;
Wherewith she sighed soft, as if his case she rewd.

The whiles some one did chaunt this louely lay:
Ah see, who so faire thing doest faine to see,
In springing flowre the image of thy day;
Ah see the Virgin Rose, how sweetly shee
Doth first peepe forth with bashfull modestee,
That fairer seemes, the lesse ye see her may;
Lo see soone after, how more bold and free
Her bared bosome she doth broad display;
Loe see soone after, how she fades, and falles away.

So passeth, in the passing of a day,
Of mortall life the leafe, the bud, the flowre,
Ne more doth flourish after first decay,
That earst was sought to decke both bed and bowre,
Of many a Ladie, and many a Paramowre:
Gather therefore the Rose, whilest yet is prime,
For soone comes age, that will her pride deflowre:
Gather the Rose of loue, whilest yet is time,
Whilest loung thou mayst loued be with equall crime.

Christopher Marlowe

1564–1593

The English poet and dramatist Christopher Marlowe was educated at Canterbury and Cambridge before reputedly becoming a government agent. He died in mysterious circumstances (possibly about to face charges of atheism) in a Deptford tavern brawl. A master of blank verse, his major work includes the plays The Jew of Malta, Doctor Faustus, *and* Edward II, *and the narrative poem* Hero and Leander *(completed by George Chapman, c. 1598).*

From **Hero and Leander** (*c.* 1598)

    'O Hero, Hero!' thus he cried full oft,
    And then he got him to a rock aloft,
    Where having spied her tower, long stared he on't,
    And prayed the narrow toiling Hellespont
    To part in twain, that he might come and go,
    But still the rising billows answered 'No'.
    With that he stripped him to the ivory skin,
    And crying, 'Love, I come,' leapt lively in.
    Whereat the sapphire-visaged god grew proud,
    And made his capering Triton sound aloud,
    Imagining that Ganymede, displeased,
    Had left the heavens; therefore on him he seized.
    Leander strived, the waves about him wound,
    And pulled him to the bottom, where the ground
    Was strewed with pearl, and in low coral groves
    Sweet singing mermaids sported with their loves
    On heaps of heavy gold, and took great pleasure
    To spurn in careless sort the shipwrack treasure.
    For here the stately azure palace stood
    Where kingly Neptune and his train abode.
    The lusty god embraced him, called him love,
    And swore he never should return to Jove.
    But when he knew it was not Ganymede,
    For under water he was almost dead,
    He heaved him up, and looking on his face,
    Beat down the bold waves with his triple mace,
    Which mounted up, intending to have kissed him,
    And fell in drops like tears because they missed him.
    Leander, being up, began to swim,
    And, looking back, saw Neptune follow him;
    Whereat aghast the poor soul 'gan to cry,
    'O let me visit Hero ere I die.'
    The god put Helle's bracelet on his arm,
    And swore the sea should never do him harm.
    He clapped his plump cheeks, with his tresses played,
    And smiling wantonly, his love bewrayed.
    He watched his arms, and as they opened wide
    At every stroke, betwixt them would he slide
    And steal a kiss, and then run out and dance,
    And as he turned, cast many a lustful glance,
    And threw him gaudy toys to please his eye,

And dive into the water, and there pry
Upon his breast, his thighs, and every limb,
And up again, and close beside him swim,
And talk of love. Leander made reply,
'You are deceived, I am no woman, I.'

William Shakespeare

1564–1616

England's greatest dramatist, Shakespeare was born and educated in Stratford-upon-Avon. From the late 1580s he established his reputation as one of London's leading playwrights, but his work also included the two narrative poems Venus and Adonis *and* The Rape of Lucrece *(1594), which, together with the* Sonnets *(published 1609), constitute one of the most impressive bodies of English erotic poetry.*

From **Venus and Adonis** (1593)

All swoln with chasing, down Adonis sits,
Banning his boisterous and unruly beast;
And now the happy season once more fits,
That love-sick Love by pleading may be blest;
For lovers say the heart hath treble wrong,
When it is barr'd the aidance of the tongue.

An oven that is stopp'd, or river stay'd,
Burneth more hotly, swelleth with more rage:
So of concealed sorrow may be said;
Free vent of words love's fire doth assuage;
But when the heart's attorney once is mute,
The client breaks, as desperate in his suit.

He sees her coming, and begins to glow,
Even as a dying coal revives with wind,
And with his bonnet hides his angry brow;
Looks on the dull earth with disturbed mind,
Taking no notice that she is so nigh,
For all askaunce he holds her in his eye.

O what a sight it was, wistly to view
How she came stealing to the wayward boy!
To note the fighting conflict of her hue!
How white and red each other did destroy!
But now her cheek was pale, and by and by
It flash'd forth fire, as lightning from the sky.

Now was she just before him as he sat,
And like a lowly lover down she kneels;
With one fair hand she heaveth up his hat,
Her other tender hand his fair cheek feels:
His tenderer cheek receives her soft hand's
    print
As apt as new-fallen snow takes any dint.

O what a war of looks was then between them!
Her eyes, petitioners, to his eyes suing:
His eyes saw her eyes as they had not seen
    them;
Her eyes woo'd still, his eyes disdain'd the
    wooing:
And all this dumb play had his acts made plain
With tears, which, chorus-like, her eyes did
    rain.

Full gently now she takes him by the hand,
A lily prison'd in a gaol of snow,
Or ivory in an alabaster band;
So white a friend engirts so white a foe:
This beauteous combat, wilful and unwilling,
Show'd like two silver doves that sit a-billing.

Once more the engine of her thoughts began:
'O fairest mover on this mortal round,
Would thou wert as I am, and I a man,

My heart all whole as thine, thy heart my
    wound;
For one sweet look thy help I would assure
    thee,
Though nothing but my body's bane would
    cure thee.'

'Give me my hand,' saith he, 'why dost thou
    feel it?'
'Give me my heart,' saith she, 'and thou shalt
    have it;
O give it me lest thy hard heart do steel it,
And being steel'd, soft sighs can never grave it;
Then love's deep groans I never shall regard,
Because Adonis' heart hath made mine hard.'

'For shame,' he cries, 'let go, and let me go;
My day's delight is past, my horse is gone,
And 't is your fault I am bereft him so;
I pray you hence, and leave me here alone:
For all my mind, my thought, my busy care,
Is how to get my palfrey from the mare.'

Thus she replies: 'Thy palfrey, as he should,
Welcomes the warm approach of sweet desire.
Affection is a coal that must be cool'd;
Else, suffer'd, it will set the heart on fire:
The sea hath bounds, but deep desire hath
    none.

'How like a jade he stood, tied to the tree,
Servilely master'd with a leathern rein!
But when he saw his love, his youth's fair fee,
He held such petty bondage in disdain;
Throwing the base thong from his bending
    crest,
Enfranchising his mouth, his back, his breast.

'Who sees his true love in her naked bed,
Teaching the sheets a whiter hue than white,
But, when his glutton eye so full hath fed,
His other agents aim at like delight?
Who is so faint that dare not be so bold
To touch the fire, the weather being cold?

'Let me excuse thy courser, gentle boy;
And learn of him, I heartily beseech thee,
To take advantage on presented joy;
Though I were dumb, yet his proceedings teach
    thee.
O learn to love; the lesson is but plain,
And, once made perfect, never lost again.'

'I know not love,' quoth he, 'nor will not
    know it,
Unless it be a boar, and then I chase it:
'Tis much to borrow, and I will not owe it;
My love to love is love but to disgrace it;
For I have heard it is a life in death,
That laughs, and weeps, and all but with a
    breath.

'Who wears a garment shapeless and unfinish'd?
Who plucks the bud before one leaf put forth?
If springing things be any jot diminish'd,
They wither in their prime, prove nothing
    worth:
The cold that's back'd and burthen'd being
    young
Loseth his pride, and never waxeth strong.

'You hurt my hand with wringing; let us part,
And leave this idle theme, this bootless chat:
Remove your siege from my unyielding heart;
To love's alarm it will not ope the gate.
Dismiss your vows, your feigned tears, your
    flattery;
For where a heart is hard, they make no
    battery.'

'What! canst thou talk,' quoth she, 'hast thou a
    tongue?
O would thou hadst not, or I had no hearing!
Thy mermaid's voice hath done me double
    wrong;
I had my load before, now press'd with bearing:
Melodious discord, heavenly tune harsh
    sounding,

Ear's deep-sweet music, and heart's deep-sore
    wounding.

'Had I no eyes, but ears, my ears would love
That inward beauty and invisible:
Or, were I deaf, thy outward parts would move
Each part in me that were but sensible:
Though neither eyes nor ears, to hear nor see,
Yet should I be in love, by touching thee.

'Say that the sense of feeling were bereft me,
And that I could not see, nor hear, nor touch,
And nothing but the very smell were left me,
Yet would my love to thee be still as much;
For from the still'tory of thy face excelling
Comes breath perfum'd, that breedeth love by
    smelling.

'But O, what banquet wert thou to the taste,
Being nurse and feeder of the other four!
Would they not wish the feast might ever last,
And bid Suspicion double-lock the door?
Lest Jealousy, that sour unwelcome guest,
Should, by his stealing in, disturb the feast.'

Once more the ruby-colour'd portal open'd,
Which to his speech did honey passage yield;
Like a red morn, that ever yet betoken'd
Wreck to the seaman, tempest to the field,
Sorrow to shepherds, woe unto the birds,
Gusts and foul flaws to herdmen and to herds.

This ill presage advisedly she marketh:
Even as the wind is hush'd before it raineth,
Or as the wolf doth grin before it barketh,
Or as the berry breaks before it staineth,
or like the deadly bullet of a gum,
His meaning struck her ere his words begun.

And at his look she flatly falleth down,
For looks kill love, and love by looks reviveth:
A smile recures the wounding of a frown,
But blessed bankrupt, that by love so thriveth!
The silly boy, believing she is dead,
Claps her pale cheek, till clapping makes it red;

And all-amaz'd brake off his late intent,
For sharply he did think to reprehend her,
Which cunning love did wittily prevent:
Fair fall the wit that can so well defend her!
For on the grass she lies as she were slain,
Till his breath breatheth life in her again.

He wrings her nose, he strikes her on the
    cheeks,
He bends her fingers, holds her pulses hard;
He chafes her lips, a thousand ways he seeks
To mend the hurt that his unkindness marr'd;
He kisses her; and she, by her good will,
Will never rise so he will kiss her still.

The night of sorrow now is turn'd to day:
Her two blue windows faintly she upheaveth,
Like the fair sun, when in his fresh array
He cheers the morn, and all the world relieveth:
And as the bright sun glorifies the sky,
So is her face illumin'd with her eye:

Whose beams upon his hairless face are fix'd,
As if from thence they borrow'd all their shine.
Were never four such lamps together mix'd,
Had not his clouded with his brow's repine;
But hers, which thro' the crystal tears gave light,
Shone like the moon in water seen by night.

'O', where am I?' quoth she, 'in earth or
    heaven,
Or in the ocean drench'd, or in the fire?
What hour is this? or morn, or weary even?
Do I delight to die, or life desire?
But now I liv'd, and life was death's annoy;
But now I died, and death was lively joy.

'O thou didst kill me; – kill me once again:
Thy eyes' shrewd tutor, that hard heart of thine,
Hath taught them scornful tricks, and such
    disdain
That they have murder'd this poor heart of
    mine;
And these mine eyes, true leaders to their
    queen,
But for thy piteous lips no more had seen.

'Long may they kiss each other, for this cure!
O never let their crimson liveries wear!
And as they last, their verdure still endure,
To drive infection from the dangerous year!
That the star-gazers, having writ on death,
May say the plague is banished by thy breath.

'Pure lips, sweet seals in my soft lip imprinted,
What bargains may I make, still to be sealing?
To sell myself I can be well contented,
So thou wilt buy, and pay, and use good dealing;
Which purchase if thou make, for fear of slips,
Set thy seal-manual on my wax-red lips.

'A thousand kisses buys my heart from me;
And pay them at thy leisure, one by one.
What is ten hundred touches unto thee?
Are they not quickly told, and quickly gone?
Say, for non-payment that the debt should
    double,
Is twenty hundred kisses such a trouble?'

'Fair queen,' quoth he, 'if any love you owe me,
Measure my strangeness with my unripe years;
Before I know myself seek not to know me;
No fisher but the ungrown fry forbears:
The mellow plum doth fall, the green sticks fast,
Or being early pluck'd is sour to taste.

'Look, the world's comforter, with weary gait,
His day's hot task hath ended in the west:
The owl, night's herald, shrieks, – 'tis very late;
The sheep are gone to fold, birds to their nest;
And coal-black clouds that shadow heaven's
    light
Do summon us to part, and bid good night.

'Now let me say "good night," and so say you;
If you will say so, you shall have a kiss.'
'Good night,' quoth she; and, ere he says
    'adieu,'
The honey fee of parting tender'd is:
Her arms do lend his neck a sweet embrace;
Incorporate then they seem; face grows to face.

Till, breathless, he disjoin'd, and backward drew
The heavenly moisture, that sweet coral mouth,
Whose precious taste her thirsty lips well knew,
Whereon they surfeit, yet complain on drouth:
He with her plenty press'd, she faint with
    dearth,
(Their lips together glued,) fall to the earth.

Now quick Desire hath caught the yielding prey,
And glutton-like she feeds, yet never filleth;
Her lips are conquerors, his lips obey,
Paying what ransom the insulter willeth;
Whose vulture thought doth pitch the price so
    high,
That she will draw his lips' rich treasure dry.

And having felt the sweetness of the spoil,
With blindfold fury she begins to forage;
Her face doth reek and smoke, her blood doth
    boil,
And careless lust stirs up a desperate courage:
Planting oblivion, beating reason back,
Forgetting shame's pure blush, and honour's
    wrack.

Sheik Umar Ibn Muhammed al-Nefzawi

16th century

Umar Ibn Muhammed al-Nefzawi was a Tunisian sheik whose work The Perfumed Garden *forms part of a long tradition of Muslim treatises which combine sex-education, philosophy and science. The work was discovered by a French army officer in Algeria in the mid-nineteenth century and championed by Guy de Maupassant in France. It was impressively translated by the great Victorian Oriental erotophile, Sir Richard Burton.*

From **The Perfumed Garden**: 'The History of Djoâidi and Fadehat el Djemal'.
Trans. Sir Richard Burton

I was in love with a woman who was all grace and perfection, beautiful of shape, and gifted with all imaginable charms. Her cheeks were like roses, her forehead lily white, her lips like coral; she had teeth like pearls, and breasts like pomegranates. Her mouth opened round like a ring; her tongue seemed to be incrusted with precious gems; her eyes, black and finely slit, had the languor of slumber, and her voice the sweetness of sugar. With her form pleasantly filled out, her flesh was mellow like fresh butter, and pure as the diamond.

As to her vulva, it was white, prominent, round as an arch; the centre of it was red, and breathed fire, without a trace of humidity; for, sweet to the touch, it was quite dry. When she walked it showed in relief like a dome or an inverted cup. In reclining it was visible between her thighs, looking like a kid couched on a hillock.

This woman was my neighbour. All the others played and laughed with me, jested with me, and met my suggestions with great pleasure. I revelled in their kisses, their close embraces and nibblings, and in sucking their lips, breasts, and necks. I had coition with all of them, except my neighbour, and it was exactly her I wanted to possess in preference to all the rest; but instead of being kind to me, she avoided me rather. When I contrived to take her aside to trifle with her and try to rouse her gaiety, and spoke to her of my desires, she recited to me the following verses, the sense of which was a mystery to me:

> Among the mountain tops I saw a tent placed firmly,
> Apparent to all eyes high up in mid-air.
> But, oh! the pole that held it up was gone.
> And like a vase without a handle it remained,
> With all its cords undone, its centre sinking in,
> Forming a hollow like that of a kettle.

Every time I told her of my passion she answered me with these verses, which to me were void of meaning, and to which I could make no reply, which, however, only excited my love all the more. I therefore inquired of all those I knew – amongst wise men, philosophers, and savants – the meaning, but not one of them could solve the riddle for me, so as to satisfy my heat and appease my passion.

Nevertheless I continued my investigations, when at last I heard of a savant named Abou Nouass, who lived in a far-off country, and who, I was told, was the only man capable of solving the enigma. I betook to him, apprised him of the discourses I had with the woman, and recited to him the above-mentioned verses.

Abou Nouass said to me, 'This woman loves you to the exclusion of every other man. She is very corpulent and plump.' I answered, 'It is exactly as you say. You have given her likeness as if she were before you, excepting what you say in respect of her love for me, for, until now, she has never given me any proof of it.'

'She has no husband.'

'This is so,' I said.

Then he added, 'I have reason to believe that your member is of small dimensions, and such a member cannot give her pleasure nor quench her fire; for what she wants is a lover with a member like that of an ass. Perhaps it may not be so. Tell me the truth about this!' When I had reassured him on that point, affirming that my member, which began to rise at the expression of his doubtings, was full-sized, he told me that in that case all difficulties would disappear, and explained to me the sense of the verses as follows:

The *tent*, firmly planted, represents the vulva of grand dimension and placed well forward, the *mountains*, between which it rises, are the thighs. The *stake* which supported its centre and has been torn up, means that she has no husband, comparing the stake or pole that supports the tent to the virile member holding up the lips of the vulva. *She is like a vase without a handle*; this means if the pail is without a handle to hang it up by it is good for nothing, the pail representing the vulva, and the handle the verge. *The cords are undone and its centre is sinking in*; that is to say, as the tent without a supporting pole caves in at the centre, inferior in this respect to the vault which remains upright without support, so can the woman who has no husband not enjoy complete happiness. From the words, *It forms a hollow like that of a kettle*, you may judge how lascivious God has made that woman in her comparisons; she likens her vulva to a kettle, which serves to prepare the *tserid* [Arabian dish]. Listen; if the *tserid* is placed in the kettle, to turn out well it must be stirred by means of a *medeleuk* [large wooden spoon shaped like a pouch] long and solid, whilst the kettle is steadied by the feet and hands. Only in that way can it be properly prepared. It cannot be done with a small spoon; the cook would burn her hands, owing to the shortness of the handle, and the dish would not be well prepared. This is the symbol of this woman's nature, O Djoâidi. If your member has not the dimensions of a respectable *medeleuk*, serviceable for the good preparation of the *tserid*, it will not give her satisfaction, and, moreover, if you do not hold her close to your chest, enlacing her with your hands and feet, it is useless to solicit her favours; finally if you let her consume herself by her own fire, like the bottom of the kettle which gets burnt if the *medeleuk* is not stirred upon it, you will not gratify her desire by the result.

You see now what prevented her from acceding to your wishes; she was afraid that you would not be able to quench her flame after having fanned it.

SEVENTEENTH AND EIGHTEENTH CENTURIES

The odalisque François Boucher

The erotic delight in human nature characteristic of the sixteenth-century humanist poets with their renewed interest in classical literature had been accompanied by the growth of a puritanical, repressive and moralizing attitude in Protestants and Catholics alike. This, and the cause of religious unity, contributed to increasing State interference in the realms of private morality and was to exert a great influence on the climate for erotic literature.

At the same time, critics detect a creeping terror, almost a horror, of sexuality in literature by the turn of the century. Three centuries later D.H. Lawrence was to attribute this to the knowledge, and increasingly widespread experience, of syphilis, which took its name from a poem, 'Syphilis sive morbus gallicus' (1530), by the Italian scientist and poet Girolamo Fracastoro (1483–1533), which tells the story of a shepherd named Syphilis whom the Sun god punished with this disease. Initially treated as an inconvenient and often amusing outcome of love-making, by 1600 it was known to be an instrument of certain death and generally believed to be caused by debauchery. The association of sex with guilt, which had played virtually no part in the erotic literature of the Renaissance, lay at the heart of the Puritan ethic.

The English metaphysical poets added another dimension to the changing attitudes towards sexual desire. These early seventeenth-century poets occupy a period of transition between the Elizabethan poets, who cultivated the Italian and French love poets, and the Restoration poets of the 1660s, who expressed a more deterministic psychology. The term 'metaphysical', first used disparagingly by Samuel Johnson in 1777, denotes a style and treatment of the erotic sensibility in which passion and argument, imagination and reason are integrated.

Foremost among the metaphysical poets is John Donne, who analysed the experience of love in a variety of moods ranging from cynical sensuality to a profound sense of union, but always with a realistic force (see page 153). Ben Jonson, turning to the Latin lyric poets and epigrammatists, translated Horace, Martial and especially Catullus into witty and spontaneous contemporary speech (see page 154). Robert Herrick responded to contemporary concerns with an appreciation of rural culture; his short verses have been aptly described as exquisite little orgasms (see page 156). Of the late metaphysicals, Thomas Carew (see page 158), one of the best-known Cavalier poets of the Court of Charles I, and Andrew Marvell (see page 161), both share an epicurean belief that the highest good is pleasure, particularly sensuous pleasure, allied with virtue.

One of the most notable works of French erotic literature of this period caused such a furore that the printer was forced out of business. The author, Nicolas Chorier, avoided punishment by throwing up a smokescreen of pseudonyms, false translators and different titles. The work in question, originally known as *Aloisae Sigeae Totelanae Satyra Sotadica de Arcanis Amoris et Venus* ('The Sotadic Satire of Louisa Sigea of Toledo on the Secrets of Love and Venus'), (see page 162), takes the form of a conversation between a young, innocent virgin and an older, sexually experienced married woman. (Sotades was an ancient Greek poet whose explicit work is marked by coarseness and scurrility.) Following in the tradition of Aretino, Chorier set the tone for a new genre of erotic literature that became known as the 'whore dialogue'.

Many other Western writers adapted this form, which on occasion rose above the tedious. Most notable was the Italian Pallavicino Ferrante (*b.* 1618) whose *Le Rettorica delle putane* (1642) combined a realistic understanding of the hard life of the whore with a strong undercurrent of male fear of female sexuality. Translated and adapted into English in 1648 as *The Whore's Rhetorik*, the work instantly became a successful classic of this sub-genre. The anonymous *L'Escholle des filles* (see page 163) has less to recommend it in literary terms, but it too became a European bestseller. The Restoration dramatist William Wycherley (1641–1715), whose licentious drama delighted the King, referred to it in *The Country Wife* (*c.* 1675), along with bawdy pictures and a reference to Aretino. Samuel Pepys (1633–1703) masturbated over it and then 'burned it that it might not be among my books to my shame'. By the nineteenth century, the 'whore dialogue' was one of the most popular forms of pornography.

The scandal caused by Chorier's 'novel' – no more than a dialogue loosely linked by an extremely thin narrative – was probably due to the fact that it was prose rather than poetry, and aimed at an audience wider than the aristocracy and an educated literary elite. This path was also taken around this time by the Japanese writer Ihara Saikaku, whose ribald and worldlywise novels were infinitely more sophisticated than anything produced by contemporary European erotic writers. In *Five Women Who Loved Love*, written for the amusement of the merchant-class citizens of his native Osaka (see page 165), Saikaku plays a slyly erotic game linking realistic detail to fantastic event. Saikaku's novels are remarkable not only when compared with European prose of this period, but also when considered in terms of contemporary Japan. His lovers were ordinary townswomen and men, not the courtesans who usually peopled traditional Japanese fiction. They appear startlingly modern, not least because the defloration of virgins which so obsessed the seventeenth- and eighteenth-century European male is almost totally absent; adultery was the taboo that Oriental erotica explored.

In China there was also a lively tradition of erotic fiction. *The Carnal Prayer Mat* by Li Yu (see page 166) tells of the enlightenment gained by the scholar Vesperus during a career of licentiousness before taking monastic vows. Written in a wholeheartedly comic spirit without pretensions, and with no attempt to disguise its theme of unrestrained sexual desire at large in society, it is a landmark in the history of the erotic novel. However, neither Saikaku's nor Li Yu's novels could influence the European erotic novel since they were not translated until the twentieth century. Europe was to wait almost another 100 years before this genre was really established.

The book which many regard as one of the biggest single influences on the development of the erotic novel in Europe was *The Love Letters of a Portuguese Nun*, which may have been written by the lovelorn Marianna Alcoforado, or perhaps by Gabriel de Lavergne de Guilleragues (see page 171). (If by the latter, he was a man with an acute nose for commercial success.) These poignant letters, which together form a loose narrative, echo an eroticism closer in spirit to that of the medieval Heloise than to the bawdy rumbustiousness of the Restoration or of French libertinism. Hugely popular, the book provided the prototype for the abandoned and passionate mistress who was to stalk the pages of the erotic novel, as well as for the epistolary novel which was to become so popular in the eighteenth century.

Of all the British Restoration erotic writers – referred to by Marvell as the 'merry gang' – perhaps the best known, the most reviled and the least understood is John Wilmot, Earl of Rochester. He wrote some of the most outrageously licentious verse of his day, and, although he denied authorship, probably penned a wicked sexually explicit play, *Sodom, or The Quintessence of Debauchery* (1668). With characters named Bolloxinian, Cuntagratia, Prickett, Prince Buggeranthus, Fuckadilla, Cunticula, Clytoris and Virtuose, who was the merkin (pubic wig) and dildo-maker to the royal family, *Sodom* (see page 168) is regarded as the first full-length modern drama deliberately written to shock and excite.

It is an over-simplification to view Rochester and his fellow courtier poets as corrupt and cynical pleasure-seekers. Rochester's mind was essentially serious. He accepted the doctrine of his contemporary, the philosopher Thomas Hobbes (1588–1679), that 'Pleasure . . . or delight is the appearance, or the sense of good; and molestation or displeasure, the . . . sense of evil', and plunged into the experiment of living the complete life of pleasure with the same ardour with which the physicists of the day devoted themselves to the investigation of nature. Voltaire considered him an '*homme de génie et grand poète*', and for D.H. Lawrence his genius lay in the 'unrestful, ingraspable poetry of the sheer present . . . the soul and the mind and the body surging at once, nothing left out'.

Little has done more to provoke an explosion of erotic indulgence than puritanical re-pression – hence the sexual licence of the Restoration, which coincided with the spread of libertinism in Europe, especially France. But court poetry and drama were not the only outlets for the Western erotic imagination. Countless anonymous ballads and broadsheets, which celebrated sexual desire with humour, bawdiness and verve, circulated throughout the seventeenth century. The best-known English collection, known as *The Roxburghe Ballads* (1774), contain some delightful folk songs which reveal unrestrained pleasure in human sexuality (see page 178).

Defying potent social restraints on female erotic expression, the poet, dramatist, novelist and some-time spy, Aphra Behn, was to be acclaimed this century by Virginia Woolf as the first Englishwoman to earn her living by writing 'with all the plebeian virtues of humour, vitality and courage'. Both Behn's lifestyle and her writing unashamedly celebrate sexual pleasure and insist upon women's right to financial and sexual independence. Her poem 'The Disappointment' (see page 173), probably the first treatment of male impotence by a female writer, was all too much for some of the male writers of the day, who were reduced to accusing her of plagiarism as well as lewdness.

Salacious stories of seduction and betrayal were the hallmarks of Eliza Haywood (?1693 –1756) and Mary Delarivier Manley. In *The New Atalantis* (see page 175) Manley satirized the Duchess of Cleveland, mistress of Charles II, inverting the traditional eroticized seduction scene by presenting the woman as the sexual predator. In the eighteenth century the female rake was to be superseded by the highly fantasized biographical sexual exploits of Giacomo Casanova (see page 209) and Restif de la Bretonne (see page 202) among others, and few women were to put their pens to erotic effect. The domestic sphere of women became increasingly emphasized, and those with intellectual or literary ambitions in any genre were condemned as slatternly if not outright licentious. (In 1732 a 'Miss W.' responded in kind to Swift's 'The Lady's Dressing Room', but the poem lacks the wit and skill of Swift's satirical pen, and is, in any case, very probably by a man.)

From the mid-seventeenth century and throughout the eighteenth century, Europe witnessed an explosion of erotic literature, causing one critic to suggest the 'Age of Enlightenment' be renamed the 'Age of Eros'. Erotica was not confined to poetry, drama and fiction. There were also scientific treatises and para-medical works, sometimes in verse, which paid lavish attention to lesbianism, female virginity and masturbation; the last was a particular taboo for eighteenth-century European society. At the same time scurrilous journalistic 'faction' exploited popular interest in adultery, rape, seduction and sodomy. Anti-aristocratic erotic satire was another popular genre, giving rise to an extraordinary increase of obscene libels, bawdy lampoons, ribald personal satire and overtly political pornography against the nobility in a literary tradition which reached back to Aretino and Pierre de Bourdeille, and perhaps even further to Suetonius.

Erotic anti-religious writings were produced in great quantity, often taking the form of erotic parodies of church sermons, the catechism, the Commandments and other aspects of the church service. But in the satirical, anti-clerical pornography of this period, Eros was frequently used as an excuse for salacity rather than as a weapon to attack the Church. Satire was not the only expression of the links between the pagan and Christian gods of love; religious and erotic expression in the confessional writings of medieval mystics had produced a terminology and formed a tradition which is clearly discernible in the hymns of English evangelist John Wesley (1703–91).

The amatory novels of post-Restoration England, the 'whore dialogue' and the plethora of other erotic genres paved the way for the sexually explicit novels of the eighteenth century, such as those by Daniel Defoe, Samuel Richardson, Henry Fielding and Tobias Smollet. These culminated in John Cleland's *Fanny Hill* (see page 192), which is widely considered to be the first Western erotic novel proper. The novels were written from a variety of motives. Defoe's *Moll Flanders* (see page 182) and *Roxana* (1724), while comic depictions of the low life, possess a high moral tone. Fielding was so outraged by what he believed to be the prurience in Richardson's *Pamela* (see page 185) that he launched a counter-attack with *Shamela* (see page 187). It is difficult, however, to place Laurence Sterne's highly original and innovative novel *The Life and Opinions of Tristram Shandy* (see page 198) within a particular tradition or genre. While the book owes much to predecessors such as Rabelais and Cervantes, as well as to the English philosophers Sir Robert Burton and John Locke, it is nonetheless a unique work which is seen as the progenitor of the 'stream-of-consciousness' fiction exemplified by James Joyce's *Ulysses* in the twentieth century.

Initially, the main target of the erotic fiction of this period was middle-class morality. It gradually degenerated into a prurience which allowed authors to present a world of crime, prostitution and sex in which money, or the lack of it, played a central role to a growing bourgeoisie avid for sexual titillation. (The term 'purse' was a popular euphemism for the vagina and 'spendings' a favourite term for female and male ejaculate). By the end of the century the intention of arousing the reader became an obvious feature of the erotic novel. The Comte de Mirabeau (1749–91), French revolutionary and author of pornographic novels, as well as a biographical account of his life as a gigolo, had made no effort to disguise his intentions, exhorting his (probably male) reader: '*Eh bien, lis, dévore, et branle-toi*' ('And now read, devour and masturbate').

While the English amatory or erotic novel mainly indulged a middle-class fascination for the sexually seamy aspects of the underworld, the French erotic novel, inspired by the newly translated *Arabian Nights* (see page 102), explored the erotic potential of exotic, Oriental worlds. Magical metamorphoses, jinn, fairies and spells were put to erotic use in novels that spelled out in licentious detail the sexual activities of pimps and prostitutes, as well as lustful clerics, sultans, Japanese war-lords and princesses in fantasies of rape, seduction, adultery, defloration, floggings and enemas. The most popular novel of this genre was *Le Sopha* (1737) by Crébillon *fils*, which the English Gothic novelist Horace Walpole (1717–97) reputedly held in as high esteem as *Don Quixote*. *Les Bijoux indiscrets* by Diderot (see page 197) dashed off in two weeks, in which a magic ring empowers women's labia-surrounded 'toys' to speak, is a fascinating example of this genre mixed with political and social satire. The eroticism in Marie Le Prince de Beaumont's famous fairy-tale *Beauty and the Beast* (see page 190) cannot be ignored when viewed in the context of the popularity of these *contes de fées érotiques* (erotic fairy-tales).

A further influence on the seemingly endless production of erotica was the new philosophy of pleasure and sexual libertinism. Originating in France where it denoted 'free-thinking', libertine literature attacked the bastions of religious, political, societal and sexual repression. The libertine novel, with its disregard for popular concepts of morality and its emphasis on sensual pleasure, reached its apotheosis in the licentious fiction of Andrea de Nerciat in the late eighteenth century, which did much to bring about its fall into disrepute. It has been said that whereas Nerciat described the feel of libertinism, Choderlos de Laclos in *Les Liaisons dangereuses* (see page 203) 'wrote down its rules in vitriol and thereby destroyed it'. It survived, however, in the works of the Marquis de Sade (see page 207), who fiercely espoused libertine philosophy. For this he was attacked by Restif de la Bretonne, but unsuccessfully: Restif's novel *L'Anti-Justine* (1798) almost outstrips de Sade in its perverse, frequently 'sadistic' detail.

Within the erotic-satirical tradition of exposing hypocrisy that characterizes some of the finest erotic poetry and prose of the eighteenth century lies a language that reveals a two-way osmotic process of influence between 'high' literature and underground erotica, or what came to be called pornography. These links between the 'high' and the 'low' are cleverly exploited in Richardson's ambiguous *Pamela*. Rarely has a heroine so apparently determined to hang on to her virginity spent more time dreaming about rape and seduction. No reader with a knowledge of popular erotic fiction and jargon could have remained unamused – or perhaps unaroused – by Pamela's tendency to break out into sweats, faint or 'die' whenever a male hand sneaks to her bosom. In *Fanny Hill*, John Cleland (see page 192) made successful use of these links by renouncing all language which might be unacceptable to middle-class sensibilities. This gives to the novel, perhaps the masterpiece of the century, some refreshingly inventive euphemisms, although there are also occasional clumsy circumlocutions.

'Essay on Woman' (see page 200), almost certainly written by John Wilkes, a dissolute Member of Parliament for Aylesbury, is another example of this trend. Written in the most vulgar of tongues in parody of the high-minded moral and philosophical poem 'An Essay on Man' (1733–4) by Alexander Pope, it caused a scandal that resulted in Wilkes being charged with obscene libel. He was arrested, expelled from Parliament and for a while banned altogether from England.

Pope himself exemplifies the osmotic influences between the two worlds of literature in 'The Rape of the Lock' (see page 180). His use of sexual allusion and outrageous punning innuendo results in highlighting rather than evading middle-class hypocritical preoccupations with seduction, rape and female virginity. Jonathan Swift goes to the other extreme in his scatological and obscene verse riddles (see page 184). But these should not be seen simply as a sign of a private pathological obsession with ordure; rather they are an indication of his closeness to contemporary folklore. The supreme master of the vulgar tongue was Robert Burns, whose direct contact with the poor and illiterate enabled him to write verse which upset his conventionally decorous editors in Edinburgh and caused many of his contemporaries and later readers to doubt his authorship of some of his more sexually explicit verse (see page 208).

Conventional bourgeois morality meant that women writers of this period who were interested in the erotic had to be discreet if they dared to approach the subject at all – and relatively few did. But censorship and invention have a long history of interconnection. The erotic undercurrents in the novels of Jane Austen (1775–1817) are seldom pointed out to the generations of schoolchildren who have been solemnly taught to regard her as the very model of gentility and propriety. The following passage from *Sense and Sensibility* (1811) makes it clear that she had a detailed knowledge and an amused understanding of the *double entendre* in Swift's 'Rape of the Lock':

> 'I am sure they will be married very soon, for he has got a lock of her hair . . . I saw him cut it off. Last night, after tea, when you and mama went out of the room, they were whispering and talking together as fast as could be, and he seemed to be begging for something of her, and presently he took up her scissors and cut off a long lock of her hair, for it was all tumbled down her back; and he kissed it, and folded it up in a piece of white paper, and put it into his pocket-book.'

In pre-revolutionary Europe erotic literature was in part an attempt to dislocate and destroy the social order, and to challenge bourgeois patterns of thought, behaviour and morality. Coming at the end of the century, the eroticism of the early Romantics, Wordsworth, Burns and Blake in Britain, and Schiller, Goethe (see page 208) and Schlegel (see page 210) in Germany, represented an anti-authoritarian reaction to French absolutism and, influenced by Rousseau, an unafraid emotionalism based on a conviction of finding in nature the sanction society denied. The novel *Lucinde* by Friedrich Schlegel is the best known and most popular novel to come out of the German Romantic movement. It was based on his own experience of abducting the wife of a Jewish merchant, an exploit made even more outrageous by the fact that she was also a mother. Schlegel's eroticism may seem mild or obscure to twentieth-century readers, but it was considered scandalously shocking at the end of the eighteenth century, perhaps because it was perceived to be one of the fullest and most probing explorations of bodily union.

Despite the poetry and prose of these early Romantics, a tradition that was to flower in the early nineteenth century, Eros had become tainted by bourgeois taste and ideology, which increasingly sought to ban sex from literature. The disgust and guilt Samuel Pepys experienced after enjoying *L'Escholle des filles* became codified in censorship laws. As twentieth-century critic Peter Wagner, author of *Eros Revived* (1990), writes: 'The newcomers among the readers of erotica, now more and more recruited from the middle class, created the notion of pornography in the eighteenth century, and first coined it as a term in the nineteenth century, the age of the bourgeois. The *ars amoris* [art of love] thus gained a dimension it had never before possessed – and so did erotic literature; morality entered the process of evaluating erotica and has affected literary judgements down to our present day and age.'

John Donne

1572–1631

John Donne, regarded as one of the most important writers of the Renaissance period, was originally a Roman Catholic but was ordained into the Anglican Church in 1615; he was made Dean of St Paul's in 1621. Donne's work covers an enormous variety of genres and subjects, from religious works to satires, epigrams and sonnets. His poetry, for the most part, did not appear until after his death when a collection was published in 1633.

'To his Mistris Going to Bed'

Come, Madam, come, all rest my powers defie,
Until I labour, I in labour lie.
The foe oft-times having the foe in sight,
Is tir'd with standing though he never fight.
Off with that girdle, like heavens Zone glistering,
But a far fairer world incompassing.
Unpin that spangled breastplate which you wear,
That th'eyes of busie fooles may be stopt there.
Unlace your self, for that harmonious chyme,
Tells me from you, that now it is bed time.
Off with that happy busk, which I envie,
That still can be, and still can stand so nigh.
Your gown going off, such beautious state reveals,
As when from flowry meads th'hills shadow steales.
Off with that wyerie Coronet and shew
The haiery Diademe which on you doth grow:
Now off with those shooes, and then safely tread
In this loves hallow'd temple, this soft bed.
In such white robes, heaven's Angels us'd to be
Receavd by men; Thou Angel bringst with thee
A heaven like Mahomets Paradice; and though

Ill spirits walk in white, we easly know,
By this these Angels from an evil sprite,
Those set our hairs, but these our flesh upright.
Licence my roaving hands, and let them go,
Before, behind, between, above, below.
O my America! my new-found-land,
My kingdome, safeliest when with one man man'd,
My Myne of precious stones, My Emperie,
How blest am I in this discovering thee!
To enter in these bonds, is to be free;
Then where my hand is set, my seal shall be.
Full nakedness! All joyes are due to thee,
As souls unbodied, bodies uncloth'd must be,
To taste whole joyes. Gems which you women use
Are like Atlanta's balls, cast in mens views,
That when a fools eye lighteth on a Gem,
His earthly soul may covet theirs, not them.
Like pictures, or like books gay coverings made
For lay-men, are all women thus array'd;
Themselves are mystick books, which only wee
(Whom their imputed grace will dignifie)
Must see reveal'd. Then since that I may know;
As liberally, as to a Midwife, shew
Thy self: cast all, yea, this white lynnen hence,
There is no pennance due to innocence.
To teach thee, I am naked first; why then
What needst thou have more covering than a man.

Ben Jonson

1572–1637

The English dramatist and poet Ben Jonson was born in London, and worked as a bricklayer and soldier before becoming an actor and playwright. His exuberantly satirical and linguistically dazzling plays include Volpone *(1605) and* The Alchemist *(1610), and despite having offended James I with the 1605 play* Eastward Hoe, *he became in effect the first poet laureate in 1616, writing verses and masques for the court.*

'To the same'

'Kisse me, sweet: The warie lover
Can your favours keepe, and cover,
When the common courting jay
All your bounties will betray.
Kisse againe: no creature comes.

Kisse, and score up wealthy summes.
On my lips, thus hardly sundred,
While you breath. First give a hundred,
Then a thousand, then another
Hundred, then unto the tother

Ritratto della fornarina Raphael

Adde a thousand, and so more:
Till you equall with the store,
All the grasse that Rumney yeelds,
Or the sands in Chelsey fields,
Or the drops in silver Thames,
Or the starres that guild his streames,

In the silent sommer-nights,
When youths ply their stolne delights.
That the curious may not know
How to tell 'hem, as they flow,
And the envious, when they find
What their number is, be pin'd.'

Robert Herrick

1591–1674

The English poet Robert Herrick was the son of a wealthy London goldsmith, a trade he was apprenticed to before going up to Cambridge. In 1623 he was ordained as a priest and given a living at Dean Prior in Devon in 1630, where he stayed for the rest of his life apart from the years of the Puritan Commonwealth, when his Royalist sympathies caused him to be expelled. His work includes the volumes Hesperides *and* Noble Numbers *(both 1647), and consists largely of short and elegant lyrics dealing with sex and the transience of life.*

'The Vine'

I dreamed this mortal part of mine
Was metamorphosed to a vine;
Which crawling one and every way,
Enthralled my dainty Lucia.
Me thought, her long small legs and
   thighs
I with my tendrils did surprise;
Her belly, buttocks, and her waist
By my soft nervelets were embraced:
About her head I writhing hung,
And with rich clusters (hid among
The leaves) her temples I behung

So that my Lucia seemed to me
Young Bacchus ravished by his tree.
My curls about her neck did crawl,
And arms and hands they did enthrall:
So that she could not freely stir,
(All parts there made one prisoner.)
But when I crept with leaves to hide
Those parts, which maids keep unespied,
Such fleeting pleasures there I took,
That with the fancy I awoke;
And found (Ah me!) this flesh of mine
More like a stock, than like a vine.

~

'Clothes do but Cheat and Cozen us'

Away with silks, away with lawn,
I'll have no scenes or curtains drawn;
Give me my mistress as she is,
Dressed in her naked simplicities –
For as my heart, e'en so my eye
Is won with flesh, not drapery.

King Candaules of Lydia showing his wife to Gyges Jacob Jordaens

Thomas Carew

1594–1640

The English poet Thomas Carew was educated at Oxford and acted as secretary to the diplomat Sir Dudley Carleton in Venice and the Hague. During the 1630s he was a member of Charles I's court, writing the masque Coelum Britannicum *for the king. His poems – elegant, witty and erotic lyrics – were published in 1640.*

From 'A Rapture'

Come, then, and mounted on the wings of Love
We'll cut the flitting air, and soar above
The monster's head, and in the noblest seats
Of those blest shades quench and renew our heats.
There shall the Queens of Love and Innocence,
Beauty and Nature, banish all offence
From our close ivy-twines; there I'll behold
Thy bared snow and thy unbraided gold;
There my enfranchised hand on every side
Shall o'er thy naked polished ivory slide.
No curtain there, though of transparent Lawn
Shall be before thy virgin-treasure drawn;
But the rich mine, to the enquiring eye
Exposed, shall ready still for mintage lie,
And we will coin young Cupids. There a bed
Of roses and fresh myrtles shall be spread
Under the cooler shade of cypress groves;
Our pillows of the down of Venus' doves,
Whereon our panting limbs we'll gently lay,
In the faint respites of our active play:
That so our slumbers may in dreams have leisure
To tell the nimble fancy our past pleasure,
And so our souls that cannot be embraced
Shall the embraces of our bodies taste.
Meanwhile the bubbling stream shall court the shore,
Th'enamoured chirping wood-choir shall adore
In varied tunes the Deity of Love;
The gentle blasts of western winds shall move
The trembling leaves, and through their close boughs breathe
Still music, whilst we rest ourselves beneath
Their dancing shade; till a soft murmur, sent
From souls entranced in amorous languishment,
Rouse us, and shoot into our veins fresh fire,
Till we in their sweet ecstasy expire.

. . .

Now in more subtle wreaths I will entwine
My sinewy thighs, my legs and arms with thine;
Thou like a sea of milk shalt lie displayed,
Whilst I the smooth calm ocean invade
With such a tempest, as when Jove of old
Fell down on Danaë in a storm of gold;
Yet my tall pine shall in the Cyprian strait
Ride safe at anchor, and unlade her freight:
My rudder with thy bold hand, like a tried
And skilful pilot, thou shalt steer, and guide
My bark into love's channel, where it shall
Dance, as the bounding waves do rise or fall.
Then shall thy circling arms embrace and clip
My willing body, and thy balmy lip
Bathe me in juice of kisses, whose perfume
Like a religious incense shall consume,
And send up holy vapours to those powers
That bless our loves and crown our sportful hours,
That with such halcyon calmness fix our souls
In steadfast peace, as no affright controls.
There no rude sounds shake us with sudden starts;
No jealous ears, when we unrip our hearts,
Suck our discourse in; no observing spies
This blush, that glance traduce; no envious eyes
Watch our close meetings; nor are we betrayed
To rivals by the bribed chambermaid.
No wedlock bonds unwreathe our twisted loves;
We seek no midnight arbour, no dark groves
To hide our kisses: there the hated name
Of husband, wife, lust, modest, chaste or shame,
Are vain and empty words, whose very sound
Was never heard in the Elysian ground.
All things are lawful there that may delight
Nature or unrestrained appetite;
Like and enjoy, to will and act is one:
We only sin when Love's rites are not done.
    The Roman Lucrece there reads the divine
Lectures of love's great master, Aretine,
And knows as well as Lais how to move
Her pliant body in the act of love.
To quench the burning ravisher, she hurls
Her limbs into a thousand winding curls,
And studies artful postures, such as be

Carved on the bark of every neighbouring tree
By learned hands, that so adorned the rind
Of those fair plants, which, as they lay entwined,
Have fanned their glowing fires.

Richard Crashaw

c. 1613–1649

The English poet Richard Crashaw was the son of a Puritan cleric, but converted to Catholicism in 1645, after which he was forced to flee to Paris and later to Italy. His poetry, both secular and religious, is unique in English for its extravagant baroque imagery, and includes the volumes Steps to the Temple *and* The Delights of the Muses *(both 1646).*

From 'Hymn to the Name and Honour of the Admirable Saint Teresa'

Thou art love's victim and must die
A death more mystical and high.
Into love's arms thou shalt let fall
A still-surviving funeral.
His is the dart must make the death
Whose stroke shall taste thy hallowed
        breath;
A dart thrice dipped in that rich flame
Which writes thy spouse's radiant name
Upon the roof of heav'n, where aye
It shines, and with a sov'reign ray
Beats bright upon the burning faces
Of souls which in that name's sweet graces
Find everlasting smiles. So rare,
So spiritual, pure, and fair
Must be th'immortal instrument
Upon whose choice point shall be sent
A life so loved. And that there be
Fit executioners for thee,
The fair'st and first-born sons of fire,
Blest seraphim, shall leave their choir
And turn love's soldiers, upon thee
To exercise their archery.

O how oft shalt thou complain
Of a sweet and subtle pain!
Of intolerable joys!
Of a death in which who dies
Loves his death, and dies again,
And would forever so be slain!
And lives and dies and knows not why
To live, but that he thus may never leave
        to die.
How kindly will thy gentle heart
Kiss the sweetly-killing dart!
And close in thine embraces keep
Those delicious wounds that weep
Balsam to heal themselves with. Thus
When these thy deaths so numerous,
Shall all at last die into one,
And melt thy soul's sweet mansion,
Like a soft lump of incense, hasted
By too hot a fire, and wasted
Into perfuming clouds, so fast
Shalt thou exhale to heav'n at last
In a resolving sigh, and then –
O what? Ask not the tongues of men.

Anon. (England)

'Arithmetic of the Lips' (1641)

Give me a kiss from those sweet lips of thine
And make it double by enjoining mine,
Another yet, nay yet and yet another,
And let the first kiss be the second's brother.
Give me a thousand kisses and yet more;
And then repeat those that have gone before.
Let us begin while daylight springs in heaven
And kiss till night descends into the even,
And when that modest secretary, night,
Discolours all but thy heaven beaming bright,
We will begin revels of hidden love
In that sweet orb where silent pleasures
   move.
In high new strains, unspeakable delight,
We'll vent the dull hours of the silent night.

Were the bright day no more to visit us,
Oh, then for ever would I hold thee thus,
Naked, enchained, empty of idle fear,
As the first lovers in the garden were.
I'll die betwixt thy breasts that are so white,
For to die there would do a man delight.
Embrace me still, for time runs on before,
And being dead we shall embrace no more.
Let us kiss faster than the hours do fly,
Long live each kiss and never know to
   die . . .
Let us vie kisses, till our eyelids cover,
And if I sleep, count me an idle lover;
Admit I sleep, I'll still pursue the theme,
And eagerly I'll kiss thee in a dream. . . .

Andrew Marvell

1621–1678

The English poet Andrew Marvell was born at Winstead in Yorkshire and educated at Hull Grammar School and Cambridge. His somewhat ambiguous loyalties during the Civil War were finally resolved in favour of Cromwell, and he assisted and subsequently replaced Milton as Latin Secretary to the Council of State, becoming MP for Hull in 1659. His complex political, satirical and lyrical poetry remained largely unread until the revival of interest in the Metaphysical poets during the 1920s.

'To His Coy Mistress'

Had we but world enough, and time,
This coyness, lady, were no crime –
We would sit down and think which way
To walk, and pass our long love's day.
Thou by the Indian Ganges' side
Should'st rubies find: I by the tide
Of Humber would complain. I would
Love you ten years before the Flood,
And you should if you please refuse
Till the Conversion of the Jews.
My vegetable love should grow
Vaster than empires, and more slow.

An hundred years should go to praise
Thine eyes, and on thy forehead gaze;
Two hundred to adore each breast,
But thirty thousand to the rest;
An age at least to every part,
And the last age should show your heart.
For, lady, you deserve this state,
Nor would I love at lower rate.

But at my back I always hear
Time's winged chariot hurrying near;
And yonder all before us lie

Deserts of vast eternity.
Thy beauty shall no more be found,
Nor in thy marble vault shall sound
My echoing song; then worms shall try
That long-preserved virginity,
And your quaint honour turn to dust,
And into ashes all my lust.
The grave's a fine and private place,
But none, I think, do there embrace.

Now, therefore, while the youthful hue
Sits on thy skin like morning dew,

And while thy willing soul transpires
At every pore with instant fires,
Now let us sport us while we may,
And now, like amorous birds of prey
Rather at once our time devour
Than languish in his slow-chapped power.
Let us roll all our strength, and all
Our sweetness, up into one ball
And tear our pleasures with rough strife
Thorough the iron gates of life.
Thus, though we cannot make our sun
Stand still, yet we will make him run.

Nicolas Chorier

1612–1692

Nicolas Chorier was a lawyer from Grenoble and the anonymous author of A Dialogue between a Married Lady
and a Maid, *written in Latin in keeping with the 'whore dialogue' tradition. He threw a smokescreen around his identity by claiming it had been written by a sixteenth-century Spanish poet, Luisa Sigea, and translated by a Dutch
philologist whom he named Johannes Mersius.*

From **A Dialogue between a Married Lady and a Maid** (*c.* 1660). *Trans. anon*

TULLIA: In thee, that inward Slit, and the Sheath, are very short and narrow. Let me see it a
little, open your legs.

OCTAVIA: I do; what do you see now?

TULLIA: Ah! Pretty Creature! How Cherry-red it is! I see all the Flower of thy Virginity, as entire
as a Morning Rose-bud, not touched by a Travellers Hand, and sweeter than any Rose in its
Enjoyment.

OCTAVIA: O hold, Tullia, you tickle me so, that I am not able to endure it; take away that wicked
Finger, it hurts me.

TULLIA: Well I pity thee strangely, this pretty shell, prettier than that out of which Venus
herself was born, will be sadly torn by Philander; nay I begin to be concerned for him too;
for the Entrance of this Paradise is so narrow, that it will be with great Difficulty, and no
small Pain, e'er that he himself will get admittance, did you ever see the Thing he has
between his legs?

OCTAVIA: I never saw it, but felt it hard, big and long.

TULLIA: Thy Mother is overjoyed with the Reputation he has of being the best provided young
Man in all this city, but it will cost thee some Tears; yet be not afraid, my Husband had the
same Reputation, and with Reason, and yet I am alive and well.

OCTAVIA: Prithee let me see how your c—t is, since it has had such a monster within it.

TULLIA: Do, my pretty Octavia; here, I open my legs a Purpose.

OCTAVIA: Lord! What a Gap is here! I can thrust my whole Hand in almost; how strong it smells! Sure the Roses are almost gone here . . .

[*After her wedding night Octavia reports back to Tullia what happened when Philander 'opened the slit of my Commodity, and conveyed the Head of his Engine to it'. After many successful pleasurings Philander ejaculates prematurely . . .*]

TULLIA: Ah! Dear Cousin, had you no Pleasure this time?

OCTAVIA: You shall hear a pleasant thing: No sooner was he off me, but I began to be tickled with a certain itching in those Parts, that I catch'd fast hold of him in my Arms, and, with Sighs and Kisses, demanded, as it were, that he should help me. He could not do it with the proper Instrument, it was not then in a Condition to obey his Desires, therefore, putting his Finger into my c—t, and stirring gently up and down, towards the upper Part of it, he made me spend so pleasantly, such a Quantity of the delicious Nectar, that it flew about his hand, and all wetted him. I beg thy Pardon, my lovely Octavia, for not expecting thy Pleasure; for nature in us men, is something so eager, that we cannot withstand first Impetuosities [*said he*].

Anon.

From **L'Escholle des filles** (*c.* 1668). *Trans. Derek Parker*

KATY: Look here, I believe very few wenches have handsomer thighs than I, for they are white, smooth and plump.

FANNY: I know it, for I have often seen and handled them before now, when we lay together.

KATY: Feeling them, he was overjoyed, protesting he never felt the like. In doing this his hat, which he had laid on his knees, fell off, and I casting my eyes downwards perceived something swelling in his breeches, as if it had a mind to get out.

FANNY: Say you so, madam?

KATY: That immediately put me in mind of that stiff thing, which you say men piss with and which pleaseth us women so much. I am sure when he first came into the chamber 'twas not so big.

FANNY: No, his did not stand then.

KATY: When I saw it I began to think there was something to be done in good earnest, so I got up and shut the door . . . Having made all sure, I returned and he, taking me about the neck and kissing me, would not let me sit as before on the bed but pulled me between his legs and, thrusting his hand into the slit of my coat behind, handled my buttocks, which he found plump, round and hard. With his other hand he takes my right hand and, looking me in the face, put it into his breeches.

FANNY: You are very tedious in telling your story.

KATY: I tell you every particular. He put his prick into my hand and desired me to hold it.

FANNY: This relation makes me mad for fucking.

KATY: This done, says he, 'I would have you see what you have in your hand,' and so made me take it out of his breeches. I wondered to see such a damned great tarse, for it is quite another thing when it stands. He perceiving me a little amazed said, 'Do not be frightened, girl, for you have about you a very convenient place to receive it,' and upon a sudden pulls up my smock.

FANNY: This is what I expected all this while.

KATY: Then he thrust me backwards, put down his breeches, put by his shirt and draws me nearer to him.

FANNY: Now begins the game.

KATY: I soon perceived he had a mind to stick it in. I desired him to hold a little for it pained me. Having breathed, he made me open my legs wider and with another hard thrust, went a little farther in. He told me that he would not hurt me much more and I should have nothing but pleasure for the pain I should endure, and that he endured a share of the pain for my sake, which made me patiently suffer two or three thrusts more. Endeavouring still to get more ground he takes and throws me backwards on the bed, but being too heavy he took my two thighs and put them on his shoulders, he standing on his feet by the bedside. This way did give me some ease, yet I desired him to get off, which he did.

FANNY: What a deal of pleasure did you enjoy! For my part, had I such a prick, I should not complain.

KATY: Stay a little, I do not complain for all this. Presently he came and kissed me and bandled my cunt afresh. Being still troubled with a standing prick and not knowing what to do with himself, he walked up and down the chamber 'till I was fit for another bout.

FANNY: Poor fellow, I pity him; he suffered a great deal.

KATY: Mournfully pulling out his prick before me, he takes down a little pot of pomatum which stood on the mantletree of the chimney. 'Oh,' says he, 'this is for our turn,' and taking some of it he rubbed his prick an over with it to make it go in the more glib.

FANNY: He had better have spit upon his hand and rubbed his prick therewith.

KATY: At last he thought of that and did nothing else. Then he placed me on a chair and by the help of the pomatum got in a little further, but seeing he could do no great good that way, he made me rise and laid me with all four on the bed, and having once more rubbed his tarse with pomatum he charged me briskly in the rear.

FANNY: What a bustle here to get one poor maidenhead! My friend and I made not half this stir. We had soon done and never flinched for it.

KATY: I tell you the truth verbatim. My coats being over my shoulders, holding out my arse I gave him a fair mark enough. This new posture so quickened his fancy that, no longer regarding my crying out, he kept thrusting on with might and main, 'till at last be perfected the break and took entire possession of all.

FANNY: Very well, I am glad you escaped a thousand little accidents which attend young lovers, but let us come to the sequel.

KATY: It now began not to be so painful. My cunt fitted his prick so well that no glove could come straighter on a man's hand. To conclude, he was sovereign at his victory, called me his love, his dear and his soul.

FANNY: Very good.

KATY: He asked me if I were pleased. I answered, 'yes'. 'So am I,' said he, hugging me close to him, his hands under my buttocks.

FANNY: This was to encourage and excite him.

KATY: The more he pushed, the more it tickled me, that at last my hands on which I leaned failed me and I fell flat on my face.

FANNY: I suppose you caught no harm by the fall?

KATY: None, but he and I dying with pleasure fell in a trance, he only having time to say, 'There have you lost your maidenhead, my fool.'

Ihara Saikaku

1642–1693

A popular novelist and prize-winning Haikai writer, Ihara Saikaku was a citizen of Osaka who wrote for the amusement of the townspeople in the new commercial centres of 17th-century Japan. His work was noted for its originality in that the lovers in his works were ordinary townswomen and men, and not the traditional courtesans of contemporary Japanese fiction.

From **Five Women who Loved Love**. *Trans. William Theodore de Barry*

When cherry trees bloom at Onoe, men's wives bloom too with a new pride in their appearance and pretty girls go strolling with their proud mothers, not so much to see the spring blossoms as to be seen themselves. That is the way people are these days; at least that is the way with women. They are witches who could enchant even the wizard fox of Himeji Castle.

. . .

Onatsu, however, was not among the onlookers. She seemed to be indisposed with a painful toothache and remained alone behind the curtains, resting on her elbow, her *sach* undone, in complete disarray. Screening her from view was a pile of extra garments, behind which she pretended to snore as if asleep.

Who would think of this as a good chance to make love, when there could be only a brief moment for consummation? None but the most determined and accomplished of lovers – certainly no city girl would ever dream of it. But Seijuro, quickly noticing that Onatsu was left alone, went round the back way, through a luxuriant growth of pines, to find his lover beckoning to him. Caring little that Onatsu's hairdress might become disarranged, the two clasped each other tight, breathing heavily, and their hearts beating fast. Fearful, however, of being discovered by Onatsu's sister-in-law, they kept their eyes on the spectators beyond the tent.

It was not until they arose that they noticed behind them a woodcutter, who had come up and laid down his load of wood. Holding his sickle in one hand and moving his underpants about with the other, he stood there watching the couple intently, amazed and amused. Truly this was a case of 'hiding one's head and leaving the tail unguarded'.

When Seijuro finally left the curtained enclosure, the performers put a stop to the entertainment outside, although some of the best parts of it remained unplayed. Many of the picnickers were disappointed by this sudden halting of the show, but already a thick mist was settling in and the evening sun was falling fast so they got their things together and started back to Himeji. Onatsu did not seem to be aware of the mess that had been made of her kimono in the back.

Seijuro, following them, was profuse in his thanks to the company of lion dancers. 'I am indeed indebted to you for your services today.'

Think of it! This passing show had actually been arranged in advance, the clever stratagem of a desperate lover. Perhaps even the wise gods knew nothing of his secret. And the others, especially that know-it-all wife of Onatsu's brother – what chance had they of knowing?

Li Yu

c. 1610–1680

Little is known of the life of Li Yu, a Chinese essayist, dramatist and novelist. The Carnal Prayer Mat, part of a strong tradition of Chinese literary erotica, is unequalled in its humorous approach to sex. Several attempts, mostly unsuccessful, have been made to ban the book in China over the centuries.

From **The Carnal Prayer Mat** (*c.* 1652). *Trans. Patrick Hanan*

She's beginning to show a little interest, thought Vesperus. I was planning to start at once, but this is the first time her desires have been aroused and her appetite is still quite undeveloped. If I give her a taste of it now, she'll be like a starving man at the sight of food – she'll bolt it down without savouring it and so miss the true rapture; I think I'll tantalize her a little before mounting the stage.

Pulling up an easy chair, he sat down and drew her onto his lap, then opened the album and showed it to her picture by picture. This album differed from others in that the first page of each leaf contained the erotic picture and the second page a comment on it. The first part of the comment explained the activity depicted, while the rest praised the artist's skill. All the comments were in the hand of famous writers.

Vesperus told Jade Scent to try to imagine herself in the place of the people depicted and to concentrate on their expressions so that she could imitate them later on. While she looked at the pictures, he read out the comments:

Picture Number One. The Releasing the Butterfly in Search of Fragrance position. The woman sits on the Lake Tai rock with her legs apart while the man sends his jade whisk into her vagina and moves it from side to side seeking the heart of the flower. At the moment depicted, the pair are just beginning and have not reached the rapturous stage, so their eyes are wide open and their expressions not much different from normal.

Picture Number Two. The Letting the Bee Make Honey position. The woman is lying on her back on the brocade quilt, bracing herself on the bed with her hands and raising her legs aloft to meet the jade whisk and let the man know the location of the heart of the flower so that he will not thrust at random. At the moment depicted, the woman's expression is almost ravenous, while the man seems so nervous that the observer feels anxiety on his behalf. Supreme art at its most mischievous.

Picture Number Three. The Lost Bird Returns to the Wood position. The woman leans back on the embroidered couch with her legs in the air, grasping the man's thighs and driving them directly downward. She appears to have entered the state of rapture and is afraid of losing her way. The couple are just at the moment of greatest exertion and show extraordinary vitality. This scene has the marvellous quality of 'flying brush and dancing ink'.

Picture Number Four. The Starving Horse Races to the Trough position. The woman lies flat on the couch with her arms wrapped around the man as if to restrict his movements. While he supports her legs on his shoulders, the whole of the jade whisk enters the vagina, leaving not a trace behind. At the moment depicted, they are on the point of spending; they are about to shut their eyes and swallow each other's tongues, and their expressions are identical. Supreme art indeed.

Picture Number Five. The Two Dragons Who Fight Till They Drop position. The woman's head rests beside the pillow and her hands droop in defeat, as soft as cotton floss. The man's head rests beside her neck, and his whole body droops too, also as soft as cotton floss. She has spent, and her soul is about to depart on dreams of the future. This is a state of calm after furious activity. Only her feet, which have not been lowered but still rest on the man's shoulders, convey any trace of vitality. Otherwise, he and she would resemble a pair of corpses, which leads the observer to understand their rapture and think of lovers entombed together.

By the time Jade Scent reached this page, her sexual desires were fully aroused and could no longer be held in check. Vesperus turned the page and was about to show her the next picture when she pushed the book away and stood up.

'A fine book this is!' she exclaimed. 'It makes one uncomfortable just to look at it. Read it yourself if you want to. I'm going to lie down.'

Vesperus caught her in his arms. 'Dear heart, there are more good ones. Let's look at them together and then go to bed.'

'Don't you have any time tomorrow? Why do you have to finish today?'

Vesperus knew she was agitated, and he put his arms around her and kissed her. When kissing her before, he had tried to insert his tongue in her mouth but her tightly clenched teeth always prevented him. As a result, she was still unacquainted with his tongue after more than a month of marriage. But on this occasion he had no sooner touched her lips than that sharp, soft tongue of his had somehow slipped past her teeth and entered her mouth.

'Dear heart,' said Vesperus, 'there's no need to use the bed. Why don't we take this easy chair as our rock and try to imitate the picture in the album. What do you say?'

Jade Scent pretended to be angry. 'People don't *do* things like that!'

'You're right,' said Vesperus, 'people don't do them. Immortals do! Let's be immortals for a little while.' He put out his hand and undid her belt. Jade Scent's heart was willing, even if her words were not, and she simply hung on his shoulder and offered no resistance. Taking off her trousers, Vesperus noticed a large damp patch in the seat caused by her secretions while she was looking at the pictures.

Vesperus took off his own trousers and pulled her over to the chair, where he made her sit with her legs apart. He then inserted his jade whisk into her vagina before removing the clothes from her upper body.

John Wilmot, 2nd Earl of Rochester

1647–1680

John Wilmot, lyric poet, satirist and leading 'court wit', is most widely known for his scurrilous, sexually explicit verse and chaotic lifestyle. However, he has gained increasing recognition as an important metaphysical poet admired by Marvell and an influence on Dryden, Swift and Pope.

From **Sodom, or the Quintessence of Debauchery** (1668)

[A grove of Cyprus trees and others cut in shapes of pricks, several arbours, figures and pleasant ornaments in a banqueting house; men are discovered playing tabours and dulciores with their pricks, and women with jews harps in their cunts; a youth is sitting under a palm tree singing in a melancholy manner.]

Song

> Oh gentle Venus, ease a tarse
> That owns that cunt's agreen;
> That lately suffered by a lars,
> And spat out blood as green as grass,
> And shankers has fifteen.
> Under hand it panting has,
> Ah faine, 'twould but cannot rise;
> And when it's got between her thighs,
> I'll grieve to feel such pocky pain,
> And draw my pintle back again.

[Exeunt]

[Enter Bolloxinian, Borastus and Pockanelle]

BOLLOX: Which of the Gods more than myself can do?
POCK: None, Sire; they are pimps compar'd to you.
BOLLOX:

> I'll heaven invade, and bugger all the Gods,
> And drain the spring of their immortal codds;
> Then make 'em rub, 'till prick and bollock cry,
> I'll frig them out of immortality.

John Dryden

1631–1700

The English dramatist, critic and poet John Dryden was born into a Puritan family in Aldwinkle, Northamptonshire. Educated at Westminster School and Trinity College, Cambridge, his time-serving career followed the political and religious vagaries of his age: by 1670 he was poet laureate and historiographer royal. Towards the end of his life he turned to translating, producing what are still considered some of the finest translations of the classics. His works represent a transitional position between Donne and the Metaphysical poets and the neoclassical reaction of which he was a leading proponent.

From **Marriage-à-la-Mode** (1672)

Whilst Alexis lay pressed
In her Arms he loved best
With his hands round her neck
And his head on her breast,
He found the fierce pleasure too hasty to stay,
And his soul in the tempest just flying away.

When Celia saw this,
With a sigh, and a kiss,
She cry'd, 'Oh my dear, I am robbed of my bliss;
'Tis unkind to your Love, and unfaithfully done,
To leave me behind you, and die all alone.'

The Youth, though in haste,
And breathing his last,
In pity died slowly, while she died more fast;
Till at length she cried, 'Now, my dear, now let us go,
Now die, my Alexis, and I will die too.'

Thus entranced they did lie,
Till Alexis did try
To recover new breath, that again he might die:
Then often they died; but the more they did so,
The Nymph died more quick, and the Shepherd more slow.

Anon. (England)

'The Maid's Complaint for want of a Dil doul' (1774)

This Girl long time had in a sickness been,
Which many maids do call the sickness green:
I wish she may some comfort find, poor Soul,
And have her belly fill'd with a Dil doul.

Young men give ear to me a while,
    if you to merriment are inclin'd,
And i'le tell you a story shall make you to smile,
    of late done by a woman kind:
And as she went musing all alone,
    I heard her to sigh, to sob and make moan,
For a dill doul, dil doul doul
(quote she) I'm undone if I ha'nt a dil doul.

For I am a Maid and a very good Maid,
    and sixteen years of age am I,
And fain would I part with my Maiden-head,
    if any good fellow would with me lye:
But none to me ever yet proffer'd such love,
    as to lye by my side and give me a shove
With his dil doul, dil doul, dil doul,
    O happy were I &c

At night when I go to bed,
    thinking for to take my rest,
Strange fancies comes in my head,
    I pray for that which I love best:
For it is a comfort and pleasure doth bring
    to women that hath such a pritty fine
        thing,
Call'd a dill doul, dill doul, dill doul doul,
    then happy were I &c

Last week I walked in the *Strand*,
    I met with my Sister, a handsome Lass,
I kindly took her by the hand,
    this question of her I did ask:
Whether she kept still a Maiden alone,
    or whether her maiden-head was fled or
        gone,

For a dill doul, dill doul, dill doul doul,
    O happy were &c

THE SECOND PART

Kind sister, quoth she, to tell you the truth,
    it has gone this twelve months day;
I freely gave it to a handsome youth,
    that us'd to sport and play:
To grieve for the loss of it I never shall,
    if I had ten thousand I would give um all
For a dill doul, dill doul, dil doul doul,
    O my &c

She making this answer, I bid her adieu,
    and told her I could no longer stay,
I let go her hand, and I straight left the *Strand*,
    and to *Covent-Garden* I hasted away:
Where lively young gallants do use to resort,
    to pick up young lasses & shew um fine
        sport
With a dil doul, dil doul, dil doul doul,
    yet none &c

I would i'de a sweet heart, as some Maids have,
    that little know how to pleasure a man,
I'de keep him frolicksome, gallant and brave,
    and make as much on him as anyone can:
Before any good thing he should lack,
    i'de sell all my Coats & Smock from my back
For his dil doul, dil doul, dill doul doul,
    and all my &c

Besides, young men, I have store of money,
    good red gold and Silver bright,
And he shall be master of every peny,
    that marries with me and yields me delight.
For why, t'other night I heard my dame *Nancy*
    declare how her master did tickle her fancy,
With his dill doul, dill doul, dill doul doul,
then what e're it cost me i'le have a dil doul.

Then come to me my bonny Lad,
   while I am in the prime, I pray,
And take a good bargain while it is to be
    had,
   and do not linger your time away.

'Tis money, you see, makes many a man rich:
   then come along rub on the place that
    doth itch
   For a dill doul, dil doul, dil doul doul,
    take all my money, give me a dill doul.

Marianna Alcoforado

Mid 17th century

Little is known of Marianna Alcoforado's life, other than that she was born into one of the most aristocratic families in Portugal, and became a Franciscan nun. The Love Letters of a Portuguese Nun, which have been attributed to her, were said to have been written to a captain billeted near her convent, who often visited her. She fell in love with him, but he deserted her and returned to France. The letters are the only known record of her life.

From **The Love Letters of a Portuguese Nun** (*c.* 1668).
Trans. Howard Wilford Bell

Think, my love, to what an extent you have been wanting in foresight. Oh, unhappy man, you have been betrayed, and have betrayed me by false hopes. A passion upon which you had planned so much happiness now causes you a mortal despair, which can be compared only to the cruelty of the absence which occasions it. What! This absence – for which my grief with all its ingenuity can find no name dark enough – will then forever prevent me from looking into those eyes where I saw so much love, and which made me conscious of feelings that filled me with joy, that took the place of everything, and left me satisfied.

Alas, my eyes are deprived of the only light which could brighten them; for them, tears alone remain, and the only use I have made of them is to weep unceasingly, since I learned that you had finally resolved upon a separation, so unbearable that it will soon kill me.

Yet it seems to me that I cling to sorrows of which you alone are the cause. I gave my life to you as soon as I saw you, and I feel a certain pleasure in sacrificing it to you. A thousand times a day my sighs go out to you, seeking you everywhere, and bringing back in return for such disquietude only too true a warning, sent by my evil fortune, which is cruel enough not to let me deceive myself, but keeps saying, 'Cease, cease, unhappy Marianna, vainly devouring your own heart, and searching for a lover whom you will never find; who has crossed the seas to escape from you; who is in France, in the midst of pleasures; who never gives a thought to your grief, and is quite willing to dispense with all these transports for which he is not in the least grateful.' But no, I cannot make up my mind to judge you so harshly; I am too interested in justifying you; I will not let myself think that you have forgotten me. Am I not unhappy enough without tormenting myself with false suspicions? And why should I make the effort not to remember all the pains you took to prove to me your love. I was so charmed by all you did for me that I should be most ungrateful did I not love you with the same ardour that my passion aroused when you gave me proof of yours.

How is it possible that the memory of such delightful moments can become so cruel? Contrary to their nature, must they serve only to torture my very soul? Alas, your last letter brought me to a strange condition; my heart suffered so keen a pang, that it seemed to make the effort to tear itself away from me and go in search of you. I was so overcome by these violent emotions that I remained more than three hours entirely without consciousness. I forbade myself to return to a life which I ought to lose for you, since I cannot keep it for you. I finally saw the light again in spite of myself. I flattered myself with the thought that I was dying of love, and moreover I was glad to be no longer exposed to have my heart torn by the grief of your absence. Since then I have suffered many other woes, but can I ever be without ills so long as I cannot see you? I bear them, however, without murmuring, since they come from you. What! is this then the reward you give me for having loved you so tenderly? But no matter, I am resolved to adore you all my life and never to look at any one else. And I assure you that you will do well also to love no one else. Could you be content with a passion less ardent than mine? You will find, perhaps, more beauty (although you used to call me beautiful) but you will never find so much love, and all the rest is nothing.

Do not fill your letters with useless things, do not write to me to remember you. I cannot forget you, and also I do not forget that you have allowed me to hope that you would come and spend some time with me. Alas! why will you not spend all your life here? If it were possible for me to leave this wretched cloister, I should not await in Portugal the fulfilment of your promises. I should go, regardless of consequences, to seek you – to follow you and love you all the world over. I do not dare flatter myself that this is possible. I will not foster hopes which would certainly give me pleasure, and I will no longer be sensible to anything but pain.

I confess, however, that the opportunity given me by my brother to write to you, surprised in me a feeling of joy, and held in check, for a moment, my despair.

I conjure you to tell me why you set your heart upon fascinating me as you did, when you knew very well that you were going to desert me? and why have you been so pitiless in making me wretched? Why did you not leave me in peace in this cloister? Had I done you any injury? But forgive me; I impute nothing to you. I am in no state to think of revenge, and I only accuse the harshness of my fate. In separating us, it seems to have done all the harm we could have feared. But our hearts cannot be separated; love, which is more powerful than destiny, has united them for our whole life. If you take any interest in mine, write to me often. I certainly deserve to have you take some trouble in letting me know the state of your heart and your fortunes. Above all, come to see me. Farewell, I cannot leave this paper; it will fall into your hands; would that I might have the same happiness. Alas! how insane I am! I see that this is not possible. Farewell! I can write no more. Farewell, love me always and make me suffer still more misery.

Aphra Behn

1640–1689

An English dramatist, poet and novelist, born in Kent, Aphra Behn's extraordinary life ranged from visiting
Surinam (which she used as the setting for her anti-slavery novel Oronooko*), acting as a government spy during the*
Dutch war, to debt and imprisonment. The first English woman to earn her living as a writer, she suffered much
prejudice and incurred charges of lewdness. Her plays include the satirical comedies The Rover *(1677–81) and* City
Heiress *(1682).*

'The Disappointment'

One day the amorous Lysander,
By an impatient passion swayed,
Surprised fair Cloris, that loved maid,
Who could defend herself no longer.
All things did with his love conspire:
The gilded planet of the day
In his gay chariot drawn by fire
Was now descending to the sea,
And left no light to guide the world
But what from Cloris' brighter eyes was
   hurled.

In a lone thicket made for love,
Silent as yielding maid's consent,
She with a charming languishment
Permits his force, yet gently strove.
Her hands his bosom softly meet,
But not to put him back designed –
Rather to draw 'em on inclined.
Whilst he lay trembling at her feet
Resistance 'tis in vain to show:
She wants the power to say, 'Ah, what
   d'ye do?'

Her bright eyes sweet, and yet severe,
Where love and shame confusedly strive,
Fresh vigour to Lysander give;
And breathing faintly in his ear
She cried: 'Cease, cease your vain desire
Or I'll call out! What would you do?
My dearer honour even to you
I cannot, must not give! Retire!

Or take this life, whose chiefest part
I gave you with the conquest of my heart.'

But he as much unused to fear
As he was capable of love
The blessed minutes to improve
Kisses her mouth, her neck, her hair.
Each touch her new desire alarms,
His burning, trembling hand he pressed
Upon her swelling, snowy breast,
While she lay panting in his arms.
All her unguarded beauties lie
The spoils and trophies of the enemy.

And now without respect or fear
He seeks the object of his vows
(His love no modesty allows),
By swift degrees advancing – where
His daring hand that altar seized
Where gods of love do sacrifice:
That awful throne, that paradise
Where rage is calmed and anger pleased,
That fountain where delight still flows
And gives the universal world repose.

Her balmy lips encountering his,
Their bodies, as their souls, are joined
Where both in transports unconfined
Extend themselves upon the moss.
Cloris half dead and breathless lay,
Her soft eyes cast a humid light
Such as divides the day and night,

Or falling stars whose fires decay;
And now no signs of life she shows
But what in short-breathed sighs returns
   and goes.

He saw how at her length she lay.
He saw her rising bosom bare,
Her loose, thin robes, through which
   appear
A shape designed for love and play,
Abandoned by her pride and shame.
She does her softest joys dispense,
Offering her virgin-innocence
A victim to love's sacred flame,
While the o'er-ravished shepherd lies
Unable to perform the sacrifice.

Ready to taste a thousand joys
The too transported, hapless swain
Found the vast pleasure turned to pain –
Pleasure which too much love destroys.
The willing garments by he laid,
And heaven all opened to his view.
Mad to possess, himself he threw
On the defenceless, lovely maid.
But oh, what envying god conspires
To snatch his power, yet leave him the
   desire!

Nature's support (without whose aid
She can no human being give)
Itself now wants the art to live;
Faintness its slackened nerves invade.
In vain th'enraged youth essayed
To call its fleeting vigour back,
No motion 'twill from motion take.
Excess of love is Love betrayed.
In vain he toils, in vain commands –
Insensible falls weeping in his hands.

In this so amorous, cruel strife
Where love and fate were too severe
The poor Lysander in despair

Renounced his reason with his life.
Now all the brisk and active fire
That should the nobler part inflame
Served to increase his rage and shame
And left no spark for new desire.
Not all her naked charms could move
Or calm that rage that had debauched his
   love.

Cloris returning from the trance
Which love and soft desire had bred,
Her timorous hand she gently laid
(Or guided by desire or chance)
Upon that fabulous priapus,
That potent god, as poets feign –
But never did young shepherdess
Gathering of fern upon the plain
More nimbly draw her fingers back
Finding beneath the verdant leaves a
   snake

Than Cloris her fair hand withdrew,
Finding that god of her desires
Disarmed of all his awful fires
And cold as flowers bathed in the morning
   dew.
Who can the nymph's confusion guess?
The blood forsook the hinder place
And strewed with blushes all her face,
Which both disdain and shame expressed;
And from Lysander's arms she fled,
Leaving him fainting on the gloomy bed.

Like lightning through the groves she
   hies,
Or Daphne from the Delphic god;
No print upon the grassy road
She leaves, t'instruct pursuing eyes.
The wind that wantoned in her hair
And with her ruffled garments played
Discovered in the flying maid
All that the gods e'er made, if fair.
So Venus, when her love was slain,

With fear and haste flew o'er that fatal
   plain.

The nymph's resentments none but I
Can well imagine or condole.
But none can guess Lysander's soul
But those who swayed his destiny.

His silent griefs swell up to storms,
And not one god his fury spares;
He cursed his birth, his fate, his stars –
But more the shepherdess's charms,
Whose soft, bewitching influence
Had damned him to the hell of
   impotence.

~

'In a cottage'

In a cottage by the mountain
Lives a very pretty maid,
Who lay sleeping by a fountain
Underneath a myrtle shade;
Her petticoat of wanton sarcenet
The amorous wind about did move
And quite unveiled
And quite unveiled the throne of love
And quite unveiled the throne of love.

Mary Delarivier Manley

1663–1724

A writer of plays and scandalous memoirs, Manley had an unconventional life. She had a bigamous marriage with her cousin, openly took the warden of Fleet Prison as her lover, and was arrested for her libellous writings against notable Whigs of her time. In 1711 she succeeded the poet and satirist Jonathan Swift as editor of the Tory periodical the Examiner.

From **The New Atalantis** (1709)

After this tender, dangerous commerce, Charlot found everything insipid, nothing but the Duke's kisses could relish with her; all those conversations she had formerly delighted in were insupportable. He was obliged to return to court, and had recommended to her reading the most dangerous books of love, Ovid, Petrarch, Tibullus, those moving tragedies that so powerfully expose the force of love and corrupt the mind. He went even farther, and left her such as explained the nature, manner and raptures of enjoyment. Thus he infused poison into the ears of the lovely virgin. She easily (from those emotions she had found in herself) believed as highly of those delights as was imaginable; her waking thoughts, her golden slumber ran all of a bliss only imagined but never proved. She even forgot, as one that wakes from sleep and visions of the night, all those precepts of airy virtue which she found had nothing to do with nature. She longed again to renew those dangerous delights. The Duke was an age absent from her, she could only in imagination possess what she believed so pleasing. Her memory was prodigious, she was indefatigable in reading. The Duke had left orders she should not be controlled in anything. Whole nights were wasted by her in the gallery; she had too well informed herself of the speculative joys of love. There are books dangerous to the community of mankind; abominable for virgins and destructive to youth; such as explain the mysteries of nature, the congregated pleasures of Venus, the full delights of mutual lovers, and which rather ought to pass the fire than the press. The Duke had laid in her way such as made no mention of Virtue or Hymen, but only advanced native, generous and undissembled love. She was become so great a proficient that nothing of the theory was a stranger to her. . . . The season of the year was come that he must make the campaign with the King; he could not resolve to depart unblessed; Charlot still refused him that last proof of her love. He took a tender and passionate farewell. Charlot, drowned in tears, told him it was impossible she should support his absence; all the court would ridicule her melancholy. This was what he wanted; he bid her take care of that. A maid was but an ill figure that brought herself to be sport of laughters; but since her sorrow (so pleasing and glorious to him) was like to be visible, he advised her to pass some days at his villa, till the height of melancholy should be over, under the pretence of indisposition. He would take care that the Queen should be satisfied of the necessity of her absence; he advised her even to depart that hour. Since the King was already on his journey he must be gone that moment and endeavour to overtake him. He assured her he would write by every courier, and begged her not to admit of another lover, though he was sensible there were many (taking advantage of his absence, would endeavour to please her). To all this she answered so as to disquiet his distrust and fears; her tears drowned her sighs, her words were lost in sobs and groans! The Duke did not show less concern, but led her all trembling to put her in a coach that was to convey her to his villa; where he had often wished to have her, but she distrusted herself and would not go with him; nor had she ventured now, but that she thought he was to follow the King, who could not be without him.

Charlot no sooner arrived, but the weather being very hot, she ordered a bath to be prepared for her. As soon as she was refreshed with that, she threw herself down upon a bed with only one thin petticoat and a loose nightgown, the bosom of her gown and shift open; her nightclothes tied carelessly with a cherry-coloured ribbon which answered well to the yellow and silver stuff of her gown. She lay uncovered in a melancholy careless posture, her head resting upon one of her hands. The other held a handkerchief, that she employed to dry those tears that sometimes fell from her eyes; when raising herself a little at a gentle noise she heard from the opening of a door that answered to the bedside, she was quite astonished to see enter the amorous Duke. Her first emotions were all joy; but in a minute she recollected herself, thinking he was not come there for nothing. She was going to rise but he prevented her by flying to her arms where, as we may call it, he nailed her down to the bed with kisses. His love and resolution gave him a double vigour, he would not stay a moment to capitulate with her; whilst yet her surprise made her doubtful of his designs, he took advantage of her constitution to accomplish them; neither her prayers, tears, nor strugglings could prevent him, but in her arms he made himself a full amends for all those pains he had suffered for her.

A lady at her toilet Jean-Antoine Watteau

Thus was Charlot undone! thus ruined by him that ought to have been her protector! It was very long before he could appease her; but so artful, so amorous, so submissive was his address, so violent his assurances, he told her that he must have died without the happiness. Charlot espoused his crime by sealing his forgiveness. He passed the whole night in her arms, pleased, transported and out of himself, whilst the ravished maid was not at all behindhand in ecstasies and guilty transports. He stayed a whole week with Charlot in a surfeit of love and joy! that week more inestimable than all the pleasures of his life before! whilst the court believed him with the King, posting to the army. He neglected Mars to devote himself wholly to Venus; abstracted from all business, that happy week sublimed him almost to an immortal. Charlot was formed to give and take all those raptures necessary to accomplish the lover's happiness; none were ever more amorous! none were ever more happy!

Anon. (England)

'The Unfortunate Miller' (often closely associated with **The Roxburghe Ballads**, 1774)

All of you that desire to hear a jest,
Come listen a while and it shall be exprest;
It is of a Miller that lived very near,
The like of this ditty you never did hear,
A handsome young Damsel she came to his Mill,
To have her Corn Ground with Ready good Will.
As soon as he saw her beauty so bright,
He caused this young Damosel to tarry all night.

Said he, my dear Jewel, it will be ne'r Morn,
Before my Man Lawrence can grind my Dears Corn,
And therefore if thou wilt be ruled by me,
At home in my Parlour thy Lodging shall be,
For I am inflam'd with thy Amorous Charms,
And therefore this Night thou shalt sleep in my arms,
I swear it, and therefore it needs must be so,
It is but in vain for to answer me no.

At this the young Damsel she blushing did stand,
But strait ways the Master took her by the hand,
And leading her home to young Gillian his wife,
Said he, my sweet honey, the joy of my Life,
Be kind to this Maid, for her Father I know,
And let her lye here in the Parlour below,
Stout Lawrence my servant, and I, we shall stay
All night in the Mill till the dawning of Day.

To what he desired she straitways agreed,
And then to the Mill did he hasten with speed,
He ready was then to leap out of his skin,
To think of the Bed which he meant to Lye in;
Now when he was gone, the Maid told his intent,
To Gillian, and they a new Project invent,
By which they well fitted his Crafty young blade;
The Miller by Lawrence a Cuckold was made.

The Maid and his Wife they changed Bed for that night.
So that when the Miller came for his delight,
Strait way to the Parlour Bed he did Repair,
Instead of the Damsel wife Gillian was there,
Which he did Imagine had been the young Lass,
When after some hours in pleasure they past,
He ris, and return'd to the Mill, like one wild,
For fear he had Got the young Damsel with child.

Then to his man Lawrence the miller did say,
I have a young damsel both bonny and Gay,
Her Eyes are like diamonds, her cheeks sweet and fair,
They may with the Rose and the Lilly Compare,
Her lips they are like rich coral for Red,
This Lass is at home in my Parlour a Bed,
And if you go home you may freely enjoy,
With her the sweet pleasure, for she is not Coy.

His masters kind Proffer he did not refuse,
But was brisk and Airy, and pleased with the News,
But said, to your self much beholding I am,
And for a Requital i'le give you my Ram;
This done lusty Lawrence away home he goes,
And stript off his Coat, Breeches, likewise shooes and hose,
And went into Bed to Gillian his dame,
Yet Lawrence for this was not worthy of blame.

He little Imagen'd his Dame was in bed,
And therefore his heart was the freer from dread,
The minutes in Pastime and pleasure they spent,
Unknown to them both she injoy'd true content,
Now after a while he his dame had Imbrac'd,
He Rose and Return'd to the mill in all hast,
Telling his master of all the delight,
Which he had injoy'd with that damsel this Night.

Next morning the maid to the mill did Repair,
The miller and Lawrence his servant was there,
His master then whisper'd this word in her Ear,
How like you to lye with a miller, my dear?
At this the young damsel then laughing out Right;
And said, I chang'd Beds with young Gillian last Night;
If you injoy'd any it was your sweet wife,
For my part I ne'r lay with a man in my Life.

At this he began for to Rave, stamp and stare,
Both scratching his Elbows and Hauling his hair,
And like one distracted about he did Run,
And often times Crying, ha! what have I done,
Was ever poor miller so finely betray'd,
By Lawrence my man, I am a Cuckold made.
The damsel she laught, and was pleas'd in her mind,
And said he was very well serv'd in his kind.

Alexander Pope

1688–1744

The English poet and satirist Alexander Pope was born the son of a London linen-draper. As a Catholic he was subject to discrimination which denied him a formal education, and was embittered throughout life because of a deformity of the spine. His biting wit gained him many literary supporters and enemies but it was his mock-heroic poem 'The Rape of the Lock' which really established his reputation.

From 'The Rape of the Lock' (1712)

The adventurous baron the bright locks
    admired;
He saw, he wished, and to the prize aspired.
Resolved to win, he meditates the way,
By force to ravish, or by fraud betray;
For when success a lover's toil attends,
Few ask, if fraud or force attained his ends.

.   .   .

The peer now spreads the glittering forfex wide,
To inclose the lock; now joins it, to divide . . .
The meeting points the sacred hair dissever
From the fair head, for ever, and for ever!

.   .   .

Then flashed the living lightning from her eyes,
And screams of horror rend the affrighted skies.
Not louder shrieks to pitying Heaven are cast,
When husbands, or when lapdogs breathe their
    last;
Or when rich China vessels fallen from high,
In glittering dust and painted fragments lie!

.   .   .

'For ever cursed be this detested day,
Which snatched my best, my favourite curl away!
Happy! ah, ten times happy had I been,
If Hampton Court these eyes had never seen!
Yet am I not the first mistaken maid,

By love of courts to numerous ills betrayed.
Oh, had I rather unadmired remained
In some lone isle, or distant northern land;
Where the gilt chariot never marks the way,
Where none learn ombre, none e'er taste
    Bohea!
There kept my charms concealed from mortal
    eye,
Like roses, that in deserts bloom and die.
What moved my mind with youthful lords to
    roam?
Oh, had I stayed, and said my prayers at home!
'Twas this, the morning omens seemed to tell;
Thrice from my trembling hand the patch-box
    fell;

The tottering China shook without a wind,
Nay, Poll sat mute, and Shock was most unkind!
A sylph, too, warned me of the threats of fate,
In mystic visions, now believed too late!
See the poor remnants of these slighted hairs!
My hands shall rend what even thy rapine
    spares:
These in two sable ringlets taught to break,
Once gave new beauties to the snowy neck;

.   .   .

Oh, hadst thou, cruel! been content to seize
Hairs less in sight, or any hairs but these!'

Anon. (England)

**From 'A Full and True Account of a Dreaded Fire, that Lately Broke
out in the Pope's Breeches' (1713)**

Pope

_____ _____ Ah! my Dear,
Come sit thee down in *Peter's* Chair;

Here's Peter's Key, and as you Sit,
Let's try how Peter's Key will fit
Thy Key-hole; for even those who Sin most
Their Secrets must unlock, tho' inmost,
Unto their Ghostly Father, who
From all their Sins does them undo;
For those who practise Holy Living,
Must to their Priests go off a Shriving.
This said, St. Peter's Key he stole,
As he suppos'd, to the Key-hole,
And then began to push it in,
In order to unlock her Sin.

She
With that, O Holy Sir, cry'd She,

I doubt you've pitch'd too low your Key:
I'll pitch it for ye, if you please,
And then you may unlock at Ease.
Then strait she did it with a Touch,
His Holiness too thank'd her much,
And withal this excuse did make,
In the behalf of his Mistake.

Pope
Saying, he seldom had of late
Us'd his Key to ope fore-gate;
Therefore, dear Madam, 'tis no wonder,
That now my Key had made a Blunder
Now as he thrust the Key in Hole,
Amaz'd, he cry'd, upon my Soul,
The Key goes in most wondrous easy,
What is the Key-hole broke, or Greasy?
Hah! it turns round not very hard,

I fear your Lock has ne'er a Ward;
Pray what's the Reason of it, Madam?
You must tell Truth by good St. Adam.

She

Ah! Sir, if it must be then spoken,
My Key-hole is a little broken;
As to the Wards, I do declare,
They were knock'd out in Angleterre.

Pope

In Angleterre, Damn'd Hereticks!
Damn 'em to the bottom of Styx!
I'm out of Patience, marry am I,
I'll turn my Key no more, G—d d—n me.
By C— and by St. Peter's Rock,
I'll put my Key out of thy Lock,
This said, he let down T—s's Smock.

Some Three Days after, this Apostle
In's holy Codpiece had strange Bustle,
Which when he found he sent forthwith
For Learned able Pintle Smith,
To Cure his Fleshly Key's disaster,
Which he soon did by Pill and Plaister.
As soon as e're the Pope grew well,
He curst poor T—s by Book and Bell,
And vow'd to keep, in fright of Whores,
His Key for to unlock back Doors.

Thus, Sirs, you see how T—s has pepper'd,
The Codpiece of the Romish Shepherd.
We could not burn the Pope at Home,
But T—s has burnt the Pope at Rome.
What may not Hereticks then hope,
Since even at Rome they've burnt the
   Pope.

Daniel Defoe

1660–1731

Born in Cripplegate, London, Defoe was educated for the Nonconformist ministry, but became a hosier instead. He took part in Monmouth's rebellion and joined the army of William III in 1688, and in 1702 was fined, imprisoned and pilloried for writing an ironical pamphlet attacking the Dissenters. A prolific writer, in all he produced some 560 books, pamphlets and journals but is best known for his adventure novel Robinson Crusoe *(1719) and picaresque novels such as* Moll Flanders *(1722).*

From **Moll Flanders** (1722)

It happen'd one Day that he came running up Stairs, towards the Room where his Sisters us'd to sit and Work, as he often us'd to do; and calling to them before he came in, as was his way too, I being there alone, step'd to the Door, and said, Sir, the Ladies are not here, they are Walk'd down the Garden; as I step'd forward, to say this towards the Door, he was just got to the Door, and clasping me in his Arms, as if it had been by Chance, O! Mrs. *Betty, says he,* are you here? that's better still; I want to speak with you, more than I do with them, and then having me in his Arms he Kiss'd me three or four times.

I struggl'd to get away, and yet did it but faintly neither, and he held me fast, and still Kiss'd me, till he was almost out of Breath, and then sitting down, says, *dear Betty* I am in Love with you.

His Words I must confess fir'd my Blood; all my Spirits flew about my Heart, and put me into Disorder enough, which he might easily have seen in my Face: He repeated it afterwards several times, that he was in Love with me, and my Heart spoke as plain as a Voice, that I lik'd it; nay, when ever he said, I am in Love with you, my Blushes plainly reply'd, *wou'd you were* Sir.

However nothing else pass'd at that time; it was but a Surprise, and when he was gone, I soon recover'd myself again. He had stay'd longer with me, but he happen'd to look out at the Window and see his Sisters coming up the Garden, so he took his leave, Kiss'd me again, told me he was very serious, and I should hear more of him very quickly, and away he went leaving me infinitely pleas'd tho' surpris'd; and had there not been one Misfortune in it. I had been in the Right, but the Mistake lay here, that Mrs. *Betty* was in Earnest, and the Gentleman was not.

From this time my Head ran upon strange Things, and I may truly say, I was not myself; to have such a Gentleman talk to me of being in Love with me, and of my being such a charming Creature, as he told me I was, these were things I knew not how to bear; my vanity was elevated to the last Degree: It is true, I had my Head full of Pride, but knowing nothing of the Wickedness of the times, I had not one Thought of my own Safety or of my Virtue about me; and had my young Master offer'd it at first Sight, he might have taken any Liberty he thought fit with me; but he did not see his Advantage, which was my happiness for that time.

After this Attack, it was not long but he found an opportunity to catch me again, and almost in the same Posture, indeed it had more of Design in it on his Part, tho' not on my Part; *it was thus*; the young Ladies were all gone a Visiting with their Mother; his Brother was out of Town; and as for his Father, he had been at *London* for a Week before; he had so well watched me, that he was in the House; and he briskly comes up the Stairs, and seeing me at Work comes into the Room to me directly, and began just as he did before with taking me in his Arms, and Kissing me for almost a quarter of an Hour together.

It was his younger Sisters Chamber, that I was in, and as there was no Body in the House but the Maids below Stairs, he was it may be the ruder: In short, he began to be in Earnest with me indeed; perhaps he found me a little too easie, for God knows I made no Resistance to him, while he only held me in his Arms and Kiss'd me; indeed I was too well pleas'd with it, to resist him much.

However as it were, tir'd with that kind of Work, we sat down, and there he talk'd with me a great while; *he said*, he was charm'd with me, and that he could not rest Night or Day till he had told me how he was in Love with me: and if I was able to Love him again, and would make him happy, I should be the saving of his Life; and many shan't catch me a Kissing of you, I told him I did not know who should be coming up Stairs, for I believ'd there was no Body in the House but the Cook and the other Maid, and they never came up those Stairs, well my Dear; *says he*, 'tis good to be sure however; and so he sits down and we began to Talk; and now, tho' I was still all on fire with his first visit, and said little, he did, as it were, put Words in my Mouth, telling me how passionately he lov'd me, and that tho' he could not mention such a thing till he came to his Estate, yet he was resolv'd to make me happy then, and himself too; *that is to say, to Marry me*, and abundance of such fine things, which I poor Fool did not understand the drift of, but acted as if there was no such thing as any kind of Love but that which tended to Matrimony; and if he had spoke of that, I had no Room, as well as no Power to have said No; but we were not come that length yet.

We had not sat long, but he got up, and stoping my very Breath with Kisses, threw me upon the Bed again; but then being both well warm'd, he went farther with me than Decency permits me to mention, nor had it been in my power to have deny'd him at that Moment, had he offer'd much more than he did.

However, tho' he took these Freedoms with me, it did not go to that, which they call the last Favour, which, to do him Justice, he did not attempt; and he made that Self-denial of his a Plea for all his Freedoms with me upon other Occasions after this: When this was over, he stay'd but a little while, but he put almost a Handful of Gold in my Hand, and left me; making a thousand Protestations of his Passion for me, and of his loving me above all the Women in the World.

.   .   .

My Colour came and went, at the Sight of the Purse, and with the fire of his Proposal together; so that I could not say a Word, and he easily perceiv'd it; so putting the Purse into my Bosom, I made no more Resistance to him, but let him do just what he pleas'd; and as often as he pleas'd; and thus I finish'd my own Destruction at once, for from this Day, being forsaken of my Virtue, and my Modesty, I had nothing of Value left to recommend me.

Jonathan Swift

1667–1745

The Anglo-Irish writer Jonathan Swift was born and educated in Dublin, ordained in 1694 and became Dean of St Patrick's in 1713. A vituperative polemicist, he had been a member of the Tory Scriblerus Club with Pope and Gay, but is mostly remembered for his poems and the prose satire Gulliver's Travels *(1726). The* Journal to Stella *(1710–1713) consists of intimate letters to Esther Johnson, who may have been his lover.*

'A Beautiful Young Nymph Going to Bed' (1731)

Corinna, Pride of Drury-Lane,
For whom no Shepherd sighs in vain;
Never did Covent Garden boast
So bright a batter'd, strolling Toast;
No drunken Rake to pick her up,
No Cellar where on Tick to sup;
Returning at the Midnight Hour;
Four Stories climbing to her Bow'r;
Then, seated on a three-legg'd Chair,
Takes off her artificial Hair:
Now, picking out a Crystal Eye,
She wipes it clean, and lays it by.
Her Eye-Brows from a Mouse's Hyde,
Stuck on with Art on either Side,
Pulls off with Care, and first displays 'em,
Then in a Play-Book smoothly lays 'em.
Now dextrously her Plumpers draws,

That serve to fill her hollow Jaws.
Untwists a Wire; and from her Gums
A Set of Teeth completely comes.
Pulls out the Rags contriv'd to prop
Her flabby Dugs and down they drop.
Proceeding on, the lovely Goddess
Unlaces next her Steel-Rib'd Bodice;
Which by the Operator's Skill,
Press down the Lumps, the Hollows fill,
Up goes her Hand, and off she slips
The Bolsters that supply her Hips.
With gentlest Touch, she next explores
Her Shankers, Issues, running Sores,
Effects of many a sad Disaster;
And then to each applies a Plaister.
But must, before she goes to Bed,
Rub off the Dawbs of White and Red;

And smooth the Furrows in her Front,
With greasy Paper stuck upon't.
She takes a *Bolus* e'er she sleeps;
And then between two Blankets creeps.
With Pains of Love tormented lies;
Or if she chance to close her Eyes,
Of *Bridewell* and the *Compter* dreams,
And feels the Lash, and faintly screams;
Or, by a faithless Bully drawn,
At some Hedge-Tavern lies in Pawn;
Or to *Jamaica* seems transported,
Alone, and by no Planter courted;
Or, near *Fleet-Ditch's* oozy Brinks,
Surrounded with a Hundred Stinks,
Belated, seems on watch to lye,
And snap some Cully passing by;
Or, struck with Fear, her Fancy runs
On Watchmen, Constables and Duns,
From whom she meets with frequent Rubs;
But, never from Religious Clubs;
Whose Favour she is sure to find,

Because she pays them all in Kind.

Corinna wakes. A dreadful Sight!
Behold the Ruins of the Night!
A wicked Rat her Plaister stole,
Half eat, and dragg'd in to his Hole.
The Crystal Eye, alas, was miss't;
And Puss had on her Plumpers pisst.
A Pigeon pick'd her Issue-Peas;
And Shock her Tresses fill'd with Fleas.
The Nymph, tho' in this mangled Plight,
Must ev'ry Morn her Limbs unite.
But how shall I describe her Arts
To recollect the scatter'd Parts?
Or shew the Anguish, Toil, and Pain,
Of gath'ring up herself again?
The bashful Muse will never bear
In such a Scene to interfere.
Corinna in the Morning dizen'd,
Who sees, will spew; who smells, be
        poison'd.

Samuel Richardson

1689–1761

Samuel Richardson, regarded as one of the chief founders of the modern novel, is most famous for his epistolary novel Pamela, *which was praised for its morality and realism but parodied by Henry Fielding in* Shamela *(1741). He wrote two other epistolary novels,* Clarissa Harlowe *(1747–48) and* The History of Sir Charles Grandison *(1753–54).*

From **Pamela** (1741)

LETTER XXV

My dear parents,

.   .   .

I went to Mrs. Jervis's chamber; and, O dreadful! my wicked master hid himself, base man as he is, in her closet, where she has a few books, a chest of drawers, and such like. I little suspected it; though I used, till this night, always to look into that closet, and another in the room, also under the bed, ever since the summer-house trick, but never found any thing; therefore I did not do it then, being resolved to be angry with Mrs. Jervis for what had happened in the day, so thought of nothing else.

.   .   .

'Hush!' said I, 'Mrs. Jervis, did you not hear something stir in the closet?' – 'No, silly girl,' said she; 'your fears are always awake.'

. . .

I was hush; but she said, 'Pr'ythee, my good girl, make haste to bed. See if the door be fast.' I did, and was thinking to look into the closet; but, hearing no more noise, thought it needless, and so went again and sat myself down on the bed-side, and went on undressing myself. And Mrs. Jervis, being by this time undressed, stepped into bed, and bid me hasten, for she was sleepy.

. . .

I don't know what was the matter, but my heart sadly misgave me. I pulled off my stays, and my stockings, and all my clothes to an under-petticoat; then hearing a rustling again in the closet, 'Heaven protect us! But before I say my prayers I must look into this closet.' And so was going to it slip-shod, when, O dreadful! out rushed my master in a rich silk and silver morning-gown.

I screamed, ran to the bed, and Mrs. Jervis screamed too; he said, 'I'll do you no harm if you forbear this noise; but otherwise take what follows.'

Instantly he came to the bed (for I had crept into it, to Mrs. Jervis, with my coat on and my shoes), and taking me in his arms, said, 'Mrs. Jervis, rise, and just step up stairs, to keep the maids from coming down at this noise: I'll do no harm to this rebel.'

'O for Heaven's sake! for pity's sake! Mrs. Jervis' said I, 'if I am not betrayed, don't leave me; and, I beseech you raise all the house.' – 'No,' said Mrs. Jervis, 'I will not stir, my dear lamb; I will not leave you. I wonder at you, Sir,' said she; and kindly threw herself upon my coat, clasping me round the waist. 'You shall not hurt this innocent,' said she; 'for I will lose my life in her defence. Are there not,' said she, 'enough wicked ones in the world, for your base purpose, but you must attempt such a lamb as this?'

He was desperate angry, and threatened to throw her out of the window; and turn her out of the house the next morning. 'You need not, Sir,' said she; 'for I will not stay in it. God defend my poor Pamela till to-morrow, and we will both go together,' – Says he, 'Let me but expostulate a word or two with you, Pamela.' – 'Pray, Pamela,' said Mrs. Jervis, 'don't hear a word, except he leaves the bed, and goes to the other end of the room.' – 'Aye, out of the room,' said I, 'expostulate to-morrow, if you must expostulate!'

I found his hand in my bosom, and when my fright let me know it, I was ready to die; I sighed, screamed and fainted away. And still he had his arms about my neck; Mrs. Jervis was about my feet, and upon my coat. And all in a cold dewy sweat was I. 'Pamela! Pamela!' says Mrs. Jervis, as she tells me since, ' – Oh!' and gave another shriek, 'my poor Pamela is dead for certain!' And so I was for a time; for I knew nothing more of the matter, one fit followed another, till about three hours after, I found myself in bed, and Mrs. Jervis sitting up on one side, with her wrapper about her, and Rachel on the other; but no master, for the wicked wretch was gone. I was so overjoyed that I hardly could believe myself; I said, which were my first words, 'Mrs. Jervis – Mrs. Rachel, can I be *sure* it is you? Tell me, can I? – Where have I been?' – 'Hush, my dear,' said Mrs. Jervis; 'You have been in fit after fit. I never saw any body so frightful in my life!'

Henry Fielding

1704–1754

Born near Glastonbury, the English novelist and dramatist Henry Fielding was the son of a high-ranking army officer. He was educated at Eton, and, after early careers as a dramatist and a lawyer, he turned to fiction – supposedly outraged by the moralism of Samuel Richardson's Pamela *(1741), which he parodied ruthlessly and hilariously in* Shamela *(1741) and* Joseph Andrews *(1749). He is, however, best remembered for his famous novel* Tom Jones, *published in 1749.*

From **Shamela** (1741)

LETTER V

HENRIETTA MARIA HONORA ANDREWS *to* SHAMELA ANDREWS

Dear Child,

Why will you give such way to your passion? How could you imagine I should be such a simpleton, as to upbraid thee with being thy mother's own daughter! When I advised you not to be guilty of folly, I meant no more than that you should take care to be well paid beforehand, and not trust to promises, which a man seldom keeps, after he hath had his wicked will. And seeing you have a rich fool to deal with, your not making a good market will be the more inexcusable; indeed, with such gentlemen as Parson Williams, there is more to be said; for they have nothing to give, and are commonly otherwise the best sort of men. I am glad to hear you read good books, pray continue so to do. I have inclosed you one of Mr. Whitefield's sermons, and also the *Dealings* with him, and am

Your affectionate Mother,
HENRIETTA MARIA, &c.

LETTER VI

SHAMELA ANDREWS *to* HENRIETTA MARIA HONORA ANDREWS

O Madam, I have strange things to tell you! As I was reading in that charming book about the Dealings, in comes my master – to be sure he is a precious one. Pamela, says he, what book is that? I warrant you Rochester's poems. – No, forsooth, says I, as pertly as I could; why how now Saucy Chops, Boldface, says he – Mighty pretty words, says I, pert again. – Yes (says he), you are a d—d, impudent, stinking, cursed, confounded jade, and I have a great mind to kick your a—. You, kiss – says I. A-gad, says he, and so I will; with that he caught me in his arms, and kissed me till he made my face all over fire. Now this served purely, you know, to put upon the fool for anger. O! What precious fools men are! And so I flung from him in a mighty rage, and pretended as how I would go out at the door; but when I came to the end of the room, I stood still, and my master cryed out, Hussy, Slut, Saucebox, Boldface, come hither – Yes, to be sure, says I; why don't you come, says he; what should I come for, says I; if you don't come to me, I'll come to you, says he; I shan't come to you, I assure you, says I. Upon which he run up, caught me in his arms, and flung me upon a chair, and began to offer to touch my under-petticoat. Sir, says I, you had better not offer to be rude; well, says he, no more I won't then; and away he went out of the room. I was so mad to be sure I could have cry'd.

Oh what a prodigious vexation it is to a woman to be made a fool of!

Mrs. Jervis, who had been without, harkening, now came to me. She burst into a violent laugh the moment she came in. Well, says she, as soon as she could speak, I have reason to bless myself that I am an old woman. Ah child! if you had known the jolly blades of my age, you would not have been left in the lurch in this manner. Dear Mrs. Jervis, says I, don't laugh at one; and to be sure I was a little angry with her. – Come, says she, my dear honeysuckle, I have one game to play for you; he shall see you in bed; he shall, my little rosebud, he shall see those pretty, little, white, round, panting – and offer'd to pull off my handkerchief. – Fie, Mrs. Jervis, says I, you make me blush, and upon my fackins, I believe she did. She went on thus: I know the squire likes you, and notwithstanding the aukwardness of his proceeding, I am convinced hath some hot blood in his veins, which will not let him rest, 'till he hath communicated some of his warmth to thee, my little angel; I heard him last night at our door, trying if it was open; now tonight I will take care it shall be so; I warrant that he makes the second trial; which if he doth, he shall find us ready to receive him. I will at first counterfeit sleep, and after a swoon; so that he will have you naked in his possession: and then if you are disappointed, a plague of all young squires, say I. – And so, Mrs. Jervis, says I, you would have me yield myself to him, would you; you would have me be a second time a fool for nothing. Thank you for that, Mrs. Jervis. For nothing! marry forbid, says she, you know he hath large sums of money, besides abundance of fine things; and do you think, when you have inflamed him, by giving his hand a liberty with that charming person; and that you know he may easily think he obtains against your will, he will not give anything to come at all? – This will not do, Mrs. Jervis, answered I. I have heard my mamma say (and so you know, Madam, I have), that in her youth, fellows have often taken away in the morning what they gave over night. No, Mrs. Jervis, nothing under a regular taking into keeping, a settled settlement, for me, and all my heirs, all my whole lifetime, shall do the business – or else crosslegged is the word, faith, with Sham; and then I snapt my fingers.

Thursday Night, Twelve O'Clock

Mrs. Jervis and I are just in bed, and the door unlocked; if my master should come – Odsbobs! I hear him just coming in at the door. You see I write in the present tense, as Parson Williams says. Well, he is in bed between us, we both shamming a sleep; he steals his hand into my bosom, which I, as if in my sleep, press close to me with mine, and then pretend to awake. – I no sooner see him, but I scream out to Mrs. Jervis, she feigns likewise but just to come to herself; we both begin, she to becall, and I to bescratch very liberally. After having made a pretty free use of my fingers, without any great regard to the parts I attack'd, I counterfeit a swoon. Mrs. Jervis then cries out, O sir, what have you done? you have murthered poor Pamela: she is gone, she is gone. –

O what a difficulty it is to keep one's countenance, when a violent laugh desires to burst forth!

The poor Booby, frightned out of his wits; jumped out of bed, and, in his shirt, sat down by my bed-side, pale and trembling, for the moon shone, and I kept my eyes wide open, and pretended to fix them in my head. Mrs. Jervis apply'd lavender water, and hartshorn, and this for a full half hour; when thinking I had carried it on long enough, and being likewise unable to continue the sport any longer, I began by degrees to come to myself.

The squire, who had sat all this while speechless, and was almost really in that condition which I feigned, the moment he saw me give symptoms of recovering my senses, fell down on his knees; and O Pamela, cryed he, can you forgive me, my injured maid? By heaven, I know not whether you are a man or a woman, unless by your swelling breasts. Will you promise to forgive me? I forgive you! D—n you, says I; and d—n you, says he, if you come to that. I wish I had never seen your bold face, saucy sow – and so went out of the room.

O what a silly fellow is a bashful young lover!

He was no sooner out of hearing, as we thought, than we both burst into a violent laugh. Well, says Mrs. Jervis, I never saw anything better acted than your part: but I wish you may not have discouraged him from any future attempt; especially since his passions are so cool, that you could prevent his hands going further than your bosom. Hang him, answer'd I, he is not quite so cold as that, I assure you; our hands, on neither side, were idle in the scuffle, nor have left us any doubt of each other as to that matter.

Friday Morning

My master sent for Mrs. Jervis, as soon as he was up, and bid her give an account of the plate and linnen in her care; and told her, he was resolved that both she and the little gipsy (I'll assure him) should set out together. Mrs. Jervis made him a saucy answer; which any servant of spirit, you know, would, tho' it should be one's ruin; and came immediately in tears to me, crying, she had lost her place on my account, and that she should be forced to take to a house, as I mentioned before; and that she hoped I would, at least, make her all the amends in my power, for her loss on my account, and come to her house whenever I was sent for. Never fear, says I, I'll warrant we are not so near being turned away as you imagine; and, i'cod, now it comes into my head, I have a fetch for him, and you shall assist me in it. But it being now late, and my letter pretty long, no more at present from

Your Dutiful Daughter,
SHAMELA

Giorgio Baffo

1694–1768

An Italian poet, Giorgio Baffo was born in Venice. A one-time tutor of the famous lover Casanova, he was elected to the Supreme Court of Justice in Venice towards the end of his life. A prolific writer, he wrote more than 600 sonnets, as well as many madrigals and other lyrics.

'Sonnet'. *Trans. Wayland Young*

> My meditation turns to thinking
> How the saints in heaven can have any fun
> When they've got no balls and no pricks
> And not a cunt to fuck.
> How can they get through eternity
> Without the great pleasure of coming,
> Which I can't see how anything can be lovelier than,
> So that my hair stands on end when I just think of it?
> But I go further in my thought,
> And I say: God is the world, and of this God
> We are each one of us a part.
> So when my prick fucks,
> As it so often does,
> God fucks too, and the saints who are with him.

Marie Le Prince de Beaumont

1711–1781

A French writer of educational prose fiction, Marie Le Prince de Beaumont was born in Rouen, and studied to be a teacher although she eventually became a governess in England and wrote moral tales for children. Her best-known fairy tale, Beauty and the Beast, *was an adaptation of an original story by Gabrielle de Villeneuve.*

From **Beauty and the Beast**

[Beauty has left the Beast and returned to her home.]

Beauty reproached herself, nevertheless, with the grief she was causing to the poor Beast; moreover, she greatly missed not seeing him. On the tenth night of her stay in her father's house she dreamed that she was in the palace garden, where she saw the Beast lying on the grass nearly dead, and that he upbraided her for her ingratitude. Beauty woke up with a start, and burst into tears.

'I am indeed very wicked,' she said, 'to cause so much grief to a Beast who has shown me nothing but kindness. Is it his fault that he is so ugly, and has so few wits? He is good, and that makes up for all the rest. Why did I not wish to marry him? I should have been a good deal

Lovers in a wood – before William Hogarth

happier with him than my sisters are with their husbands. It is neither good looks nor brains in a husband that make a woman happy; it is beauty of character, virtue, kindness. All these qualities the Beast has. I admit I have no love for him, but he has my esteem, friendship, and gratitude. At all events I must not make him miserable, or I shall reproach myself all my life.'

With these words Beauty rose and placed her ring on the table.

Hardly had she returned to her bed than she was asleep, and when she woke the next morning she saw with joy that she was in the Beast's palace. She dressed in her very best on purpose to please him, and nearly died of impatience all day, waiting for nine o'clock in the evening. But the clock struck in vain: no Beast appeared. Beauty now thought she must have caused his death, and rushed about the palace with loud despairing cries. She looked everywhere, and at last, recalling her dream, dashed into the garden by the canal, where she had seen him in her sleep. There she found the poor Beast lying unconscious, and thought he must be dead. She threw herself on his body, all her horror of his looks forgotten, and feeling his heart still beat, fetched water from the canal and threw it on his face.

The Beast opened his eyes and said to Beauty:

'You forgot your promise. The grief I felt as having lost you made me resolve to die of hunger; but I die content since I have the pleasure of seeing you once more.'

'Dear Beast, you shall not die,' said Beauty: 'you shall live and become my husband. Here and now I offer you my hand, and swear that I will marry none but you. Alas, I fancied I felt only friendship for you, but the sorrow I have experienced clearly proves to me that I cannot live without you.'

Beauty had scarce uttered these words when the castle became ablaze with lights before her eyes: fireworks, music – all proclaimed a feast. But these splendours were lost on her: she turned to her dear Beast, still trembling for his danger.

Judge of her surprise now! At her feet she saw no longer the Beast, who had disappeared, but a prince, more beautiful than Love himself, who thanked her for having put an end to his enchantment. With good reason were her eyes riveted upon the prince.

John Cleland

1709–1789

The novelist and journalist John Cleland was educated at Westminster School, then went on to join the consular service, and travelled extensively in Europe. He is best known for his novel Fanny Hill, or the Memoirs of a Woman of Pleasure *which, despite being a bestseller, earned him little money and a summons before the Privy Council for indecency. The book was again prosecuted for obscenity in 1963.*

From **Fanny Hill, or the Memoirs of a Woman of Pleasure** (*c.* 1748)

Hitherto I had been indebted only to the girls of the house for the corruption of my innocence; their luscious talk, in which modesty was far from respected, their descriptions of their engagements with men, had given me a tolerable insight into the nature and mysteries of their profession, at the same time that they highly provoked an itch of florid

Lovers in a wood – after William Hogarth

warm-spirited blood through every vein: but above all, my bedfellow, Phoebe, whose pupil I more immediately was, exerted her talents in giving me the first tinctures of pleasure: whilst nature now warmed and wantoned with discoveries so interesting, piqued a curiosity which Phoebe artfully whetted, and leading me from question to question of her own suggestion, explained to me all the mysteries of Venus. But I could not long remain in such an house as that, without being an eye-witness of more than I could conceive from her descriptions.

One day about twelve at noon, being thoroughly recovered of my fever, I happened to be in Mrs Brown's dark closet, where I had not been half an hour, resting on the maid's settle-bed, before I heard a rustling in the bed-chamber, separated from the closet only by two sash-doors, before the glasses of which were drawn two yellow damask curtains, but not so close as to exclude the full view of the room from any person in the closet.

I instantly crept softly, and posted myself so that, seeing everything minutely, I could not myself be seen; and who should come in but the venerable mother abbess herself! handed in by a tall, brawny, young horse-grenadier, moulded in the Hercules-style; in fine, the choice of the most experienced dame, in those affairs, in all London.

Oh! how still and hush did I keep at my stand, lest any noise should balk my curiosity, or bring madam into the closet!

But I had not much reason to fear either, for she was so entirely taken up with her present great concern that she had no sense of attention to spare to anything else.

Droll was it to see that clumsy fat figure of her's flop down on the foot of the bed, opposite to the closet door, so that I had a full front view of all her charms.

Her paramour sat down by her. He seemed to be a man of very few words, and a great stomach, for proceeding instantly to essentials, he gave her some hearty smacks, and thrusting his hand into her breasts, disengaged them from her stays, in scorn of whose confinement they broke loose and swagged down, navel low at least. A more enormous pair did my eyes behold, nor of a worse colour, flagging soft, and most lovingly contiguous: yet such as they were, this neck-beef-eater seemed to paw them with a most unenviable gust, seeking in vain to confine or cover one of them with a hand scarce less than a shoulder of mutton. After toying with them thus some time, as if they had been worth it, he laid her down pretty briskly, and canting up her petticoats, made barely a mask of them to her broad red face, that blushed with nothing but brandy.

As he stood on one side for a minute or so, unbottoning his waistcoat and breeches, her fat brawny thighs hung down; and the whole greasy landscape lay fairly open to my view: a wide open-mouthed gap, overshaded with a grizzly bush seemed held out like a beggar's wallet for its provision.

But I soon had my eyes called off by a more striking object, that entirely engrossed them.

Her sturdy stallion had now unbuttoned, and produced naked, stiff, and erect, that wonderful machine, which I had never seen before, and which, for the interest my own seat of pleasure began to take furiously in it, I stared at with all the eyes I had. However, my senses were too much flurried, too much concentered in that now burning spot of mine, to observe anything more than in general the make and turn of that instrument, from which the instinct of nature, yet more than all I had heard of it, now strongly informed me I was to expect that supreme pleasure which she has placed in the meeting of those parts so admirably fitted for each other.

Long, however, the young spark did not remain, before, giving it two or three shakes, by way of brandishing it, he threw himself upon her, and his back being now towards me, I could only take his being engulfed for granted, by the direction he moved in, and the impossibility of missing so staring a mark; and now the bed shook, the curtains rattled so, that I could scarce hear the sighs and murmurs, the heaves and pantings that accompanied the action, from the beginning to the end: the sound and sight of which thrilled to the very soul of me, and made every vein of my body circulate liquid fires: the emotion grew so violent that it almost intercepted my respiration.

Prepared then, and disposed as I was by the discourse of my companions, and Phoebe's minute detail of everything, no wonder that such a sight gave the last dying blow to my native innocence.

Whilst they were in the heat of the action, guided by nature only, I stole my hand up my petticoat, and with fingers all on fire, seized and yet more inflamed that center of all my senses; my heart palpitated, as if it would force its way through my bosom; I breathed with pain; I twisted my thighs, squeezed and compressed the lips of that virgin slit, and following mechanically the example of Phoebe's manual operation on it, as far as I could find admission, brought on at last the critical ecstasy, the melting flow, into which nature, spent with excess of pleasure, dissolves and dies away.

. . .

As soon as I heard them go downstairs, I stole up softly to my own room, out of which I had been luckily not missed. There I began to breathe a little freer, and to give a loose to those warm emotions which the sight of such an encounter had raised in me, I laid me down on the bed, stretched myself out, joining, and ardently wishing, and requiring any means to divert or allay the rekindled rage and tumult of my desires, which all pointed strongly to their pole, man. I felt about the bed, as if I sought for something that I grasped in my waking dream, and not finding it, could have cried for vexation, every part of me glowing with stimulating fires. At length, I resorted to the only present remedy, that of vain attempts at digitation, where the smallness of the theater did not yet afford room enough for action, and where the pain my fingers gave me in striving for admission, though they procured me a slight satisfaction for the present, started an apprehension which I could not be easy till I had communicated to Phoebe and received her explanations upon it.

François Voltaire

1694–1778

A French philosopher, historian, novelist, poet and dramatist, Voltaire was born in Paris and educated by the Jesuits. His constant criticism of the ancien régime *led to imprisonment in the Bastille and temporary exile in England (1726–29), and his religious scepticism finally led the church to refuse him burial. His work includes the* Lettres philosophiques *(1734) and the great satire of Enlightment complacency,* Candide.

From **Candide** (1758). *Trans. John Bull*

'One night when I was fast asleep in bed, the Bulgars (by grace of God) arrived at our lovely Thunder-ten-tronckh and slaughtered my parents. They cut my father's throat and my brother's, and made mincemeat of my mother. A great lout of a Bulgar, six foot tall, noticed that I had fainted at the sight of this butchery, and set about ravishing me. That was enough to bring me round. I recovered my senses and cried for help, struggling, biting, and scratching as hard as I could. I wanted to tear the fellow's eyes out. You see, I didn't appreciate that what was happening in my father's house was in no way unusual. The brute gave me a wound in my left thigh, and I still bear the scar.'

'Oh, how I should like to see it!' exclaimed Candide, innocently.

'You shall,' said Cunégonde; 'but first let me go on with my story.'

'By all means,' said Candide.

Cunégonde continued: 'A Bulgar captain came in. He noticed that I was bleeding and that the soldier made no attempt to move. This lack of respect for an officer so enraged the captain that he slew the brute across my body. He then had my wound dressed and took me to his quarters as a prisoner of war. I used to wash his shirts for him (he hadn't many) and cook his meals. There is no denying he thought me pretty as well as useful, and I admit that he was quite handsome himself. His skin was certainly both white and soft, but apart from that I can say little for him. He had not much intelligence and little understanding of philosophy: it was quite clear that he had not been brought up by Dr. Pangloss. At the end of three months he had no money left, and as he had grown tired of me he sold me to Don Issachar, a Jew with business connexions in Holland and Portugal, who had a weakness for women. This Jew was much attached to my person, but he could not get his way with me, for I was more successful in resisting him than the Bulgar soldier. A woman of honour can be ravished once, but the experience is a tonic for her virtue. To make me more amenable, the Jew brought me to this country house where we are sitting. I used to think,' she continued, as she looked round her boudoir, 'that there was no place so beautiful as Castle Thunder-ten-tronckh, but I see that I was wrong.

'One day the Grand Inquisitor noticed me at Mass. He ogled me persistently, and sent a message to say he had something to discuss with me in private; so I was brought to his palace. I told him of my birth, whereupon he showed me how I was degrading myself in belonging to an Israelite. A proposal was then made to Don Issachar that he should surrender me to His Eminence. Don Issachar, who is the Court banker, and therefore a man of some standing, would not hear of the proposition, until the Inquisitor threatened him with an auto-da-fé. This forced the Jew's hand, but he made a bargain by which this house and I should belong to both of them in common, to the Jew on Mondays, Wednesdays, and Sabbath days, and to the Inquisitor the other days of the week. This agreement has now lasted for six months. There has been some quarrelling, as they cannot decide whether Saturday night belongs to the old law or to the new. For my part I have resisted both of them so far, and I think that is why they love me still.

'In course of time His Eminence made up his mind to prevent the disaster of another earthquake, and to intimidate Don Issachar, by celebrating an auto-da-fé, to which he did me the honour of inviting me. I had an excellent seat, and delicious refreshments were served to the ladies between Mass and the execution. I confess I was horrified at seeing those two Jews burned, and that honest Basque who had married his godmother; but imagine my surprise, my fright and distress, at seeing a figure that looked like Pangloss, dressed in the sacrificial cassock and paper mitre! I rubbed my eyes and watched attentively till I saw him hanged. Then I fainted; but scarcely had I recovered my senses when my eyes lighted on you, standing there stark naked. You can fancy what horror and consternation, what grief and despair I felt. Your skin, I assure you, is much whiter than my Bulgar captain's; it has a much more delicate bloom. The sight roused feelings which overwhelmed and consumed me. I screamed, and wanted to shout: "Stop, you Barbarians!" But my voice failed me, and indeed my cries would have been useless. When you had been thoroughly flogged, I said to myself, "What can have brought my adorable Candide and our wise Pangloss to Lisbon, one to receive a hundred lashes and the other to be hanged at the orders of that same Cardinal Inquisitor who is so devoted to me? I am afraid Pangloss cruelly deceived me when he told me that all is for the best in this world."

'You can well imagine how distracted I was. One moment I was almost beside myself with frenzy, the next I was at death's door from very faintness. And all the time my mind kept recurring to my parents' butchery and my brother's slaughter, then to the insolence of that brutal Bulgar soldier and the wound he gave me, then to my slavery as a kitchen-maid and to my Bulgar captain, and that wretched Don Issachar and the hateful Inquisitor, then back to Dr. Pangloss's execution and the magnificent anthem in counterpoint performed while you were being flogged. But above all my mind dwelt on the kiss you gave me behind the screen that day when I saw you for the last time, and I praised God for bringing you back to me through so many trials. I ordered my old servant to take care of you and bring you here as soon as she could, and she has faithfully carried out my wishes. It gives me inexpressible pleasure to see you again and to listen to you and talk to you; but you must be ravenous. I am feeling famished myself. So let's have supper.'

They sat down to table together, and after supper reclined on the beautiful couch already mentioned. There they were when Don Issachar, one of the masters of the house, arrived. It being the Sabbath day, he had come to enjoy his rights and unfold the tenderness of his love.

Denis Diderot

1713–1784

The French writer Denis Diderot was the son of a Langres cutler and educated by the Jesuits. For some 30 years from 1745 he was largely responsible for L'Encyclopédie, *that great enterprise of the French Enlightenment. A religious sceptic, philosopher and natural scientist, Diderot's other work includes* Pensées philosophiques *(1746), the licentious romance* Les Bijoux indiscrets *and the satirical moral fable* Jacques le fataliste *(published posthumously 1796).*

From **Les Bijoux indiscrets** (1748)

A wealthy lord, travelling through France, dragg'd me to London. Ay, that was a man indeed! He water'd me six times a day, and as often o' nights. His prick like a cornet's tail shot flaming darts: I never felt such quick and thrilling thrusts. It was not possible for mortal prowess to hold out long, at this rate; so he dropped by degrees, and I received his soul distilled through his Tarse. He gave me fifty thousand guineas. This noble lord was succeeded by a couple of privateer-commanders lately return'd from cruising: being intimate friends they fuck'd me, as they had sailed, in company, endeavouring who should show most vigour and serve the rediest fire. Whilst one was riding at anchor, I towed the other by his Tarse and prepared him for a fresh time. Upon a modest computation, I reckon'd in about eight days time I received a hundred and eighty shot. But I soon grew tired with keeping so strict an account, for there was no end of their broad-sides. I got twelve thousand pounds from them for my share of prizes they had taken. The winter quarter being over, they were forced to put to sea again, and would fain have engaged me as a tender, but I had made a prior contract with a German count.'

Laurence Sterne

1713–1768

A sharply witty, often salacious novelist, Laurence Sterne was born in Tipperary, Ireland, the son of an infantry ensign. He was educated at the Halifax Grammar School, then at Jesus College, Cambridge, and was ordained a priest in 1738. He wrote several sermons and journals, but is best known for this famous novel, The Life and Opinions of Tristram Shandy, *which brought him great success as well as criticism on literary and moral grounds. He is widely regarded today as the begetter of the 'stream-of-consciousness' novel.*

From **The Life and Opinions of Tristram Shandy** (1759)

CHAPTER TWENTY-THREE

We are ruined and undone, my child, said the abbess to Margarita, – we shall be here all night – we shall be plundered – we shall be ravished –

– We shall be ravished, said Margarita, as sure as a gun. *Sancta Maria!* cried the abbess (forgetting the *O!*) – why was I governed by this wicked stiff joint? why did I leave the convent of Andoüillets? and why didst thou not suffer thy servant to go unpolluted to her tomb?

O my finger! my finger! cried the novice, catching fire at the word *servant* – why was I not content to put it here, or there, any where rather than be in this strait?

– Strait! said the abbess.

Strait – said the novice; for terror had struck their understandings – the one knew not what she said – the other what she answered.

O my virginity! virginity! cried the abbess.

– inity! – inity! said the novice, sobbing.

CHAPTER TWENTY-FOUR

MY dear mother, quoth the novice, coming a little to herself, – there are two certain words, which I have been told will force any horse, or ass, or mule, to go up a hill whether he will or no; be he never so obstinate or ill-willed, the moment he hears them uttered, he obeys. They are words magic! cried the abbess in the utmost horror – No; replied Margarita calmly – but they are words sinful – What are they? quoth the abbess, interrupting her: They are sinful in the first degree, answered Margarita, – they are mortal – and if we are ravished and die unabsolved of them, we shall both – but you may pronouce them to me, quoth the abbess of Andoüillets – They cannot, my dear mother, said the novice, be pronounced at all; they will make all the blood in one's body fly up into one's face – But you may whisper them in my ear, quoth the abbess.

Heaven! hadst thou no guardian angel to delegate to the inn at the bottom of the hill? was there no generous and friendly spirit unemployed – no agent in nature, by some monitory shivering, creeping along the artery which led to his heart, to rouse the muleteer from his banquet? – no sweet minstrelsy to bring back the fair idea of the abbess and Margarita, with their black rosaries!

Rouse! rouse! – but 'tis too late – the horrid words are pronounced this moment –

– and how to tell them – Ye, who can speak of every thing existing, with unpolluted lips – instruct me – guide me –

CHAPTER TWENTY-FIVE

ALL sins whatever, quoth the abbess, turning casuist in the distress they were under, are held by the confessor of our convent to be either mortal or venial: there is no further division. Now a venial sin being the slightest and least of all sins, – being halved – by taking, either only the half of it, and leaving the rest – or, by taking it all, and amicably halving it betwixt yourself and another person – in course becomes diluted into no sin at all.

Now I see no sin in saying, *bou, bou, bou, bou, bou*, a hundred times together; nor is there any turpitude in pronouncing the syllable *ger, ger, ger, ger, ger*, were it from our matins to our vespers: Therefore, my dear daughter, continued the abbess of Andoüillets – I will say *bou*, and thou shalt say *ger*; and then alternately, as there is no more sin in *fou* than in *bou* – Thou shalt say *fou* – and I will come in (like fa, sol, la, re, me, ut, at our complines) with *ter*. And accordingly the abbess, giving the pitch note, set off thus:

Abbess,	}	Bou - - bou - - bou - -
Margarita,		—ger, - - ger, - - ger.
Margarita,	}	Fou - - fou - - fou - -
Abbess,		—ter, - - ter, - - ter.

The two mules acknowledged the notes by a mutual lash of their tails; but it went no further – 'Twill answer by an' by, said the novice.

Abbess,	}	Bou- bou- bou- bou- bou- bou-
Margarita,		—ger, ger, ger, ger, ger, ger.

Quicker still, cried Margarita.

Fou, fou, fou, fou, fou, fou, fou, fou, fou.

Quicker still, cried Margarita.

Bou, bou, bou, bou, bou, bou, bou, bou, bou.

Quicker still – God preserve me! said the abbess – They do not understand us, cried Margarita – But the Devil does, said the abbess of Andoüillets.

John Wilkes

1727–1797

The English politician and author John Wilkes was born in London, the son of a distiller. A dissolute man, though a brave and popular politician (winning grudging respect even from his foe Dr Johnson), he was twice expelled from Parliament for libel, once for attacking Bute's administration and again on account of his splenetic satirical poem 'Essay on Woman', condemned as obscene.

From **'Essay on Woman'** (1763)

Awake my Fanny! leave all meaner things;
This morn shall prove what rapture swiving brings!
Let us (since life can little more supply
Than just a few good fucks, and then we die)
Expatiate free o'er that loved scene of man,
A mighty maze, for mighty pricks to scan;
A wild, where PAPHIAN THORNS promiscuous shoot,
Where flows the monthly Rose, but yields no Fruit.

.   .   .

He who the hoop's immensity can pierce,
Dart thro' the whalebone fold's vast universe,
Observe how circle into circle runs,
What courts the eye, and what all vision shuns,
All the wild modes of dress our females wear,
May guess what makes them thus transform'd appear.

But of their cunts the bearings and ties,
The nice connexions, strong dependencies,
The latitude and longitude of each
Hast thou gone through, or can thy Pego reach?
Was that great Ocean, that unbounded Sea,
Where pricks like whales may spout, fathom'd by Thee?
Presumptuous Prick! The reason would'st thou find
Why form'd so weak, so little, and so blind?

.   .   .

Then, in the scale of Pricks, 'tis plain,
God-like erect, BUTE stands the foremost man
And all the question (wrangle e'er so long)
Is only this, if Heaven placed his wrong.

.   .   .

Then, say not Man's imperfect, Heaven in fault,
Say rather, Man's as perfect as he ought;
His Pego measured to the female Case,
Betwixt a woman's thighs his proper place;
And if to fuck in a proportion'd sphere,
What matters how it is, or when, or where?
Fly fuck'd by fly may be completely so,
As Hussey's Duchess, or your well-bull'd cow.

. . .

Pleased to the last, she likes the luscious food,
And grasps the prick just raised to shed her blood.
Oh! Blindness to the Future, kindly given,
That each may enjoy what fucks are mark'd by Heaven.
Who sees with equal Eye, as God of all,
The Man just mounting, and the Virgin's fall;
Prick, cunt, and bollocks in convulsions hurl'd
And now a Hymen burst, and now a World.
Hope humbly, then, clean girls; nor vainly soar;
But fuck the cunt at hand, and God adore.
What future fucks he gives not thee to know,
But gives that Cunt to be thy Blessing now.

Anon.

From **Kitty's Atalantis for the year 1766**

What's that in which good housewives take delight,
Which, though it has no legs, will stand upright,
'Tis often us'd, both sexes must agree,
Beneath the navel, yet above the knee;
At the end it has a hole; 'tis stiff and strong,
Thick as a maiden's wrist and pretty long:
To a soft place 'tis very oft apply'd,
And makes the thing 'tis us'd to, still more wide;
The women love to wriggle it to and fro,
That what lies under may the wider grow:
By giddy sluts sometimes it is abus'd,
But by good housewives rubb'd before it's us'd,
That it may fitter for their purpose be,
When they to occupy the same are free.
Now tell me merry lasses if you can,
What this must be, that is no part of man?
[Answer: A Rolling Pin]

Restif de la Bretonne

1734–1806

Born at Sacy, the French novelist Restif de la Bretonne worked as a printer in Paris before embarking on an extra-ordinarily prolific career as a writer (he produced over 200 volumes). Most of his work is crudely realistic and morally didactic, and includes the 16-volume erotic autobiography Monsieur Nicolas, *largely set in the Paris underworld.*

From **Monsieur Nicolas** (1778). *Trans. Robert Baldick*

I was now fully developed; infrequent but fairly numerous acts of virility had given me practice and fired my senses. I often went a whole week without seeing the beloved sweetheart who inspired me with the love of virtue; truth to tell, my imagination was excited by her on my way to ring the bells at noon; but on my return I found Marguerite, a woman of forty, I agree, but as fresh as a devout Christian, or rather as a woman, who, having private means, had never known want. Besides, it is well-known that that age in a woman is no obstacle to desire for boys reaching adolescence; it seems indeed as if Nature tends to make them prefer mature women, not to love them tenderly, but to enjoy them. Marguerite Pâris was well made, and clean in dress and person; she dressed her hair tastefully and exactly like Mademoiselle Rousseau; her shoes came from Paris and were as graceful as those of our prettiest women; if she wore clogs, they were well made, with high heels. On the day of the Assumption, she wore new slippers of black morocco whose seams retained their dazzling whiteness, with a narrow heel which made her shapely legs seem even thinner; these legs were clad in fine cotton stockings with blue clocks. My eyes fastened in spite of myself on Marguerite's pretty feet; I could not tear them away. It was very hot; after Vespers, the housekeeper undressed and changed into white: her shortened skirt revealed the lower part of her legs. I found myself in a situation similar to that in which, four years earlier, Madame Rameau's Nannette had placed me; it was even more decisive, since I had passed the stage when the voice breaks and becomes masculine; I already needed a razor. Marguerite noticed the attention I was paying her, and the good woman seemed to find it flattering. She knew that I had a sentimental passion; she regarded it as a misfortune for me, and was afraid that I might suffer as much in loving the daughter as she herself had suffered in loving the father. It seemed to her that a distraction would do me good and she was not displeased at the idea of providing it. We were alone; my comrades were playing; the Abbé Thomas was busy; I was studying at my little table by the window. Not far from me, Marguerite was cleaning a salad, with her legs crossed, thus showing me one leg up to the calf, with her pretty slipper hanging on to her foot by the toe. Once my imagination had been fired, my burning senses would not allow me to stay where I was. I could not resist an automatic rubbing motion, either because Nature was calling for necessary relief, or simply because of a feeling of irritation. I got up in a fury of excitement; I went over to Marguerite. She did not take fright. 'My dear boy,' she said gently, 'what is the matter? Well, what do you want?' I made no reply, but I held her hands, which I squeezed without trying to go any further. But then she was disturbed by the sight of my wild eyes. 'Monsieur Nicolas, are you feeling ill? I'll give you some water.' I gripped her strongly without replying, pressing her in my arms fit to stifle her. She was afraid that I might double my efforts if she resisted; she clasped me to her breast. I felt weak, a cloud covered my eyes, my legs gave way beneath me; I would have fallen if Marguerite had not supported me. It was the first time that this had happened to me without copulation and without my losing consciousness completely. Delighted at having felt it all, I said to myself: 'At last I am a man!' And once again Jeannette was the principal cause of my joy. 'I could be Mademoiselle Rousseau's husband.' I recovered from my excessive perturbation, and Marguerite, seeing that I was calm, reproved me, although she had no idea (at least so I imagine) what had just happened to me. I assured her that it was a sort of involuntary aberration, that I had suddenly lost my composure, I did not know how, and that I had been a long way from wishing to do her any harm. She seemed to believe me, for she smiled. Then she asked me: 'But what put you into that state?' 'It must,' I said, I was still so innocent, 'have been the sight of your slipper or your leg, for I could not prevent myself from looking at them when the envy took me: I was like a bird spellbound by a viper. He senses the danger and cannot avoid it.' 'But if you are in love with Jeannette Rousseau?' This remark was like a thunderbolt. A sort of shudder ran through me; my blood froze. The bell rang for Vespers and I went to church. It was there that, plunged in meditation, I blushed at my action, involuntary though it had been; indeed, it had some peculiar effects on my imagination and my organs. To prevent a recurrence of the excessive emotion engendered by Marguerite's leg and voluptuous foot, I was obliged to resort to my antipathy for blood, by imagining a furious soldier plunging his sword into Madame Chevrier or some other pretty woman of the village. But I had a more effective remedy against the curé's exhortations from the pulpit: the sight of Jeannette; the beautiful, modest Rousseau girl restored calm to my senses. She had never disturbed them; her power was exerted upon the noblest part of me; she inspired every virtue in me, even chastity. I am not trying to impress you, reader: if I wanted to lie, or simply to conceal the truth, you would not have the pages you have just been reading.

Choderlos de Laclos

1741–1803

Laclos was born in Amiens and pursued a career as a soldier until he was imprioned in 1793 as a Jacobin, although he was later allowed to return to the army. As a writer, he is remembered for the epistolary novel Les Liaisons dangereuses, *which recounts the intricate sexual schemings of the libertines Vicomte de Valmont and Madame de Merteuil.*

From **Les Liaisons dangereuses** (1782). *Trans. P.W.K. Stone*

LETTER 96: *The Vicomte de Valmont to Madame de Merteuil*

. . . For some days, during which I had been better treated by my tender devotee and was consequently less concerned about: her, I had been conscious that the little Volanges was in fact extremely pretty; and that, if it was absurd to be enamoured of her as Danceny is, it was perhaps equally so for me not to look to her for the distraction my solitude compels me to find. It seemed to be only just, too, that I should have some reward for my efforts on her behalf, and

I remembered, besides, that you had offered her to me before Danceny had any pretensions in the matter. I decided I could legitimately claim certain rights in a property which was his only because I had refused and relinquished it. The pretty look of the little creature, her fresh little mouth, her childish air, even her gaucherie, confirmed me in these wise determinations. I decided to act upon them, and success has crowned my enterprise.

You are already wondering how I arrived so soon at supplanting the cherished lover, and what method of seduction can have been appropriate to such lack of years and experience. Spare yourself the trouble: I took none at all myself. While, with your skill in handling the weapons of your sex, yours was a triumph of cunning, I, restoring to man his inalienable rights, conquered by force of authority. Sure of seizing my prey if I could come within reach of her, I had no need of strategem, except to secure a means of approach, and the ruse I employed for that purpose was hardly worthy of the name.

I took my opportunity as soon as I received Danceny's next letter to his mistress. Having given her the signal of warning agreed upon between us, I exercised all my ingenuity, not in giving her the letter, but in failing to find a means of doing so. I pretended to share her resulting impatience, and having caused the evil I pointed out the remedy.

The young lady occupies a room, one door to which gives on to the corridor. The mother had, as was to be expected, removed the key, and it was only a question of recovering it. Nothing could have been easier: I asked only to have it at my disposal for two hours whereupon I should be responsible for procuring a duplicate. After that everything, correspondence, meetings, nocturnal rendez-vous, would have become convenient and safe. Yet – would you believe it? – the cautious child took fright and refused. Another man would have been crushed by this: I saw in it no more than an occasion for pleasure of a more piquant kind. I wrote to Danceny complaining of the refusal, and did it so well that the blockhead would not be satisfied till he had obtained, exacted rather, a promise from his timorous mistress to grant my request and leave everything to my discretion.

I was very pleased, I must say, with my change of role, and with the young man's doing for me what he thought I would be doing for him. The idea doubled the worth of the enterprise in my eyes, so that as soon as I had possession of the precious key, I hastened to make use of it. That was last night.

Having made sure that all was quiet throughout the house, armed with my dark lantern and clothed as befitted the hour and the circumstances, I paid my first visit to your pupil. I had everything arranged (she herself had obliged me) so that I could enter without noise. She was in her first sleep, the deep sleep of youth, so that I arrived at her bedside without waking her. I thought at first of proceeding further and attempting to pass myself off as a dream. But, fearing the effect of surprise and the consequent alarms, I decided instead to wake the sleeping beauty with every caution, and eventually succeeded in preventing the outcry I had anticipated.

When I had calmed her initial fears, and since I was not there to chat, I risked a few liberties. There is no doubt she was not taught enough at the convent either about the many different perils to which fearful innocence is exposed, or about all that it has to protect, or be taken by surprise: for, directing her whole attention and all her energies to defending herself from a kiss, which was nothing but a feint, she left everything else defenceless. How could I let my advantage slip? I changed my line of attack and immediately seized a position. At this point we both thought all was lost. The little creature, quite horrified, made in good earnest to cry out: fortunately her voice was strangled in tears. She then threw herself towards the bell-rope, but I had the presence of mind to take hold of her arm in time.

'What are you trying to do?' I said to her. 'Ruin yourself for ever?' What will it matter to me if someone comes? How will you convince anyone that I am not here with your permission? Who else but you could have provided me with a means of entering your room? As for the key which I have from you, which I can only have obtained from you, will you undertake to explain its purpose?' This short harangue pacified neither grief nor rage; but it inspired submission. I don't know whether my tones were eloquent; my gestures, at all events, were not. One hand was needed for power, the other for love: where is the orator that could aspire to grace in such a position? If you can picture the circumstances you will agree that they were favourable for attack: but I am a blockhead, and as you say, the simplest woman, a mere convent girl, has me by the leading-strings like a child.

The girl in question, in the midst of her despair, knew that she must find some way of coming to terms with me. Entreaties found me inexorable and she was reduced to making offers. You will suppose I set a high price upon my important position: no, I promised everything away for a kiss. True, once I had taken the kiss I did not keep my promise: but I had good reason not to. Had we agreed that the kiss should be taken or given? After much bargaining we decided upon a second, and this one was to be received. Having guided her timid arms around my body, I clasped her more lovingly in the one of mine that was free, and the sweetest kiss was in fact received: properly, perfectly received: love itself could not have done better.

So much good faith deserved its reward, and I immediately granted the request. The hand was withdrawn; but by some extraordinary chance I found that I myself had taken its place. You imagine me very breathless and busy at this point, don't you? Not at all. I have acquired a taste for dawdling, I tell you. Why hurry when one's destination is in sight?

Seriously, I was glad for once to observe the power of opportunity, deprived in this case of all extraneous aid, with love in combat against it; love, moreover, sustained by modesty and shame, and encouraged by the bad humour I had provoked, which had been given free rein. Opportunity was alone; but it was there, offering itself, continually present, whereas love was not.

To confirm my observations, I was malicious enough to exert no more strength than could easily have been resisted. It was only when my charming enemy, taking advantage of my lenity, seemed about to escape me that I restrained her with the threats of which I had already felt the happy effects. Oh well, to go no further, our sweet inamorata, forgetting her vows, first yielded and then consented: of course, tears and reproaches were resumed at the first opportunity. I don't know whether they were real or pretended, but, as always happens, they ceased the moment I set about giving her reason for more. At length, having proceeded from helplessness to indignation, and from indignation to helplessness, we separated quite satisfied with one another and looking forward with equal pleasure to this evening's rendezvous.

I did not return to my room till daybreak, dying of sleep and fatigue: I sacrificed both, however, to my desire to appear this morning at breakfast. I have a passion for the mien of the morning after. You have no idea of this one. Such embarrassment of gesture, such difficulty of movement! Eyes kept steadily lowered, so large, and so haggard! The little round face so drawn! Nothing was ever so amusing. And for the first time her mother, alarmed at this extreme alteration, displayed some sympathetic interest! The Présidente, too, danced attendance round her. Oh, *her* sympathy is only borrowed, believe me! The day will come for its return, and that day is not far off. Good-bye, my love.

Château de —

1 October 17—

LETTER 97: *Cécile Volanges to the Marquise de Merteuil*

Oh God, Madame, how heavy-hearted, how miserable I am! Who will console me in my distress? Who will advise me in my difficulties? This Monsieur de Valmont . . . and Danceny? No: the very thought of Danceny throws me into despair . . . How shall I tell you? How shall I say it? . . . I don't know what to do. But my heart is full . . . I must speak to someone, and in you alone can I, dare I confide. You have been so kind to me! What shall I say? I do not want you to be kind. Everyone here has offered me sympathy today . . . they have only increased my wrechedness: I was so very much aware that I did not deserve it! Scold me instead; give me a good scolding, for I am very much to blame. But then save me. If you will not have the kindness to advise me I shall die of grief.

Know then . . . my hand trembles, as you see. I can scarcely write. I feel my cheeks on fire . . . Oh, it is the very blush of shame. Well, I shall endure it. It shall be the first punishment for my fault. Yes, I shall tell you everything.

You must know, then, that Monsieur de Valmont who hitherto has delivered Monsieur Danceny's letters to me, suddenly found it too difficult to continue in the usual way. He wanted a key to my room. I can certainly assure you that I did not want to give him one: but he went so far as to write to Danceny, and Danceny wanted me to do so. I am always so sorry to refuse him anything, particularly since our separation which has made him so unhappy, that I finally agreed. I had no idea of the misfortune that would follow.

Last night Monsieur de Valmont used the key to come into my room as I slept. I was so little expecting this that he really frightened me when he woke me. But as he immediately began to speak, I recognized him and did not to cry out; then, too, it occurred to me at first that he had come to bring me a letter from Danceny. Far from it. Very shortly afterwards he attempted to kiss me; and while I defended myself, as was natural, he cleverly did what I should not have wished for all the world . . . but first he wanted a kiss. I had to: what else could I do? The more so since I had tried to ring, but besides the fact that I could not, he was careful to tell me that if someone came he would easily be able to throw all the blame on me; and, in fact, it would have been easy on account of the key. After this he budged not an inch. He wanted a second kiss; and, I don't know why, but this time I was quite flustered and afterwards it was even worse than before. Oh, really, it was too wicked. Then, after that . . . you will spare my telling you the rest, but I am as unhappy as anyone could possibly be.

Marquis de Sade

1740–1814

The French writer Donatien-Alphonse-François-Comte de Sade was born in Paris, the son of a diplomat, and fought in the Seven Years War. He spent most of his life in and out of prison (including the Bastille) for his notoriously violent libertine practices, until in 1803 Napoleon had him confined for good to the Charenton lunatic asylum, where he directed his own plays. His pornographic romances include Justine *(1791) and* Les Crimes de l'amour *(1800). Sadism, the infliction of pain for sexual pleasure, is named after him.*

From **The One Hundred and Twenty Days of Sodom** (1785).
Trans. Austryn Wainhouse and Richard Seaver

The time has finally arrived, my Lords, to relate the passion of the Marquis de Mesanges to whom, you will recall, I sold the daughter of the unfortunate shoemaker, Petignon, who perished in jail with his wife while I enjoyed the inheritance his mother had left for him. As 'twas Lucile who satisfied him, you will allow me to place the story in her mouth.

'I arrive at the Marquis' mansion,' that charming girl told me, 'at about ten o'clock in the morning. As soon as I enter, all the doors are shut.

' "What are you doing here, little bitch?" says the Marquis, all afire. "Who gave you permission to disturb me?"

' And since you gave me no prior warning of what was to happen, you may readily imagine how terrified I was by this reception.

' "Well, take off your clothes, be quick about it," the Marquis continues. "Since I've got my hands on you, whore, you'll not get out of here with your skin intact . . . indeed, you're going to perish – your last minutes have arrived."

'I burst into tears, I fall down at the Marquis' feet, but nothing would bend him. And as I was not quick enough in undressing, he himself tore my clothes off, ripping them away by sheer force. But what truly petrified me was to see him throw them one after another into the fire.

' "You'll have no further use for these," he muttered, casting each article into a large grate. "No further need for this mantelet, this dress, these stockings, this bodice, no,' said he when all had been consumed, "all you'll need now is a coffin."

'And there I was, naked; the Marquis, who had never before seen me, contemplated my ass for a brief space, he uttered oaths as he fondled it, but he did not bring his lips near it.

' "Very well, whore," said he, "enough of this, you're going to follow your clothes, I'm going to bind you to those andirons; yes, by fuck, yes indeed, by sweet Jesus, I'm going to burn you alive, you bitch, I'm going to have the pleasure of inhaling the aroma of your burning flesh."

'And so saying he falls half-unconscious into an armchair and discharges, darting his fuck upon the remnants of my burning clothes. He rings, a valet enters and then leads me out, and in another room I find a complete new outfit, clothes twice as fine as those he has incinerated.'

That is the account of it I had from Lucile; it remains now to discover whether 'twas for that or for worse he employed the girl I sold him.

Johann Wolfgang von Goethe

1749–1832

The German poet, novelist and dramatist Goethe was born at Frankfurt into a wealthy and influential family. His studies (at Leipzig University) and subsequent legal career were interrupted by successive love affairs, which provided the inspiration for his 1774 novel The Sorrows of Young Werther, *whose suicidally sensitive artist-hero brought him European fame. Perhaps the leading German intellectual of his time, Goethe met Napoleon and Beethoven, and was a friend of Schiller. His enormously varied work includes the archetypal* Bildungsroman, Wilhelm Meister *(1829) and the two parts of his panoramic verse tragedy* Faust *(1808 and 1832).*

From **Roman Elegies**. *Trans. David Luke*

Here my garden is growing, the flowers of Eros I tend here;
They are the Muse's own choice, bedded out wisely they bloom.
Branches that bear ripe fruit, the golden fruit of the life-tree:
Gladly I planted them once, gladly I nurture them now.
Stand here beside them, Priapus! I've nothing to fear from marauders;
Anyone's welcome, it's all free to be picked and enjoyed.
But keep the hypocrites out those miscreants flaccid and shamefaced!
If one should dare to approach, peep at our charming domain,
Turn up his nose at the fruits of pure Nature, just punish his backside
With one thrust of that red stake-shaft that sprouts from your hips.

Robert Burns

1759–1796

The Scottish poet Robert Burns was born into a poor cottar's family near Alloway in Ayrshire, and had to support himself through school by working as a farm labourer. The publication in 1786 of Poems, chiefly in the Scottish Dialect *turned him into a literary celebrity (and national hero), despite or perhaps because of his notorious philandering. From 1791 he worked as an excise officer in Dumfries, though he continued collecting and writing ballads for James Johnson's* Scots Musical Museum *(1793–1803).*

'Wat ye what my Minnie did' (**Merry Muses of Caledonia**, *c.* 1800)

O wat ye what my Minnie did
My Minnie did, My Minnie did
O wat ye what my Minnie did
My Minnie did to me jo

She pat me in a dark room
A dark room, a dark room
She pat me in a dark room
A styme I couldna see jo

An' there cam' in a lang man
A merkle man, a strang man
An' there cam' in a lang man
He might hae worried me jo

For he pou'd out a lang thing
A merkle thing, a strang thing
For he pou'd out a lang thing
Just like a stannin' tree jo

An' I had but a wee thing
A little thing, a wee thing
An' I had but a wee thing
Just like a needle e'e jo

But an I had wanted that
Had wanted that, had wanted that
But an I had wanted that
He might hae sticket me jo

For he shot in hislang thing
His merkle thing, his strang thing
For he shot in hislang thing
Into my needle e'e jo

But had it no come out again
Out again, out again
But had it no come out again
It might hae stay't for me jo

Giacomo Casanova

1725–1798

The Italian adventurer and autobiographer Casanova came from a Venetian theatrical family and was a gifted student at Padua University. Twice forced to leave Venice, he travelled round Europe, becoming librarian for a Bohemian nobleman in Austria in 1782. His 12-volume unfinished History of My Life *records the gossip of European court life and his own sexual libertinism. He is also thought to have helped Lorenzo da Ponte with the libretto for Mozart's* Don Giovanni *(1787).*

From **History of My Life** (1828–38). *Trans. Willard R. Trask*

'Tell me, Marta and Nanetta, do you consider me a man of honour?'

'Yes, certainly.'

'Well and good. Do you want to convince me of it? You must both lie down beside me completely undressed, and count on my word of honour, which I now give you that I will not touch you. You are two and I am one – what have you to fear? Won't you be free to leave the bed if I do not behave myself? In short, if you will not promise to show me this proof of your confidence, at least when you see that I have fallen asleep, I will not go to bed.'

I then stopped talking and pretended to fall asleep, and they whispered together; then Marta told me to get into bed and said they would do likewise when they saw that I was asleep. Nanetta made the same promise, whereupon I turned my back to them, took off all my clothes, got into the bed, and wished them good night. I pretended to fall asleep at once, but within a quarter of an hour I was asleep in good earnest. I woke only when they came and got into the bed, but I at once turned away and resumed my sleep, nor did I begin to act until I had reason to suppose that they were sleeping. If they were not, they had only to pretend to be. They had turned their backs to me and we were in darkness. I began with the one toward whom I was turned, not knowing whether it was Nanetta or Marta. I found her curled up and covered by her shift, but by doing nothing to startle her and proceeding step by step as gradually as possible, I soon convinced her that her best course was to pretend to be asleep and let me go on. Little by little I straightened her out, little by little she uncurled, and little by little, with slow, successive, but wonderfully natural movements, she put herself in a position which was the most favourable she could offer me without betraying herself. I set to work, but to crown my labours it was necessary that she should join in them openly and undeniably, and nature finally forced her to do so. I found this first sister beyond suspicion, and suspecting the pain she must have endured, I was surprised. In duty bound religiously to respect a prejudice to which I owed a pleasure the sweetness of which I was tasting for the first time in my life, I let the victim alone and turned the other way to do the same thing with her sister, who must be expecting me to demonstrate the full extent of my gratitude.

I found her motionless, in the position often taken by a person who is lying on his back in deep, untroubled sleep. With the greatest precautions, and every appearance of fearing to waken her, I began by delighting her soul, at the same time assuring myself that she was as untouched as her sister; and I continued the same treatment until, affecting a most natural movement without which I could not have crowned my labours, she helped me to triumph; but at the moment of crisis she no longer had the strength to keep up her pretense. Throwing off the mask, she clasped me in her arms and pressed her mouth on mine. After the act, 'I am sure,' I said, 'that you are Nanetta.'

'Yes, and I consider myself fortunate, as my sister is, if you are honourable and loyal.'

'Even unto death, my angels! All that we have done was the work of love.'

Friedrich Schlegel

1772–1829

A German novelist and critic, born in Hanover, Schlegel studied law and classics at Göttingen and Leipzig, then moved to Berlin where he became a leading figure in the German Romantic movement, contributing critical articles on writers such as Goethe and Lessing to periodicals. His novel Lucinde *caused a sensation by seeming to record his adulterous affair with Dorothea Veit, then married to a wealthy banker. Increasingly conservative as he got older, he became a civil servant to the Austrian government.*

From **Lucinde** (1799). *Trans. Peter Firchow*

Lucinde had a decided bent for the romantic. He was struck by this further similarity to himself and was always discovering new ones. She also belonged to that part of mankind that doesn't inhabit the ordinary world but rather a world that it conceives and creates for itself. Only whatever she loved and respected in her heart had any true reality for her; everything else was spurious: and she knew what was valuable. Also she had renounced all ties and social rules daringly and decisively and lived a completely free and independent life.

This wonderful similarity soon attracted the young man to her. He noticed that she felt their kinship too, and both became aware that they weren't indifferent to each other. They hadn't known each other for very long and Julius only dared to speak single, disconnected words to her, words full of meaning but not very clear. He longed to know more about her fate and former life, something she had been extremely secretive about to others. She confessed to him – but not without severe emotional agony – that she had been the mother of a lovely boy who had died soon after birth. He, too, recalled his past, and by telling her about it saw his life for the first time as a connected whole. How happy Julius was when he talked with her about music and heard from her mouth his own inmost thoughts about the sacred enchantment of this romantic art! How happy he was when he heard her singing and listened to that

Nightmare Henry Fuseli

pure and powerfully formed voice softly rising from the depths of her soul! How happy when he accompanied her, and their voices merged into one, and when they exchanged unspoken questions and answers in the language of the tenderest feelings. He couldn't resist the temptation and pressed a bashful kiss on her fresh lips and fiery eyes. With eternal rapture he felt the divine head of this noble creature sink upon his shoulder, and saw the black hair flow over the snow of her full breasts. Softly he said 'magnificent woman!' – and just then some accursed guests came into the room.

According to his principles, she had now actually granted him everything. It wasn't possible for him to begin quibbling in a relationship which had been so purely and nobly conceived, and yet every delay was intolerable. It seemed to him that one shouldn't ask a goddess to grant something that one conceives of only as a means to an end, a transition to something else, but admit openly and confidently just what it is one wants. And so he asked her with unaffected innocence for everything a lover can grant, and described to her with flowing eloquence how his passion would destroy him if she was going to be too feminine. She was quite surprised but foresaw that he would be more loving and faithful to her after her surrender than before. She was unable to arrive at a decision and so left the matter to arrange itself by chance. They had been alone a few days when she gave herself to him forever and opened up to him the depths of her soul and all the power, nature, and holiness that was in her. She had also lived long in enforced seclusion, and now all at once from the depths of their hearts their suppressed faith and sympathy broke out in streams of words that were interrupted only by embraces. In a single night they alternated more than once between passionate tears and loud laughter. They were completely devoted and joined to each other, and yet each was wholly himself, more than he had ever been before, and every expression was full of the deepest feeling and the most unique individuality. At one moment an everlasting rapture would seize them, at another they would flirt and tease each other, and Cupid was here truly what he is so seldom – a happy child.

It became clear to Julius from what was revealed to him that only a woman could be truly unhappy and truly happy, and that, having remained the creatures of nature in the midst of human society, women alone possessed that childlike consciousness with which one has to accept the favours and gifts of the gods. He learned to value the beautiful happiness he had found, and when he compared it with that ugly, false happiness that he had earlier tried to extort artfully from stubborn chance, then his happiness seemed to him like a natural rose on a living branch compared to an artificial one.

NINETEENTH
CENTURY

Proserpine Dante Gabriel Rossetti

Rejecting the rationalism of the Enlightenment, the late eighteenth-century Romantics had opened the door and welcomed in experience. The precursory Gothic movement made popular by Horace Walpole and the more overtly macabre erotic fantasies in the drawings of Henry Fuseli (1741–1825) had emphasized emotional experience in their portrayal of mysterious danger and sexually tinged evil. In Germany, widely considered the birthplace of Romanticism, Goethe's *Young Werther* (1774) and the *Sturm und Drang* movement placed an overwhelming emphasis on intensity of passion. In England William Blake (1757–1827) demanded that daylight be shed on Eros: 'Can delight,/Chain'd in night,/The virgins of youth and morning bear?'

Romanticism burst into full bloom in the nineteenth century with the English poets who were unafraid of fantasy as a means of giving expression to emotional experience. Wordsworth, Shelley and, above all, Keats (see page 222), revolted against classical form, conservative morality and human moderation, giving full rein to the power of joy and love in nature. The rebellious spirit of the movement was perhaps epitomized by the life of Lord Byron, although his views were closer in spirit to contemporary conventional aristocratic attitudes than to the Romantics. Violently antipathetic towards the works of Keats and Wordsworth, his preference for sense rather than sensibility expressed in the scepticism of *Don Juan* (see page 221), marks him as an anti-Romantic.

In France, where Romanticism was in part a reaction against the authoritarian attitudes of the court, Jean Jacques Rousseau (1712–78) had explored the conflict between reason and emotion, allowing emotion to triumph in his influential novel *La Nouvelle Héloïse* (1761). French Romanticism reached a peak in writers such as Théophile Gautier, Victor Hugo, Honoré de Balzac, Stendhal, Alfred de Musset, Prosper Merimée and the prolific George Sand, all of whom made use of human love and sexual feeling as the paradigm of social solidarity. Balzac's erotic *Les Contes drôlatiques* (see page 232), written in carefully researched medieval French, were a not altogether successful attempt to recreate the bawdy anti-clerical medieval tales of Marguerite de Navarre (see page 119). Sand's fiction (see page 230) mirrored her own life-style – passionate, romantic and sexually liberated – but it was primarily as a novelist of Nature rather than the erotic that she was to influence writers such as George Eliot, the Brontës, Thomas Hardy and Henry James.

Sand's novels outraged society, and not simply because she was a woman. At the same time there was a huge demand for lubricity; pornography poured off the printing presses and sold in its thousands. In *The Other Victorians* (1966) Steven Marcus makes a case for one notorious example, *The Lustful Turk* (see page 229), as an example of the juncture of literature and pornography through its use of the trappings of the Gothic romance:

> 'The Abbots, monasteries, novices, burials alive, illicit relations, etc., all function as parts of a tissue of reference through which the whole of reality is sexualized. Such a circumstance confirms again what has often been suspected. Romanticism, especially in its more popular forms, has often been regarded as a movement from beneath upward, as gestures from the underground, a giving of articulation to what had hitherto been ignored, denied or constrained. We are doubly confirmed in this notion when we see that Romanticism, once it establishes itself above ground, could then with consummate ease feed back into the underground, the real underground, the underworld or underlife of pornography.'

'It is better every way that what cannot be spoken and ought not to have been written should not be written,' thundered the *Edinburgh Review*. Economics reinforced moralistic convention in dictating that the novel was aimed at public or family reading. The new circulating libraries promoted the three-volume, morally safe Victorian novel, censoriously ensuring their members were edified and protected from so much as a hint of eroticism. Paradoxically, pornography also shared something in common with much of the verbally prudish, morally 'correct' bourgeois fiction of the period. While drawing upon fantasy, pornography often purported to be didactically 'social realist' or 'autobiographical' to acquire a spurious authenticity. This was nothing new; the whore dialogues of the preceding centuries had often been deliberately educational as well as purposely arousing. In the nineteenth century the supposedly factual aspect of pornography reflected the scientism of an age which quickly grasped the erotic potential of photography. The new psychologists and pornographers alike used this invention to show, for instance, 'nymphomaniac' women in lewd poses.

In their different ways both *My Secret Life* by 'Walter' (see page 272) and *The Memoirs of Dolly Morton* by 'Hughes Rebell' (see page 268) appealed to the prurient Victorian mind by blending real life with fantasy. *My Secret Life* is the meticulously recorded sexual memoirs of a British Casanova, who may have been the erotic bibliophile Henry Spencer Ashbee. Among the stories of troilism, female 'spendings', improbable virile prowess and that peculiarly English obsession with flagellation to which Swinburne and Beardsley were so drawn, 'Walter' also provides a mine of information about nineteenth-century social and sexual mores comparable to the work of the English social reformer Henry Mayhew, as well as serious treatises on copulation and male and female genitalia.

It is more difficult to believe in the 'realism' of *Dolly Morton* (actually written by Georges Grassall, a friend and admirer of Oscar Wilde). While claiming to be an attack on Southern white American male chauvinism and racism, the book makes use of the traditional devices of pornography – the pleasures in store for raped virgins, huge phalluses and whipped slaves – in what today seems to be an example of racist and sexist pornography.

To censorious Victorian sensibilities it became important to mark clear boundaries between 'high' literature, often classified as erotica, and low pornography, a newly coined term. Fears of social upheaval and of masturbation underlay much of the moral condemnation towards anything remotely erotic, but the boundaries between the two were not always easy to delineate. The sense of shame Puritans associated with sexual relations and which drove pornography underground also affected literary erotica. Bowdlerism, initiated in Regency England, was codified in the 1857 Obscene Publications Act, and American 'comstockery' (from the name of the zealous censor who made it illegal to post any obscene publication through the US mails) attempted to suppress the sort of literature which had been widely praised in the previous century. Although both Gustave Flaubert (1821–80) and Charles Baudelaire (see page 241) were fined for offending public morality, Europeans tended to rely on public moral outrage to curb the erotic excesses of writers, making France, Germany and Italy a safe haven for British writers to print and publish their erotic books.

The eroticism in the poetry of Emily Dickinson (see page 244), of the Jesuit Gerard Manley Hopkins (see page 254) and of his fellow Catholic Francis Thompson (see page 256) went largely unnoticed, partly because literary poetry was not deemed to constitute a threat to the fabric of society, but also, perhaps, because it derived from an unconscious impulse. However, not all 'high' literature was safe from a fear of the supposed harm that Eros would cause. The erotic imaginings of Christina Rossetti so disturbed her brother when editing her posthumously published poem 'A Nightmare' (see page 244), that he changed the word 'love' to 'friend' and 'rides' to 'hunts'. (Riding as a metaphor for sexual intercourse went back at least to the late sixteenth century and was put to extraordinarily transparent use in the poem 'The Last Ride Together' (see page 238) by Robert Browning.

The English erotophile Sir Richard Burton (1829–90) circumvented risk of prosecution for publishing his unexpurgated translations of the *Arabian Nights*, *The Kama Sutra*, *The Perfumed Garden* and other Oriental erotic texts by printing them in Paris. His widow, however, burnt his journals and an unpublished translation of an Oriental classic. The wealthy gentleman-traveller Henry Ashbee felt it necessary to print privately his mammoth three-volume annotated bibliography devoted to erotic writing, and did so under the pseudonym of Pisanus Fraxi. Ashbee's possibly tongue-in-cheek aim in publishing his *Index Librorum Prohibitorum* (1877), whose very title cocked a snook at the Papal Index of forbidden books, was 'to catalogue, as thoroughly, and at the same time, as tersely as possible, books which, as a rule, have not been mentioned by former bibliographers, and to notice them in such a way that the student or collector may be able to form a pretty just estimate of their value or purport, without having recourse to the books themselves'. Ashbee bequeathed his vast collection of erotica to the British Museum, where it forms the nucleus of the Private Case of erotica, which were kept under lock and key and excluded from the printed catalogue until recently.

Much nineteenth-century English and European fiction responded to the aristocratic licentious excesses of the late eighteenth century, with increasing puritanical verbal prudery. The French 'naturalist' writers, led by Honoré de Balzac (see page 232) and followed by Gustave Flaubert, the brothers Goncourt, Alphonse Daudet (see page 260) and Émile Zola (see page 252), as well as Gerhart Hauptmann in Germany (see page 261), refused to be affected by conventional bourgeois notions of morality. Zola's realistic portrayals of poverty, prostitution, murder and sexual nightmare reflected his belief that 'love and death, possessing and killing, are the dark foundations of the human soul'. His fiction, especially *Thérèse Raquin*, scandalized the moralizing critics, who dubbed him a pornographer and regarded this work as a quagmire of filth. The Austrian lawyer Leopold Sacher-Masoch whose novel *Venus in Furs* (see page 245) is responsible for the word 'masochism', the English critic, poet and novelist Algernon Swinburne (see page 251), and the French High Romantics, Charles Baudelaire (see page 241), Arthur Rimbaud (see page 256) and Paul Verlaine (see page 260) were all considered hugely shocking to societies in which underworld pornography circulated furiously.

Nowhere was puritanism so strong as in the New World. There is a sense of the erotic impulse being so deeply buried in the American puritan unconscious that some critics have been persuaded that it did not exist until the mid-nineteenth century, when Walt Whitman's startling, sexually emancipated verse, *Leaves of Grass*, was published (see page 240). But Eros had lurked in the fervid misogynist fantasies of seventeenth-century New England witch-hunters as clearly as it had in the minds of the Elizabethan Puritans and the earlier papally-endorsed, sex-obsessed Inquisitors. It is unmissable in the teasing *Advice on the Choice of a Mistress* (1745) by Benjamin Franklin (1706–90), who concluded that an old woman was preferable to a young one because 'the sin is less. The debauching of a virgin may be her ruin, and make her for life unhappy'.

No pornography was produced in the USA until the middle of the nineteenth century, and even then the racy stories of George Thompson (see page 237) display a certain coyness, hinting at taboos rather than describing them explicitly. They may, however, have proved even more exciting than the overtly sexual English and European imports which were widely read. (This technique was most famously used – who can say whether with the deliberate intention to arouse – by the French medieval writer Chrétien de Troyes; we never learn exactly what Lancelot and his Queen got up to, but we know it was naughty and we suspect they enjoyed it precisely because of the veil he draws.) In 1879 Mark Twain rather surprisingly entered the world of pornography with *1601 or Conversation As It Was by the Social Fireside in the Time of the Tudors* (see page 249), dedicated to his friend the Reverend Josiah Twichell, whom he described as 'that robust divine . . . who had no special scruples concerning Shakespearian parlance and customs'. Scatological and bawdy rather than erotic, Twain used satire to attack hypocrisy and conventional morality in much the same way as Aretino (see page 117) had done.

The verbal prudery that characterized so much of Victorian middle-class literature was an important factor in the USA, where there was an almost fanatical concern for decency arising from the elevated importance of family life. The eroticism in Nathaniel Hawthorne's *The Scarlet Letter* (see page 235) is a subtle, shimmering affair, only just discernible. The phallic imagery of Herman Melville's contemporaneous *Moby Dick* (1851), a novel that embodies a belief in the close connections between the sources of artistic and sexual creativity, was, and doubtless still is, lost on those keen only to see a vigorous sea tale. Emily Dickinson (see page 244) – none of whose verse was published in her lifetime, although this may not be connected to its homoerotic and sado-masochistic content – had an ingrained sense of decorum, complaining of those who 'talk of hallowed things aloud, and embarrass my dog'. Her brilliantly intense poems have been described as reaching personal erotic feelings buried so deep that they could only be touched with circumspection.

In the 1880s male novelists in England began to revolt against the trend of the three-volume novel designed primarily for family reading, and the moralistic stranglehold of the circulating libraries. The novelist George Gissing (1857–1903) wrote of 'sexual anarchy'; it was a period during which conventional laws governing sexual identity and behaviour seemed to be breaking down. The *fin de siècle* writers Pierre Louÿs (see page 262), Oscar Wilde (see page 264) and Aubrey Beardsley (see page 266) deliberately blurred the boundaries between 'high' literature and underworld pornography. Underlining the onanistic nature of such writings, American literary critic Elaine Showalter notes, 'Unsuitable for family consumption, these books were more likely to be read alone and perhaps even under the covers. Sex and the single book became the order of the day.'

During most of the nineteenth century women writers, while largely mute on matters erotic, ruled the fiction scene. The American Kate Chopin (see page 267) was an exception. Not only was she one of the few women at the end of the century to write fiction that looked directly at the sensuous and the erotic, she was also one of the very few women to be writing fiction at all. Unwilling to pay obeisance to 'comstockery', she wrote uncompromisingly about the modern woman's dilemma in confronting sexual passion with a sensuous awareness which caused such outrage that it ended her literary career.

The novels, dramas and poetry of *fin de siècle* decadent male writers in England were peopled by inverts, hermaphrodites, single men and by 'new' and 'odd' women. They were strongly influenced by the early French decadents such as Baudelaire (variously described as 'late Romantic', 'early Symbolist' and a 'lyricist of moral decay') and the French writer Joris-Karl Huysmans (1848–1907), whose erotic novel *À Rebours* (1884), with its often perverse detail, Wilde claimed as a direct inspiration for his novel *A Picture of Dorian Gray* (1891). French erotica had long held sway over the English, not simply because of the immunity offered by publishing across the English Channel, but because of an alluring glamour which Robert Browning well understood: 'Or, my scrofulus French novel/On grey paper with blunt type!/Simply glance at it, you grovel/Hand and foot in Belial's gripe.'

Not that the English decadents were interested in reproducing shoddy French pornography. *The Yellow Book*, a beautifully-produced *fin de siècle* quarterly magazine, and Wilde's erotic masterpiece *Salome* (see page 264) which he originally wrote in French, were both illustrated by Beardsley and represented Wilde's view that beauty was the highest sense of which a human was capable and that only a badly written book could produce a sense of disgust.

Gender confusion and sexual sadism also bloodied the pages of highly popular novels like H.G. Wells's *The Island of Dr Moreau* (1896) and Bram Stoker's *Dracula* (1897). Wells wrote his novel in response to the scandal caused by Wilde's highly publicized trial for homosexuality in 1895, which created a moral panic and ushered in a period of oppression and censorship affecting both early feminists and homosexuals throughout Western society. The merest suggestion of lesbianism in Thomas Hardy's *Jude the Obscure* (1895) caused one reviewer to denounce it as 'Jude the Obscene'. The scientific works of sexologists and sex reformers, including Havelock Ellis (1859–1939), Edward Carpenter (1844–1929) and Richard von Krafft-Ebing (1840–1902), who were busy defying conventional attitudes by writing openly about (and defining) homosexuality and perversion, were prosecuted with vigour.

But, as the twentieth-century French philosopher Michel Foucault convincingly argued, it is simplistic to analyse nineteenth-century attitudes towards erotic literature only in terms of repression and censorship. 'Mrs Grundyism', a term originating in Tom Morton's play *Speed the Plough* (1798), meant not that sex had been negated but that the boundaries of what could be said and written about sex were actually enlarged. Contrary to popular belief, all social relations were sexualized and sex was transformed into discourse. The autobiographical erotic work of writers as diverse as Colette (see page 287) and Frank Harris (see page 297) followed hard on the heels of 'Walter' in spelling out 'not only consummated acts, but all sensual touchings, all impure gazes, all obscene remarks . . . all consenting thoughts'. (Michel Foucault, *The History of Sexuality*, 1979).

Fear, however, continued to smother Blake's visionary call for delight to be unchained from night. When a petition in Wilde's defence was circulated in France, no member of the literary establishment, many of whom had themselves suffered from the moral condemnation of prudish and moralizing bourgeois society, would sign it.

Lord Byron

1788–1824

The English poet George Gordon (Lord) Byron was educated at Harrow and Cambridge. He recorded his extensive travels in Childe Harold's Pilgrimage *(1812 and 1818), which helped foster the legend of the Byronic hero: romantic, handsome, melancholy, and an outsider. The scandals following his love affairs – with Lady Caroline Lamb and (reputedly) his half-sister Augusta – forced him to leave England for Venice, where he wrote his great epic satire* Don Juan. *He died from fever at Missolonghi, on his way to help liberate Greece from Turkish rule.*

From **Don Juan** (1819–24)

Alas, they were so young, so beautiful,
So lonely, loving, helpless, and the hour
Was that in which the heart is always full,
And having o'er itself no further power,
Prompts deeds eternity cannot annul,
But pays off moments in an endless shower
Of hell-fire, all prepared for people giving
Pleasure or pain to one another living.

Alas for Juan and Haidée! They were
So loving and so lovely; till then never,
Excepting our first parents, such a pair
Had run the risk of being damned forever.
And Haidée, being devout as well as fair,
Had doubtless heard about the Stygian river
And hell and purgatory, but forgot
Just in the very crisis she should not.

They look upon each other, and their eyes
Gleam in the moonlight, and her white arm
    clasps

Round Juan's head, and his around hers lies
Half buried in the tresses which it grasps.
She sits upon his knee and drinks his sighs,
He hers, until they end in broken gasps;
And thus they form a group that's quite antique,
Half naked, loving, natural, and Greek.

And when those deep and burning moments
    passed,
And Juan sunk to sleep within her arms,
She slept not, but all tenderly, though fast,
Sustained his head upon her bosom's charms.
And now and then her eye to heaven is cast,
And then on the pale cheek her breast now
    warms,
Pillowed on her o'erflowing heart, which pants
With all it granted and with all it grants.

An infant when it gazes on a light,
A child the moment when it drains the breast,
A devotee when soars the Host in sight,

An Arab with a stranger for a guest,
A sailor when the prize has struck in fight,
A miser filling his most hoarded chest
Feel rapture, but not such true joy are reaping
As they who watch o'er what they love while
    sleeping.

For there it lies so tranquil, so beloved;
All that it hath of life with us is living,
So gentle, stirless, helpless, and unmoved,
And all unconscious of the joy 'tis giving.
All it hath felt, inflicted, passed, and proved,
Hushed into depths beyond the watcher's
    diving,
There lies the thing we love with all its errors
And all its charms, like death without its terrors.

The lady watched her lover; and that hour
Of love's and night's and ocean's solitude

O'erflowed her soul with their united power.
Amidst the barren sand and rocks so rude
She and her wave-worn love had made their
    bower,
Where nought upon their passion could
    intrude,
And all the stars that crowded the blue
    space
Saw nothing happier than her glowing face.

Alas, the love of women! It is known
To be a lovely and a fearful thing,
For all of theirs upon that die is thrown,
And if 'tis lost, life hath no more to bring
To them but mockeries of the past alone,
And their revenge is as the tiger's spring,
Deadly and quick and crushing; yet as real
Torture is theirs, what they inflict they feel.

John Keats

1795–1821

The son of a London livery-stable manager, Keats abandoned a career in medicine to devote himself to poetry. He published volumes of poems in 1817 and 1820; the second was written when he was already becoming ill with the tuberculosis that was to kill him. His work received scathing reviews at the time, but his reputation grew throughout the 19th century, with the Victorians particularly revering his poignant lyricism.

From 'The Eve of St Agnes' (1818)

Sudden a thought came like a full-blown rose,
Flushing his brow, and in his painèd heart
Made purple riot; then doth he propose
A strategem, that makes the beldame start:
'A cruel man and impious thou art:
Sweet lady, let her pray, and sleep, and dream
Alone with her good angels, far apart
From wicked men like thee. Go, go! – I deem
Thou canst not surely be the same that thou didst seem.'

'I will not harm her, by all saints I swear,'
Quoth Porphyro: 'O may I ne'er find grace
When my weak voice shall whisper its last prayer,
If one of her soft ringlets I displace,

Or look with ruffian passion in her face:
Good Angela, believe me by these tears,
Or I will, even in a moment's space,
Awake, with horrid shout, my foeman's ears,
And beard them, though they be more fanged than wolves and bears.'

'Ah! why wilt thou affright a feeble soul?
A poor, weak, palsy-stricken, churchyard thing,
Whose passing-bell may ere the midnight toll;
Whose prayers for thee, each morn and evening,
Were never missed.' – Thus plaining, doth she bring
A gentler speech from burning Porphyro,
So woeful, and of such deep sorrowing,
That Angela gives promise she will do
Whatever he shall wish, betide her weal or woe.

Which was, to lead him, in close secrecy,
Even to Madeline's chamber, and there hide
Him in a closet, of such privacy
That he might see her beauty unespied,
And win perhaps that night a peerless bride,
While legioned faeries paced the coverlet,
And pale enchantment held her sleepy-eyed.
Never on such a night have lovers met,
Since Merlin paid his Demon all the monstrous debt.

'It shall be as thou wishest,' said the Dame:
'All cates and dainties shall be storèd there
Quickly on this feast-night; by the tambour frame
Her own lute thou wilt see. No time to spare,
For I am slow and feeble, and scarce dare
On such a catering trust my dizzy head.
Wait here, my child, with patience; kneel in prayer
The while. Ah! thou must needs the lady wed,
Or may I never leave my grave among the dead.'

So saying, she hobbled off with busy fear.
The lover's endless minutes slowly passed;
The dame returned, and whispered in his ear
To follow her; with agèd eyes aghast
From fright of dim espial. Safe at last,
Through many a dusky gallery, they gain
The maiden's chamber, silken, hushed, and chaste;
Where Porphyro took covert, pleased amain.
His poor guide hurried back with agues in her brain.

Her faltering hand upon the balustrade,
Old Angela was feeling for the stair,
When Madeline, St Agnes' charmèd maid,
Rose, like a missioned spirit, unaware:
With silver taper's light, and pious care,
She turned, and down the agèd gossip led
To a safe level matting. Now prepare,
Young Porphyro, for gazing on that bed –
She comes, she comes again, like ring-dove frayed and fled.

Out went the taper as she hurried in;
Its little smoke, in pallid moonshine, died:
She closed the door, she panted, all akin
To spirits of the air, and visions wide –
No uttered syllable, or, woe betide!
But to her heart, her heart was voluble,
Paining with eloquence her balmy side;
As though a tongueless nightingale should swell
Her throat in vain, and die, heart-stiflèd, in her dell.

A casement high and triple-arched there was,
All garlanded with carven imag'ries
Of fruits, and flowers, and bunches of knot-grass,
And diamonded with panes of quaint device,
Innumerable of stains and splendid dyes,
As are the tiger-moth's deep-damasked wings;
And in the midst, 'mong thousand heraldries,
And twilight saints, and dim emblazonings,
A shielded scutcheon blushed with blood of queens and kings.

Full on this casement shone the wintry moon,
And threw warm gules on Madeline's fair breast,
As down she knelt for heaven's grace and boon;
Rose-bloom fell on her hands, together pressed,
And on her silver cross soft amethyst,
And on her hair a glory, like a saint:
She seemed a splendid angel, newly dressed,
Save wings, for Heaven – Porphyro grew faint;
She knelt, so pure a thing, so free from mortal taint.

Anon his heart revives; her vespers done,
Of all its wreathèd pearls her hair she frees;
Unclasps her warmèd jewels one by one;
Loosens her fragrant bodice; by degrees
Her rich attire creeps rustling to her knees:

Half-hidden, like a mermaid in sea-weed,
　　Pensive awhile she dreams awake, and sees,
　　In fancy, fair St Agnes in her bed,
But dares not look behind, or all the charm is fled.

Soon, trembling in her soft and chilly nest,
　　In sort of wakeful swoon, perplexed she lay,
　　Until the poppied warmth of sleep oppressed
　　Her soothèd limbs, and soul fatigued away –
　　Flown, like a thought, until the morrow-day;
　　Blissfully havened both from joy and pain;
　　Clasped like a missal where swart Paynims pray;
　　Blinded alike from sunshine and from rain,
As though a rose should shut, and be a bud again.

Stolen to this paradise, and so entranced,
　　Porphyro gazed upon her empty dress,
　　And listened to her breathing, if it chanced
　　To wake into a slumbrous tenderness;
　　Which when he heard, that minute did he bless,
　　And breathed himself: then from the closet crept,
　　Noiseless as fear in a wide wilderness,
　　And over the hushed carpet silent, stepped,
And 'tween the curtains peeped, where, lo! – how fast she slept.

Then by the bed-side, where the faded moon
　　Made a dim, silver twilight soft he set
　　A table, and, half anguished threw thereon
　　A cloth of woven crimson, gold, and jet –
　　O for some drowsy Morphean amulet:
　　The boisterous, midnight, festive clarion,
　　The kettle-drum, and far-heard clarinet
　　Affray his ears, though but in dying tone; –
The hall door shuts again, and all the noise is gone.

And still she slept an azure-lidded sleep,
　　In blanchèd linen, smooth, and lavendered,
　　While he from forth the closet brought a heap
　　Of candied apple, quince, and plum, and gourd,
　　With jellies soother than the creamy curd,
　　And lucent syrups, tinct with cinnamon:
　　Manna and dates, in argosy transferred
　　From Fez; and spicèd dainties, every one,
From silken Samarkand to cedared Lebanon.

These delicates he heaped with glowing hand
On golden dishes and in baskets bright
Of wreathèd silver; sumptuous they stand
In the retirèd quiet of the night,
Filling the chilly room with perfume light.
'And now, my love, my seraph fair, awake!
Thou art my heaven, and I thine eremite:
Open thine eyes, for meek St Agnes' sake,
Or I shall drowse beside thee, so my soul doth ache.'

Thus whispering, his warm, unnervèd arm
Sank in her pillow. Shaded was her dream
By the dusk curtains – 'twas a midnight charm
Impossible to melt as iced stream:
The lustrous salvers in the moonlight gleam;
Broad golden fringe upon the carpet lies.
It seemed he never, never could redeem
From such a steadfast spell his lady's eyes;
So mused awhile, entoiled in woofèd fantasies.

Awakening up, he took her hollow lute,
Tumultuous, and, in chords that tenderest be,
He played an ancient ditty, long since mute,
In Provence called, 'La belle dame sans mercy',
Close to her ear touching the melody –
Wherewith disturbed, she uttered a soft moan:
He ceased – she panted quick – and suddenly
Her blue affrayèd eyes wide open shone.
Upon his knees he sank, pale as smooth-sculptured stone.

Her eyes were open, but she still beheld,
Now wide awake, the vision of her sleep –
There was a painful change, that nigh expelled
The blisses of her dream so pure and deep.
At which fair Madeline began to weep,
And moan forth witless words with many a sigh,
While still her gaze on Porphyro would keep;
Who knelt, with joinèd hands and piteous eye,
Fearing to move or speak, she looked so dreamingly.

'Ah, Porphyro!' said she, 'but even now
Thy voice was at sweet tremble in mine ear,
Made tuneable with every sweetest vow,
And those sad eyes were spiritual and clear:
How changed thou art! How pallid, chill, and drear!

Give me that voice again my Porphyro.
Those looks immortal, those complainings dear!
O leave me not in this eternal woe,
For if thou diest, my Love, I know not where to go.'

Beyond a mortal man impassioned far
At these voluptuous accents, he arose,
Ethereal, flushed, and like a throbbing star
Seen mid the sapphire heaven's deep repose;
Into her dream he melted, as the rose
Blendeth its odour with the violet –
Solution sweet. Meantime the frost-wind blows
Like Love's alarum pattering the sharp sleet
Against the window-panes; St Agnes' moon hath set.

'Tis dark: quick pattereth the flaw-blown sleet.
'This is no dream, my bride, my Madeline!'
'Tis dark: the icèd gusts still rave and beat.
'No dream, alas! alas! and woe is mine!
Porphyro will leave me here to fade and pine. –
Cruel! what traitor could thee hither bring?
I curse not, for my heart is lost in thine,
Though thou forsakest a deceivèd thing –
A dove forlorn and lost with sick unprunèd wing.'

'My Madeline! sweet dreamer! lovely bride!
Say, may I be for aye thy vassal blessed?
Thy beauty's shield, heart-shaped and vermeil dyed?
Ah, silver shrine, here will I take my rest
After so many hours of toil and quest,
A famished pilgrim – saved by miracle.
Though I have found, I will not rob thy nest
Saving of thy sweet self; if thou think'st well
To trust, fair Madeline, to no rude infidel.

Hark! 'tis an elfin-storm from faery land,
Of haggard seeming, but a boon indeed:
Arise – arise! the morning is at hand.
The bloated wassailers will never heed –
Let us away, my love, with happy speed –
There are no ears to hear, or eyes to see,
Drowned all in Rhenish and the sleepy mead;
Awake! arise! my love, and fearless be,
For o'er the southern moors I have a home for thee.'

She hurried at his words, beset with fears,
For there were sleeping dragons all around,
At glaring watch, perhaps, with ready spears –
Down the wide stairs a darkling way they found.
In all the house was heard no human sound.
A chain-drooped lamp was flickering by each door;
The arras, rich with horseman, hawk, and hound,
Fluttered in the besieging wind's uproar;
And the long carpets rose along the gusty floor.

They glide, like phantoms, into the wide hall;
Like phantoms, to the iron porch, they glide;
Where lay the Porter, in uneasy sprawl,
With a huge empty flaggon by his side:
The wakeful bloodhound rose, and shook his hide,
But his sagacious eye an inmate owns.
By one, and one, the bolts full easy slide –
The chains lie silent on the footworn stones –
The key turns, and the door upon its hinges groans.

And they are gone – ay, ages long ago
These lovers fled away into the storm.
That night the Baron dreamt of many a woe,
And all his warrior-guests, with shade and form
Of witch, and demon, and large coffin-worm,
Were long be-nightmared. Angela the old
Died palsy-twitched, with meagre face deform;
The Beadsman, after thousand aves told,
For aye unsought for slept among his ashes cold.

Heinrich Heine

1797–1856

A German Jewish poet, born in Düsseldorf, Heine's original careers as banker and businessman and then in the law came to nothing, and he turned increasingly to literature. After converting to Christianity in 1825, he moved to Paris in 1831, where he worked as a journalist, though his revolutionary sympathies led briefly to his works being banned in Germany. His poetry is alternately profoundly introspective and polemical, and includes the volume Buch der Lieder *(1827), whose poems have been set to music by composers from Schumann to Richard Strauss.*

'The Song of Songs'

Woman's white body is a song,
And God Himself's the author;
In the eternal book of life
He put the lines together.

It was a thrilling hour; the Lord
Felt suddenly inspired;
Within his brain the stubborn stuff
Was mastered, fused, and fired.

Truly, the Song of Songs is this,
The greatest of his trophies:
This living poem where soft limbs
Are a rare pair of strophes.

Oh, what a heavenly masterpiece
That neck and its relation
To the fair head, like an idea
Crowned with imagination.

In pointed epigrams, the breasts
Rise under teasing rallies;
And a caesura lies between
The loveliest of valleys.

He published the sweet parallel
Of thighs – what joy to be there!
The fig-leaf grotto joining them
Is not a bad place either.

It is no cold, conceptual verse,
No patterned abstract study!

This poem sings with rhyming lips,
With sweet bones and warm body.

Here breathes the deepest poetry!
Beauty in every motion!
Upon its brow it bears the stamp
Of His complete devotion.

Here in the dust, I praise Thee, Lord.
We are – and well I know it –
Rank amateurs, compared to Thee:
Heaven's first major poet!

I'll dedicate myself to learn
This song, the lyric body;
With ardour and with energy
All day – and night – I'll study!

Yes, day and night, I'll never lack
For constant application;
And though the task may break my back
I'll ask for no vacation!

Anon. (England)

From **The Lustful Turk** (1828)

'Never, oh never shall I forget the delicious transport that followed the stiff insertion; and then, ah me! by what thrilling degrees did he, by his luxurious movements, fiery kisses, and strange touches of his hand to the most crimson parts of my body, reduce me to a voluptuous state of insensibility. I blush to say so powerfully did his ravishing instrument stir up nature within me, that by mere instinct I returned him kiss for kiss, responsively meeting his fierce thrusts, until the fury of the pleasure and the ravishing became so overpowering that, unable longer to support the excitement I so luxuriously felt, I fainted in his arms with pleasure . . . '

George Sand

1804–76

The French novelist George Sand (Lucile-Aurore Duderant, née Dupin) was born in Paris and educated at her country home and in a Paris convent. Her marriage to a retired army officer in 1822 produced two sons, but in 1831 she left him to pursue a literary career, writing in support of the 1848 Revolution, and taking a series of lovers, among them Alfred de Musset, Liszt and Chopin. Her novels, often romantic and pastoral, include Indiana *(1832) and* La Mare au diable *(1846).*

From **Lélia** (1833). *Trans. Joseph Barry*

'You are right, my dear sister, we were not alike. Wiser and happier than I, you lived only for enjoyment; I, more ambitious and perhaps less obedient to God, lived only to desire. Do you recall that sultry summer's day when we rested on the bank of a brook under the cedars of the valley, in a mysterious dark retreat where the murmur of water falling from stone to stone mingled with the sad song of the cicadas? We lay down on the grass, and as we looked up through the trees at the burning sky above our heads we were overcome by a deep untroubled slumber. We woke up in each other's arms unaware that we had slept.'

At these words Pulchérie started and squeezed her sister's hand.

'Yes, I recall this better than you, Lélia. It stands as a glowing memory in my life, and I have often thought of that day with emotion full of charm, and maybe also of shame.'

'Of shame?' said Lélia, drawing back her hand.

'You have never known, you have never guessed this,' said Pulchérie. 'I would never have dared to tell you of it then. But now I can confess all, and you can learn all. Listen, dear sister, it was in your innocent arms, on your virgin breast, that God revealed to me for the first time the power of life. Please do not withdraw this way. Put aside your prejudices and listen to me.'

'Prejudices!' exclaimed Lélia, drawing closer again. 'If only I had prejudices! That at least would be some kind of belief. Speak, tell me all, dear sister.'

'Well,' said Pulchérie, 'we were sleeping peacefully in the warm, moist grass. The cedars gave off their exquisite, sweet-smelling scent and the noon wind fanned our damp foreheads with its burning wings. Until then, carefree and merry, I had greeted each day of my life as a new blessing. At times sudden, deep-reaching sensations would stir my blood. A strange ardour would seize my imagination; the colours of nature would seem more sparkling; youth would throb more vivaciously and more cheerfully in my breast; and if I looked at myself in the mirror, I found myself flushed and more beautiful at such moments. I felt like kissing my own reflected image which inspired me with an insane love. Then I would start laughing, and I would run, stronger and lighter, over the grass and the flowers; for nothing was ever revealed to me through suffering. I would not, like you, tire myself out trying to divine things; I would find because I did not seek.

'On that day, happy and calm as I was, the hitherto impenetrable and calmly unquestioned mystery was revealed to me through a strange, delirious, extraordinary dream. Oh, dear sister! you may deny the heavenly influence! You may deny the sanctity of pleasure! But had you been granted this moment of ecstasy, you would have said that an angel from the very bosom of God had been sent to initiate you into the sacred mysteries of human life. As for me, I dreamed simply of a dark-haired man bending over me to brush my lips with his burning red mouth; and I woke up overwhelmed, palpitating and happier than I had ever imagined I could possibly be. I looked around me: the sun was glinting on the depths of the wood; the air was good and sweet and the cedars were lifting their majestic, spreading branches like immense arms and long hands stretching up towards heaven. Then I looked at you. Oh, my dear sister, how beautiful you were! I had never considered you as such before that day. In my complacent girlish conceit I preferred myself to you. I thought that my glowing cheeks, my rounded shoulders, my golden hair made me the more beautiful. But at that moment the meaning of beauty was revealed to me in another creature. I no longer loved only myself: I felt the need to find an object of admiration and love outside myself. Gently I raised myself and I gazed at you with strange curiosity and unusual pleasure. Your thick black hair was sticking to your forehead, its tight curls twisting and intertwining, clinging as if endowed with life to your neck, velvet with shade and perspiration. I ran my fingers through it: your hair seemed to tighten around them and to draw me toward you. Tight over your breast, your thin white shirt displayed skin tanned by the sun to an even darker shade than usual; and your long eyelids, heavy with sleep, stood out against your cheeks which were of a fuller colour than they are today. Oh, how beautiful you were, Lélia! But your beauty was different from mine, and that I found strangely disturbing. Your arms, thinner than mine, were covered by an almost imperceptible dark down which has long since disappeared under the treatment that luxury imposes. Your feet, so perfect in their loveliness, were dipping in the brook, and long blue veins stood out on them. Your breast rose and fell as you breathed with a regularity that seemed to betoken calm and strength; and in all your features, in your posture, in your shape more clear-cut than mine, in the darker shade of your skin, and especially in the proud, cold expression on your sleeping face there was something so masculine and strong that I scarcely recognized you. I felt that you looked like the beautiful dark-haired child I had just been dreaming of, and trembling I kissed your arm. Then you opened your eyes and their expression filled me with an unknown shame; I turned away as if I had done something shameful. And yet, Lélia, no impure thought had even crossed my mind. How did this happen? I was totally ignorant. I was receiving from nature and from God, my creator and my master, my first lesson in love, my first sensation of desire. Your eyes were mocking and severe as they had always been. But never before had they intimidated me as they did at that instant. Do you not recall my confusion and the way I blushed?'

'I even recall a remark that I could not explain,' replied Lélia. 'You made me bend over the water and said: "Look at yourself, dear sister; do you not think that you are beautiful?" I answered that I was less so than you. "Oh, no! much more so," you continued. "You look like a man."'

'And that made you shrug your shoulders contemptuously,' Pulchérie went on.

'And I did not guess,' replied Lélia, 'that destiny had just been achieved for you, while for me no destiny would ever be accomplished.'

'Begin your story,' said Pulchérie.

Honoré de Balzac

1799–1850

The French novelist Balzac, born at Tours, worked as a lawyer's clerk while studying at the Sorbonne. Success as a writer came with the Comédie humaine, *his panoramic and inter-connecting cycle of novels – including* Eugénie Grandet *(1833),* Le Père Goriot *(1834) and* La Cousine Bette *(1834) – which proved formative in the development of the nineteenth-century realist novel. His prolific output (he wrote over 90 novels) also includes the Rabelaisian* Les Contes drôlatiques.

From **Les Contes drôlatiques**: 'The Merry Tattle of the Nuns of Poissy'
(1832–37)

I cannot leave them without relating an adventure which took place in their house, when Reform was passing a sponge over it, and making them all saints, as before stated. At that time, there was in the episcopal chair of Paris a veritable saint, who did not brag about what he did, and cared for naught but the poor and suffering, whom the dear old bishop lodged in his heart, neglecting his own interests for theirs, and seeking out misery in order that he might heal it with words, with help, with attentions, and with money, according to the case: as ready to solace the rich in their misfortunes as the poor, patching up their souls and bringing them back to God; and tearing about hither and thither, watching his troop, the dear shepherd! Now the good man went about careless of the state of his cassocks, mantles, and breeches, so that the naked members of his church were covered. He was so charitable that he would have pawned himself, to save an infidel from distress. His servants were obliged to look after him carefully. Ofttimes he would scold them when they changed unasked his tattered vestments for new; and he used to have them darned and patched, as long as they would hold together. Now this good archbishop knew that the late Sieur de Poissy had left a daughter, without a sou or a rag, after having eaten, drunk, and gambled away her inheritance. This poor young lady lived in a hovel, without fire in winter or cherries in spring; and did needlework, not wishing either to marry beneath her or sell her virtue. Awaiting the time when he should be able to find a young husband for her, the prelate took it into his head to send her the outside case of one to mend, in the person of his old breeches, a task which the young lady, in her present position, would be glad to undertake. One day that the archbishop was thinking to himself that he must go to the convent of Poissy, to see after the reformed inmates, he gave to one of his servants, the oldest of his nether garments, which was sorely in need of stitches, saying, 'Take this, Saintot, to the young ladies of Poissy,' meaning to say, 'the young lady of Poissy.' Thinking of affairs connected with the cloister, he did not inform his varlet of the situation of the lady's house; her desperate condition having been by him discreetly kept a secret. Saintot took the breeches and went his way towards Poissy, gay as a grasshopper, stopping to chat with friends he met on the way, slaking his thirst at the wayside inns, and showing many things to the breeches during their journey that might hereafter be useful to them. At last he arrived at the convent, and informed the abbess that his master had sent him to give her these articles. Then the varlet departed, leaving with the reverend mother, the garment accustomed to model in relief the archiepiscopal proportions of the continent nature of the good man, according to the fashion of the period, beside the image of those things of which the Eternal Father has

Les Diableries érotiques Anonymous

deprived His angels, and which in the good prelate did not want for amplitude. Madame the abbess having informed the sisters of the precious message of the good archbishop, they came in haste, curious and hustling, as ants into whose republic a chestnut husk as fallen. When they undid the breeches, which gaped horribly, they shrieked out, covering their eyes with one hand, in great fear of seeing the devil come out, the abbess exclaiming, 'Hide yourselves, my daughters! This is the abode of mortal sin!'

The mother of the novices, giving a little look between her fingers, revived the courage of the holy troop, swearing by an Ave that no living head was domiciled in the breeches. Then they all blushed at their ease, while examining this Habitavit, thinking that perhaps the desire of the prelate was that they should discover therein some sage admonition or evangelical parable. Although this sight caused certain ravages in the hearts of these most virtuous maidens, they paid little attention to the fluttering of their reins, but sprinkling a little holy water in the bottom of the abyss, one touched it, another passed her finger through a hole, and grew bolder looking at it. It has even been pretended that, their first stir over, the abbess found a voice sufficiently firm to say, 'What is there at the bottom of this? With what idea has our father sent us that which consummates the ruin of women?'

'It's fifteen years, dear mother, since I have been permitted to gaze upon the demon's den.'

'Silence, my daughter. You prevent me thinking what is best to be done.'

Then so much were these archiepiscopal breeches turned and twisted about, admired and re-admired, pulled here, pulled there, and turned inside out – so much were they talked about, fought about, thought about, dreamed about, night and day, that on the morrow a little sister said, after having sung the matins, to which the convent had a verse and two responses – 'Sisters, I have found out the parable of the archbishop. He has sent us as a mortification his garment to mend, as a holy warning to avoid idleness, the mother abbess of all the vices.'

Thereupon there was a scramble to get hold of the breeches; but the abbess, using her high authority, reserved to herself the meditation over this patchwork. She was occupied during ten days, praying, and sewing the said breeches, lining them with silk, and making double hems, well sewn, and in all humility. Then the chapter being assembled, it was arranged that the convent should testify by a pretty souvenir to the said archbishop their delight that he thought of his daughters in God. Then all of them, to the very youngest, had to do some work on these blessed breeches, in order to do honour to the virtue of the good man.

Meanwhile, the prelate had had so much to attend to, that he had forgotten all about his garment. This is how it came about. He made the acquaintance of a noble of the court, who, having lost his wife – a she-fiend and sterile – said to the good priest, that he had a great ambition to meet with a virtuous woman, confiding in God, with whom he was not likely to quarrel, and was likely to have pretty children. Such a one he desired to hold by the hand, and have confidence in. Then the holy man drew such a picture of Mademoiselle de Poissy, that this fair one soon became Madame de Genoilhac. The wedding was celebrated at the archiepiscopal palace, where was a feast of the first quality, and a table bordered with ladies of the highest lineage, and the fashionable world of the court, among whom the bride appeared the most beautiful, since it was certain that she was a virgin, the archbishop guaranteeing her virtue.

When the fruits, conserves, and pastry were, with many ornaments, arranged on the cloth, Saintot said to the archbishop, 'Monseigneur, your well-beloved daughters of Poissy send you a fine dish for the centre.'

'Put it there,' said the good man, gazing with admiration at an edifice of velvet and satin, embroidered with wire ribbon, in the shape of an ancient vase, the lid of which exhaled a thousand superfine odours.

Immediately the bride, uncovering it, found therein sweetmeats, cakes, and those delicious confections to which the ladies are so partial. But one of them – some curious devotee – seeing a little piece of silk, pulled it towards her, and exposed to view the habitation of the human compass, to the great confusion of the prelate, for laughter rang round the table like a discharge of artillery.

'Well have they made the centre dish,' said the bridegroom. 'These young ladies are of good understanding. Therein are all the sweets of matrimony.'

Can there be any better moral than that deduced by Monsieur de Genoilhac? Then no other is needed.

Nathaniel Hawthorne

1804–1864

The American novelist and short-story writer Nathaniel Hawthorne was born in Boston, Massachusetts, and educated at Bowdoin College, Maine. From 1839 he worked as a surveyor in the Boston Custom House, and later became US Consul in Liverpool. Briefly involved with the Transcendentalist movement, he lived for a short time in a commune. His novels include The House of Seven Gables *(1851) and* The Scarlet Letter, *the latter set in 17th-century Boston against the background of the witch-hunts (his ancestor John Hathorne [sic] had been a judge during the notorious 1692 Salem witch trials).*

From The Scarlet Letter (1850)

'Thou wilt go,' said Hester calmly, as he met her glance.

The decision once made, a glow of strange enjoyment threw its flickering brightness over the trouble of his breast. It was the exhilarating effect – upon a prisoner just escaped from the dungeon of his own heart – of breathing the wild, free atmosphere of an unredeemed, unchristianized, lawless region. His spirit rose, as it were, with a bound, and attained a nearer prospect of the sky, than throughout all the misery which had kept him grovelling on the earth. Of a deeply religious temperament, there was inevitably a tinge of the devotional in his mood.

'Do I feel joy again?' cried he, wondering at himself. 'Methought the germ of it was dead in me! O Hester, thou art my better angel! I seem to have flung myself – sick, sin-stained, and sorrow-blackened – down upon these forest-leaves, and to have risen up all made anew, and with new powers to glorify Him that hath been merciful! This is already the better life! Why did we not find it sooner?'

'Let us not look back,' answered Hester Prynne. 'The past is gone! Wherefore should we linger upon it now? See! With this symbol, I undo it all, and make it as it had never been.'

So speaking, she undid the clasp that fastened the scarlet letter, and, taking it from her bosom, threw it to a distance among the withered leaves. The mystic token alighted on the hither verge of the stream. With a hand's breadth farther flight it would have fallen into the water, and have given the little brook another woe to carry onward, besides the unintelligible tale which it still kept murmuring about. But there lay the embroidered letter, glittering like a lost jewel, which some ill-fated wanderer might pick up, and thenceforth be haunted by strange phantoms of guilt, sinkings of the heart, and unaccountable misfortune.

The stigma gone, Hester heaved a long, deep sigh, in which the burden of shame and anguish departed from her spirit. O exquisite relief! She had not known the weight, until she felt the freedom! By another impulse, she took off the formal cap that confined her hair; and down it fell upon her shoulders, dark and rich, with at once a shadow and a light in its abundance, and imparting the charm of softness to her features. There played around her mouth, and beamed out of her eyes, a radiant and tender smile, that seemed gushing from the very heart of womanhood. A crimson flush was glowing on her cheek, that had been long so pale. Her sex, her youth, and the whole richness of her beauty, came back from what men call the irrevocable past, and clustered themselves, with her maiden hope, and a happiness before unknown, within the magic circle of this hour. And, as if the gloom of the earth and sky had been but the effluence of these two mortal hearts, it vanished with their sorrow. All at once, as with a sudden smile of heaven, forth burst the sunshine, pouring a very flood into the obscure forest, gladdening each green leaf, transmuting the yellow fallen ones to gold, and gleaming adown the grey trunks of the solemn trees. The objects that had made a shadow hitherto, embodied the brightness now. The course of the little brook might be traced by its merry gleam afar into the wood's heart of mystery, which had become a mystery of joy.

Such was the sympathy of Nature – that wild, heathen Nature of the forest, never subjugated by human law, nor illumined by higher truth – with the bliss of these two spirits! Love, whether newly born, or aroused from a deathlike slumber, must always create a sunshine, filling the heart so full of radiance, that it overflows upon the outward world. Had the forest still kept its gloom, it would have been bright in Hester's eyes, and bright in Arthur Dimmesdale's!

Hester looked at him with the thrill of another joy.

'Thou must know Pearl!' said her. 'Our little Pearl! Thou hast seen her, – yes, I know it! – but thou wilt see her now with other eyes. She is a strange child! I hardly comprehend her! But thou wilt love her dearly, as I do, and wilt advise me how to deal with her.'

'Dost thou think the child will be glad to know me?' asked the minister, somewhat uneasily. 'I have long shrunk from children, because they often show a distrust, – a backwardness to be familiar with me. I have even been afraid of little Pearl!'

'Ah, that was sad!' answered the mother. 'But she will love thee dearly, and thou her. She is not far off. I will call her! Pearl! Pearl!'

'I see the child,' observed the minister. 'Yonder she is, standing in a streak of sunshine, a good way off, on the other side of the brook. So thou thinkest the child will love me?'

Hester smiled, and again called to Pearl, who was visible, at some distance, as the minister had described her, like a bright-apparelled vision, in a sunbeam, which fell down upon her through an arch of boughs. The ray quivered to and fro, making her figure dim or distinct, –

now like a real child, now like a child's spirit, – as the splendour went and came again. She heard her mother's voice, and approached slowly through the forest.

Pearl had not found the hour pass wearisomely, while her mother sat talking with the clergyman. The great black forest – stern as it showed itself to those who brought the guilt and troubles of the world into its bosom – became the playmate of the lonely infant, as well as it knew how. Sombre as it was, it put on the kindest of its moods to welcome her. It offered her the partridge-berries, the growth of the preceding autumn, but ripening only in the spring, and now red as drops of blood upon the withered leaves. These Pearl gathered, and was pleased with their wild flavour. The small denizens of the wilderness hardly took pains to move out of her path. A partridge, indeed, with a brood of ten behind her, ran forward threateningly, but soon repented of her fierceness, and clucked to her young ones not to be afraid. A pigeon, alone on a low branch, allowed Pearl to come beneath, and uttered a sound as much of greeting as alarm. A squirrel, from the lofty depths of his domestic tree, chattered either in anger or merriment, – for a squirrel is such a choleric and humorous little personage that it is hard to distinguish between his moods, – so he chattered at the child, and flung down a nut upon her head. It was a last year's nut, and already gnawed by his sharp tooth. A fox, startled from his sleep by her light footstep on the leaves, looked inquisitively at Pearl, as doubting whether it were better to steal off, or renew his nap on the same spot. A wolf, it is said, – but here the tale has surely lapsed into the improbable, – came up, and smelt of Pearl's robe, and offered his savage head to be patted by her hand. The truth seems to be, however, that the mother-forest, and these wild things which it nourished, all recognized a kindred wildness in the human child.

And she was gentler here than in the grassy-margined streets of the settlement, or in her mother's cottage. The flowers appeared to know it; and one and another whispered, as she passed, 'Adorn thyself with me, thou beautiful child, adorn thyself with me!' – and, to please them, Pearl gathered the violets, and anemones, and columbines, and some twigs of the freshest green, which the old trees held down before her eyes. With these she decorated her hair, and her young waist, and became a nymph-child, or an infant dryad, or whatever else was in closest sympathy with the antique wood. In such guise had Pearl adorned herself, when she heard her mother's voice, and came slowly back.

Slowly; for she saw the clergyman!

George Thompson

Little is known of the life of the American author George Thompson, who wrote under the pseudonym 'Greenhorn'. His prolific output included Venus in Boston *(1840),* The House Breaker *(1848),* Jack Harold *(1851) and* Blueskin! *(1866).*

From **Delights of Love** (185?)

[The heroine and hero have been admiring a painting of Venus and Adonis . . .]

The eyes of both Julie and Eurgen now simultaneously turned upon this exciting gem of art, and, like electricity, there passed from one to the other a bursting declaration of their mutual wishes.

'Be my Adonis!' murmured the lady libertine, as she pantingly sank into the arms of the eager youth, who whispered, as he pressed her yielding form to his widly throbbing heart –

'I am yours, my Venus!'

It is a great pity, we know, and the reader may blame us for it; but we are here reluctantly compelled to drop the curtain.

Alfred Lord Tennyson

1809–1892

Tennyson was born in Somersby, Lincolnshire, the son of an impoverished and alcoholic rector, and educated at Cambridge. By the 1840s his poetry had won an almost unprecedented audience, partly through its voicing of major Victorian concerns – religious doubt in the face of science, love and loss – couched in a lyrical melancholy, and in 1850 he succeeded Wordsworth as poet laureate. His work includes In Memoriam *(1850), written after the death of his close friend A.H.Hallam in 1833,* Maud *(1855) and the* Arthurian Idylls of the King *(1859–85).*

From 'The Princess' (1847)

Deep in the night I woke: she, near me, held
A volume of the Poets of her land:
There to herself, all in low tones, she read.

'Now sleeps the crimson petal, now the white;
Nor waves the cypress in the palace walk;
Nor winks the gold fin in the porphyry font:
The fire-fly wakens: waken thou with me.

Now droops the milkwhite peacock like a ghost,
And like a ghost she glimmers on to me.

Now lies the Earth all Danaë to the stars,
And all thy heart lies upon unto me.

Now slides the silent meteor on, and leaves
A shining furrow, as thy thoughts in me.

Now folds the lily all her sweetness up,
And slips into the bosom of the lake:
So fold thyself, my dearest, thou, and slip
Into my bosom and be lost in me.'

Robert Browning

1812–1889

An English poet, born and educated in London, Browning's early work brought him into contact with literary figures such as Dickens and Carlyle. In 1845 he met the poet Elizabeth Barrett, with whom he eloped to Italy, returning with their son after her death in 1861. His poetry – including Men and Women *(1855),* Dramatis Personae *(1864) and* The Ring and the Book *(1868–69) – is remarkable for its use of dramatic monologues, with their original and vividly realized characterizations.*

'The Last Ride Together'

I said – Then, dearest, since 'tis so,
Since now at length my fate I know,
Since nothing all my love avails,
Since all, my life seemed meant for, fails,

Since this was written and needs must
     be –
My whole heart rises up to bless
Your name in pride and thankfulness!

Take back the hope you gave, – I claim
Only a memory of the same,
– And this beside, if you will not blame,
 Your leave for one more last ride with me.

My mistress bent that brow of hers;
Those deep dark eyes where pride demurs
When pity would be softening through,
Fixed me a breathing-while or two
 With life or death in the balance: right!
The blood replenished me again;
My last thought was at least not vain:
I and my mistress, side by side
Shall be together, breathe and ride,
So, one day more am I deified.
 Who knows but the world may end to-night?

Hush! if you saw some western cloud
All billowy-bosomed, over-bowed
By many benedictions – sun's
And moon's and evening star's at once –
 And so, you, looking and loving best,
Conscious grew, your passion drew
Cloud, sunset, moonrise, star-shine too,
Down on you, near and yet more near,
Till flesh must fade for heaven was here –
Thus leant she and lingered – joy and fear!
 Thus lay she a moment in my breast

Then we began to ride. My soul
Smoothed itself out, a long-cramped scroll
Freshening and fluttering in the wind.
Past hopes already lay behind.
 What need to strive with a life awry?
Had I said that, had I done this,
So might I gain, so might I miss.
Might she have loved me just as well
She might have hated, who can tell!
Where had I been now if the worst befell?
 And here we are riding, she and I.

Fail I alone, in words and deeds?
Why, all men strive and who succeeds?
We rode; it seemed my spirit flew,
Saw other regions, cities new,

As the world rushed by on either side
I thought, – All labour, yet no less
Bear up beneath their unsuccess.
Look at the end of work, contrast
The petty done, the undone vast,
This present of theirs with the hopeful past!
 I hoped she would love me; here we ride.

What hand and brain went ever paired?
What heart alike conceived and dared?
What act proved all its thought had been?
What will but felt the fleshly screen?
 We ride and I see her bosom heave.
There's many a crown for who can reach.
Ten lines, a statesman's life in each!
The flag stuck on a heap of bones,
A soldier's doing! what atones?
They scratch his name on the Abbey-
 stones.
 My riding is better, by their leave.

What does it all mean, poet? Well,
Your brains beat into rhythm, you tell
What we felt only; you expressed
You hold things beautiful the best,
 And pace them in rhyme so, side by side.
'Tis something, nay 'tis much: but then,
Have you yourself what's best for men?
Are you – poor, sick, old ere your time –
Nearer one whit your own sublime
Than we who never have turned a rhyme?
 Sing, riding's a joy! For me, I ride.

And you, great sculptor – so, you gave
A score of years to Art, her slave,
And that's your Venus, whence we turn
To yonder girl that fords the burn!
 You acquiesce, and shall I repine?
What, man of music, you grown grey
With notes and nothing else to say,
Is this your sole praise from a friend,
'Greatly his opera's strains intend,
But in music we know how fashions end!'
 I gave my youth; but we ride, in fine.

Who knows what's fit for us? Had fate
Proposed bliss here should sublimate
My being – had I signed the bond –
Still one must lead some life beyond,
  Have a bliss to die with, dim-descried.
This foot once planted on the goal,
This glory-garland round my soul,
Could I descry such? Try and test!
I sink back shuddering from the quest.
Earth being so good, would heaven seem
      best?
  Now, heaven and she are beyond this ride.

And yet – she has not spoke so long!
What if heaven be that, fair and strong
At life's best, with our eyes upturned
Whither life's flower is first discerned,
  We, fixed so, ever should so abide?

What if we still ride on, we two
With life for ever old yet new,
Changed not in kind but in degree,
The instant made eternity, –
And heaven just prove that I and she
  Ride, ride together, for ever ride?

Walt Whitman

1819–1891

One of the most important and influential of American poets, Walt Whitman was born in Long Island, New York. After working variously as a printer, teacher, and army nurse, he eventually found his strength as a poet and champion of political and sexual emancipation. His masterpiece, the boldly innovative homoerotic collection Leaves of Grass, *was derided by some critics and considered offensive by others, but was greatly admired abroad.*

From 'From Pent-up Aching Rivers' (Leaves of Grass, 1855)

From pent-up aching rivers,
From that of myself without which I were nothing,
From what I am determin'd to make illustrious, even if I stand sole among men,
From my own voice resonant, singing the phallus,
Singing the song of procreation,
Singing the need of superb children and therein superb grown people,
Singing the muscular urge and the blending,
Singing the bedfellow's song, (O resistless yearning!
O for any and each the body correlative attracting!
O for you whoever you are your correlative body! O it, more than all else, you delighting!)
From the hungry gnaw that eats me night and day,
From native moments, from bashful pains, singing them,
Seeking something yet unfound though I have diligently sought it many a long year,
Singing the true song of the soul fitful at random,
Renascent with grossest Nature or among animals,
Of that, of them and what goes with them my poems informing,
Of the smell of apples and lemon, of the pairing of birds,
Of the wet of woods, of the lapping of waves,
Of the mad pushes of waves upon the land, I them chanting,

The overture lightly sounding, the strain anticipating,

The welcome nearness, the sight of the perfect body,

The swimmer swimming naked in the bath, or motionless on his back lying and floating,

The female form approaching, I pensive, love-flesh tremulous aching,

The divine list for myself or you or for any one making,

The face, the limbs, the index from head to foot, and what it arouses,

The mystic deliria, the madness amorous, the utter abandonment,

(Hark close and still what I now whisper to you,

I love you, O you entirely possess me,

O that you and I escape from the rest and go utterly off, free and lawless,

Two hawks in the air, two fishes swimming in the sea not more lawless than we;)

The furious storm through me careering, I passionately trembling.

The oath of the inseparableness of two together, of the woman that loves me and whom I
    love more than my life, that oath swearing,

(O I willingly stake all for you,

O let me be lost if it must be so!

O you and I! what is to it us what the rest do or think?

What is all else to us? only that we enjoy each other and exhaust each other if it must
    be so;)

From the master, the pilot I yield the vessel to,

The general commanding me, commanding all, from him permission taking,

From time the programme hastening, (I have loiter'd too long as it is).

Charles Baudelaire

1821–1867

Charles Baudelaire, French poet and critic, was born in Paris and educated in Lyons. He lived for a time in Mauritius, where he met Jeanne Duval, his mistress and the 'Venus noire' of his poems. Returning to Paris in 1842, he worked as a reviewer and translator (of Edgar Allan Poe, among others) before the succès de scandale *of his volume of poems* Les Fleurs du mal *(1857), for which he was prosecuted on grounds of impropriety. The work's preoccupation with evil and with the city had a profound influence on Symbolist and modernist writers.*

'The Snake that Dances'.

I love to watch, while you are lazing,
   Your skin. It iridesces
Like silk or satin, smoothly-glazing
   The light that it caresses.

Under your tresses dark and deep
   Where acrid perfumes drown,
A fragrant sea whose breakers sweep
   In mazes blue or brown,

My soul, a ship, to the attraction
   Of breezes that bedizen
Its swelling canvas, clears for action
   And seeks a far horizon.

Your eyes where nothing can be seen
   Either of sweet or bitter
But gold and iron mix their sheen,
   Seem frosty gems that glitter.

To see you rhythmically advancing
    Seems to my fancy fond
As if it were a serpent dancing
    Waved by the charmer's wand.

Under the languorous moods that weight
    it,
    Your childish head bows down:
Like a young elephant's you sway it
    With motions soft as down.

Your body leans upon the hips
    Like a fine ship that laves

Its hull from side to side, and dips
    Its yards into the waves.

When, as by glaciers ground, the spate
    Swells hissing from beneath,
The water of your mouth, elate,
    Rises between your teeth –

It seems some old Bohemian vintage
    Triumphant, fierce, and tart,
A liquid heaven that showers a mintage
    Of stars across my heart.

Dora Greenwell

1821–1882

Dora Greenwell, English poet and essayist, was born in Lanchester, County Durham. She combined her religious conviction with an interest in social reform, and was a friend of Josephine Butler, the women's rights campaigner. Her poetry includes Stories That Might Be True *(1850) and* Songs of Salvation *(1873), the latter often set as hymns.*

'The Sun-Flower'

Till the slow daylight pale,
    A willing slave, fast bound to one above,
I wait; he seems to speed, and change, and fail;
    I know he will not move.

I lift my golden orb
    To his, unsmitten when the roses die,
And in my broad and burning disk absorb
    The splendours of his eye.

His eye is like a clear
    Keen flame that searches through me; I must
        droop
Upon my stalk, I cannot reach his sphere;
    To mine he cannot stoop.

I win not my desire,
    And yet I fail not of my guerdon; lo!
A thousand flickering darts and tongues of
        fire
    Around me spread and glow.

All rayed and crowned, I miss
    No queenly state until the summer wane,
The hours flit by; none knoweth of my bliss,
    And none has guessed my pain.

I follow one above,
    I track the shadow of his steps, I grow
Most like to him I love
    Of all that shines below.

Rolla Henri Gervex

Christina Rossetti

1830–1894

The English poet Christina Rossetti was born in London, sister to the poet and painter Dante Gabriel and the art critic William Michael Rossetti. Ill health prevented her from working as a governess, and after she had broken off an engagement to the painter James Collinson in 1850, she lived a life of retirement. Her work ranges from verses for children, love lyrics, sonnets to fantasy and religious poetry, and includes Goblin Market *(1862) and* The Prince's Progress *(1866).*

'A Nightmare' (1857)

I have a love in ghostland –
Early found, ah me how early lost! –
Blood-red seaweeds drip along that coastland.
By the strong sea wrenched and tost.

If I wake he rides me like a nightmare:
I feel my hair stand up, my body creep:
Without light I see a blasting sight there,
See a secret I must keep.

Emily Dickinson

1830–1886

The American poet Emily Dickinson was born and educated in Amherst, Massachusetts. Her father was a public figure – a Congressman and judge – but from the age of about 30 she herself lived an almost entirely reclusive life. Her prolific poetic output was published posthumously, consisting mainly of short lyrics dealing with religious doubt, love and nature, and framed in her unique, fragmented and elliptical idiom.

'Wild Nights' (*c.* 1861)

Wild Nights – Wild Nights!
Were I with thee
Wild Nights should be
Our luxury!

Futile – the Winds –
To a Heart in port –
Done with the Compass –
Done with the Chart!

Rowing in Eden –
Ah, the Sea!
Might I but moor – Tonight –
In Thee!

Leopold von Sacher-Masoch

1836–1895

Sacher-Masoch was born in Lemberg, Austria and educated in Prague and Graz. He is remembered for his novels of sexual domination and submission, including Venus in Furs *(1870), from which the term 'masochism' was coined by the Viennese psychiatrist Richard Krafft-Ebing.*

From **Venus in Furs** (1870). *Trans. Clive Moeller and Laura Lindgren*

'Give me the whip, Haydée,' commands Wanda, with unearthly calm.

The negress hands it to her mistress, kneeling.

'And now take off my heavy furs,' she continues. 'They impede me.'

The negress obeyed.

'The jacket there!' Wanda commanded.

Haydée quickly brought her the *kazabaika* set with ermine, which lay on the bed, and Wanda slipped into it with two inimitably graceful movements.

'Now tie him to the pillar here!'

The negresses lifted me up and twisting a heavy rope around my body, tied me standing against one of the massive pillars which supported the top of the wide Italian bed.

Then they suddenly disappeared, as if the earth had swallowed them.

Wanda swiftly approached me. Her white satin dress flowed behind her in a long train, like silver, like moonlight; her hair flared like flames against the white fur of her jacket. Now she stood in front of me with her left hand firmly planted on her hips, her right hand holding the whip. She uttered an abrupt laugh.

'Now play has come to an end between us,' she said with heartless coldness. 'Now we will begin in dead earnest. You fool, I laugh at you and despise you; you who in your insane infatuation have given yourself as a plaything to me, a frivolous and capricious woman. You are no longer the man I love, but my *slave*, at my mercy even unto life and death.

'You shall know me!

'First of all you shall have a taste of the whip in all seriousness, without having done anything to deserve it, so that you may understand what to expect if you are awkward, disobedient, or refractory.'

With a wild grace she rolled back her fur-lined sleeve and struck me across the back.

I winced, for the whip cut like a knife into my flesh.

'Well, how do you like that?' she exclaimed.

I was silent.

'Just wait, you will yet whine like a dog beneath my whip,' she threatened, and simultaneously began to strike me again.

The blows fell quickly, in rapid succession, with terrific force upon my back, arms, and neck; I had to grit my teeth not to scream aloud. Now she struck me in the face, warm blood ran down, but she laughed and continued her blows.

'It is only now I understand you,' she said. 'It really is a joy to have someone so completely in one's power, and a man at that, who loves you – you do love me' – No – Oh! I'll tear you to shreds yet, and with each blow my pleasure will grow. Now, twist like a worm, scream, whine! You will find no mercy in me!'

Finally she seemed tired. She tossed the whip aside, stretched out on the ottoman, and rang. The negresses entered.

'Untie him!'

As they loosened the rope, I fell to the floor like a lump of wood. The black women grinned, showing their white teeth.

'Untie the rope around his feet.'

They did it, but I was unable to rise.

'Come over here, Gregor.'

I approached the beautiful woman. Never did she seem more seductive to me than today in spite of all her cruelty and contempt.

'One step further,' Wanda commanded. 'Now kneel down, and kiss my foot.'

She extended her foot beyond the hem of white satin, and I, the suprasensual fool, pressed my lips upon it.

'Now, you won't lay eyes on me for an entire month, Gregor,' she said seriously. 'I want to become a stranger to you so you will more easily adjust yourself to our new relationship. In the meantime you will work in the garden and await my orders. Now, off with you, slave!'

'And the moral of the story?' I asked Severin when I put the manuscript down on the table.

'That I was a donkey,' he said without turning around, for he seemed to be embarrassed. 'If only I had beaten her!'

'A curious remedy,' I remarked, 'which might answer with your peasant women –'

'Oh, they are used to it,' he replied eagerly, 'but imagine the effect upon one of our delicate, nervous, hysterical ladies –'

'But the moral?'

'That woman, as nature has created her, and as man at present is educating her, is man's enemy. She can only be his slave or his despot, but never his *companion*. This she can become only when she has the same rights as he and is his equal in education and work.

'At present we have only the choice of being hammer or anvil, and I was the kind of donkey who let a woman make a slave of him, do you understand?

'The moral of the tale is this: Whoever allows himself to be whipped, deserves to be whipped.

'The blows, as you see, have agreed with me; the roseate suprasensual mist has dissolved, and no one can ever make me believe again that these "sacred apes of Benares or Plato's rooster" are the image of God.'

Anon. (Afghan)

'Black Hair'.

Last night my kisses drowned in the softness of black hair,
And my kisses like bees went plundering the softness of black hair.
Last night my hands were thrust in the mystery of black hair,
And my kisses like bees went plundering the sweetness of pomegranates
And among the scents of the harvest above my queen's neck, the harvest of black hair;
And my teeth played with the golden skin of her two ears.
Last night my kisses drowned in the softness of black hair,
And my kisses like bees went plundering the softness of black hair.

Your kisses went plundering the scents of my harvest, O friend,
And the scents laid you drunk at my side. As sleep overcame Bahram
In the bed of Sarasya, so sleep overcame you on my bed.
I know one that has sworn your hurt for stealing the roses from my cheeks,
Has sworn your hurt even to death, the Guardian of black hair.
Last night my kisses drowned in the softness of black hair,
And my kisses like bees went plundering the softness of black hair.
My hurt, darling? The sky will guard me if you wish me guarded.
But now for my defence, dearest, roll me a cudgel of black hair;
And give me the whiteness of your face, I am hungry for it like a little bird.
Still, if you wish me there, loosen me among the wantonness of black hair.
Last night my kisses drowned in the softness of black hair,
And my kisses like bees went plundering the softness of black hair.

Sweet friend, I will part the curtain of black hair and let you into the white garden of my
     breast.
But I fear you will despise me and not look back when you go away.
I am so beautiful and so white that the lamp-light faints to see my face,
And also God has given me for adornment my heavy black hair,
Last night my kisses drowned in the softness of black hair,
And my kisses like bees went plundering the softness of black hair.

He has made you beautiful even among his most beautiful;
I am your little slave. O queen, cast me a little look.
I sent you the message of love at the dawn of day,
But my heart is stung by a snake, the snake of black hair.
Last night my kisses drowned in the softness of black hair,
And my kisses like bees went plundering the softness of black hair.

Fear not, dear friend, I am the Charmer,
My breath will charm the snake upon your heart;
But who will charm the snake on my honour, my sad honour?

If you love me, let us go from Pakli. My husband is horrible.
From this forth I give you command over black hair.
Last night my kisses drowned in the softness of black hair,
And my kisses like bees went plundering the softness of black hair.

Muhammadji has power over the poets of Pakli,
He takes tax from the Amirs of great Delhi.
He reigns over an empire and governs with a sceptre of black hair,
Last night my kisses drowned in the softness of black hair,
And my kisses like bees went plundering the softness of black hair.

Yü Ch'ing-Tsêng

Late 19th century

Yü Ch'ing-Tsêng was the granddaughter of the celebrated Chinese scholar Yu Yueh. She married the scholar Tsing Sun-nien when she was very young, and according to legend, committed suicide due to her mother-in-law's jealousy and ill-treatment of her.

To the tune 'Intoxicated with shadows of flowers'.
Trans. Kenneth Rexroth and Ling Chung

A brush of evening clouds.
The perfume of flowers in the darkness.
A harp melody
Accompanies the chanting of poetry.
Smoke rises from the incense clock's seal characters.
We lock the silk sliding doors,
And let down the curtains of the bed,
And whisper the words
We do not want others to hear.
The moonlight flows like water.
All the world is still.
My young lover can read my mind.
Laughing, we wash away my makeup,
And watch our love making in the mirror.

Mark Twain
1835–1910

Born in Florida, Missouri, Mark Twain grew up in Hannibal on the Mississippi River, the setting for his two most popular novels Tom Sawyer *(1876) and* Huckleberry Finn *(1884). As a young man he travelled through the States, working variously as a printer, journalist and silver prospector, and when his writing became well-known, as a public speaker. His work is characteristically humorous and satirical, though progressively pessimistic.*

From **1601, or Conversation As It Was by the Social Fireside in the Time of the Tudors** (1876)

Then felle they to talk about ye manners and customs of many peoples, and Master Shaxpur spake of ye boke of ye sieur Michael de Montaine, wherein was mention of ye customs of widows of Perigord to wear uppon ye headdress, in signe of widowhood, a jewel in ye similitude of a man's member wilted and limber, whereat ye queene did laffe and say, *Widows in England doe wear prickes too, but betwixt the thighs, and not wilted neither, till coition hath done that office for them.* Master Shaxpur did likewise observe how yt ye sieur de Montaine hath also spoken of a certain emperor of such mightie prowess yt he did take ten maidenheddes in ye compass of a single night, ye while his empress did entertain two and twenty lusty knights between her sheetes, yet was not satisfied; wherat ye merrie Countesse Granby saith a ram is yet ye emperor's superior, sith he will tup a hundred yewes 'twixt sun and sun; and after, if he can have none more to shag, will masturbate until he hath enrich'd whole acres wh his seed.

Then spake ye damned windmill, Sr Walter, of a people in ye utermost parts of America, yt copulate not until they be five and thirty yeres of age, ye women being eight and twenty, and do it then but once in seven yeres.

Ye Queene: How doth yt like mine little Lady Helen? Shall we send thee thither and preserve thy belly?

Lady Helen: Please your highness grace, mine old nurse hath told me there are more ways of serving God than by locking the thighs together; yet am I willing to serve him yt way too, sith your highnesses grace hath set ye ensample.

Ye Queene: God's wowndes, a good answer, childe.

Lady Alice: Mayhap 'twill weaken when ye hair sprouts below ye navel.

Lady Helen: Nay, it sprouted two yeres syne. I can scarce more than cover it with my hand now.

Ye Queene: Hear ye that, my little Beaumonte? Have ye not a little birde about ye yt stirs at hearing tell of so sweete a neste?

Beaumonte: 'Tis not insensible, illustrious madam; but mousing owls and bats of low degree may not aspire to bliss so whelming and ecstatic as is founde in ye downie nestes of birdes of Paradise.

Ye Queene: By ye gullet of God, 'tis a neat-turned compliment. With such a tong as thine, lad, thou'lt spread the ivory thighs of many a willing maide in thy good time, an thy cod-piece be as handie as thy speeche.

Then spake ye queene of how she met olde Rabelais when she was turned of fifteen, and he did tell her of a man his father knew yt hadde a double pair of bollocks, wheron a controversy followed as concerning the most just way to spell the word, ye contention running high betwixt ye learned Bacon and ye ingenious Jonson, until at last ye olde Lady Margery, wearying of it all, Saith, *Gentles, what mattereth it how ye shall spell the word? I warrant ye when ye use your bollocks ye shall not think of it: and my Lady Granby, be ye content: let the spelling be, ye shall enjoy the beating of them on your buttocks just the same. I trow. Before I hadde gained my fourteenth yere I hadde learned yt them yt wolde explore a cunte stop't not to consider the spelling o't.*

Sr W: In soothe, when a shift's turned uppe, delay is mete for naught but dalliance. Boccaccio hath a story of a prieste yt did beguile a maide into his cell, then knelt him in a corner to praye for grace to be rightly thankful for this tender maidenhedde ye Lord hath sent him; but ye abbot, spying through ye key-hole, did see a tuft of brownish hair with fair white flesh about it, wherfore when ye priestes prayer was done, his chance was gone, forasmuch as ye little maide hadde but ye one cunte, and yt was already occupied to her content.

Then conversed they of religion, and ye mightie work ye olde dead Luther did doe by ye grace of God. Then next about poetry, and Master Shaxpur did rede a part of his King Henry IV, ye which, it seemeth unto me, is not of the value of an arseful of ashes, yet they praised it bravely, one and all.

Ye same did rede a portion of his 'Venus and Adonis' to their prodigious admiration, whereas I, being sleepy and fatigued withal, did deme it but paltrie stuff, and was the more discomfited in yt ye blodie bucanier hadde got his secconde wynde, and did turn his mind to farting wh such villain zeal that presently I was like to choke once more. God damn this wyndie ruffian and all his breed. I wolde yt hell mighte get him.

They talked about ye wonderful defense which olde Sr Nicholas Throgmorton did make for himself before ye judges in ye time of Mary; which was an unlucky matter to broach, sith it fetched out ye queene wh a *Pity yt he, having so much wit, hadde yet not enough to save his doter's maidenhedde sounde for her marriage-bedde.* And ye queene did give ye damn'd Sr Walter a look yt made hym wince – for she hath not forgot he was her own lover in yt olde day. There was silent uncomfortableness now; 'twas not a good turn for talk to take, sith if ye queene must find offense in a little harmless debauching, when prickes were stiff and cuntes not loath to take ye stiffness out of them, who of this companie was sinless? Beholde, was not ye wife of Master Shaxpur four months gone wh childe when she stood uppe before ye altar? Was not her Grace of Bilgewater roger'd by four lords before she hadde a husband? Was not ye little Lady Helen borne on her mother's wedding-day? And, beholde, were not ye Lady Alice and ye Lady Margery there, mouthing religion, whores from ye cradle?

In time came they to discourse of Cervantes, and of the new painter, Rubens, that is beginning to be heard of. Fine words and dainty-wrought phrases from the ladies now, one or two of them being, in other days, pupils of yt poor arse, Lille himself; and I marked how that Jonson and Shaxpur did fidget to discharge some venom of sarcasm, yet dared they not in the presence, ye queenes grace being ye very flower of ye Euphuists herself. But beholde, these be they yt, having a specialtie, and admiring in it themselves, be jealous when a neighbour doth essaye it, nor can abide it in them long. Wherfore 'twas observable yt ye queene waxed uncontent; and in time a labor'd grandiose speeche out of ye mouthe of Lady Alice, who manifestly did mightily pride herself theron, did quite exhauste ye queenes endurance, who listened till ye gaudie speeche was done, then lifted uppe her brows, and wh vaste ironie, mincing saith, *O shitte*! Wherat they alle did laffe, but not ye Lady Alice, yt olde foolish bitche.

Now was Sr Walter minded of a tale he once did heare ye ingenious Margarette of Navarre relate, about a maide, which being like to suffer rape by an olde archbishoppe, did smartly contrive a device to save her maidenhedde, and said to him, *First, my lord, I prithee, take out thy holy tool and pisse before me;* which doing, lo! his member felle, and wolde not rise again.

Algernon Charles Swinburne

1837–1909

The English poet and critic Swinburne was born in London and educated at Eton and Oxford. His eclectic poetry includes Poems and Ballads *(1866) and* Tristram of Lyonesse *(1882). He scandalized his Victorian contemporaries with his renunciation of Christianity and his dissolute life style (especially his notorious predilection for flagellation), though this anti-Victorianism influenced the younger Aesthetic movement.*

From **Lesbia Brandon** (1877)

For the last month or two of his free childish life Herbert clung daily to the sea, diving in and out among cliffs and coves, and tracking with small rapid feet miles of the blown sand and stormy seabanks. Under the March winds the sea gained strength and splendour, and its incessant beauty maddened him with pleasure. His blood kept time with its music, his breath and pulse felt and answered the sweet sharp breath that lifted and the long profound pulse that shook the stormy body of the sea. The reefs clashed and the banks chafed with violent and variable waves; the low rocks thundered and throbbed underfoot as the water rang round them, and wave by wave roared out its heavy heart and lost its fierce fleet life in lavish foam. Beyond the yellow labouring space of sea that heaved and wallowed close inshore, the breakers crashed one upon another, white and loud beyond the sudden green line of purer sea. In thunder that drowned his voice, wind that blew over his balance, and snowstorms of the flying or falling foam that blinded his eyes and salted his face, the boy took his pleasure to the full; this travail and triumph of the married wind and sea filled him with a furious luxury of the senses that kindled all his nerves and exalted all his life. From these haunts he came back wet and rough, blown out of shape and beaten into colour, his ears full of music and his eyes of dreams: all the sounds of the sea rang through him, all its airs and lights breathed and shone upon him: he felt land-sick when out of the sea's sight, and twice alive when hard by it. It was in this guise that he first met the man who was to rule and form his life for years to come. Drenched and hot and laughing, salt and blown and tumbled, he was confronted with a tall dark man, pale and strong, with grey hard features and hair already thinned. Mr. Denham had noticeable eyes, clear brown in colour, cold and rapid in their glance; his chest and arms were splendid, the whole build of him pliant and massive, the limbs fleshless and muscular. But for the cold forehead and profound eyes he seemed rather a training athlete than trained student. The forehead was large in all ways, and the strong prominent bones made the outlines coarse. Nothing in his face seemed mobile but the nostrils; and these were its weakest feature. The nose and mouth had a certain Irish air, corrected by the strong compression of the lips which if relaxed would have changed the whole face; but they never did relax, whether in talking or laughing, drinking or sleeping; they should have been full and soft, and were thin it seemed not because they had grown thin through natural change but by dint of purpose and compulsion. Life repressed and suppressed strength were not indiscernible after sharp scrutiny of his face. The skin looked blasted and whitened, as if it had once been brilliant and smooth: it was now colourless and dry, lined and flaked with dull tints of diseased colour. As his eyes fell on Herbert, the boy felt a sudden tingling in his flesh, his skin was aware of danger, and his nerves winced. He blushed again at his blushes, and gave his small wet hand shyly into the wide hard grasp of the strong and supple fingers that closed on it. Denham had broad hands on which the veins and muscles stood in hard relief; well-shaped and strong, good at handling oar and bat, the nails wide and flat and pale, the joints large and the knuckles wrinkled; hands as significant as the face. The soft sunburnt hand with feminine fingers lay in his almost like a roseleaf taken up and crushed; his grasp was close and retentive by instinct; he kept hold of the boy and read his face sharply over, watching it redden and flinch. Lord Wariston who was by recollected the look, and remembered how quiet and tough a hold the man had as a boy, and how when young and fresh he had made an excellent tyrant, notable as scholar and bully alike. 'I hope you won't begin by giving Herbert such a licking as you gave me once,' he said for a fragment of a laugh. 'I wouldn't have been your fag then for something.'

'Don't remember the licking myself,' said Mr. Denham. 'However, if your brother is to fag for me I shall keep him up to his work. Twelve next month, is he? Ever been flogged yet, my boy?'

Émile Zola

1840–1902

The French novelist Émile Zola was born in Paris and brought up in Aix-en-Provence. He settled in Paris in 1858, where he worked as a publisher's assistant and journalist. Through his 20-novel cycle Les Rougon-Macquart – *including* L'Assommoir *(1887),* Nana *(1880) and* Germinal *(1885) – which described life during the Second Empire, he sought to realize his influential theory of literary naturalism, combining extreme realism with a form of social-Darwinism. He became embroiled in the Dreyfus affair by writing the pro-Dreyfus pamphlet* J'accuse *(1898), for which he was charged with libel, escaping imprisonment only by fleeing to England.*

From **Nana** (1880). *Trans. George Holden*

Then he looked up. Nana had grown absorbed in her ecstatic contemplation of herself. She had bent her neck and was gazing attentively in the mirror at a little brown mole just above her right hip. She was touching it with the tip of her finger, and by leaning backwards was making it stand out more than ever; situated where it was, it presumably struck her as both quaint and pretty. Then she studied other parts of her body, amused by what she was doing, and filled once more with the depraved curiosity she had felt as a child. The sight of herself always surprised her, and she looked as astonished and fascinated as a young girl who has just discovered her puberty. Slowly she spread out her arms to set off her figure, the torso of a plump Venus, bending this way and that to examine herself in front and behind, lingering over the side-view of her bosom and the sweeping curves of her thighs. And she ended up by indulging in a strange game which consisted of swinging to right and left, with her knees apart, and her body swaying from the waist with the continuous quivering of an almeh performing a belly-dance.

Muffat sat looking at her. She frightened him. The newspaper had dropped from his hands. In that moment of clarity and truth, he despised himself. Yes, that was it: she had corrupted his life, and he already felt tainted to the core of his being, by undreamt-of impurities. Now everything was going to rot within him, and for a moment he realized how this evil would develop; he saw the havoc wrought by this ferment, himself poisoned, his family destroyed, a section of the social fabric cracking and crumbling. And, unable to take his eyes away, he stared at Nana, trying to fill himself with disgust for her nakedness.

Nana had stopped moving. With one arm behind her neck, one hand clasped in the other, and her elbows far apart, she had thrown back her head, so that he could see a fore-shortened reflection of her half-closed eyes, her parted lips, her face lit up with loving laughter, while behind, her mane of loosened yellow hair covered her back with the fell of a lioness. Bending back with her hips thrust out, she displayed the solid loins and the firm bosom of an Amazon, with strong muscles beneath the satin texture of the skin. A delicate line, curving only slightly at the shoulder and thigh, ran from one of her elbows to her foot. Muffat's eyes followed this charming profile, noticing how the lines of the fair flesh vanished in golden gleams, and how the rounded contours shone like silk in the candle-light. He thought of his former dread of Woman, of the Beast of the Scriptures, a lewd creature of the jungle. Nana's body was covered with fine hair, reddish down which turned her skin into velvet; while there was something of the Beast about her equine crupper and franks, about the fleshy curves and deep hollows of her body, which veiled her sex in the suggestive mystery of their shadows. She was the Golden Beast, as blind as brute force, whose very odour corrupted the world. Muffat gazed in fascination, like a man possessed, so intently that when he shut his eyes to see no more, the Beast reappeared in the darkness, larger, more awe-inspiring, more suggestive in its posture. Henceforth it would remain before his eyes, in his very flesh, for ever.

But Nana was hunching her shoulders. A little shiver of emotion seemed to have run through her limbs, and with tears in her eyes she was trying, as it were, to make herself small, as if to become more conscious of her body. She unclasped her hands and slid them down as far as her breasts, which she squeezed in a passionate grasp. Then, holding herself erect, and embracing her whole body in a single caress, she rubbed her cheeks coaxingly first against one shoulder and then against the other. Her greedy mouth breathed desire over her flesh. She put out her lips and pressed a lingering kiss on the skin near her armpit, laughing at the other Nana who was likewise kissing herself in the mirror.

Muffat gave a long, weary sigh. This solitary self-indulgence was beginning to exasperate him. Suddenly his self-control was swept away as if by a mighty wind. In a fit of brutal passion he seized Nana round the waist and threw her down on the carpet.

'Let go!' she cried. 'You're hurting me!'

Gerard Manley Hopkins

1844–1889

An English poet, Hopkins was born in Stratford, Essex. While at Oxford he came under the influence of Newman's Oxford Movement, and converted to Catholicism. From 1868 he was a Jesuit, working in North Wales, Liverpool and Dublin among other places. He suffered from increasing ill health and depression until his early death from typhoid. His work was largely unpublished until 1918, partly due to its ambitious syntax, prosody and subject matter, and includes such poems as 'The Wreck of the Deutschland' and the so-called 'Dark Sonnets'.

'Harry Ploughman' (*c.* 1885–89)

Hard as hurdle arms, with a broth of goldish flue
Breathed round, the rack of ribs; the scooped flank; lank
Rope-over thigh; knee-nave; and barrelled shank –

                Head and foot, shoulder and shank –
By a grey eye's heed steered well, one crew, fall to;
Stand at stress. Each limb's barrowy brawn, his thew
That onewhere curded, onewhere sucked or sank –
                Soared or sank –,
Though as a beechbole firm, finds his, as at a roll-call, rank
And features, in flesh, what deed he each must do –
                His sinew-service where do.

He leans to it, Harry bends, look. Back, elbow, and liquid waist
In him, all quail to the wallowing o' the plough: 's cheek crimsons; curls
Wag or crossbridle, in a wind lifted, windlaced –
                See his wind lilylocks -laced;
Churlsgrace, too, child of Amansstrength, how it hangs or hurls
Them – broad in bluff hide his frowning feet lashed! raced
With, along them, cragiron under and cold furls –
                With-a-fountain's shining-shot furls.

Guy de Maupassant

1850–1893

A French short story writer and novelist, born in Normandy, Maupassant fought with the army and worked as a minor civil servant before being encouraged to write by Flaubert. Taking Zola's naturalism as his model, he led a highly successful literary career, producing detached and simple narratives of the supernatural, war and provincial life – such as Mademoiselle Fifi *(1882) and* Contes du jour et de la nuit *(1885) – though his dissolute lifestyle led to mental breakdown and an early death.*

From **The Colonel's Nieces**. *Trans. Howard Nelson*

'Look Julia', said Florentine. 'See what a contrast there is between your black hair and my blonde tresses.'

'Yes, that's so,' agreed her sister as she removed the combs and pins from the yellow tresses which tumbled down over her shoulders. The blending of blonde and brunette offered an enchanting picture.

In the meantime, Florentine was undoing the button of her sister's blouse, bringing into view a superb pair of breasts, the rosy tips of which she gently nibbled with her teeth.

'Let's compare,' Julia exclaimed. 'I never dreamed you were so lovely. I want to see the rest of you, in the costume that Eve wore when she met the snake.'

'But shouldn't there be an even exchange?' Florentine softly asked.

'Of course. We shall stand before the mirror and look at ourselves.'

As they were so chatting, they started to remove their clothing, letting each piece drop on the carpet. Soon the corsets, the shoes, the stockings, and the batiste lingerie formed a jumbled heap on the floor. Now each contemplated the nude body of the other, each embodying in its own way the apex of feminine pulchritude.

'How beautiful you are!' Florentine exclaimed.

'Not in comparison with you,' replied Julia.

The sisters vied with one another in their cries of admiration.

For several moments they looked at each other warmly, like two prize-fighters just entering the ring. Then, with her left hand, Julia grasped her sister's hips, drew them gradually to her, and began to kiss the nape of her neck, which sent her into a pitch of excitement. Involuntarily, Florentine returned the kisses, starting with the throat and descending to the breasts with their hardening nipples.

'You certainly are impudent,' Julia said reprovingly, 'and I am going to punish you.'

She took the eager pink tips into her mouth, each in turn, and rolled and sucked them with her compressed mouth. This produced squeals of rapture from Florentine.

After this foreplay, Florentine let herself sink down on the divan under her sister's body.

'I bet nobody has ever done what I am going to do to you,' Julia challenged her.

Arthur Rimaud

1854–1891

The French poet Rimbaud was born in the Ardennes. His precocious literary career spanned less than ten years from the age of 15. During this time, he had a notoriously passionate and violent relationship with Verlaine in Brussels and London, and wrote the poems Une Saison en enfer *(1873), a kind of modern spiritual autobiography, and the prose work* Les Illuminations *(published 1886), both couched in a style anticipating the Symbolist movement.*

'Obscur et froncé'. *Trans. Kenneth McLeish*

Dark, wrinkled as a purple pink,
It breathes, it nestles in that bed of moss,
Still damp from love, which hugs the slope,
The white thighs' slope, to crater's heart.

Threads, gossamer, milky tears
Wept, wept, in scouring wind
That drove them on clots of scarlet scree
Till they tumbled on the edge, were gone.

My dreams touch kisses, kisses to the gate.
Soul envies couplings of the flesh,
Its tear-bottle this, its nest of sobs.

Ecstatic olive! Seductive flute!
Throat sucking almond-sweet sublime!
Moss-circled, female, promised land!

Francis Thompson

1859–1907

Born in Preston, Lancashire, Francis Thompson's plans for the Catholic priesthood and medicine fell victim to his eventual opium addiction, which almost caused him to starve in London until he was rescued by the writers Alice and Wilfred Meynell. His three volumes of highly ornate religious verse include the poems 'The Kingdom of God' and 'The Hound of Heaven'.

From 'The Hound of Heaven' (1890)

I fled Him, down the nights and down the days;
I fled Him, down the arches of the years;
I fled Him, down the labyrinthine ways
Of my own mind; and in the mist of tears
I hid from Him, and under running laughter.
Up vistaed hopes I sped;
And shot, precipitated,
Adown titanic glooms of chasmèd fears,
From those strong feet that followed, followed
     after.
But with unhurrying chase,
And unperturbèd pace,
Deliberate speed, majestic instancy,
They beat – and a voice beat
More instant than the feet –
'All things betray thee, who betrayest Me.'

I pleaded outlaw-wise,
By many a hearted casement, curtained red,
Trellised with intertwining charities;
(For, though I knew His love Who followed,
 Yet was I sore adread
Lest, having Him, I must have naught
        beside).
But, if one little casement parted wide,
The gust of His approach would clash it to.
Fear wist not to evade, as Love wist to pursue.
Across the margent of the world I fled,
And troubled the gold gateways of the stars,
Smiting for shelter on their clangèd bars;
Fretted to dulcet jars
And silvern chatter the pale ports o' the moon.
I said to Dawn: Be sudden – to Eve: Be soon;
With thy young skeyey blossoms heap me over
From this tremendous Lover –
Float thy vague veil about me, lest He see!
I tempted all His servitors, but to find
My own betrayal in their constancy,
In faith to Him their fickleness to me,
Their traitorous trueness, and their loyal deceit.
To all swift things for swiftness did I sue;
Clung to the whistling mane of every wind.
But whether they swept, smoothly fleet,
The long savannahs of the blue;
Or whether, Thunder-driven,
They clanged His chariot 'thwart a heaven,
Plashy with flying lightnings round the spurn o'
        their feet: –
Fear wist not to evade as Love wist to pursue.
Still with unhurrying chase,
And unperturbèd pace,
Deliberate speed, majestic instancy,
Came on the following Feet,
And a Voice above their beat –
'Naught shelters thee, who wilt not shelter
        Me.'

I sought no more that after which I strayed
In face of man or maid;
But still within the little children's eyes

Seems something, something that
        replies,
They at least are for me, surely for me!
I turned me to them very wistfully;
But just as their young eyes grew sudden fair
With dawning answers there,
Their angel plucked them from me by the
        hair.
'Come then, ye other children, Nature's –
        share
With me' (said I) 'your delicate fellowship;
Let me greet you lip to lip,
Let me twine with you caresses,
Wantoning
With our Lady-Mother's vagrant tresses,
Banqueting
With her in her wind-walled palace,
Underneath her azured dais,
Quaffing, as your taintless way is,
From a chalice
Lucent-weeping out of the dayspring.'
So it was done:
I in their delicate fellowship was one –
Drew the bolt of nature's secrecies.
I knew all the swift importings
On the willful face of skies;
I knew how the clouds arise
Spumèd of the wild sea-snortings;
All that's born or dies
Rose and drooped with; made them
        shapers
Of mine own moods, or wailful or divine;
With them joyed and was bereaven.
I was heavy with the even,
When she lit her glimmering tapers
Round the day's dead sanctities.
I laughed in the morning's eyes.
I triumphed and I saddened with all weather,
Heaven and I wept together,
And its sweet tears were salt with mortal
        mine;
Against the red throb of its sunset-heart
I laid my own to beat,

And share commingling heat;
But not by that, by that, was eased my human
    smart.
In vain my tears were wet on Heaven's grey
    cheek.
For ah! we know not what each other says,
These things and I; in sound *I* speak –
Their sound is but their stir, they speak by
    silences.
Nature, poor stepdame, cannot slake my
    drouth;
Let her, if she would owe me,
Drop yon blue bosom-veil of sky, and show me
The breasts o' her tenderness:
Never did any milk of hers once bless
My thirsting mouth.
Nigh and nigh draws the chase,
With unperturbèd pace,
Deliberate speed, majestic instancy;
And past those noisèd Feet
A Voice comes yet more fleet –

'Lo! naught contents thee, who content'st
    not Me.'

Naked I wait Thy love's uplifted stroke!
My harness piece by piece Thou hast hewn from
    me,
And smitten me to my knee;
I am defenseless utterly.
I slept, methinks, and woke,
And, slowly gazing, find me stripped in sleep.
In the rash lustihead of my young powers,
I shook the pillaring hours
And pulled my life upon me; grimed with
    smears,
I stand amid the dust o' the mounded years –
My mangled youth lies dead beneath the
    heap.
My days have crackled and gone up in
    smoke,
Have puffed and burst as sun-stars on a
    stream.

Thomas Hardy

1840–1928

Thomas Hardy, the English poet and novelist, was born near Dorchester, and worked as an architect until the success of his 1874 novel Far From the Madding Crowd *enabled him to take up writing full-time. Many novels followed, but the hostile critical reception to* Jude the Obscure *(1896) over its alleged immorality caused Hardy to turn to poetry, of which he produced eight volumes, also dealing with nature and rural life. The 1914 volume* Satires of Circumstances *describes frankly his reactions to the death of his first wife Emma Gifford.*

From **Tess of the D'Urbervilles** (1891)

Approaching the hay-trussers she could hear the fiddled notes of a reel proceeding from some building in the rear; but no sound of dancing was audible – an exceptional state of things for these parts, where as a rule the stamping drowned the music. The front door being open she could see straight through the house into the garden at the back as far as the shades of night would allow; and nobody appearing to her knock she traversed the dwelling and went up the path to the outhouse whence the sound had attracted her.

It was a windowless erection used for storage, and from the open door there floated into the obscurity a mist of yellow radiance, which at first Tess thought to be illuminated smoke. But on drawing nearer she perceived that it was a cloud of dust, lit by candles within the outhouse, whose beams upon the haze carried forward the outline of the doorway into the wide night of the garden.

When she came close and looked in she beheld indistinct forms racing up and down to the figure of the dance, the silence of their footfalls arising from their being overshoe in 'scroff' – that is to say, the powdery residuum from the storage of peat and other products, the stirring of which by their turbulent feet created the nebulosity that involved the scene. Through this floating, fusty *débris* of peat and hay, mixed with the perspirations and warmth of the dancers, and forming together a sort of vegeto-human pollen, the muted fiddles feebly pushed their notes, in marked contrast to the spirit with which the measure was trodden out. They coughed as they danced, and laughed as they coughed. Of the rushing couples there could barely be discerned more than the high lights – the indistinctness shaping them to satyrs clasping nymphs – a multiplicity of Pans whirling a multiplicity of Syrinxes; Lotis attempting to elude Priapus, and always failing.

It was a typical summer evening in June, the atmosphere being in such delicate equilibrium and so transmissive that inanimate objects seemed endowed with two or three senses, if not five. There was no distinction between the near and the far, and an auditor felt close to everything within the horizon. The soundlessness impressed her as a positive entity rather than as the mere negation of noise. It was broken by the strumming of strings.

Tess had heard those notes in the attic above her head. Dim, flattened, constrained by their confinement, they had never appealed to her as now, when they wandered in the still air with a stark quality like that of nudity. To speak absolutely, both instrument and execution were poor; but the relative is all, and as she listened Tess, like a fascinated bird, could not leave the spot. Far from leaving she drew up towards the performer, keeping behind the hedge that he might not guess her presence.

The outskirt of the garden in which Tess found herself had been left uncultivated for some years, and was now damp and rank with juicy grass which sent up mists of pollen at a touch; and with tall blooming weeds emitting offensive smells – weeds whose red and yellow and purple hues formed a polychrome as dazzling as that of cultivated flowers. She went stealthily as a cat through this profusion of growth, gathering cuckoo-spittle on her skirts, cracking snails that were underfoot, staining her hands with thistle-milk and slug-slime, and rubbing off upon her naked arms sticky blights which, though snow-white on the apple-tree trunks, made madder stains on her skin; thus she drew quite near to Clare, still unobserved of him.

Tess was conscious of neither time nor space. The exaltation which she had described as being producible at will by gazing at a star, came now without any determination of hers; she undulated upon the thin notes of the second-hand harp, and their harmonies passed like breezes through her, bringing tears into her eyes. The floating pollen seemed to be his notes made visible, and the dampness of the garden the weeping of the garden's sensibility. Though near nightfall, the rank-smelling weed-flowers glowed as if they would not close for intentness, and the waves of colour mixed with the waves of sound.

The light which still shone was derived mainly from a large hole in the western bank of cloud; it was like a piece of day left behind by accident, dusk having closed in elsewhere. He concluded his plaintive melody, a very simple performance, demanding no great skill; and she waited, thinking another might be begun. But, tired of playing, he had desultorily come round the fence, and was rambling up behind her. Tess, her cheeks on fire, moved away furtively, as if hardly moving at all.

Paul Verlaine

1844–1896

The French poet Paul Verlaine was born in Metz and educated in Paris, and then entered the civil service and became involved in Parisian literary life. His disastrous relationship with the young poet Rimbaud between 1871 and 1873 ended in two years' imprisonment, after which he taught at schools in England and France. His poetry includes Romances sans paroles *(1874) and* Amour *(1888), largely written for his 'adopted son' Lucien Létinois. His essays* Les Poètes Maudits *(1884) heavily influenced the emergent Symbolist movement.*

'He's an awkward bedfellow and I love to keep . . .' **(Femmes/Hombres)**.
Trans. Alistair Elliot

He's an awkward bedfellow and I love to keep
Feeling him there, proud captive of my sleep,
Strong partner in the best of companies
(No small-hour waking, no miscarriages),
So near me, like a threat, contentedly
Growling, so near I think he's kissing me
With his great prick whose little red mouth lies
Wet on my quivering belly or my thighs
If we're confronted; if he's turned himself,
Like a good loaf slid down the oven shelf
His arse (perhaps in some sweet dream of lust)

And doughy cheeks (in fact, well-kneaded)
   thrust
Suddenly in my lap and with a thump
Pump and provoke a steeple from my stump;
Or if I turn away, he seems . . . he tries . . .
To thread my ring; if back to back, with nice
Animal carelessness he claps his bum
To mine, so (overjoyed) I rise and come
And sink and rise again in endless stands.

Happy? My whole world lies in His kind hands.

Alphonse Daudet

1840–1897

The French novelist Alphonse Daudet was born in Nîmes and educated in Lyons. In 1857 he moved to Paris, where he began contributing to periodicals, and from 1861 he was private secretary to the Duc de Mornay, Napoleon III's half-brother. His work – including Lettres de mon moulin *(1868), sketches of Provençal life, and the novel* Sappho *– belongs to the school of naturalism, but with a sharp eye for satirical and humorous detail.*

From **Sappho** (1883)

They stopped in the Rue Jacob, outside an hotel catering for students. There were four flights of stairs, a long, hard climb. 'Would you like me to carry you?' he asked, laughing, though softly in this sleeping house. She took him in with a slow look, scornful and tender, a gaze full of experience, measuring him up and quite distinctly saying: 'Poor boy. . . . '

And with the lovely fierce energy of youth and of the South he came from, he took her up in his arms and carried her like a child; he was sturdy and strapping, for all his girlish fair skin, and he went up the first flight without stopping for breath, rejoicing in his burden and the two beautiful, bare, rosy arms linked round his neck.

The second flight was longer, less delightful. The woman let herself go, and weighed the more heavily. The iron of her dangling ornaments, which was at first a caressing, a tickling of his skin, began to prick more cruelly and enter into his flesh.

On the third flight he was gasping like a furniture remover shifting a piano. He was too breathless to speak, while she, with fluttering eyelids, rapturously murmured: 'Oh, sweetheart, how lovely . . . how I do enjoy this. . . . ' And the last steps, which he climbed one at a time, were like the treads of a giant staircase and the walls, banisters, and narrow windows seemed to be turning in an endless spiral. It was no longer a woman he carried in his arms, but some heavy and dreadful thing that was stifling him, a thing that he was at every instant tempted to fling angrily from him, even at the risk of doing some brutal hurt.

When they reached the narrow landing – 'So soon?' she said, opening her eyes. What he thought was: 'At last!' But he could not have said it, standing there pale as death with both hands pressed to his chest, which seemed to be bursting.

Their whole story was there in that climbing of the stairs, in the grey gloom of the dawn.

Gerhart Hauptmann

1862–1946

A German dramatist, novelist and poet, Gerhart Hauptmann was born in Silesia and studied philosophy and history at Jena and sculpture in Rome. His early plays are naturalistic and polemical, and include Before Dawn *(1889), a sensational account of alcoholism, and* The Weavers *(1892). His later verse dramas turned to historical and mythological subjects. His novels include* Lineman Thiel *and* The Heretic of Soana *(1918), the latter concerning a priest who succumbs to an erotic paganism.*

From **Lineman Thiel** (1887). *Trans. Stanley Radcliffe*

When this had been done, three shrill bursts on the bell, which were repeated, announced that a train travelling from Breslau had been cleared by the next station down the line. Showing not the slightest sign of haste, Thiel remained a good while yet inside the cabin, finally emerging into the open, flag and detonator-bag in hand, to walk with a lazy, shambling gait along the narrow sandy path to the level-crossing that was about twenty paces distant. Thiel was conscientious in the closing and opening of his barriers before and after each train, although the road was scarcely ever used.

His job finished, he leaned waiting against the black and white barrier.

The track cut a straight line to right and left through the never-ending green of the forest; at either side of it the masses of green foliage seemed to check themselves, leaving a lane free between them, which was taken up by the reddish-brown, gravel-covered permanent way. The black, parallel-lying rails upon it resembled overall a gigantic iron mesh, whose narrow strands converged at points on the horizon to the extreme south and north.

The wind had risen and stirred the fringe of the wood into gentle waves, passing on into the distance. From the telegraph posts which ran alongside the track came a harmonious humming. To the wires which spun themselves from post to post like the web of some giant spider, flocks of twittering birds clung in serried rows. A woodpecker flew over Thiel's head with its laughing call, unacknowledged by so much as a glance.

The sun, which emerged at that moment beneath a bank of massive clouds to sink into the dark-green sea of crests, poured streams of purple over the forest. The colonnades of pine-trunks on the other side of the track seemed to flame incandescently and glow like iron.

The rails too began to glow, like fiery snakes; but they were the first to die out. And now the glow slowly rose from the ground into the air, leaving first the shafts of the pines and then the greater part of their crowns in the cold stagnant light, until finally only the topmost points of the crests were touched by a reddish shimmer. Silently and solemnly the sublime spectacle was enacted. The lineman was still standing motionless at the barrier. At last he took a step forward. A dark point on the horizon where the lines met was increasing in size. Growing from second to second, it yet seemed to remain in one place. Suddenly it acquired motion and approached. Through the lines there went a vibration and a humming, a rhythmical clatter, a muffled commotion, becoming louder and louder until it was not unlike the pounding of an approaching cavalry squadron.

From the distance a snorting and thundering came in waves through the air. Then suddenly the stillness was rent. A furious raging and roaring filled the whole place, the lines bent, the ground trembled – a mighty pressure of air – a cloud of dust, steam and smoke, and the black, snorting monster was past. Just as they had grown, the sounds gradually died away. The vapour dispersed. Shrunk to a point, the train disappeared into the distance, and the old sacred silence closed in again over the woods.

Pierre Louÿs

1870–1925

The French poet and novelist Pierre Louÿs was born in Ghent and educated in Paris, where, with Gide and Valéry, he founded the two symbolist literary reviews La Conque *(1891) and* Le Centaure *(1896). His own work includes* The Songs of Bilitis, *prose poems purporting to be translations from ancient Greek, and the novel* Aphrodite *(1896), describing the life of a courtesan in ancient Alexandria.*

From **The Songs of Bilitis**: 'Desire' (1894). *Trans. Alvah C. Bessie*

At night, they left us on a high white terrace, fainting among the roses. Warm perspiration flowed like heavy tears from our armpits, running on our breasts. An over-whelming pleasure-lust flushed our thrown-back heads.

Salome Franz von Stuck

Four captive doves, bathed in four different perfumes, fluttered silently above our heads. Drops of scent fell from their wings upon the naked women. I was streaming with the odour of the iris.

Oh, weariness! I laid my cheek upon a young girl's belly, who cooled her body with my humid hair. My open mouth was drunken with her saffron-scented skin. She slowly closed her thighs about my neck.

I dreamed, but an exhausting dream awakened me: the iynx, bird of night-desires, sang madly from afar. I coughed and shivered. An arm, as languid as a flower, rose in the air stretching towards the moon.

Oscar Wilde

1854–1900

Oscar Wilde, Irish dramatist, poet and novelist, was born in Dublin. His father was a surgeon and his mother a popular writer. Whilst at Oxford, he became a living embodiment of Aestheticism, renowned for his dandyism and brilliant wit. His work includes the social comedies Lady Windermere's Fan *(1892) and* The Importance of Being Earnest *(1895), and the novel* The Picture of Dorian Gray *(1891). After a sensational trial in 1895, Wilde was sentenced to two years' hard labour for homosexual offences, which gave rise to the poem 'The Ballad of Reading Gaol' (1898) and the posthumously published justificatory letter* De Profundis *(1905).*

From **Salome** (1894)

(A great black arm, the arm of the executioner, rises from the cistern, bearing on a silver shield the head of Jokanaan. Salome seizes it. Herod hides his face in his mantle. Herodias smiles and fans herself. The Nazarenes kneel and begin to pray.)

Ah! Thou didst not wish to let me kiss thy mouth, Jokanaan. Ah, well! I will kiss it now. I will bite it with my teeth as I bite a ripe fruit. Yes, I will kiss thy mouth, Jokanaan. I told thee I would, did I not? I told thee I would. Well! I will kiss it now . . . But why dost thou not look at me, Jokanaan? Thine eyes which were so terrible, which were so full of anger and scorn are now shut. Why are they shut? Open thine eyes! Lift thine eyelids, Jokanaan. Why dost thou not look at me? Hast thou fear of me, Jokanaan, that thou wilt not look at me? . . . and thy tongue which was like a red serpent darting out poison, it no longer moves, it says nothing now, Jokanaan, that red viper which spat its venom on me. It is strange, is it not? How is it the red viper moves not? . . . Thou wouldst have nothing of me, Jokanaan. Thou hast rejected me. Thou hast said infamous things of me. Thou hast treated me as a courtesan, as a prostitute, I, Salome, daughter of Herodias, Princess of Judæa! Ah, well! Jokanaan, I live still, but thou art dead and thy head belongs to me. I can do with it what I will. I can throw it to the dogs and the birds of the air. That which the dogs leave the birds will eat . . . Ah! Jokanaan, Jokanaan, thou wast the only man I have loved. All other men disgust me. But thou wast lovely. Thy body was a column of ivory upon a pedestal of silver. It was a garden full of doves and silver lilies. It was a silver tower adorned with ivory shields. Nothing in the world was as white as thy body. In the world was nothing so black as thy hair. In the whole world nothing was as red as thy lips. Thy voice was a swinging censer which spreads strange perfumes, and when I looked at thee

Lucian's True History Aubrey Beardsley

I heard mysterious music. Ah! why didst thou not look upon me, Jokanaan? Behind thy hands and thy blasphemies thou hast hidden thy countenance. Thou hast put over thine eyes the bandage of him who wishes only to see his God. Ah, well, thou hast seen Him, thy God, Jokanaan, whereas I . . . I, thou hast never seen me. If thou hadst looked upon me, thou wouldst have loved me. As to me, I have looked upon thee, Jokanaan, and I have loved thee. Oh! How I have loved thee. I love thee still, Jokanaan. I love only thee . . . I have thirst for thy beauty. I am hungry for thy body. Neither wine, nor fruit can satisfy my desire. What shall I do now, Jokanaan? Neither the floods nor the great waters can quench my desire. I was a princess, thou hast scorned me. I was a virgin, thou hast deflowered me. I was chaste, thou didst fill my veins with fire . . . Ah! Ah! why didst thou not look upon me, Jokanaan? If thou hadst looked upon me, thou wouldst have loved me. I know well thou wouldst have loved me, and the mystery of love is greater than the mystery of death. Love only shall be heeded.

Aubrey Beardsley

1872–1898

Best known for his unorthodox illustrations, Brighton-born Beardsley became one of the founders of the Art Nouveau style in Europe. His illustrations for Sir Thomas Malory's Le Morte d'Arthur *and Oscar Wilde's* Salome *were considered outrageously decadent, as were his contributions to the literary and artistic quarterly,* The Yellow Book. *His erotic novel* The Story of Venus and Tannhauser *(subsequently published in expurgated form as* Under the Hill*) contains a vicious caricature of Oscar Wilde.*

From **The Story of Venus and Tannhauser** (1907)

When all was said and done, the Chevalier tripped off to bid good morning to Venus. He found her wandering, in a sweet white muslin frock, upon the lawn outside, plucking flowers to deck her little déjeuner. He kissed her lightly upon the neck.

'I'm just going to feed Adolphe,' she said, pointing to a little reticule of buns that hung from her arm. Adolphe was her pet unicorn. 'He is such a dear,' she continued; 'milk-white all over excepting his black eyes, rose mouth and nostrils, and scarlet John.'

The unicorn had a very pretty palace of its own, made of green foliage and golden bars – a fitting home for such a delicate and dainty beast. Ah, it was indeed a splendid thing to watch the white creature roaming its artful cage, proud and beautiful, and knowing no mate except the Queen herself.

As Venus and Tannhauser approached the wicket, Adolphe began prancing and curvetting, pawing the soft turf with his ivory hoofs, and flaunting his tail like a gonfalon. Venus raised the latch and entered.

'You mustn't come in with me – Adolphe is so jealous,' she said, turning to the Chevalier who was following her; 'but you can stand outside and look on; Adolphe likes an audience.' Then in her delicious fingers she broke the spicy buns, and with affectionate niceness, breakfasted her ardent pet. When the last crumbs had been scattered, Venus brushed her hands together and pretended to leave the cage, without taking any more notice of Adolphe. Every morning she went through this piece of play, and every morning the amorous unicorn was cheated into a distressing agony lest that day should have proved the last of Venus's love. Not for long, though, would she leave him in that doubtful, piteous state, but running back passionately to where he stood, make adorable amends for her unkindness.

Poor Adolphe! How happy he was, touching the Queen's breasts with his quick tongue-tip. I have no doubt that the keener scent of animals must make women much more attractive to them than to men; for the gorgeous odour that but faintly fills our nostrils must be revealed to the brute creation in divine fulness. Anyhow Adolphe sniffed as never a man did around the skirts of Venus. After the first charming interchange of affectionate delicacies was over, the unicorn lay down upon his side, and, closing his eyes, beat his stomach wildly with the mark of manhood!

Venus caught that stunning member in her hands and lay her cheek along it; but few touches were wanted to consummate the creature's pleasure. The Queen bared her left arm to the elbow, and with the soft underneath of it made amazing movements horizontally upon the tightly-strung instrument. When the melody began to flow, the unicorn offered up an astonishing vocal accompaniment. Tannhauser was amused to learn that the etiquette of the Venusberg compelled everybody to await the outburst of these venereal sounds before they could sit down to déjeuner.

Adolphe had been quite profuse that morning.

Venus knelt where it had fallen, and lapped her little aperitif!

Richard Wagner

1813–1883

The German composer Richard Wagner was born and educated in Leipzig. His operas, for which he wrote his own libretti, include Tannhäuser *(1845),* Lohengrin *(1850),* Tristan and Isolde *and the 'Ring Cycle' (1854–1876). Always a controversial figure, not least for his revolutionary and nationalistic politics and tempestuous domestic life, his innovative music and critical writings represented the culmination of German Romanticism, his work becoming enormously influential in literature as well as in music.*

From **Tristan and Isolde** (1857–59). *Trans. Alfred Forman*

ISOLDE

(who, unconscious of everything around her, has been gazing vacantly before her, fixes her eyes at last upon TRISTAN.)

A smile his lips
has softly lighted;
his eyes are sweetly
on me opened;
friends, you see not?
Say you so?
More he beams
and more he brightens;
mightier grows

his mien and gladder;
with stars beset
aloft he soars;
friends, you see not?
Say you so?
How his heart,
too high to rest,
burns and pulses
in his breast;

how apart   is it waves
his lips are pressed   of breezes blended?
by swell of breath   Is it seas
he through them sends? –   of scent unended?
                                         How they stream
You see not, friends,   and storm and darken!
and feel not what I say? –   Shall I breathe them?
For me alone   Shall I hearken?
can be the sound   Shall I drink,
that fills and fades   or dive below,
and floats around;   spend my breath
for gladness grieves,   beneath their flow? –
unspoken leaves   Where the ocean of bliss
nought at all;   is unbounded and whole,
in rise and fall   where in sound upon sound
seems, by bringing   the scent-billows roll,
peace, his singing?   in the World's yet one
Will not wane,   all-swallowing soul –
burns my brain,   to drown –
sweeter round me   go down –
swells again?   to nameless night –
Clearer growing,   last delight!
deeper flowing,

(She sinks, as if transfigured, softly, in BRANGÆNE'S *arms, down upon* TRISTAN'S *body. Emotion and awe among the bystanders.* MARKE *blesses the bodies. The curtain falls slowly.)*

Georges Grassall

1867–1905

Georges Grassall wrote The Memoirs of Dolly Morton, *under the pen-name 'Hughes Rebell'. A prolific poet, novelist and essayist, he was also a friend and admirer of Oscar Wilde.*

From **The Memoirs of Dolly Morton** (1899)

Although I had often seen the marks of the lash on the bodies of the runaways who had passed through our station, I hitherto had never seen a slave whipped. Dinah, in her capacity of housekeeper, maintained strict discipline, so she often brought one of the women or one of the girls before Randolph for neglecting her work or some other offence, and sometimes he himself gave the offender a whipping on her bottom with the switch. I occasionally had heard the squeaks of a cuplrit, but I always avoided being present at the punishment.

Whipping a girl seemed to have an exciting effect on Randolph, for, after switching one he invariably used to come to me, wherever I happened to be, and poke me with great vigour.

I thought it strange at the time, but I since found out that men's passions are inflamed by whipping the bottom of a female until she cries and writhes with pain, and, if they can't do it themselves, they like seeing it done. This is a curious, but undoubted fact, and it shows what cruel creatures men are . . .

Kate Chopin

1851–1904

Novelist and story-writer Kate Chopin was born in St Louis, Missouri of part-French descent and lived both there and in New Orleans at different stages of her life. A great admirer of the French short story writer, Guy de Maupassant, she mainly wrote stories set among the Creoles and Cajuns. A consistent theme in her fiction was the oppression of women and the suppression of the female self.

From **The Awakening** (1899)

She leaned over and kissed him – a soft, cool, delicate kiss, whose voluptuous sting penetrated his whole being – then she moved away from him. He followed, and took her in his arms, just holding her close to him. She put her hand up to his face and pressed his cheek against her own. The action was full of love and tenderness. He sought her lips again. Then he drew her down upon the sofa beside him and held her hand in both of his.

'Now you know,' he said, 'now you know what I have been fighting against since last summer at Grand Isle, what drove me away and drove me back again.'

'Why have you been fighting against it?' she asked. Her face glowed with soft lights.

'Why? Because you were not free; you were Léonce Pontellier's wife. I couldn't help loving you if you were ten times his wife, but so long as I went away from you and kept away I could help telling you so.' She put her free hand up to his shoulder, and then against his cheek, rubbing it softly. He kissed her again. His face was warm and flushed.

'There in Mexico I was thinking of you all the time, and longing for you.'

'But not writing to me,' she interrupted.

'Something put into my head that you cared for me, and I lost my senses. I forgot everything but a wild dream of your some way becoming my wife.'

'Your wife!'

'Religion, loyalty, everything would give way if only you cared.'

'Then you must have forgotten that I was Léonce Pontellier's wife.'

'Oh! I was demented, dreaming of wild, impossible things, recalling men who had set their wives free, we have heard of such things.'

'Yes, we have heard of such things.'

'I came back full of vague, mad intentions. And when I got here –'

'When you got here you never came near me!' She was still caressing his cheek.

'I realized what a cur I was to dream of such a thing, even if you had been willing.'

She took his face between her hands and looked into it as if she would never withdraw her eyes more. She kissed him on the forehead, the eyes, the cheeks, and the lips.

'You have been a very, very foolish boy, wasting your time dreaming of impossible things when you speak of Mr. Pontellier's setting me free! I am no longer one of Mr. Pontellier's possessions to dispose of or not. I give myself where I choose. If he were to say, "Here, Robert, take her and be happy, she is yours," I should laugh at you both.'

His face grew a little white. 'What do you mean?' he asked.

There was a knock at the door. Old Celestine came in to say that Madame Ratignolle's servant had come around the back way with a message that Madame had been taken sick and begged Mrs. Pontellier to go to her immediately.

'Yes, yes,' said Edna, rising; 'I promised. Tell her yes – to wait for me. I'll go back with her.'

'Let me walk over with you,' offered Robert.

'No,' she said; 'I will go with the servant.' She went into her room to put on her hat, and when she came in again she sat once more upon the sofa beside him. He had not stirred. She put her arms about his neck.

'Good-bye, my sweet Robert. Tell me good-bye.' He kissed her with a degree of passion which had not before entered into his caress, and strained her to him.

'I love you,' she whispered, 'only you, no one but you. It was you who awoke me last summer out of a life-long, stupid dream. Oh! you have made me so unhappy with your indifference. Oh! I have suffered, suffered! Now you are here we shall love each other, my Robert. We shall be everything to each other. Nothing else in the world is of any consequence. I must go to my friend; but you will wait for me? No matter how late; you will wait for me, Robert?'

'Don't go, don't go! Oh! Edna, stay with me,' he pleaded. 'Why should you go? Stay with me, stay with me.'

'I shall come back as soon as I can; I shall find you here.' She buried her face in his neck, and said good-bye again. Her seductive voice, together with his great love for her, had enthralled his senses, had deprived him of every impulse but the longing to hold her and keep her.

Stefan George

1868–1933

The German poet Stefan George was born near Bingen, the son of a wealthy vintner. Influenced by Mallarmé and the Symbolist movement, his own poetry – including Hymnen *(1890) – and the journal he produced between 1890 and 1919,* Blätter fur die Kunst, *were characterized by a stylized aestheticism. His later work –* Das neue Reich *(1928), for example – expressed the hope for civilization's renewal through a youthful elite epitomized by Maximin, a boy he had met in Munich in 1903. These poems were eagerly appropriated by the Nazis, though George himself refused their honours.*

'Have you his lovely image'. *Trans. Carol North Valhope and Ernst Morwitz*

Have you his lovely image still in mind,
Who boldly at the chasm's roses caught,
Who passing day forgot in such a find,
Who heavy nectar from the clusters sought?

Who when the sheen of wings had driven him
Too far, for resting turned into the park,

Who musing sat at yonder water's rim
And listened to the deep and secret dark?

The swan by falling waters left his stand,
His island built of stones that mosses deck,
And led within a child's caressing hand,
And delicate – his slender neck.

Anon. (England)

'Nine Times a Night'

A buxom young fellow from London came down
To set up his trade in Ramsbottom town;
They asked who he was and he answered them right,
'I belong to a family called "Nine times a night".'

A buxom young widow who still wore her weeds,
Whose husband had left her her riches and deeds,
Resolvèd she was by her conjugal right,
To fill up her chisum with nine times a night.

She ordered her waiting maids, Betty and Nan,
To keep a lookout for that wonderful man,
And whenever they saw him appear in their sight,
To bring her glad tidings of nine times a night.

Fortune favoured the joke on the very next day,
Those giggling girls saw him coming that way.
Then upstairs they ran with amorous delight,
'Upon my word, madam, here's nine times a night.'

From a chair she arose (what I say is true),
And down to the hall door like lightning they flew,
She viewed him all over and gave him a smack,
The bargain was struck and done in a crack.

The marriage being over, the bride tolled the bell,
He did six times and pleased her so well,
She vowed from her heart she was satisfied quite,
Still she gave him a hint of nine times a night.

He said, 'My dear bride, you mistook the wrong thing,
I said to that family I did belong.
Nine times a night is too much for a man,
I can't do it myself, but my sister, she can.'

'Walter'

Little is known of 'Walter', the pen-name of a Victorian gentleman who wrote My Secret Life, *an eleven-volume account of his wide-ranging and explicit sexual adventures. It has been suggested by some that 'Walter' may have been the erotic bibliophile Henry Spencer Ashbee.*

From **My Secret Life** (*c.* 1890)

The abbess liked to introduce others and no doubt got paid for it. One day a Miss D**sy was named. – 'Speaks three languages, has been kept, not long been gay, and now only on the quiet, quite up to fun.' – So we had Miss D. a tallish, quite fair haired woman of say eight and twenty, a genteel woman who spoke French and German as I found, and who really knew much about Europe. She like all the others took a letch for H. – they all do – and of course I fucked her whilst minetting H. – the usual formula. But somehow her cunt didn't fit me at all, and I cared not about fucking her. Yet we had her several times, she was so conversable, and talked erotic philosophy in chaste language in the way poor Camille used, and for some reason or other – who can give reasons for letches tho we try? – the two women used to examine very curiously each other's cunts – a thing which usually H. did not care about doing, tho she'd frig any cunt near her when I was fucking her.

Miss D.'s cuntal fringe was silky but not very curly, and at half way down the sides of the lips the curls ceased and the hair became actually straight and long. It continued so nearly round the division between prick hole and bum hole, and when she squatted to piddle – of course I made her do that, her cunt looked – as indeed it did when she stood upright or lay on the bed with thighs apart, – not unlike the end of a broom. I told her of this, saying it was ugly. – H. agreed with me.

Miss D. said she didn't like it and looked carefully at H.'s one day – whose lips as they die away towards her bum hole are slightly covered by the shortest hairs with a charming tendency to curl – I said that if D.'s were clipped short they would look nicer to me – tho perhaps not to others, for tastes vary. – It ended in my artistically trimming Miss D**sy's straggling cuntal fringe with the scissors. – Next time seen she was delighted, for the short hairs had actually curled partially, she examined them with a hand glass before us, and we without the glass. The beauty of her cunt was really enhanced by my tonsorial skill, and particularly when she knelt on the bed and we viewed her quim from behind.

Yet as her cunt after several trials didn't fit me, we discontinued seeing her. She was soon after again kept by a gentleman, the abbess said. – She was a conversable woman, and no doubt her cunt had found a suitable partner. – Some cunts never seem to fit me – others are delicious.

.   .   .

One afternoon the abbess said as we entered, 'He's coming, I've just got a letter and have sent for a lady for him, he'll consent to masks, or anything else to have your friend.' We were a little startled at first. H. said she couldn't till she'd seen what sort of man he was. She wasn't going to let any ugly, old, common man have her.

When he arrived she went down to be introduced him, and came back approving, he was a fine tall handsome man of thirty and wanted to fuck her there and then. Her eyes glistened with lust, she had the exquisitely voluptuous look in her face which she has when randy. I layed down the conditions. He was to be naked all but his shirt, I to see his prick, and feel it if I liked. – 'No,' said the abbess, 'he won't allow that.' – 'Then he shan't have her.' – Down the abbess went and returning said that I might feel him if I liked. – 'Let him come,' – said H. impatiently. Up he came with mask on and soon divested himself of his clothes. H. without mask sat on his knee and pulled about a grand, stiff tool, triumphantly, whilst he fingered her quim. He was well made but rather hairy on his legs which I didn't like – many men are hairy legged.

Then she played one or two baudy tricks, and lastly turned her bum to him whilst he sat on a chair and got his prick up her. I sitting on a low chair opposite saw it hidden in her cunt, his balls hanging outside, his hands round her belly, one finger rubbing her clitoris. – 'Aha, go to the bed,' murmured he. He didn't attempt to disguise his voice as I did. To the bed they went where side by side she fondled his love staff, then he mounted her. – 'You shan't fuck me with that on,' said she, and suddenly pulled off his mask and dropped it on the floor. He cared about nothing now but possessing her, put his prick in her cunt rapidly, whilst she raised the thigh nearest the bedside high up, so that I who now approached the bed could see his prick ramming between her cunt lips – see the in and out movement, an exciting sight.

He'd given some rapid strokes when I threw up his shirt to his waist, to see the wag of his buttocks which were white but nothing remarkably handsome, and I didn't admire a central furrow strongly haired up to his backbone, but the come and go of his priapean shaft pleased me. He gave a sigh of pleasure and then I laid hold of his testicles. – 'Ho,' said he with a loud cry, and with a violent start uncunted. 'Don't do that.' – 'What is it?' said H., ceasing her bum wagging. – I told. – 'Fuck me, put it in, let him feel them, you will like it.' Before she'd said it all, his glowing tipped machine was again hidden, his balls wagged more than ever, soon the violent movement of her thighs and buttocks heralded her coming joy, and I heard, 'Fuck dear – aha – spunk,' and heard his murmurs of love. His ample balls were now soon steady over her bumhole, and both were quiet. *She* with closed eyes enjoying the blissful oozings of her cunt, the soothing influence of spermatic injection, his buttocks moving with the slightest gentlest jogs, rubbing his tender gland within the innermost recesses of her sexual treasure, whilst I held his balls, he seemingly unconscious of it.

TWENTIETH CENTURY

You get more salami with Modigliani Mel Ramos

As the façade of Victorian propriety began to crumble, although the radical dream of 'one culture' failed to materialize, the gap between 'high' culture and mass culture slowly began to narrow. There was a reaction against the idea expressed by Wilde that literature, being art, stood apart from life, and a growing insistence that literary values were ultimately at one with those of living itself. The movement was influenced by higher literacy rates, the mass production of cheap books and sensational censorship trials. Well into the second half of the twentieth century the seizing, banning, burning and bowdlerization of literary erotica continued throughout the Western world, as did the prosecution of its authors, publishers and sellers. But whereas official censorship once reflected public attitudes of middle-class prudery (despite the private habits of Victorian males), it now began to seem at odds with the views of readers or would-be readers.

The trials of books by such major literary figures as James Joyce (see page 299), D.H. Lawrence (see page 302), Henry Miller (see page 306), Jean Genet (see page 310), Hubert Selby Jr (see page 318) and William Burroughs (see page 321), to name but a few, were given prominent coverage by the popular newspapers, thereby popularizing works that might not otherwise have come to the public's attention. It is also likely that many more people bought books (often pirated and published abroad) by long-dead writers, such as Aristophanes, Petronius, Defoe, Cleland, Boccaccio, Rabelais, Balzac, Rousseau, Casanova and Voltaire, than they would have done had the censors not been hard at work.

Except in communist, fascist and other politically extreme states where no dissident voice was safe (Eros, being notoriously difficult to control, has always been suspected – and often accused and found guilty – of dissidence), poets, on the whole, remained relatively safe from public accusations of obscenity, legal proceedings and banning. Poetry seldom aroused the passions of censors who strove to 'protect' supposedly weaker members of society who might be depraved and corrupted by their reading matter, basically because it was assumed, largely correctly, that only the elite – who were deemed beyond corruption – ever read it. Prose fiction was viewed differently. During the trial of *Lady Chatterley's Lover* in 1960 the prosecution counsel still thought it relevant to demand of the jury, 'Is it a book that you would even wish your wife or servants to read?'

Another major influence on twentieth-century erotic literature was that of European sexologists and Sigmund Freud (1856–1939) who succeeded in codifying sexuality and both dismembering and connecting the relationship between Eros and Psyche in a startlingly new way. Freud's view of the powerful role of the unconscious became widely accepted and released writers from a sense of self-responsibility and the self-regulated codes of behaviour on which human nature – especially sexual nature – had been thought to depend. 'Stream of consciousness', a term borrowed directly from psychoanalysis to describe the flow of thoughts between the conscious and the unconscious mind, was put to erotic effect most notably by James Joyce in *Ulysses* (see page 299), and Marcel Proust (1871–1922) in *Remembrance of Things Past* (1913–27).

The virtual disappearance of sexual renunciation from western European literature in the twentieth century was part of the Freudian bequest. In defence of sexual explicitness in literature, D.H. Lawrence attacked sexual repression – a crucial tenet of psychoanalytic theory:

> 'Now our business is to realize sex. . . . After centuries of obfuscation, the mind demands to know, and know fully . . . The mind has to catch up . . . Mentally, we lag behind in our sexual thought, in a dimness, a lurking, grovelling fear which belongs to our raw, somewhat bestial ancestors . . . Now we have to catch up, and make a balance between the consciousness of the body's sensations and experiences, and these sensations and experiences themselves. Balance up the consciousness of the act, and the act itself.'
>
> (*À Propos of Lady Chatterley's Lover*)

Lady Chatterley's Lover, first published in 1928, is generally thought of as the single most important – and scandalous – erotic novel of the twentieth century. This is probably due to its long history of banning and censorship and its unbanning at a widely publicized obscenity trial rather than its actual content, which has been attacked for being too didactic and too naïvely sensualist to be considered an erotic novel of great merit. But famous, or infamous, it certainly is. As Philip Larkin (1922–85) wrote in his poem 'Annus Mirabilis': 'Sexual intercourse began/In nineteen sixty-three/(Which was rather late for me)/Between the end of the *Chatterley* ban/And the Beatles' first LP.' What seems to have got the would-be censors in a lather was Lawrence's description of anal intercourse enjoyed by Lady C. and her gamekeeper lover. But the prosecution was too coy to mention this and they lost their case, thereby discrediting the British obscenity laws as a means of banning erotica. That Lawrence was capable of some of the best erotic writing is, however, indisputable, as his poem 'Figs' (see page 302) proves. (For a more exuberantly erotic depiction of the pleasures of the palate the novel *Dona Flor and Her Two Husbands* (see page 342) by the Brazilian writer Jorge Amado is hard to beat.)

In countries where Freud's influence was negligible – in communist states, for example – heavy censorship did not have the effect of contributing to the sexual discourse. In China under Mao Tse-tung (1893–1976) and successive repressive regimes, all classical erotic literature was banned and all contemporary writers discouraged or coerced. In Russia bawdy proverbs and folk-tales were popular, but apart from the scatological *Junker* verse of Mikhail Lermontov (1814–41) and some youthful erotica by Aleksandr Pushkin (1799–1837), there was no strong erotic literary tradition. In the early years of the Soviet Union Aleksandra

Kollontai (1872–1952) challenged the increasingly authoritarian and sexually repressive attitudes of her male comrades, by defending the love poems of Anna Akmátova (1889–1966). In an article entitled 'Make Way for Winged Eros' (1923) Kollontai argued: 'The task of proletarian ideology is not to drive Eros from social life, but to rearm him according to the new social formation, and to educate sexual relationships in the spirit of the great new psychological force of comradely solidarity.' But Kollontai was dismissed as a *petit bourgeois* intellectual, and poets like Marina Tsevetayeva (an opponent of the Revolution) whose long poem cycle, 'The Poem of the End' (see page 295), records a passionate love affair she had while exiled in Prague, were unacceptable to the ruling party. It was not until the 1980s, as the union itself began to crumble, that the literary denial of Eros could be openly challenged.

Increasingly, twentieth-century writers portrayed an Eros uncontrolled by either nature or reason, with human beings completely dominated by their sex instincts. Henry Miller is perhaps the most obvious example. In *Tropic of Cancer* (see page 306) and *Tropic of Capricorn* (1939), as well as in his autobiographical trilogy, *The Rosy Crucifixion* (1949–60), he revealed a narcissistic, androcentric society in which men are emotionally far removed from women by both convention and idealism. They are stuck at an early stage of infant development, living their lives by what Freud termed the 'pleasure principle' – grabbing for what they can get before it disappears.

Freud's accompanying notion of a death instinct was another theme constantly explored in twentieth-century erotica. Thanatos (death) as a companion to Eros was nothing new. In *Eros Revived* (1990) Peter Wagner suggests that the association originated in the late medieval period, citing a picture by the sixteenth-century German artist Niklaus Manuel which portrays Death as a skeleton seducing a young woman. In the sixteenth century 'to die' became a popular literary euphemism for an orgasm; in *Much Ado About Nothing* (*c.* 1598), Benedick says to Beatrice: 'I will live in thy heart, die in thy lap, and be buried in thy eyes.' Similarly, the French term *le petit mort* perhaps owes something to the views of the early Christian fathers, who likened the male orgasm to the *petit mal* of 'falling sickness' (epilepsy) on the grounds that the froth from an epileptic's mouth was similar to ejaculate. But the relationship goes back much further. Sappho's 'bitter-sweetness' contains elements of both life- and death-giving forces, but before her, in a rare mention of sexual desire in *The Odyssey*, Homer describes Penelope's suitors as having 'loosened knees' – his phrase for a war-weary soldier who is about to face death because his legs can no longer bear him.

Early twentieth-century writers who explored the association between Eros and Thanatos, most notably in France with the Surrealist Apollinaire (see page 291), Georges Bataille (see page 301), 'Pauline Reage' (see page 316) and 'Jean de Berg' (see page 322), drew upon eighteenth-century libertine and Gothic traditions, as well as the decadent tradition of the mid- to late-nineteenth century. Refusing to dismiss these seminal French erotic writers as 'pornographers', the American critic Susan Sontag questioned contemporary assumptions that the 'human sexual appetite is, if untampered with, a natural, pleasant function; and that "the obscene" is a convention, the fiction imposed upon nature by a society convinced there is something vile about the sexual functions'. Pointing out that it is precisely these assumptions that are challenged by the French tradition represented by de Sade, Bataille and the authors of *The Story of O* and *The Image*, she continues:

'Human sexuality is, quite apart from Christian repressions, a highly questionable phenomenon, and belongs, at least potentially, among the extreme rather than the ordinary experiences of humanity. Tamed as it may be, sexuality remains one of the demonic forces in human conscious-ness – pushing us at intervals close to taboo and dangerous desires, which range from the impulse to commit sudden arbitary violence upon another person to the voluptuous yearning for the extinction of one's consciousness, for death itself. Even on the level of simple physical sensation and mood, making love surely resembles having an epileptic fit at least as much, if not more, than does eating a meal or conversing with someone. Everyone has felt (at least in fantasy) the erotic glamour of physical cruelty and an erotic lure in things that are vile and repulsive. These phenomena form part of the genuine spectrum of sexuality . . . '

(*The Pornographic Imagination*, 1967)

A fascination with death did not remain the sole preserve of European erotic fiction. In Japan, while Yukio Mishima (see page 312) explored the 'erotic glamour' of violence, Yasunari Kawabata examined the deathly lure of Lethe implicit in female passivity in *The House of the Sleeping Beauties* (see page 339). In the USA Hubert Selby Jr and William Burroughs pushed violence to what seemed to many the ultimate extreme in fiction, but the result was widely regarded as anaphrodisiac. The furore surrounding the publication of Selby's *Last Exit to Brooklyn* (see page 318) and Burroughs's *The Naked Lunch* (see page 321), in which all the old censorship arguments about literature versus pornography were re-enacted, was repeated in the 1990s with Bret Easton Ellis's *American Psycho* and with an outpouring of highly explicit sado-masochistic lesbian and gay fiction. To some critics it seemed that in the modern and post-modern novel Eros had been ascribed a multi-functional role he has never had before and which he is unable to fulfil.

Perversion and fetishism appear as major themes of twentieth-century erotic literature. Again, this is nothing new. De Sade, Sacher-Masoch and Swinburne, who wrote some of the flagellation pornography so popular in the eighteenth and nineteenth centuries, provided the most obvious templates for this sub-genre. As Michel Foucault wrote in *Madness and Civilization* (1961):

'Sadism is not a name finally given to a practice as old as Eros; it is a massive cultural fact which appeared precisely at the end of the eighteenth century, and which constitutes one of the greatest conversions of Western imagination: unreason transformed into delirium of the heart, madness of desire, the insane dialogue of love and death in the limitless presumption of appetite.'

But the codification of perversion by the turn-of-the-century sexologists and by Freud (to whom the term 'perversion' was completely neutral) perhaps provided a new impetus to those intent upon exploring the spectrum of human sexuality. Although the old obsessions with defloration, flagellation, incest and sodomy never died away completely, in a post-Freudian era perversion was treated as something infinitely more complex and varied.

Following the scandal caused by the imprisonment of Oscar Wilde for homosexual offences in 1895, which reverberated far beyond the shores of Great Britain, homosexuality as an erotic focus in fiction and verse during the early years of the twentieth century was largely covert and often reflected the view propagated by sexologists that same-sex love was a sickness. E.M. Forster (1879–1970) felt unable to publish his homosexual novel *Maurice* during his lifetime, but the Greek poet C.P. Cavafy (see page 295), while still using the model of 'disease', celebrated gay love with a directness and openness that is reminiscent of the ancient Greeks. In 1911 Thomas Mann (1875–1955) published *Death in Venice*, one of the most poignant of all erotic gay works of this period, in which it is love rather than gender that is central. The same is true of the poem 'Ode to Walt Whitman' by the Spanish writer Federico Garcia Lorca (see page 290 for another of Lorca's erotic poems).

Of all the gay writers who addressed the erotic in the twentieth century it is perhaps Jean Genet who stands out most prominently (see page 310). Befriended by Jean-Paul Sartre (1905–80), who wrote his biography, significantly entitled *Saint Genet* (1952), this French poet, novelist and playwright drew upon his personal knowledge of underworld crime, drugs and male prostitution to explore a ritualistic and mystical universe of violence, betrayal and death. The French Surrealist and Dadaist Jean Cocteau (1889–1963), himself the author of some subtly fine homoerotic novels and poems, considered Genet to be a *moraliste*; Genet's obituary in *The Times* maintained, 'not even the Marquis de Sade went further in exploring the potentialities and disappointments of evil'.

Since Aretino in the 16th century, female homosexuality had been treated by male writers as a subject for straight male sexual arousal and was a highly popular topic for nineteenth-century 'low' literature, or pornography – as it still is. Lesbian literature by lesbians was rare until the twentieth century when, despite the entirely negative view of the sexologists, they began to seize the right to explore the nature of their love for each other more openly. Unlike male homosexuality, lesbianism was not illegal, but as the English novelist Radclyffe Hall (1880–1943) discovered, society was no more kindly disposed towards gay women. Her novel, *The Well of Loneliness* (1928), with its masculine 'invert' heroine – a male soul trapped in a woman's body – and its famously coy line, ' . . . and that night they were not divided', today seems more romantic than erotic. But the prurient and lurid publicity surrounding its obscenity trial and eventual banning (until 1948) ensured that many lesbians would never be quite so lonely again.

The emergence of lesbian and gay subcultures by the 1970s was greatly influenced by this and other seminal homoerotic literary texts, notably *Giovanni's Room* (1956) by James Baldwin (1924–87) *Les Guerillères* (see page 338) by Monique Wittig and *Rubyfruit Jungle* by Rita Mae Brown (1944–1973). Male poets who addressed the homoerotic include James Kirkup, whose poem 'The Love That Dares to Speak Its Name' appeared in the British magazine *Gay News* (which was prosecuted for blasphemous libel and therefore cannot be published in this volume); the Italian film director Pier Paolo Pasolini (1922–75); the American beat poet Allen Ginsberg (*b.* 1926); and W.H. Auden, whose outrageously pornographic poem 'The Platonic Blow' (see page 324) appeared in the American magazine *Fuck You* (published by The Fuck You Press, who proclaimed themselves a 'name of distinction, representing four years of quality production in the slurping, slarfing, gobbling, golden shower and rim queen industries'). The best-known lesbian poets who in recent years have celebrated their sexuality include Adrienne Rich (see page 348), Judy Grahn (*b.* 1940) and Marilyn Hacker (*b.* 1942). In the 1980s lesbian writers in the USA, led by Pat Califia (see page 351), were at the forefront of a movement that extended the boundaries between erotica and pornography by exploring the erotic potential of gay sado-masochism.

Modern technology plays a significant role in twentieth-century explorations of perverse sexual gratification, with the communications industry receiving special attention. The eroticism of travel, implicit in so many sexual metaphors connected to horse-riding (see Browning's 'The Last Ride Together', page 238), became mechanized. While Flann O'Brien stuck to his bike (see page 309), e.e. cummings (see page 307) and an anonymous Trinidadian calypso composer (see page 315) exploited the erotic potential of the motor car. In *Lineman Thiel* (see page 261), the nineteenth-century writer Gerhart Hauptmann had used the steam engine as a metaphor for his protagonist's repressed erotic fantasies; a century later American novelist Erica Jong took to the skies to reveal an aggressive female libido in her novel *Fear of Flying* (1973). The speed, power and sense of disembodiment in air travel provided South African novelist Nadine Gordimer with the means to explore female passivity and male transgression in *The Conservationist* (see page 344); Terry Southern milks the *double entendres* of film-industry language ('shoot', 'cut' 'turn over', etc.) in his humorous erotic novel *Blue Movie* (1970); Leslie Dick's short story *Minitel 3615* tells of a love affair by electronics (see page 354), which makes Nicholson Baker's *Vox* (see page 358) seem positively outdated in its reliance upon the telephone. Modern technology seems to offer a mixture of 'dangerous' fantasy and safe sex – not altogether inappropriate in an age when millions die each year from Aids, mostly transmitted by sex.

The sexuality in much twentieth-century fiction has been described as sterile and frequently sickening, rather than erotic, in its preoccupation with violence, death, narcissism, fetishism and impersonal sex, with an insistence upon a grisly realism. The critic Allan Rodway offers an explanation in his essay on the modern erotic novel:

> 'Like the sense of smell, our sexual sense tires rapidly. To counter this process by enlisting the aid of imagination, unihibited introspection and controlled invention may indeed be one of the main justifications . . . for the preservation of this particular literary species. Unfortunately, mind and body seem much alike in this area: arousal being relatively easy . . . prolongation relatively hard, and re-arousal positively difficult – eventually becoming impossible no matter what the stimulation. In short, this is an area in which the law of diminishing returns applies with particular force.'
>
> Peter Webb, (ed.) (*The Erotic Arts*, 1975)

Humour was one means of countering this process. Eros dropped the humourless mask behind which he had been hidden since the eighteenth century. Here again, the influence of Freud can be detected, although perhaps the best example of the Freudian joke is to be found in Pierre de Bourdeille's mid-seventeenth-century novel *The Lives of Gallant Ladies* (see page 130). The *double entendre*, so popular with Pope and other eighteeth-century erotic satirists and novelists, was adopted with vigour by e.e. cummings (see page 307) and by the composers of many West Indian calypsos intent on circumventing fairly strict cultural taboos (see page 306). Terry Southern's approach to both humour and the erotic is altogether more full-frontal. His novel *Candy*, written with Mason Hoffenberg (see page 334), cleverly satirizes contemporary passions for guru cults in much the same way that Voltaire had satirized religion in *Candide* (see page 196). The title of Southern's eponymous heroine is no coincidence. In Philip Roth's

Portnoy's Complaint (1969), the erotic is subordinated to the comic psychological pictures he paints of Portnoy himself and his powerful Jewish mother. After reading this novel it is difficult to look at a slice of raw liver without blushing or with a straight face. (After reading Alina Reyes's entirely humourless novel *The Butcher* (see page 353), it may prove impossible to look at any raw meat ever again.)

One of the two novels that Rodway exempts from his criticism is Gore Vidal's hilarious *Myra Breckinridge* (see page 332), which combines the erotic with the comic, while also exploiting modern uncertainties of sexual identity. This issue is also explored, although without humour, with surprising erotic sensitivity and absence of machismo by Ernest Hemingway (1898–1961) in his posthumously published novel *Garden of Eden* (1968). Vladimir Nabokov's *Lolita* (1955) is the other novel exempted by Rodway. It too uses humour, but its eroticism lies in the exploration of a middle-aged man's unrequited passion for his 'nymphet' – a term coined by Nabokov as follows: 'Between the age limits of nine and fourteen there occur maidens who, to certain bewitched travellers twice or many times older than they, reveal their true nature which is not human, but nymphic (that is, demoniac); and these chosen creatures I propose to designate as "nymphets".' Although statutory rape was a crime at the time *Lolita* was written (and still is), it was to be some time before the full horror of childhood sexual abuse was more widely understood. Nowadays, Nadine Gordimer's opening chapter in *The Conservationist* (see page 344) seems very shocking indeed. But, like the Peruvian writer Mario Vargas Llosa in his novel *In Praise of the Stepmother* (1988), Nabokov also showed that incestuous desire did not have to be the sole preserve of 'low' pornography.

Freud's 'discovery' of infantile sexuality, initially received with horror and fear, and of teenage latency, stripped childhood and young adulthood of 'innocence', gave it a literary status it had previously only achieved in Rousseau's day. While the strong taboo surrounding very young child sexuality was largely heeded in erotic literature (although not in under-the-counter pornography), the teenage rite of passage became a subject that was explored over and over again in twentieth-century erotic fiction. At first it was mostly the young male sexual awakening that was examined by writers such as Thomas Mann (*Death in Venice*, 1913), Marcel Proust (*Remembrance of Things Past*), James Hanley (*Boy*, 1931), Günter Grass (*Cat and Mouse*, 1961) and Philip Roth (*Portnoy's Complaint*). But Colette, Violette Leduc, Rita Mae Brown and Marguerite Duras also explored this subject from the female perspective in their auto-biographical fiction, as did Angela Carter in her finely drawn novels and short stories, which frequently probed the dark side of adolescent sexuality.

Greater awareness of the importance of the sex instinct also meant that older texts, myths and fairy tales could be submitted to informed scrutiny to reveal rich veins of eroticism. In *The Uses of Enchantment* (1976), the psychologist Bruno Bettelheim shows how Marie Le Prince de Beaumont's mid-eighteenth-century children's story *Beauty and the Beast* (see page 190) is less 'innocent' than it might at first appear: 'it offers the child the strength to realize that his fears are the creations of his anxious sexual fantasies; and that while sex may at first seem beast-like, in reality love between woman and man is the most satisfying of all emotions, and the only one which makes for permanent happiness.' In the nineteenth century many children's tales were 'bowdlerized', which Angela Carter described as 'part of the project of turning the universal entertainment of the poor into the refined pastime of the middle classes, and especially of the middle-class nursery. The excision of references to sexual and excremental functions, the toning down of sexual situations and the reluctance to include "indelicate" material – that is, dirty jokes – helped to denaturize the fairy-tale and, indeed, helped to denaturize its vision of everyday life.' Carter herself drew upon the subliminal eroticism of 'Little Red Riding Hood' for one of her own novels, *Company of Wolves* (1984), and in an anthology she explored the erotic content of folk- and fairy-tales from all over the world (see page 357).

Perhaps the most notable trend of twentieth-century erotic literature was the re-emergence of women writers who, whether consciously or unconsciously, challenged a situation described by the American critic Leslie Fiedler: 'All the idealizations of the female from the earliest days of courtly love have been, in fact, devices to deprive her of freedom and self-determination.' (*Love and Death in the American Novel*, 1967). Colette in France, Sibilla Alermo in Italy, Charlotte Mew in England, Uno Chiyo in Japan, and the Americans (many of whom lived in Europe) Edith Wharton, Elinor Glyn, Edna St Vincent Millay, H.D. (Hilda Doolittle), Gertrude Stein and Djuna Barnes (who made the perceptive comment, 'Children know something they can't tell; they like Red Riding Hood and the wolf in bed!'), all broke free from the oppressive chains which had previously bound women by writing sometimes romantic but also highly sensual or sexually explicit poetry and prose. Like Kate Chopin (see page 269), many had to face hostility, but a greater awareness of female sexuality and a diminishing of Victorian prudery gave them the support that their nineteenth-century sisters had lacked. When, in 1926, Mae West wrote, produced and starred in her play succinctly entitled *SEX* – about a tough, bitter, imperious madame who ran the roughest brothel in town – male reviewers were outraged, but it drew huge, and predominantly female, audiences.

Remarkable for writing in the 1940s and 1950s, two decades in which conservative attitudes towards women and female sexuality prevailed, Anaïs Nin (see page 336) was possibly the most prolific of all twentieth-century female erotic writers, as well as one of the more problematic for feminists. In an essay entitled 'Eroticism in Women' she insisted, 'One point is established, that the erotic writings of men do not satisfy women, that it is time we write our own, that there is a difference in erotic needs, fantasies and attitudes.' But whether in her own work she succeeded in shedding what she termed the 'imitation of Henry Miller' and in making a distinction between pornography and eroticism, as she claimed for herself, is open to debate.

In the 1960s and 1970s, when the second wave of feminism burgeoned, the voice of the liberated female writer burst upon the literary scene in the Western world. Lisa Alther, Erica Jong, Marilyn French, Kate Millet, Monique Wittig, Luce Irigaray, Nicole Brossard, Marguerite Duras and Elfriede Jelinek are among the women who, in their fiction, poetry and prose, took up Nin's challenge and proved that Eros's misogynistic literary male acolytes – Lawrence, Miller, Genet, Norman Mailer, etc. – no longer ruled supreme. In the late 1970s and 1980s they were joined by Black American women such as Ntozake Shange and Alice Walker, by the Guyanese-born Grace Nichols (see page 350), by Mercedes Abad in Spain, by the Bombay-born Suniti Namjoshi and by Alina Reyes, Elisabeth Barille and Regine Deforges in France, among others.

In the 1980s and 1990s the debate concerning erotica and pornography, which had simmered and on occasions erupted into open confrontation whenever the State attempted to implement censorship laws, became dominated by feminist theory which focused on representations of sexual violence and by theories of 'political correctness'. While American feminist anti-pornographers like Andrea Dworkin and Katherine Mackinnon pursued the legislative path towards outlawing books and films that any woman considered had harmed her, other feminists pursued a policy of 'diff'rent strokes for diff'rent folks' in an unprecedented spate of anthologies of erotic stories by straight and lesbian women and by gay men, many of which were overtly sado-masochistic. Increasingly 'eroticism' became defined in terms of transgression. And yet no consensus exists; the plot summary of Andrea Dworkin's own novel, *Mercy* (1990), could be easily mistaken for that of the Marquis de Sade's *Justine* (1791).

Traditionally conservative literary genres have become increasingly sexually explicit. The once sexually sedate detective story gained sexually rapacious private eyes, straight and gay of both genders, and the woman's 'romance' was turned first into the 'bodice-ripper' and then into the 'S & F' or 'shopping and fucking' novel, for example. The label 'erotic' is given to novels which perhaps only twenty years earlier would have been condemned as 'pornography'.

Victorian pornography, once considered 'harmful' or dismissed as rubbish, is now interpreted as part of a 'discerning' erotic tradition. The American Anne Rice's gender-bending Gothic vampire novels and her more sexually explicit 'Sleeping Beauty' series have become 'mainstream' erotica. The links between Thanatos and Eros have never seemed closer than in the literary fantasies of bondage and sado-masochism by lesbian and gay writers such as Pat Califia and Dennis Cooper. Can this be one of the literary outcomes of Aids, which is otherwise avoided by writers of fiction and poetry?

It does not seem fanciful to posit that another literary outcome of Aids has been the growing popularity, perhaps largely unconscious, of the Dracula story. Vampires with their in-built predilection for blood have become an obvious metaphor for the transmission of the disease. Writers like Anne Rice and the film-maker Francis Ford Coppola lead the way for an eroticism in which the analogy is obvious, just as it had been in late Victorian times when syphilis – another disease spread by the transmission of bodily fluids – was rampant and Bram Stoker wrote the original tale.

Fears about the power of the written word to deprave and corrupt, or even to arouse, have become largely subordinated to fears about the visual media of magazine and movie culture. These were reinforced by the 1986 report of the US Attorney General, Edwin Meese, on the nature, extent and impact of pornography in the USA which, in the words of American academic Walter Kendrick, author of *The Secret Museum, Pornography in Modern Culture* (1990), 'stamped approval on America's split into a two-class culture, the top that reads and the bottom that does not or cannot ... Pictureless books can say what they please; they are impotent.' Feminist and politically correct theories notwithstanding, a wide belief prevails that the only difference between pornography and erotica is that the latter is what the rich can afford and the former what everyone else buys.

Colette

1873–1954

Sidonie Gabrielle Colette, the French writer who came to be known as simply Colette, was born in St-Saveur-en Puisaye. At the age of 20 she married Henri Gauthier-Villars, a journalist known as 'Willy', and under this name published her 'Claudine' novels, which were based on her early life. After the couple were divorced in 1906 she became a music-hall artist for a while, but continued to write. Her fiction, which is characterized by a preoccupation with sensory experience, questions traditional gender roles and explores the nature of female identity.

From **The Innocent Libertine** (1904–5). *Trans. Antonia White*

'What shall we do?'

'I don't know. Read?'

'No, it keeps one hot.'

Antoine examined Minne from head to foot. How slim she was in her transparent frock!

'A dress like that can't weigh much!'

'It still feels too heavy. Though I've got almost nothing on underneath. Look . . .'

She lifted the hem of her dress a little between her thumb and finger, like a skirt-dancer. Antoine had a glimpse of brown lisle stockings which had openwork over the pearly ankles and little lace-edged drawers, fitting tight above the knees. The patience cards slipped out of his trembling hands and fell on the floor.

'I shan't be such a fool as the last time,' he thought wildly.

He swallowed a great mouthful of saliva and managed to feign indifference.

'That's down below. But perhaps you're hot up above, under the top of your dress?'

'All I've got under that is my bra and my chemise . . . feel!'

She presented her back, with her head turned towards him, her elbows raised and her chest thrown out. He thrust out his hands, hurriedly searching for the almost flat side of the little breasts. Minne, who he had barely touched, jumped away from him with a squeak like a mouse and burst into spasms of laughter that brought tears to her eyes.

'Idiot! Idiot! Oh, that's strictly forbidden! Don't ever touch me under the arms! I think I'd have hysterics!'

She was giggling with sheer nerves, but he thought she was being provocative. Besides, he had just caught a scent from her moist armpits that went to his head. He had a frantic desire to touch Minne's skin, the secret skin that never saw daylight, to pull open her white under-clothes as one pulls open the petals of a rose – oh! not to do her any harm, only to see. He forced himself to be gentle, feeling his hands all at once extraordinarily clumsy and powerful.

'Don't laugh so loud,' he whispered, advancing on her.

She gradually calmed down, still laughing and twitching her shoulders, and dried her eyes with her fingertips.

'Have a heart! I can't stop myself. For mercy's sake, don't start again! . . . No, Antoine, or I'll scream!'

'Don't scream,' he implored, very low.

But, as he continued to advance, Minne retreated, her elbows pressed close to her sides to safeguard the ticklish place. Soon she was driven back against the door. Buttressing herself against it, she stretched out two threatening, pleading hands. Antoine seized her slender wrists and forced her timorous arms apart, thinking, when he had done so, how useful two extra hands would be at this moment for he dared not let go of Minne's wrists. She stood there, silent and uncertain, and he could see her eyes shifting uneasily, like troubled pools.

Stray strands of her hair tickled Antoine's chin and set up a furious itching which ran all over his body like a flame. To appease, without letting go of Minne's wrists, he pushed her arms further apart, plastered himself against her and rubbed his body against hers like a young, ignorant, excited dog.

A snake-like writhing repulsed him; the slender wrists turned and twisted in his fingers like the necks of strangled swans.

'You brute! You brute! Let go of me!'

He recoiled with a bound against the window and Minne remained against the door as if she were nailed to it; a white seagull with black, restless eyes.

She had not really understood. She had felt herself in danger. The whole body of a boy had pressed so hard against hers that she could still feel its hard muscles and its bruising bones. A belated anger flared up in her, she wanted to burst into furious abuse. Instead she burst into great, scalding tears which she hid in her upturned apron.

'Minne!'

Antoine, stupefied, watched her crying, tormented with grief and remorse and also with the fear that Mamma might come back.

'Minne, please, *please* stop crying!'

'Yes,' she sobbed. 'I'll tell . . . I'll tell.'

Antoine flung his handkerchief on the floor in a fury.

'Oh, of course! "I'll tell Mamma all about it!" Girls are all the same, all they can do is tell tales. You're no better than the rest.'

Instantly, Minne uncovered an offended face, dripping with tears and tumbled strands of hair.

'Oh, so that's what you think? Oh, so all I can do is tell tales? Oh, so I don't know how to keep secret, don't I? There are girls, let me tell you, who are bullied and insulted . . . '

'Minne!'

' . . . And who have more loads on their minds than all the schoolboys in the world!'.

L'École des Biches Anonymous

That innocent word 'schoolboy' stung Antoine on the raw. Schoolboy! It summed up everything: the awkward age when one's sleeves are too short and one's moustache not long enough, when one's heart dilates at a scent or the rustle of a skirt – all the melancholic, feverish years of waiting. The sudden rage that flamed up in Antoine freed him from his fuddled intoxication: Mamma could safely come in now.

Federico Garcia Lorca

1889–1936

The Spanish dramatist and poet Lorca was born in Andalucia and educated in Granada and Madrid. His plays – including Blood Wedding *(1933),* Yerma *(1934) and* The House of Bernarda Alba *(1936) – explore the themes of love, sterility and murder with an almost classical simplicity. He was murdered, probably by Nationalists, at the start of the Civil War.*

'The Unfaithful Wife'. *Trans. Alan Bold*

So I took her to the riverside
taking her for a virgin
but she had taken a husband.
Midsummer night, the Feast of St James:
it was a point of honour.
The streetlamps went off
and the crickets went on.
On the outskirts
I touched her sleeping breasts
and instantly they blossomed
like sprays of hyacinth.
The starch in her underskirt
grated on my ears like
a sheet of silk
lacerated by ten knives.
Without silver glinting on their leaves
the trees looked massive.
A horizon of dogs
Howls in the distance.

Past the blackberries,
the rushes, the hawthorn,
under her hair in the sand
I made a hollow for her head.
I took off my tie,
she took off her dress.
I removed my gunbelt,
she removed her underwear.
Neither petals nor shells

match such delicate skin,
nor do moonlit mirrors
glow with such shine.
Her thighs struggled
like astonished fish
caught in a torrent
now fiery, now frozen.
That night I rode
on the best of roads,
my mother-of-pearl mount
free and unbridled.
As a man I hesitate to say
the things she said to me:
the seeds of understanding
breed discretion.
Covered in kisses and sand
I removed her from the riverside.
The swords of the lillies
cut through the atmosphere.

I acted like the man I am,
a decent gypsy.
I gave her a big sewing-basket
of straw-coloured satin,
and preferred not to fall in love
because she had taken a husband
yet told me she was a virgin
when I took her by the riverside.

Guillaume Apollinaire

1880–1918

A French poet and critic of Polish descent, Apollinaire worked in Paris from the turn of the century as a literary journalist and editor, championing the emergent Cubist and Futurist movements. His own work includes the two volumes of formally experimental poetry Alcools *(1913) and* Calligrammes *(1918), some pseudonymously-published pornographic novels, and the play* Les Mamelles de Tiresias *(1918), one of the earliest examples of Surrealism.*

From **Les onze mille verges** or **The Amorous Adventures of Prince Mony Vibesco** (1907). *Trans. Nina Cootes*

'I am a Roumanian prince and a hereditary Hospodar.'

'And I am Culculine d'Ancône,' she said, 'I am nineteen years old and I have already drained the balls of ten men who were masters in the art of love and emptied the purses of fifteen millionaires.'

Chatting pleasantly on a number of whimsical and titillating subjects, the prince and Culculine reached the house on the rue Duphot. They took the lift to the first floor.

'Prince Mony Vibescu . . . my friend, Alexine Mangetout.'

Culculine made the introductions very gravely in a luxurious boudoir decorated with obscene Japanese prints.

The two friends kissed each other, using their tongues. Both women were tall, but not excessively so.

Culculine was dark, her grey eyes flashed with malice and a beauty spot with a little tuft of hair on it graced the bottom of her left cheek. Her complexion was matt, the blood coursed beneath her skin, her cheeks and forehead wrinkled frequently, attesting to her preoccupation with money and love.

Alexine was a blonde of that particular shade tending towards ash which one sees only in Paris. Her complexion was clear, almost transparent. In her charming rose-coloured négligé, this pretty girl looked as dainty and as roguish as a naughty eighteenth-century marchioness.

The formal introductions were soon over and Alexine, who had had a Roumanian lover, went into her bedroom to fetch his photograph. The prince and Culculine followed her. The pair threw themselves at her and laughingly undressed her. Her peignoir fell off, leaving her in a batiste chemise which revealed a charmingly buxom body, dimpled in the appropriate places.

Mony and Culculine tumbled her over on to the bed and exposed her lovely rosy tits, which were large and hard. Mony sucked the nipples. Culculine bent down and lifted her chemise, uncovering strong round thighs which met beneath a pussy of the same ash blonde as the hair of her head. Gurgling with pleasure, Alexine drew her little feet up on to the bed, letting her slippers fall to the floor with a sharp slap. Her legs spread wide, she lifted her arse to meet her friend's licking tongue and clasped her hands around Mony's neck.

It was not long before the desired result was achieved, her buttocks clenched, her body lashed more violently. Then she came, crying out:

'Beasts! You have excited me, now you must satisfy me.'

'He has sworn to do it twenty times!' said Culculine, taking off her clothes.

The prince followed her example. At the same moment each of them stood naked, admiring the other's body while Alexine lay swooning on the bed. Culculine's large bottom swayed deliciously below a very narrow waist. She grabbed hold of Mony's enormous prick, swelling over a huge pair of balls.

'Give it to her,' she said, 'you can do it to me afterwards.'

As the prince's member approached Alexine's half-open cunt, the girl trembled in anticipation:

'You'll kill me!' she cried.

But the prick sank in right up to the balls and was withdrawn and rammed in again like a piston. Culculine climbed on to the bed and laid her black bush on Alexine's mouth, while Mony licked her arsehole. Alexine moved her bottom like a woman possessed, she put one finger up Mony's arsehole and this caress made his cock still harder. He moved his hands round under Alexine's buttocks, while she clenched them together with unbelievable strength, gripping Mony's prick in her inflamed cunt in such a stranglehold that he could scarcely move.

Soon the three of them were thrashing about in a transport, panting and gasping. Alexine came three times, then it was Culculine's turn. Immediately afterwards, she moved down to nibble Mony's balls. Alexine began to cry out like a damned soul and when Mony shot his Roumanian spunk into her belly, she writhed like a serpent. Culculine at once wrenched him out of the hole and her mouth took the place of his cock, lapping up the sperm which was dribbling out in large droplets. Meanwhile, Alexine had taken Mony's weapon into her mouth and licked it clean, giving him a new erection at the same time.

A minute later, the prince threw himself on Culculine, but his prick remained at the entrance, titillating her clitoris. He seized one of the young woman's breasts in his mouth. Alexine caressed them both.

'Put it in,' cried Culculine, 'I can't bear it any longer.'

But his prick still lingered outside. She came twice, and was on the point of desperation when suddenly he penetrated her, right up to the womb. Wild with excitement and voluptuous delight, she bit Mony's ear so hard that a piece of it came away in her mouth. She swallowed it, shouting at the top of her voice and heaving her arse majestically. This wound, gushing with blood, seemed to excite Mony, for he began to plough her with increased vigour and did not leave Culculine's cunt until he had discharged three times, while she herself came ten times.

When he withdrew, they found to their amazement that Alexine had disappeared. She soon came back carrying pharmaceutical preparations for dressing Mony's ear and a huge coachman's whip.

'I bought this for 50 francs,' she exclaimed. 'I got it from the driver of Hackney-Carriage No. 3269, it will help us to make the Roumanian hard again. Let him bandage his ear, Culculine my love, while we do 69 to stimulate him.'

While he was staunching the blood, Mony watched the provocative spectacle of Culculine and Alexine, head to tail, greedily licking one another. Alexine's large backside, white and dimpled, dangled over Culculine's face; their tongues, as long as little boys' cocks, worked steadily, saliva and vaginal juices mingled, wet hairs stuck together and sighs – which would have been heart-rending if they had not been sighs of love – rose from the bed as it creaked and squeaked beneath the agreeable weight of the two pretty creatures.

'Come and bugger me!' cried Alexine.

But Mony was losing so much blood that he no longer had the strength to get an erection. Alexine stood up and, seizing the whip from Hackney-Carriage No. 3269, a superb brand new *perpignan*, brandished it and set about lashing Mony over the back and buttocks. Under the onslaught of this new pain, he forgot his bleeding ear and started to yell, but the naked Alexine, like a frenzied bacchante, kept on striking.

'Come and beat me too!' she cried to Culculine, who, with blazing eyes, began to thump Alexine's large, quivering arse as hard as she could. Soon Culculine was as excited as her friend.

'Beat me, Mony!' she pleaded, and the prince who was growing accustomed to the flagellation, although it had already drawn blood, started to slap her handsome, dusky buttocks, which opened and shut rhythmically. By the time his cock was stiff, the blood was flowing not only from his ear but from every weal left by the cruel whip.

Alexine then turned round and proffered her lovely reddened arse to the enormous prick, which pierced her little rosebud, while she, impaled, cried out, wriggling her backside and shaking her tits. But Culculine laughed and separated them, so that she and Alexine could resume their game of 69. Mony, streaming with blood, again buried his weapon up to the hilt in Alexine's arse and buggered her so vigorously that she was soon over-whelmed with joy. His balls swung to and fro like the bells of Notre-Dame and bounced against Culculine's nose. At a certain moment, Alexine squeezed her arsehole so tightly around the root of Mony's prick that he could no longer move. Then he came, his sperm sucked out in long jets by Alexine Mangetout's avid anus.

Meanwhile, out in the street, a crowd had gathered round Hackney-Carriage No. 3269, whose driver had no whip.

A policeman asked him what he had done with it.

'I sold it to a lady in rue Duphot.'

'Then go and get it back or I'll fine you.'

'All right, I'll go,' said the coachman, a Norman of exceptional strength. He asked the concierge for directions, then rang the bell on the first floor.

Alexine answered the doorbell stark naked; the coachman's eyes nearly started out of his head and when she fled into the bedroom he ran after her, caught hold of her and thrust a respectably-sized cock into her from the rear. He soon climaxed, shouting: 'Hell's bells, heaven's brothel and the Whore of Babylon!'

Alexine jerked her arse against him and came at the same moment, while Mony and Culculine were splitting their sides with mirth. The coachman, thinking they were laughing at him, flew into a terrible rage.

'Ugh, you whores, pimps, vultures, sewer rats, you're taking the piss out of me! My whip, where's my whip?'

And, catching sight of it, he snatched it up and began to flay Mony, Alexine and Culculine with all his might. Their naked bodies flinched under the blows which left bloody stripes.

Then, his cock swelling again, he pounced on Mony and buggered him.

The front door had been left open and the police sergeant, tired of waiting for the coach-man to return, had come in search of him, and it was at this precise moment that he entered the bedroom. Without wasting a moment, he pulled out his regulation-size prick and slipped it into Culculine's backside; she clucked like a hen and shivered at the cold contact of his uniform buttons.

Alexine, left to herself, took the white truncheon from its holster at the policeman's side. She inserted it into her cunt and soon all five of them were enjoying themselves immensely, while the blood from their wounds ran down on to the carpets, the sheets and the furniture and while, outside, the abandoned Hackney-Carriage No. 3269 was being led away to the police pound. The horse farted all the way, filling the street with a nauseating stench.

Rainer Maria Rilke

1875–1976

The Austrian poet Rilke was born in Prague and educated there and in Munich and Berlin. His extensive travels took him to Russia, where he met Tolstoy, and to Paris, where he acted as secretary to the sculptor Auguste Rodin. His poetry – including the Duineser Elegies *(published 1923, but mainly written during the war) and* Sonnets to Orpheus *(1923) – is often angst-ridden, but also possesses a visionary lyricism that has made Rilke one of the most widely-read poets in German.*

'The Birth of the Smile' (1920). *Trans. J.B. Leishman*

> *Vinse il Dio quella chi sola al mondo*
> *Ebbe la fonte nel suo angelico viso.*
> *Cantimi, incelita Musa, il primo giocondo*
> *Quello, nostro ancora, raro sorriso*

It was not always so. The shaping hand
that moulded our first ancestors from clay
attempted them in a more massive way,
so that the finished figure might withstand

life's flood, that snatches each created kind.
True, in the kernel of this new existence
the shaper had concealed the counter-distance,
that shapingly-encountered thing, the mind;

which, since its narrow home would not allow
it room to spread, flared up and burnt its way
through what constricted. Marks remain to-day
in the loins' surging flame, the arching brow.

The power was indeed power. But it shot
through every limb, and plied its fiery play

so fervently within the brain, the hot
charred mouth below it almost fell away.

Lovers that came together in desire
would stare like blacksmiths in their dusky
    den,
burst into flame and scream 'We are on fire!'
There was no gentleness in either then.

In primal wind their kindled atoms roared.
The fiery Deluge. The blind human blaze,
Those were the generations of the sword:
no land, one gulf of flames would meet the
    gaze.

Who tamed that maddened mind, breaking
    away
from narrow bodies where it felt afraid?
A god, a tall cool god, the people say,
appeared and beckoned to a youngest maid,

and under them an isle of coolness rose.

C.P. Cavafy

1863–1933

One of the greatest poets in modern Greek, C. P. (Constantine) Cavafy (Kafavis) was born into a prosperous Alexandrian merchant family, and spent much of his youth in England and Constantinople (Istanbul) before return- ing to Alexandria, where he worked as a civil servant. His work tackles historical, philosophical and erotic themes, and he was one of the first modern writers to deal explicitly with homosexuality.

'One Night' (1915). *Trans. Edmund Keeley and Phillip Sherrard*

The room was cheap and sordid,
hidden above the suspect taverna.
From the window you could see the alley,
dirty and narrow. From below
came the voices of workmen
playing cards, enjoying themselves.

And there on that ordinary, plain bed
I had love's body, knew those intoxicating lips,
red and sensual,
red lips so intoxicating
that now as I write, after so many years,
in my lonely house, I'm drunk with passion again.

Marina Tsvetayeva

1892–1941

The Russian poet Marina Tsvetayeva was born into an intellectual Moscow family. In 1922 she emigrated to Prague and then Paris in order to avoid Bolshevik persecution, returning to Russia in 1939 even though her husband had been shot and her daughter placed in a prison camp. After the Nazi invasion in 1941, Tsvetayeva was evacuated to Yelabuga, where she committed suicide. Her poetry – including the volumes Evening Album *(1910) and* After Russia *(1928) – is formally innovative and often darkly passionate.*

From **'The Poem of the End'**. *Trans. Elaine Feinstein*

Last   bridge   I won't
give up or take out my hand
this is the last bridge
the last bridging between

water   and firm land:
and I am saving these
coins for death
for Charon, the price of Lethe

this   shadow money
from my dark hand I press
soundlessly into
the shadowy darkness of his

shadow money it is
no gleam and tinkle in it
coins for shadows:
the dead have enough poppies

This bridge

Lovers for the most
part are without hope: passion
also is just
a bridge, a means of connection

It's warm: to nestle
close at your ribs, to move in
a visionary pause
towards nothing, beside nothing

no   arms no   legs
now, only the bone of my
side is alive where
it presses directly against you

life in that side
only, ear and echo is it: there
I stick like white to
egg yolk, or an eskimo to his fur

adhesive, pressing
joined to you: Siamese
twins are no nearer.
The woman you call mother

when she forgot
all things in motionless triumph
only to carry you:
she did not hold you closer.

Understand: we have
grown into one as we slept and
now I can't jump
because I can't let go your hand

and I won't be torn off
as I press close to you: this
bridge is no husband
but a lover: a just slipping past

our support: for the
river is fed with bodies!
I bite in like a tick
you must tear out my roots to be rid
     of me

like ivy   like a tick
inhuman   godless
to throw me away like a thing, when
     there is

no thing I ever prized
in this empty world of things.
Say this is only dream,
night still and afterwards morning

an express   to Rome?
Granada? I won't know myself
as I push off
the Himalayas of bedclothes.

But this dark is deep:
now I warm you with my blood, listen
to this flesh.
It is far truer than poems.

If you are warm, who
will you go to tomorrow for that?
This is delirium,
please say this bridge cannot

end
     as it ends.

W. B. Yeats

1865–1939

William Butler Yeats was born in Dublin and brought up in County Sligo and London. His early work draws from Walter Pater's Aesthetic Movement, though later he developed his own unmistakable idiom, marked by a visionary austerity and demanding symbolism. An ardent nationalist (in love with the revolutionary Maud Gonne), he helped found the Irish National Theatre, and his poems often deal with Irish mythology. In the 1920s he served as a senator of the newly-established Irish Free State, and was awarded the Nobel Prize for Literature.

'Leda and the Swan' (1923)

A sudden blow: the great wings beating still
Above the staggering girl, her thighs caressed
By the dark webs, her nape caught in his bill,
He holds her helpless breast upon his breast.

How can those terrified vague fingers push
The feathered glory from her loosening thighs?
And how can body, laid in that white rush,
But feel the strange heart beating where it lies?

A shudder in the loins engenders there
The broken wall, the burning roof and tower
And Agamemnon dead.
                Being so caught up,
So mastered by the brute blood of the air,
Did she put on his knowledge with his power
Before the indifferent beak could let her drop?

Frank Harris

1856–1931

Born either in Ireland or Wales (according to which of his yarns you believe), the journalist and writer Frank Harris went to America at the age of 15, progressing from bootblacker to cowboy. Back in London, he became a newspaper and magazine editor, with a taste for the sensational. As well as biographies of Shakespeare, Shaw and Wilde, Harris wrote several autobiographical works, including the salacious My Life and Loves.

From **My Life and Loves**, Volume 2 (1926)

As we turned off towards our bedrooms on the left, I saw that her face was glowing. At her door I stopped her: 'my kiss' I said and as in a dream she kissed me: *L'heure du berger* had struck.

'Won't you come to me tonight?' I whispered, 'that door leads into my room'. She looked at me with that inscrutable woman's glance and for the first time her eyes gave themselves.

That night I went to bed early and moved away the sofa which on my side barred her door. I tried the lock but found it closed on her side, worse luck!

As I lay in bed that night about eleven o'clock I heard and saw the handle of the door move: at once I blew out the light; but the blinds were not drawn and the room was alight with moonshine. 'May I come in?' she asked; 'May you?' I was out of bed in a jiffy and had taken her adorable soft round form in my arms: 'You Darling sweet' I cried and lifted her into my bed. She had dropped her dressing-gown, had only a nightie on and in one moment my hands were all over her lovely body. The next moment I was with her in bed and on her; but she moved aside and away from me.

'No, let's talk' she said. I began kissing her but acquiesced: 'let's talk'. To my amazement she began: 'Have you read Zola's latest book *Nana*?' 'Yes', I replied. 'Well' She said, 'you know what the girl did to Nana?' 'Yes' I replied with sinking heart. 'Well', she went on, 'why not do that to me? I'm desperately afraid of getting a child, you would be too in my place, why not love each other without fear?' A moment's thought told me that all roads lead to Rome and so I assented and soon I slipped down between her legs. 'Tell me please how to give you most pleasure' I said and gently, I opened the lips of her sex and put my lips on it and my tongue against her clitoris. There was nothing repulsive in it; it was another and more sensitive mouth. Hardly had I kissed it twice when she slid lower down in the bed with a sigh whispering; 'that's it; that's heavenly!'

Thus encouraged I naturally continued: soon her little lump swelled out so that I could take it in my lips and each time I sucked it, her body moved convulsively and soon she opened her legs further and drew them up to let me in, to the uttermost. Now I varied the movement by tonguing the rest of her sex and thrusting my tongue into her us far as possible; her movements quickened and her breathing grew more and more spasmodic and when I went back to the clitoris again and took it in my lips and sucked it while pushing my forefinger back and forth into her sex, her movements became wilder and she began suddenly to cry in French, 'oh, c'est fou! oh, c'est fou! oh, oh!' and suddenly she lifted me up, took my head in both her hands and crushed my mouth with hers as if she wanted to hurt me.

The next moment my head was between her legs again and the game went on. Little by little I felt that my finger rubbing the top of her sex while I tongued her clitoris gave her the most pleasure and after another ten minutes of this delightful practice she cried 'Frank, Frank, stop! kiss me! Stop and kiss me, I can't stand any more. I am rigid with passion and want to bite or pinch you.'

Naturally I did as I was told and her body melted itself against mine while our lips met – 'You dear' she said, 'I love you so, and oh how wonderfully you kiss'.

'You've taught me' I said. 'I'm your pupil'. While we were together my sex was against hers and seeking an entry, each time it pushed in, she drew away; at length she said; 'I'd love to give myself to you, dear, but I'm frightened'. 'You need not be'; I assured her 'if you let me enter I'll withdraw before my seed comes and there'll be no danger.' But do what I would, say what I would, that first night she would not yield to me in the usual way.

I knew enough about women to know that the more I restrained myself and left her to take the initiative, the greater would be my reward.

James Joyce

1882–1941

The Irish novelist James Joyce was born in Dublin, which provided the setting for all his fiction despite his self-imposed exile – from 1904 he lived successively in Paris, Zurich and Trieste. His work is marked by a radical shift from the early realism of Dubliners *(1914) to the extraordinary literary and linguistic experimentation of* Finnegans Wake *(1939).* Ulysses *– recording one day in the life of three Dubliners, and employing stream-of-consciousness narrative and encyclopaedic allusiveness – is his most influential novel, although it was banned in Britain for some forty years, thought to be obscene.*

From **Ulysses** (1922)

. . . Id love a big juicy pear now to melt in your mouth like when I used to be in the longing way then Ill throw him up his eggs and tea in the moustachecup she gave him to make his mouth bigger I suppose hed like my nice cream too I know what Ill do Ill go about rather gay not too much singing a bit now and then mi fa pietà Masetto then Ill start dressing myself to go out presto non son più forte Ill put on my best shift and drawers let him have a good eyeful out of that to make his micky stand for him Ill let him know if thats what he wanted that his wife is fucked yes and damn well fucked too up to my neck nearly not by him 5 or 6 times handrunning theres the mark of his spunk on the clean sheet I wouldnt bother to even iron it out that ought to satisfy him if you dont believe me feel my belly unless I made him stand there and put him into me Ive a mind to tell him every scrap and make him do it in front of me serve him right its all his own fault if I am an adulteress as the thing in the gallery said O much about it if thats all the harm ever we did in this vale of tears God knows its not much doesnt everybody only they hide it I suppose thats what a woman is supposed to be there for or He wouldnt have made us the way He did so attractive to men then if he wants to kiss my bottom Ill drag open my drawers and bulge it right out in his face as large as life he can stick his tongue 7 miles up my hole as hes there my brown part then Ill tell him I want £1 or perhaps 30/- Ill tell him I want to buy underclothes then if he gives me that well he wont be too bad I dont want to soak it all out of him like other women do I could often have written out a fine cheque for myself and write his name on it for a couple of pounds a few times he forgot to lock it up besides he wont spend it Ill let him do it off on me behind provided he doesnt smear all my good drawers O I suppose that cant be helped Ill do the indifferent 1 or 2 questions Ill know by the answers when hes like that he cant keep a thing back I know every turn in him Ill tighten my bottom well and let out a few smutty words smellrump or lick my shit or the first mad thing comes into my head then Ill suggest about yes O wait now sonny my turn is coming Ill be quite gay and friendly over it O but I was forgetting this bloody pest of a thing pfooh you wouldnt know which to laugh or cry were such a mixture of plum and apple no Ill have to wear the old things so much the better itll be more pointed hell never know whether he did it nor not there thats good enough for you any old thing at all then Ill wipe him off me just like a business his omission then Ill go out Ill have him eying up at the ceiling where is she gone now make him want me thats the only way a quarter after what an unearthly hour I suppose theyre just getting up in China now combing out their pigtails for the day well soon have the nuns ringing the angelus theyve nobody coming in to spoil their sleep except an odd priest or two for his night office the alarmclock next door at cockshout clattering the brains out of itself let me see if I can doze off 1 2 3 4 5 what kind of flowers are those they invented like the stars the wallpaper in Lombard street was much nicer the apron he gave me was like that something only I only wore it twice better lower this lamp and try again so as I can get up early Ill go to Lambes there beside Findlaters and get them to send us some flowers to put about the place in case he brings him home tomorrow today I mean no no Fridays an unlucky day first I want to do the place up someway the dust grows in it I think while Im asleep then we can have music and cigarettes I can accompany him first I must clean the keys of the piano with milk whatll I wear shall I wear a white rose or those fairy cakes in Liptons I love the smell of a rich big shop at 7½d a lb or the other ones with the cherries in them and the pinky sugar 11d a couple of lbs of course a nice plant for the middle of the table Id get that cheaper in wait wheres this I saw them not long ago I love flowers Id love to have the whole place swimming in roses God of heaven theres nothing like nature the wild mountains then the sea and the waves rushing then the beautiful country with fields of oats and wheat and all kinds of things and all the fine cattle going about that would do your heart good to see rivers and lakes and flowers all sorts of shapes and smells and colours springing up even out of the ditches primroses and violets nature it is as for them saying theres no God I wouldnt give a snap of my two fingers for all their learning why dont they go and create something I often asked him atheists or whatever they call themselves go and wash the cobbles off themselves first then they go howling for the priest and they dying and why why because theyre afraid of hell on account of their bad conscience ah yes I know them well who was the first person in the universe before there was anybody that made it all who ah that they dont know neither do I so there you are they might as well try to stop the sun from rising tomorrow the sun shines for you he said the day we were lying among the rhododendrons on Howth head in the grey tweed suit and his straw hat the day I got him to propose to me yes first I gave him the bit of seedcake out of my mouth and it was leapyear like now yes 16 years ago my God after that long kiss I near lost my breath yes he said I was a flower of the mountain yes so we are flowers all a womans body yes that was one true thing he said in his life and the sun shines for you today yes that was why I liked him because I saw he understood or felt what a woman is and I knew I could always get round him and I gave him all the pleasure I could leading him on till he asked me to say yes and I wouldnt answer first only looked out over the sea and the sky I was thinking of so many things he didnt know of Mulvey and Mr Stanhope and Hester and father and old captain Groves and the sailors playing all birds fly and I say stoop and washing up dishes they called it on the pier and the sentry in front of the governors house with the thing round his white helmet poor devil half roasted and the Spanish girls laughing in their shawls and their tall combs and the auctions in the morning the Greeks and the jews and the Arabs and the devil knows who else from all the ends of Europe and Duke street and the fowl market all clucking outside Larby Sharons and the poor donkeys slipping half asleep and the vague fellows in the cloaks asleep in the shade on the steps and the big wheels of the carts of the bulls and the old castle thousands of years old yes and those handsome Moors all in white and turbans like kings asking you to sit down in their little bit of a shop and Ronda with the old windows of the posadas glancing eyes a lattice hid for her lover to kiss the iron and the wineshops half open at night and the castanets and the night we missed the boat at Algeciras the watchman going about serene with his lamp and O that awful deepdown torrent O and the sea the sea crimson sometimes like fire and the glorious sunsets and the figtrees in the Alameda gardens yes and all the queer little streets and pink and blue and yellow houses and the rosegardens and the jessamine and geraniums and cactuses and Gibraltar as a girl where I was a Flower of the mountain yes when I put the rose in my hair like the Andalusian girls used or shall I wear a red yes and how he kissed me under the Moorish wall and I thought well as well him as another and then I asked him with my eyes to ask again yes and then he asked me would I yes to say yes my mountain flower and first I put my arms around him yes and drew him down to me so he could feel my breasts all perfume yes and his heart was going like mad and yes I said I will Yes.

Georges Bataille

1897–1962

The French novelist and critic Bataille worked for many years at the Bibliothèque Nationale in Paris. As well as many critical works on art, literature and eroticism, he wrote the experimental erotic novels The Story of the Eye *and* Madame Edwarda *(The Naked Beast at Heaven's Gate) (1937), published under the respective pseudonyms Lord Auch and Pierre Angelique.*

From **The Story of the Eye** (1928). *Trans. Joachim Neugroschel*

Our hearts were still booming in our chests, which were equally burning and equally lusting to press stark naked against wet unslaked hands, and Simone's cunt was still as greedy as before and my cock stubbornly rigid, as we returned to the first row of the arena. But when we arrived at our places next to Sir Edmund, there, in broad sunlight, on Simone's seat, lay a white dish containing two peeled balls, glands the size and shape of eggs, and of a pearly whiteness, faintly bloodshot, like the globe of an eye: they had just been removed from the first bull, a black-haired creature, into whose body Granero had plunged his sword.

'Here are the raw balls,' Sir Edmund said to Simone in his British accent.

Simone was already kneeling before the plate, peering at it in absorbed interest, but in something of a quandary. It seemed she wanted to do something but didn't know how to go about it, which exasperated her. I picked up the dish to let her sit down but she grabbed it away from me with a categorical 'no' and returned it to the stone seat.

Sir Edmund and I were growing annoyed at being the focus of our neighbours' attention just when the bullfight was slackening. I leaned over and whispered to Simone, asking what had got into her.

'Idiot!' she replied. 'Can't you see I want to sit on the plate, and all these people watching!'

'That's absolutely out of the question,' I rejoined, 'sit down.'

At the same time, I took away the dish and made her sit, and I stared at her to let her know that I understood, that I remembered the dish of milk, and that this renewed desire was unsettling me. From that moment on, neither of us could keep from fidgeting, and this state of malaise was contagious enough to affect Sir Edmund. I ought to say that the fight had become boring, unpugnacious bulls were facing matadors who didn't know what to do next; and to top it off, since Simone had demanded seats in the sun, we were trapped in something like an immense vapour of light and muggy heat, which parched our throats as it bore down upon us.

It really was totally out of the question for Simone to lift her dress and place her bare behind in the dish of raw balls. All she could do was hold the dish in her lap. I told her I would like to fuck her again before Granero returned to fight the fourth bull, but she refused, and she sat there, keenly involved, despite everything, in the disembowelments of horses, followed, as she childishly put it, by 'death and destruction', namely the cataract of bowels.

Little by little, the sun's radiance sucked us into an unreality that fitted our malaise – the wordless and powerless desire to explode and get up off our behinds. We grimaced, because our eyes were blinded and because we were thirsty, our senses ruffled, and there was no possibility of quenching our desires. We three had managed to share in the morose dissolution that leaves no harmony between the various spasms of the body. We were so far gone that even Granero's return could not pull us out of that stupefying absorption. Besides, the bull opposite him was distrustful and seemed unresponsive; the combat went on just as drearily as before.

The events that followed were without transition or connection, not because they weren't actually related, but because my attention was so absent as to remain absolutely dissociated. In just a few seconds: first, Simone bit into one of the raw balls to my dismay; then Granero advanced towards the bull, waving his scarlet cloth; finally, almost at once, Simone, with a blood-red face and a suffocating lewdness, uncovered her long white thighs up to her moist vulva, into which she slowly and surely fitted the second pale globule – Granero was thrown back by the bull and wedged against the balustrade; the horns struck the balustrade three times at full speed; at the third blow, one horn plunged into the right eye and through the head. A shriek of unmeasured horror coincided with a brief orgasm for Simone, who was lifted up from the stone seat only to be flung back with a bleeding nose, under a blinding sun; men instantly rushed over to haul away Granero's body, the right eye dangling from the head.

D.H. Lawrence

1885–1930

D.H. Lawrence, English novelist and poet, was the son of a coal-miner and a teacher. He briefly became a teacher himself before eloping to Italy with Frieda Weekley in 1912, after which he spent much of his life abroad. A prophet-like critic of English society, Lawrence believed in the liberating power of sensual passion, and two of his novels – The Rainbow *(1915) and* Lady Chatterley's Lover *(1928) – fell infamously foul of the censors.*

'Figs'

> The proper way to eat a fig, in society,
> Is to split it in four, holding it by the stump,

And open it, so that it is a glittering, rosy, moist, honied, heavy-petalled four-petalled
    flower.

Then you throw away the skin
Which is just like a four-petalled calex,
After you have taken off the blossom with your lips.

But the vulgar way
Is just to put your mouth to the crack, and take out the flesh in one bite.

Every fruit has its secret.

The fig is a very secretive fruit.
As you see it standing growing, you feel at once it is symbolic:
And it seems male.
But when you come to know it better, you agree with the Romans, it is female.

The Italians vulgarly say, it stands for the female part; the fig-fruit:
The fissure, the yoni,
The wonderful moist conductivity towards the centre.

Involved,
Inturned,
The flowering all inward and womb-fibrilled;
And but one orifice.

The fig, the horse-shoe, the squash-blossom.
Symbols.

There was a flower that flowered inward, womb-ward;
Now there is a fruit like a ripe womb.
It was always a secret.
That's how it should be, the female should always be secret.

There never was any standing aloft and unfolded on a bough
Like other flowers, in a revelation of petals;
Silver-pink peach, venetian glass of medlars and sorb-apples,
Shallow wine-cups on short, bulging stems
Openly pledging heaven:
Here's to the thorn in flower! Here is to Utterance!
The brave, adventurous rosaceae.

Folded upon itself, and secret unutterable,
And milk-sapped, sap that curdles milk and makes *ricotta,*
Sap that smells strange on your fingers, that even goats won't taste it;
Folded upon itself, enclosed like any Mohammedan woman,
Its nakedness all within-walls, its flowering forever unseen,
One small way of access only, and this close-curtained from the light;

Fig, fruit of the female mystery, covert and inward,
Mediterranean fruit, with your covert nakedness,
Where everything happens invisible, flowering and fertilisation, and fruiting
In the inwardness of your you, that eye will never see
Till it's finished, and you're over-ripe, and you burst to give up your ghost.

Till the drop of ripeness exudes,
And the year is over.

That's how the fig dies, showing her crimson through the purple slit
Like a wound, the exposure of her secret, on the open day.
Like a prostitute, the bursten fig, making a show of her secret.

That's how women die too.

The year is fallen over-ripe,
The year of our women.
The year of our women is fallen over-ripe.
The secret is laid bare.
And rottenness soon sets in.
The year of our women is fallen over-ripe.

When Eve once knew *in her mind* that she was naked
She quickly sewed fig-leaves, and sewed the same for the man.
She'd been naked all her days before,
But till then, till that apple of knowledge, she hadn't had the fact on her mind.

She got the fact on her mind, and quickly sewed fig-leaves.
And women have been sewing ever since.
But now they stitch to adorn the bursten fig, not to cover it.
They have their nakedness more than ever on their mind,
And they won't let us forget it.

Now, the secret
Becomes an affirmation through moist, scarlet lips
That laugh at the Lord's indignation.

What then, good Lord! cry the women.
We have kept our secret long enough.
We are a ripe fig.
Let us burst into affirmation.

They forget, ripe figs won't keep.
Ripe figs won't keep.

Honey-white figs of the north, black figs with scarlet inside, of the south.
Ripe figs won't keep, won't keep in any clime.
What then, when women the world over have all bursten into self-assertion?
And bursten figs won't keep?

Eve Eric Gill

Raphael de Leon

Little is known of the life of Raphael de Leon, who was highly popular as a calypso singer and composer in Trinidad during the 1920s and 1930s.

'Have you not heard the gossip' (*c.* 1930s)

> Have you not heard the gossip and the rumour going around
> It's all about men and women that they have today in town
> It would appear that both sexes are playing a funny game
> It's rumoured around – I've heard the talk – but cannot call a name
> Do, Re, Mi, and they're whoopsin
> Fa, Sol, La, they are polishing
> Whoopsin, whoopsin, La, Ti, Do
> And pots for soldering
>
> *[Solderer: male gay; polisher: lesbian]*

Henry Miller

1891–1980

The American novelist Henry Miller spent the 1930s in Paris, where he wrote the autobiographical works Tropic of Cancer *and* Tropic of Capricorn *(1939), banned in the US and Britain until the 1960s due to their frank accounts of his sexual exploits. Friend to Lawrence Durrell and Anaïs Nin, his other novels include the trilogy* The Rosy Crucifixion *(1949–60).*

From Tropic of Cancer (1934)

Strolling past the Dôme a little later suddenly I see a pale, heavy face and burning eyes – and the little velvet suit that I always adore because under the soft velvet there were always her warm breasts, the marble legs, cool, firm, muscular. She rises up out of a sea of faces and embraces me, embraces me passionately – a thousand eyes, noses, fingers, legs, bottles, windows, purses, saucers all glaring at us and we in each other's arms oblivious. I sit down beside her and she talks – a flood of talk. Wild consumptive notes of hysteria, perversion, leprosy. I hear not a word because she is beautiful and I love her and now I am happy and willing to die.

We walk down the Rue du Château, looking for Eugene. Walk over the railroad bridge where I used to watch the trains pulling out and feel all sick inside wondering where the hell she could be. Everything soft and enchanting as we walk over the bridge. Smoke coming up between our legs, the tracks creaking, semaphores in our blood. I feel her body close to mine – all mine now – and I stop to rub my hands over the warm velvet. Everything around us is crumbling, crumbling and the warm body under the warm velvet is aching for me. . . .

Back in the very same room and fifty francs to the good, thanks to Eugene. I look out on the court but the phonograph is silent. The trunk is open and her things are lying around everywhere just as before. She lies down on the bed with her clothes on. Once, twice, three times, four times . . . I'm afraid she'll go mad . . . in bed, under the blankets, how good to feel her body again! But for how long? Will it last this time? Already I have a presentiment that it won't.

She talks to me so feverishly – as if there will be no tomorrow. 'Be quiet, Mona! Just look at me . . . *don't talk!*' Finally she drops off and I pull my arm from under her. My eyes close. Her body is there beside me . . . it will be there till morning surely. . . . It was in February I pulled out of the harbour in a blinding snowstorm. The last glimpse I had of her was in the window waving good-bye to me. A man standing on the other side of the street, at the corner, his hat pulled down over his eyes, his jowls resting on his lapels. A foetus watching me. A foetus with a cigar in its mouth. Mona at the window waving good-bye. White heavy face, hair streaming wild. And now it is a heavy bedroom, breathing regularly through the gills, sap still oozing from between her legs, a warm feline odour and her hair in my mouth. My eyes are closed. We breathe warmly into each other's mouth. Close together, America three thousand miles away. I never want to see it again. To have her here in bed with me, breathing on me, her hair in my mouth – I count that something of a miracle. Nothing can happy now till morning . . .

I wake from a deep slumber to look at her. A pale light is trickling in. I look at her beautiful wild hair. I feel something crawling down my neck. I look at her again, closely. Her hair is alive. I pull back the sheet – more of them. They are swarming over the pillow.

e.e. cummings

1894–1962

cummings was born in Cambridge, Massachusetts, and graduated from Harvard in 1916. He drove an ambulance in France during World War 1, and stayed on in Paris after the armistice. His first published work was a novel, The Enormous Room *(1922), an exceptional prose account of his war-time internment in France. This was followed by several collections of verse, mostly characterized by his eccentric use of language and typography.*

'she being Brand'

she being Brand

-new; and you
know consequently a
little stiff i was
careful of her and (having

thoroughly oiled the universal
joint tested my gas felt of
her radiator made sure her springs were O.

K.) i went right to it flooded-the-carburetor cranked her

up, slipped the

clutch (and then somehow got into reverse she
kicked what
the hell) next
minute i was back in neutral tried and

again slo-wly; bare,ly nudg. ing (my

lev-er Right-
oh and her gears being in
A I shape passed
from low through
second-in-to-high like
greasedlightning) just as we turned the corner of Divinity

avenue i touched the accelerator and give

her the juice, good

                    (it
was the first ride and believe i we was
happy to see how nice she acted right up to
the last minute coming back down by the Public
Gardens i slammed on
the
internalexpanding
&
externalcontracting
brakes Bothatonce and

brought allof her tremB
-ling
to a:dead.

stand-
;Still)

Anon. (England)

'I Sometimes think'

I sometimes think that I should like
To be the saddle of a bike.

Flann O'Brien

1911–1966

*The Irish novelist Flann O'Brien (Brian ó Nuallain) was born in Strabane and educated at University College Dublin,
after which he worked for many years as a civil servant. His fantastical and satirical novels include* At Swim-Two-
Birds *(1939) and* The Third Policeman, *and he also wrote a long-running bilingual column for the* Irish Times
as Myles na Gopaleen, renowned for its exuberant linguistic inventiveness.

From **The Third Policeman** (1967)

The bicycle itself seemed to have some peculiar quality of shape or personality which gave it
distinction and importance far beyond that usually possessed by such machines. It was
extremely well-kept with a pleasing lustre on its dark-green bars and oil-bath and a clean
sparkle on the rustless spokes and rims. Resting before me like a tame domestic pony, it
seemed unduly small and low in relation to the Sergeant yet when I measured its height against
myself I found it was bigger than any other bicycle that I knew. This was possibly due to the
perfect proportion of its parts which combined merely to create a thing of surpassing grace
and elegance, transcending all standards of size and reality and existing only in the absolute
validity of its own unexceptionable dimensions. Notwithstanding the sturdy cross-bar it seemed
ineffably female and fastidious, posing there like a mannequin rather than leaning idly like a
loafer against the wall, and resting on its prim flawless tyres with irreproachable precision, two
tiny points of clean contact with the level floor. I passed my hand with unintended tenderness
– sensuously, indeed – across the saddle. Inexplicably it reminded me of a human face, not
by any simple resemblance of shape or feature but by some association of textures, some
incomprehensible familiarity at the fingertips. The leather was dark with maturity, hard with a
noble hardness and scored with all the sharp lines and finer wrinkles which the years with
their tribulations had carved into my own countenance. It was a gentle saddle yet calm and
courageous, unembittered by its confinement and bearing no mark upon it save that of
honourable suffering and honest duty. I knew that I liked this bicycle more than I had ever
liked any other bicycle, better even than I had liked some people with two legs. I liked her
unassuming competence, her docility, the simple dignity of her quiet way. She now seemed to
rest beneath my friendly eyes like a tame fowl which will crouch submissively, awaiting with
out-hunched wings the caressing hand. Her saddle seemed to spread invitingly into the most
enchanting of all seats while her two handlebars, floating finely with the wild grace of alighting
wings, beckoned to me to lend my mastery for free and joyful journeyings, the lightest of light
running in the company of the swift ground-winds to safe havens far away, the whir of the true
front wheel in my ear as it spun perfectly beneath my clear eye and the strong fine back wheel
with unadmired industry raising gentle dust on the dry roads. How desirable her seat was, how
charming the invitation of her slim encircling handle-arms, how unaccountably competent
and reassuring her pump resting warmly against her rear thigh!

   With a start I realized that I had been communing with this strange companion and – not
only that – conspiring with her. Both of us were afraid of the same Sergeant, both were
awaiting the punishments he would bring with him on his return, both were thinking that this

was the last chance to escape beyond his reach; and both knew that the hope of each lay in the other, that we would not succeed unless we went together, assisting each other with sympathy and quiet love.

Jean Genet

1910–1986

The French novelist, poet and dramatist Jean Genet was brought up in orphanages and by a foster family, before turning to a life of crime and prostitution around Europe. His first novel, Our Lady of the Flowers, *an ironical and highly stylized treatment of male prostitution, drew him to the attention of the French intelligentsia, notably Sartre, who managed to obtain him a pardon from a life sentence, and wrote his biography,* Saint Genet *(1952).*

From **Our Lady of the Flowers** (1943). *Trans. Bernard Frechtman*

Darling has 'fallen' in love.

I should like to play at inventing the ways love has of surprising people. It enters like Jesus into the heart of the impetuous; it also comes slyly, like a thief.

A gangster, here in prison, related to me a kind of counterpart of the famous comparison in which the two rivals come to know Eros:

'How I started getting a crush on him? We were in the jug. At night we had to undress, even take off our shirts in front of the guard to show him we weren't hiding anything (ropes, files, or blades). So the little guy and me were both naked. So I took a squint at him to see if he had muscles like he said. I didn't have time to get a good look because it was freezing. He got dressed again quick. I just had time to see he was pretty great. Man, did I get an eyeful (a shower of roses!). I was hooked. I swear! I got mine (here one expects inescapably: I knocked myself out). It lasted a while, four or five days . . . '

The rest is of no further interest to us. Love makes use of the worst traps. The least noble. The rarest. It exploits coincidence. Was it not enough for a kid to stick his two fingers in his mouth and loose a strident whistle just when my soul was stretched to the limit, needing only this stridency to be torn from top to bottom? Was that the right moment, the moment that made two creatures love each to the very blood? 'Thou art a sun unto my night. My night is a sun unto thine!' We beat our brows. Standing, and from afar, my body passes through thine, and thine, from afar, through mine. We create the world. Everything changes . . . and to know that it does!

Loving each other like two young boxers who, before separating, tear off each other's shirt, and, when they are naked, astounded by their beauty, think they are seeing themselves in a mirror, stand there for a second open-mouthed, shake – with rage at being caught – their tangled hair, smile a damp smile, and embrace each other like two wrestlers (in Greco-Roman wrestling), interlock their muscles in the precise connections offered by the muscles of the other, and drop to the mat until their warm sperm, spurting high, maps out on the sky a milky way where other constellations which I can read take shape: the constellations of the Sailor, the Boxer, the Cyclist, the Fiddle, the Spahi, the Dagger. Thus a new map of the heavens is outlined on the wall of Divine's garret.

Divine and Darling. To my mind, they are the ideal pair of lovers. From my evil-smelling hole, beneath the coarse wool of the covers, with my nose in the sweat and my eyes wide open, alone with them, I see them.

Darling is a giant whose curved feet cover half the globe as he stands with his legs apart in baggy, sky-blue silk underpants. He rams it in. So hard and calmly that anuses and vaginas slip onto his member like rings on a finger. He rams it in. So hard and calmly that his virility, observed by the heavens, has the penetrating force of the battalions of blond warriors who on June 14, 1940, buggered us soberly and seriously, though their eyes were elsewhere as they marched in the dust and sun. But they are the image of only the tensed, buttressed Darling. Their granite prevents them from being slithering pimps.

I close my eyes. Divine: a thousand shapes, charming in their grace, emerge from my eyes, mouth, elbows, knees, from all parts of me. They say to me: 'Jean, how glad I am to be living as Divine and to be living with Darling.'

I close my eyes. Divine and Darling. To Darling, Divine is barely a pretext, an occasion. If he thought of her, he would shrug his shoulders to shake off the thought, as if the thought were a dragon's claws clinging to his back. But to Divine, Darling is everything. She takes care of his penis. She caresses it with the most profuse tenderness and calls it by the kind of pet names used by ordinary folk when they feel horny. Such expressions as Little Dicky, the Babe in the Cradle, Jesus in His Manger, the Hot Little Chap, your Baby Brother, without her formulating them, take on full meaning. Her feeling accepts them literally. Darling's penis is in itself all of Darling: the object of her pure luxury, an object of pure luxury. If Divine is willing to see in her man anything other than a hot, purplish member, it is because she can follow its stiffness, which extends to the anus, and can sense that it goes farther into his body, that it is this very body of Darling erect and terminating in a pale, tired face, a face of eyes, nose, mouth, flat cheeks, curly hair, beads of sweat.

I close my eyes beneath the lice-infested blankets. Divine has opened the fly and arranged this mysterious area of her man. Has beribboned the bush and penis, stuck flowers into the buttonholes of the fly. (Darling goes out with her that way in the evening.) The result is that to Divine, Darling is only the magnificent delegation on earth, the physical expression, in short, the symbol of a being (perhaps God), of an idea that remains in heaven. They do not commune. Divine may be compared to Marie-Antoinette, who, according to my history of France, had to learn to express herself in prison, willy-nilly, in the slang current in the eighteenth century. Poor dear Queen!

Dennis Brutus

b. 1924

The South African poet Dennis Brutus was born in Salisbury, Rhodesia (now Harare, Zimbabwe) and educated in South Africa, where his anti-Apartheid activities led to his writings being banned, 18 months' hard labour, and in 1965, enforced emigration. His collections of poems include Sirens *and* Letters to Martha, *which describe his experiences as a political prisoner and deal with questions of African identity.*

'Let not this plunder be misconstrued'

Let not this plunder be misconstrued:
This is the body's expression of need –
Poor wordless body in its fumbling way
Exposing heart's-hunger by raiding and hurt;

Secret recesses of lonely desire
Gnaw at the vitals of spirit and mind
When shards of existence display eager blades
To menace and savage the pilgriming self:

Bruised though your flesh and all-aching my arms
Believe me, my lovely, I too reel from our pain –
Plucking from you these your agonized gifts
Bares only my tenderness-hungering need.

Yukio Mishima

1925–1970

Yukio Mishima was born in Tokyo, and educated at the Imperial University there. From the appearance of his first stories in the 1940s, Mishima courted both controversy and popularity through his preoccupations with homosexuality, chivalry and death. After a series of increasingly militaristic public pronouncements, in 1970 he forced his way into an army post, where after failing to incite the troops he committed hara-kiri. His novels include Confessions of a Mask *(1949) and the tetralogy* The Sea of Fertility *(1969–71), characteristically working Western and classical Japanese influences into his own experimental idiom.*

From **Thirst For Love** (1950). *Trans. Alfred H. Marks*

Etsuko heard the bamboo exploding at her side and was delighted. Any violent noise would have sounded pleasant to her ears now. Those delicate ears of hers no longer reacted to trifles and enjoyed the risk of being strained to bursting-point. She must really have been listening intently to the rhythm of some emotion deep inside her.

Suddenly the lion's head, its mane streaming, its golden teeth exposed above their heads, moved towards another gateway. Pandemonium ensued as human beings flowed in waves to right and left. Something dazzling cut across Etsuko's line of vision. It was a band of half-naked young men moving together in the glare of the flames. Some wore their hair loose and dishevelled; some wore white headbands tied so the ends streamed behind them. Uttering animal shouts, they churned past Etsuko filling the breeze with a musky smell. As they passed, the dark reverberation of hard flesh striking hard flesh, the bright squeal of sweaty skin clinging to and breaking away from sweaty skin, filled the air. So entwined were their legs in the darkness that they looked like some meaninglessly entangled mass of inhuman creatures. It seemed as though not one of them knew which legs were his.

'I wonder where Saburo is,' said Kensuke. 'When they're naked, you can't tell one from the other.'

He was taking no chances of losing one of the women, and had his arm around each of them. Etsuko's slippery shoulder threatened to slide from his grasp at any moment.

'It's true,' he said, agreeing with himself. 'When people are naked you really understand why human individuality is such a fragile thing. And when it comes to thinking, there are only four kinds: the thinking of a fat man, the thinking of a skinny man, the thinking of a tall, gangly man, and the thinking of a little man. When it comes to faces, now – whatever ones you look at – they never have more than two eyes, one nose, and one mouth apiece. You don't see anyone with one eye.

'Take even the most individualistic face – all it's good for is to symbolize the difference between its owner and other people. What's love? Nothing more than symbol falling for symbol. And when it comes to sex – that's anonymity falling for anonymity. Chaos and chaos, the unisexual mating of depersonalization with depersonalization. Masculinity? Femininity? You can't tell the difference. See, Chieko?'

Even Chieko looked bored as she grunted agreement.

Etsuko couldn't help laughing. *This man mumbling in her ear, constantly, almost incontinently. Yes, that's it! It's 'cerebral incontinence'! What pitiful weakness! His thoughts are as ridiculous as his appearance.*

The real absurdity, though, is that what he is saying is so out of tempo with all the shouting, the excitement, the smells, the activity and the life around him here. If he were a musician, no conductor would have him in his orchestra. But what can you do with a village orchestra except recognize it's out of tune and make do?

Etsuko opened her eyes wide. Her shoulder slid gently out of Kensuke's sticky hand. She had found Saburo. His usually taciturn lips were open wide – shouting. His sharp teeth showed white and shining, sparkling in the light of the bonfires.

In his eyes – never turned towards her – Etsuko saw another glowing, resplendent bonfire.

Again the lion's head stood out above the crowd, seeming to survey the scene. Then it capriciously changed direction and headed straight into the spectators, its green mane floating proudly, and moved towards the main gateway at the front of the shrine. A band of half-naked young men thundered behind it.

Etsuko relinquished all power over her legs and followed the procession. Behind her she could hear Kensuke call, 'Etsuko Etsuko!' and the shrill laughter of Chieko. She did not look back. Something inside her seemed to stand forth out of a vague, mushy quagmire and to flash forward with almost herculean physical power.

Occasionally human beings are imbued with the belief that they can accomplish anything. At such times they seem to glimpse much that is normally invisible to human eyes. Later, even after these moments have sunk to the bottom of memory's well, they sometimes revive and again suggest to men the miraculous abundance of the world's pains and joys. No one can avoid these moments of destiny; nor can anyone – no matter who he is – avoid the misfortune of seeing more than his eyes can take in.

Etsuko felt she could do anything. Her cheeks burned like fire. Jostled by the expressionless throng, she sped, half stumbling, towards the front gateway. The fan of a marshal struck her on the breast, but she did not feel the blow. She was caught up in a fierce clash of torpor and frenzy.

Saburo did not know she was near. His marvellously fleshed, lightly tanned back was turned to the pushing spectators. His face was turned towards the lion in the centre, shouting at it and challenging it. His lithe arm held his lantern high, no longer lighted though unmarred by the tears and punctures that disfigured the others. The ceaselessly twisting lower half of his body was lost in darkness, but his barely moving back was given over to a mad kaleidoscope of flame and shadow. The ripples of flesh round his shoving shoulder bones looked like the wings of a powerful bird in flight.

Etsuko longed to touch him with her fingers. She did not know what kind of desire this was. Metaphorically that back was a bottomless ocean depth to her; she longed to throw herself into it. Her desire was close to that of a person who drowns himself; he does not necessarily covet death so much as what comes after the drowning – something different from what he had before, at least a different world.

Another strong, wave-like movement in the crowd thrust everyone forward. The half-naked youths moved against this, backing up in concert with the capricious lion's head. Etsuko stumbled forward, pushed by the throng, and collided with a bare back, warm as fire, coming from the opposite direction. She reached out her hands and held it off. It was Saburo's back. She savoured the touch of his flesh. She savoured the majestic warmth of him.

The mob behind her pushed again, and her fingernails gouged into Saburo's back. He did not even feel it. In the mad pushing and shoving he had no idea what woman was pressing against him. Etsuko felt his blood dripping between her fingers.

The marshals didn't seem to have the crowd very well under control. The mad young men banded together in a mass and, shouting, moved close to one brightly blazing bamboo pole. Embers fell at their feet and were trampled upon. The barefoot men were past feeling the heat of them. The pole stood wrapped in fire, lighting up the limbs of the old cypress tree with flame and scarlet smoke. The burning bamboo leaves were yellow, as if caught by sunlight. The slim fiery pillar shook and exploded, then dipped deep from side to side like the mast of a sailing boat, and suddenly toppled into the middle of the jostling crowd.

Etsuko thought she saw a woman with her hair alight laughing loudly. That was about all she remembered with any clarity. Somehow she got away, and found herself standing by the stone steps in front of the shrine. She later remembered a moment when all the sky she could see was filled with sparks. Yet she felt no sense of horror. The young men were struggling again to plunge towards another gateway. The spectators seemed to have forgotten their fear of a few minutes ago and were streaming after them as before. Nothing had happened.

Octavio Paz

b. 1914

The Mexican poet and critic Octavio Paz travelled extensively as a diplomat (he was the Mexican ambassador in New Delhi in the mid-1960s) and more recently as a professor of literature. Influenced by the Surrealists, his poems deal with themes of isolation and sexual union, and in the prose-work Labyrinth of Solitude *(1950) he explores notions of Mexican identity. He was awarded the 1990 Nobel Prize for Literature.*

'Shrine' (1976). *Trans. Michael Edwards*

                          The name
              Its   umbras
                  The man   The Woman
              The hammer   The gong
          The i   The o
          The tower   The well
          The pointer   The hour
      The bone   The rose
      The shower   The grave
          The spring   The flame
          The brand   The night
          The river   The city
              The keel   The anchor
          The manwomb The wombman
                  The man
              His body of names
          Your name in my name I your name my name
  One facing the other one against the other one around the other
                  The one in the other
                      Nameless

Anon. (Trinidad)

Trinidad Calypso from Small Island Pride's **'Experiences as a taxi-driver in Venezuela'** (1953)

When I start my fast driving
Lots of funny things start happening
The wire cross one another
The water hose buss lose the radiator
Well the gearbox started a grinding
This gear so hard I can't get to go in
So I pull out me gear lever

Water fly through the muffler
And the whole car went on fire
CHORUS: All you got to do is drive it fast
            Don't mind if she run out o' gas
            But if the radiator start to boil
            Don't stop till the water overflow the coil

Pauline Reage

'Pauline Reage' is the pseudonym of a French author who stirred furious debate over erotica versus pornography with the publication of The Story of O.

From **The Story of O** (1954)

O struggled with all her might, she believed that the straps were going to cut through her skin. She did not want to plead, she did not want to beg to be spared. But Anne-Marie intended to drive her to that, to begging and pleading. 'Faster,' she told Colette, 'and harder.' O's body stiffened, she braced herself, but in vain. A minute later she gave way to tears and screams, while Anne-Marie caressed her face. 'Just a little more,' she said, 'and then it will be all over. Just five minutes more. You can scream for five minutes, can't you? Surely. It's twenty-five past. Colette, you'll stop at half-past, when I tell you.' But O screamed no, no, for God's sake no, she couldn't bear it any longer, no, she couldn't stand this another second. However, she did have to stand it until the end and, at half-past, Anne-Marie smiled at her. Colette left the stage. 'Thank me,' Anne-Marie said to O, and O thanked her. She knew very well why Anne-Marie had judged it above all else necessary to have her whipped. That a woman was so cruel, and more implacable than a man, O had never once doubted. But O had thought that Anne-Marie was seeking less to manifest her power than to establish a complicity between O and herself. O had never understood, but had finally come to recognize as an undeniable and very meaning-ful truth, the contradictory but constant entanglement of her feelings and attitudes: she liked the idea of torture, when she underwent it she would have seen the earth go up in fire and smoke to escape it, when it was over with she was happy to have undergone it, and all the happier the crueller and more prolonged it had been. Anne-Marie had correctly calculated upon O's acquiescence and revolt, and knew very well that her pleadings for mercy had been genuine and her final thanks authentic. There was a third reason for what she had done, and she explained it to O. She felt it important to make each girl who entered her house and who thus entered an entirely feminine society sense that her condition as a woman would not lose its importance from the fact that, here, her only contacts would be with other women, but, to the contrary, would be increased, heightened, intensified. It was for this reason she required the girls to be naked at all times; the manner in which O had been flogged, as well as the position in which she had been tied, had the same purpose. Today, it would be O who would remain for the rest of the afternoon – for three more hours – with her legs spread and raised exposed upon the platform and facing the garden. She would have the incessant desire to close her legs; it would be thwarted. Tomorrow, it would be Claire and Colette, or again

Yvonne, whom O would watch in her turn. The process was far too gradual, far too minute (as, likewise, this manner of applying the whip), to be used at Roissy. But O would discover how effective it was. Apart from the rings and the insignia she would wear, upon her departure, and restored to Sir Stephen, she would find herself much more openly and profoundly a slave than she could imagine possible.

The following morning after breakfast Anne-Marie told O and Yvonne to come with her into her room. From her secretary she took a green leather coffer which she set on the bed and opened. The two girls were seated at her feet. 'Yvonne has told you nothing?' Anne-Marie asked of O. O shook her head. What was there for Yvonne to tell her? 'Nor Sir Stephen, of course. Well, here are the rings he wishes you to wear.' They were rings of dull stainless steel, like the iron in the iron-and-gold ring.

The metal was round, about the thickness of a pencil, the shape of each ring oblong: similar to the links of heavy chains. Anne-marie showed O that each was composed of two U-shaped halves, one of which tenoned into the other. 'This is simply the trial model,' said she. 'It can be removed. Whereas, if you'll look closely, you'll see that here, in the permanent variety, there are spring catches inside the hollow prongs: one inserts the other half and it locks. Once locked, it can't be opened – can't be taken off. One would have to file the ring in two.' Each ring was as long as two little fingers, and just wide enough to admit one's little finger. From each ring was suspended, like a second link, or like the loop which supports the pendant of an ear-ring, a disk of the same metal and as large in its diameter as the ring was long. On one side, gold inlay; on the other, nothing. 'On the blank side,' said Anne-Marie, 'your name will be engraved, also your title, Sir Stephen's first and last names, and beneath that, a device: a crossed whip and riding-crop. Yvonne wears a similar disk on her collar. But you'll wear yours on your belly.' 'But –' O began. 'I know,' Anne-Marie interrupted, 'that's why I brought Yvonne in. Show your belly, Yvonne.' The red-haired girl rose and lay down on the bed. Anne-Marie opened her thighs and had O notice that one of her labia, midway down and close to its base, had been pierced: a clean hole, such as a ticket-puncher makes. A clean hole: the trial model ring would just pass through it. 'I'll make the hole for you in a moment or two, O,' said Anne-Marie, 'there's nothing to it, what takes time is putting the clamp in place: the epidermis outside and the membrane inside have to be sutured properly, the holes must coincide. It's much less painful than the whip.' 'But aren't you going to give me an anaesthetic?' O cried, trembling. 'Certainly not,' replied Anne-Marie, 'you'll simply be tied, somewhat tighter than yesterday. That's altogether sufficient. Come.'

A week later, Anne-Marie removed the clamps and slipped the trial model in place. Light as it was – it was lighter than it looked, for it was hollow – it hung heavily. The hard metal, very visibly penetrating the flesh, resembled an instrument of torture; what would it be when the second ring was added and it hung even more heavily? This barbarous apparatus would immediately catch any glance. 'Of course,' Anne-Marie admitted when O made the remark, 'but you did understand what Sir Stephen wants, didn't you? You do now: whoever, at Roissy or elsewhere, Sir Stephen or anyone else, you too before the mirror, whoever lifts up your skirt will immediately see the rings on your belly, and, if he turns you around, the insignia on your buttocks. It's possible that you someday succeed in having the rings filed off, but you'll never get rid of the insignia.' 'I used to think,' said Colette, 'that tattoos could be removed very easily.' (It was she who, upon Yvonne's fair skin, just above the triangle of her belly, had tattooed the initials of Yvonne's master; the ornate blue script letters resembled embroidery.) 'O won't be tattooed.' Anne-Marie declared. O stared at Anne-Marie. Colette and Yvonne, dumbfounded, fell silent. Anne-Marie hesitated a moment. 'Well?' said O. 'Say it.' 'Ah, my dear,' said Anne-Marie, 'I hardly dare. You will be marked with an iron. Sir Stephen sent me the iron two days ago.' 'Iron?' cried Yvonne. 'A red-hot one.'

Hubert Selby Jr

b. 1928

The American novelist Hubert Selby was born and brought up in Brooklyn, which provides the setting for most of his work. His novels include Last Exit to Brooklyn, The Room *(1971) and* The Demon *(1976), all of which deal starkly with the violence of urban life and sexual obsession.*

From **Last Exit to Brooklyn** (1957)

When they got to the apartment Harry sprawled on the couch. He felt drunk. Everything was alright. My name is Alberta, handing him a drink. Whats yours? Harry. She sat next to him. Why dont you take your shirt off. Its rather warm in here. Yeah, sure, fumbling with the buttons. Here, let me help you, leaning over and slowly unbuttoning Harry's shirt, glancing up at Harry pulling the shirt out of his trousers then sliding it off the shoulders and arms and letting it fall behind the couch. Harry watched her as she unbuttoned his shirt, felt the slight pressure of her fingers. He almost thought about the guys and what they would say if they saw him now; but the thought was easily absorbed by the alcohol before it formed and he closed his eyes and enjoyed the closeness of Alberta.

She stayed close to him, resting one hand gently on his shoulder, looking up at him, sliding her hand along his shoulder to his neck, watching his face, his eyes, for any reaction; feeling a little uneasy with Harry, not absolutely certain how he would react. Usually she knew how rough trade would react before she attempted anything, but with Harry she wasnt too certain; there was something strange in his eyes. She thought she understood what was behind them, but she still preferred a little caution to recklessness. And too, this was exciting. Occasionally she just had to cruise and bring home trade that looked dangerous; but, slowly, as she caressed his neck and back and looked into his face, she realized that she didnt have to fear Harry; and she understood too that this was a new experience to Harry. The puzzled expectant look on his face excited her. She had a cherry. She tingled. She rubbed his chest with the palm of her other hand. Your chest is so strong and hairy, the tip of her tongue showing between her lips; rubbing his back, touching gently the pimples and pockmarks. Youre so strong, moving closer, touching his neck with her lips, her hand moving from his chest to his stomach, to his belt, his fly; her mouth on his chest, then his stomach. Harry raised himself slightly as she tugged at his pants then relaxed, then tensed as she kissed his thighs and put his cock in her mouth. Harry pushed against the back of the couch, squirmed with pleasure; almost screamed with pleasure at the image of his wife being split in two with a large cock that turned into an enormous barbed pole, then he was there smashing her face with his fist and laughing, laughing and spitting and punching until the face was just a blob that oozed and then she became an old

Apollo Palace Francese Domingo i Segura

man and he stopped punching and then once more it was Mary, or it almost looked like Mary but it was a woman and she screamed as a burning white hot cock was shoved and hammered into her cunt then slowly pulled out, pulling with it her entrails and Harry sat watching, laughing his laugh and groaning, groaning with pleasure and then he heard the groan, heard it not only from inside, but heard it enter his ear from outside and he opened his eyes and saw Albertas head moving furiously and Harry moaned and squirmed frantically.

Alberta kept her head still for many minutes before getting up and going to the bathroom. Harry watched her walk away then looked at his prick hanging half rigidly between his legs. It hypnotised him and he stared at it for a moment knowing it was his yet not recognising it, as if he had never seen it before yet knowing he had. How many times had he held it in his hands as he pissed; why did it seem new to him? Why did it suddenly fascinate him so? He blinked his eyes and heard the water running in the bathroom. He looked at his penis again and the strangeness disappeared. He wondered briefly about his thoughts of a moment ago. He couldnt remember them. He felt good. He looked toward the bathroom waiting to see Albertas face.

Her face had a polished wax glow and her long hair was neatly combed. She wiggled toward him, smiling. She laughed, lightly, at Harrys surprised look when he noticed she was wearing nothing but a pair of womans lace panties. She poured two more drinks and sat beside him. Harry took a gulp of his drink and touched her panties. Do you like my silks? Harrys hand jerked back. He felt Albertas hand on the back of his neck. She gently guided his hand to her leg. I love them. They're so smooth, holding his hand on her leg and kissing his neck, his mouth, sliding her tongue into his mouth, searching for his, feeling the bottom of it as Harry curled his tongue back in his mouth, caressing the base of his tongue with hers, Harrys tongue slowly unfolding and lapping against hers, his hand grabbing her cock. Alberta moving his hand away and back on her leg, letting her saliva drip from the tip of her tongue onto Harrys, squirming as he clutched her leg tightly, almost feeling the drops of spit being absorbed by Harrys mouth, feeling his tongue lunging into her mouth as if he were trying to choke her; she sucked on his tongue then let him suck on hers, rolling her head with his, moving her hand over his lumpy back; slowly moving her head back and away from his. Lets go into the bedroom, darling. Harry pulled her toward him and sucked on her lips. She slowly separated her mouth from his and tugged him from the back of his neck. Lets go to bed, slowly standing, still tugging. Harry stood, staggering slightly. Alberta looked down and laughed. You still have your shoes and socks on. Harry blinked. He was standing with legs spread, penis standing straight before him, naked except for his black socks and shoes. Alberta giggled then took his shoes and socks off. Come on lover. She grabbed him by the prick and led him to the bedroom.

Harry flopped onto the bed and rolled over and kissed her, missing her mouth and kissing her chin. She laughed and guided him to her mouth. He pushed at her side and at first Alberta was puzzled, trying to understand what he was trying to do, then realised that he was trying to turn her over. She giggled again. You silly you. You never have fucked a fairy before, have you? Harry grumbled, still fumbling and kissing her neck and chest. We make love just like anybody else honey, a little peeved at first then once more relishing the charm of having a cherry. Just relax, rolling over on her side and kissing him, whispering in his ear. When she finished the preparations she rolled back onto her back, Harry rolling over on her, and moved rhythmically with Harry, her legs and arms wrapped around him, rolling, squirming, groaning.

Harry lunged at first, then, looking at Alberta, slowed to an exciting movement; and as he moved he was conscious of his movements, of his excitement and enjoyment and not wanting it to end; and though he clenched his teeth from lust and pinched her back and bit her neck there was a comparative relaxing, the tautness and spasms being caused by pleasure and desire to be where he was and to do what he was doing. Harry could hear hers and his moans blending, could feel her under him, could feel her flesh in his mouth; there were many tangible things and yet there was still a confusion, but it stemmed from inexperience, from the sudden overpowering sensations of pleasure, a pleasure he had never known, a pleasure that he, with its excitement and tenderness, had never experienced – he wanted to grab and squeeze the flesh he felt in his hands, he wanted to bite it, yet he didnt want to destroy it; he wanted it to be there, he wanted to come back to it. Harry continued to move with the same satisfying rhythm; continued to blend his moans with hers through the whirlygig of confusion; bewildered but not distracted or disturbed by these new emotions giving birth to each other in his mind, but just concentrating on the pleasure and allowing it to guide him as Alberta had. When he stopped moving he lay still for a moment hearing their heavy breathing then kissed her, caressed her arms then rolled slowly and gently onto the bed, stretched out and soon slept. Harry was happy.

William Burroughs

b. 1914

The American novelist William Burroughs was born in St Louis, Missouri and educated at Harvard. He lived in Paris and Tangier before moving back to New York. His novels include Junkie *(1953),* The Naked Lunch, The Wild Boys *(1979) and* Queer *(1985), fragmented and often surrealistic accounts of heroin-addiction and homosexuality.*

From **The Naked Lunch** (1959)

Hassan's Rumpus Room. Gilt and red plush Rococo bar backed by pink shell. The air is cloyed with a sweet evil substance like decayed honey. Most women in evening dress sip mousse-cafes through alabaster tubes. A Near East Mugwump sits naked on a bar stool covered in pink silk. He licks warm honey from a crystal goblet with a long black tongue. His genitals are perfectly formed – circumcized cock, black shiny pubic hairs. His lips are thin and purple-blue like the lips of a penis, his eyes are black with insect calm. The Mugwump has no liver, maintaining himself exclusively on sweets. The Mugwump pushes a slender blond youth to a couch and strips him expertly. 'Stand up and turn around', he orders . . . He ties the boy's hands behind him with a red silk cord. 'Tonight we make it all the way.'

'No. No!' screams the boy.

'Yes Yes.'

Cocks ejaculate in silent 'yes'. The Mugwump parts silk curtains, reveals a teak wood gallows against lighted screen of red flint. Gallows is on a dais of Aztec mosaics.

The boy crumples to his knees with a long 'Oooooooooh', shitting and pissing in terror. He feels the shit warm between his thighs. A great wave of hot blood swells his lips and throat. His body contracts into a foetal position and sperm spurts hot into his face. The Mugwump dips hot perfumed water from an alabaster bowl, perversely washes the boy's ass and cock, drying him with a soft blue towel. A warm wind plays over the boy's body and the hairs float free. The Mugwump puts a hand under the boy's chest and pulls him to his feet. Holding him by both pinioned elbows, propels him up the steps and under the noose. He stands in front of the boy holding the noose in both hands.

The boy looks into Mugwump eyes, black as obsidian mirrors, pools of black blood, glory holes in a toilet wall closing on the Last Erection . . .

The Mugwump slips the noose over the boy's head and tightens the knot caressingly behind the left ear. The boy's penis is retracted, his balls tight. He looks straight ahead breathing deeply. The Mugwump sidles around the boy goosing him and caressing his genitals in hieroglyphs of mockery. He moves in behind the boy with a series of bumps and shoves his cock up the boys ass. He stands there moving in circular gyrations.

The guests shush each other, nudge and giggle.

Suddenly the Mugwump pushes the boy forward into space, free of his cock. He steadies the boy with hands on the hip bones and snaps the boy's neck. A shudder passes through the boy's body. His penis rises in three great surges pulling his pelvis up, ejaculates immediately.

Green sparks explode behind his eyes. A sweet toothache pain shoots through his neck, down his spine to the groin, contracting the body out through his cock. A final spasm throws a great spurt of sperm across the red screen like a shooting star.

The boy falls with a soft gutty suction through a maze of penny arcades and dirty pictures.

Jean de Berg

'Jean de Berg' is the pseudonym of an anonymous author who dedicated the novel The Image *to 'Pauline Reage' (see page 316). Reage wrote a teasing foreword to the book speculating on the identity of the author.*

From **The Image** (1956). *Trans. Patsy Southgate*

Clare handed me the photographs one after the other, first carefully examining each one herself while I was occupied with the preceding one . . .

In the first one Anne is wearing a short black slip with nothing underneath but her stockings and a simple garter belt like the one I had already admired in the Bagatelle gardens. But these stockings do not have embroiderd tops.

She is standing next to a column in the same position Clare made her assume to hide the stolen rose under her dress. Only she is not wearing any shoes and instead of the dress she only has the slip whose thin material she is holding up with both hands, exposing the half-opened thighs and the triangle of her fleece. One leg is straight, the other slightly bent at the knee, the foot only half resting on the floor.

A lace inset decorates the top of the slip but one can't really make it out because it is pulled to one side, the right shoulder strap not being on at all and the left one having fallen off the shoulder. The black lingerie is therefore twisted around covering half of one breast and freeing the other breast almost entirely. The breasts are perfect, not too full, far enough apart, with the brown halo that encircles the nipple clearly marked but not too large. The arms are well-rounded and gracefully curved.

The face, under the loose curls, is a real triumph: the eyes consenting, the lips parted, a mingled look of ingenue charm and submissiveness . . .

In the next one the girl is entirely naked, hands chained behind her back, kneeling on the black and white checkerboard floor. The picture is taken in profile and also from above. One sees nothing but the girl, kneeling naked on the floor, and the whip.

Her head is lowered, her hair falls on either side of her face, hiding it, exposing her neck which is bent down as far as it will go. The tip of one breast appears below the shoulder. The thighs are together, leaning backward, and the trunk is bent forward in a way that makes the buttocks protrude most fetchingly as they await their punishment. The wrists are bound together behind the back, at waist height, by a slender chain of shiny metal . . .

The girl is still naked and on her knees, chained now to the foot of the bed. One sees her from the rear. The ankles are closely bound together but crossed, one foot over the other, which forces the knees wide apart . . . The buttocks are marked in every direction by deep lines, very clear and distinct, which criss cross the central crack, more or less stressed according to how hard the whip fell. This picture of little Anne chained to her bed on her knees in a most uncomfortable position is obviously more moving because of the cruel evidence of the torture she had undergone. The black ironwork frames a pattern of elegant arabesques behind her.

The nude girl is bound to the stone column by thick ropes, she is facing the camera, her legs open, her arms raised. A black band covers her eyes, her mouth is screaming, or else distorted by the extremity of her suffering . . . The ropes bite deeply into her flesh . . . The tortured body whose reflexes clearly show that it is struggling against its bonds, has two deep wounds from which blood flows freely.

One extends from the tip of the breast to the armpit, on the side where there are no ropes. The blood pours down one whole side in little rivers of varying force which run together and separate again in an elaborate network which covers one hip and a good part of the stomach. It even flows into the navel and the pubic hair in a thick stream which runs down the belly.

The second wound in the lower part of the body, ornaments the other side. It pierces the groin just above the pubis, penetrating the lower belly and coming down to the inner part of the thigh. The blood from this wound flows in large rivers, almost covering the whole area, running down to the rope which binds the body above the knees. There it accumulates a moment and then pours out directly onto one of the white flagstones where a pool has formed.

The last photograph was a logical conclusion. The tortured body of the girl, apparently lifeless, is stretched out on the black and white checkerboard floor. She still wears nothing but the black band across her eyes . . . Blood trickles out of her half-opened mouth and down her cheek before dripping to the floor. Apart from this detail the face seems peaceful, almost happy. One might almost think, for a moment, that the mouth is smiling.

W. H. Auden

1907–1973

W. H. Auden, English poet and dramatist, was educated at Oxford, where he established himself as the dominant voice of the 1930s group of left-wing poets and intellectuals. His precocious early work was characteristically terse and political, but later, especially after his emigration to the US in 1939, his tone became increasingly expansive and contemplative. Auden collaborated with Christopher Isherwood in the 1930s to produce several plays, and later with his lover Chester Kallman on opera libretti.

From 'The Platonic Blow' (1965)

Mad to be had, to be felt and smelled. My lips
Explored the adorable masculine tits. My eyes
Assessed the chest I caressed the athletic hips
And the slim limbs. I approved the grooves of the thighs.

I hugged, I snuggled into an armpit, I sniffed
The subtle whiff of its tuft, I lapped up the taste
Of his hot hollow. My fingers began to drift
On a trek of inspection, a leisurely tour of the waist.

Downward in narrowing circles they playfully strayed,
Encroached on his privates like poachers, approached the prick.
But teasingly swerved, retreating from the meeting. It betrayed
Its pleading need by a pretty imploring kick.

'Shall I rim you' I whispered. He shifted his limbs in assent,
Turned on his side and opened his legs, let me pass
To the dark parks behind. I kissed as I went
The great thick cord that ran from his balls to his arse.

Prying the buttocks aside, I nosed my way in
Down the shaggy slopes. I came to the puckered goal.
It was quick to my licking. He pressed his crotch to my chin.
His thighs squirmed as my tongue wormed in his hole.

His sensations yearned for consummation. He untucked
His legs and lay panting, hot as a teen-age boy
Naked, enlarged, charged, aching to get sucked,
Clawing the sheet, all his pores open to joy.

I inspected his erection. I surveyed his parts with a stare
From scrotum level. Sighting alongside the underside
Of his cock I looked through the forest of pubic hair
To the range of his chest beyond, rising lofty and wide.

I admired the texture, the delicate wrinkles and the neat
Sutures of the capacious bag. I adored the grace
Of the male genitalia. I raised the delicious meat
Up to my mouth, brought the face of its hard-on to my face.

Slipping my lips round the Byzantine dome of its head
With the tip of my tongue I caressed the sensitive groove,
He thrilled to the thrill. 'That's lovely!' he hoarsely said,
'Go on! Go on!' Very slowly I started to move.

Gently, intently, I slid to the massive base
Of his tower of power, paused there a moment down
In the warm moist thicket, then began to retrace
Inch by inch the smooth way to the throbbing crown.

Indwelling excitements swelled at delights to come
As I descended and ascended those thick distended walls.
I grasped his root between left forefinger and thumb
And with my right hand tickled his heavy voluminous balls.

I plunged with a rhythmical lunge, steady and slow
And at every stroke made a corkscrew roll with my tongue.
His soul reeled in the feeling. He whimpered 'Oh!'
As I tongued and squeezed and rolled and tickled and swung.

Then I pressed on the spot where the groin is joined to the cock,
Slipped a finger into his arse and massaged him from inside.
The secret sluices of his juices began to unlock.
He melted into what he felt. 'O Jesus!' he cried.

Waves of immeasurable pleasures mounted his member in quick
Spasms. I lay still in the notch of his crotch inhaling his sweat.
His ring convulsed round my finger. Into me, rich and thick,
His hot spunk spouted in gouts, spouted in jet after jet.

Violette Leduc

1907–1972

The French writer Violette Leduc was brought up by her grandmother after being abandoned by both her parents. After a series of ill-paid jobs, she was taken up by Simone de Beauvoir, who encouraged her to write her autobiography. The result was La Bâtarde *(1964), which dealt frankly with her lesbian relationships and mental breakdown, blending factual account with a highly stylized Surrealism.*

From **La Bâtarde** (1964). *Trans. Derek Coltman*

'Come and read in my room.'

She was leaving again, she was scattering crystals of frost between her request and my answer.

'Will you come?'

Isabelle left my cubicle.

She had seen me with the bed-clothes up to my neck. She didn't know I was wearing a special nightgown, a nightgown from a lingerie boutique. I thought one's personality could be changed by wearing expensive clothes. The silk nightgown brushed against my flanks with the softness of a spider's web. I dressed myself in my regulation nightgown, then I too left my cubicle, wrists gripped tightly by my regulation cuffs. The monitor was asleep. I hesitated in front of Isabelle's curtain. I went in.

'What's the time?' I asked coldly.

I stayed by the curtain, I shone my torch toward the bedside table.

'Come over here,' Isabelle said.

I didn't dare. Her long hair, all undone, seemed to belong to a stranger and it intimidated me. Isabelle was looking at the time.

'Come closer,' she said to her wrist-watch.

The luxuriance of the hair sweeping down the bars at the head of the bed. It made a shimmering screen hiding the face of a recumbent girl, it frightened me. I put out the light.

Isabelle got out of bed. She took my torch and my book away from me.

'Now come here,' she said.

Isabelle was back in bed.

She lay in bed directing the beam of my torch.

I sat down on the edge of the mattress. She stretched her arm over my shoulder, took my book from the bedside table and gave it to me. She reassured me. I turned the pages of the book because she was staring at me, I didn't know which page to stop at. She waited for what I was waiting for.

I fastened my eyes on the first letter of the first line.

'Eleven o'clock,' Isabelle said.

I gazed at the first page, at the words I could not see. She took the book from my hands and put out the light.

Isabelle pulled me backwards, she laid me down on the eiderdown, she raised me up, she kept me in her arms: she was taking me out of a world where I had never lived so that she could launch me into a world I had not yet reached; the lips opened mine a little, they moistened my teeth. The too fleshy tongue frightened me; but the strange virility didn't force its way in. Absently calmly, I waited. The lips moved over my lips. My heart was beating too hard and I wanted to prolong the sweetness of the imprint, the new experience brushing at my lips. Isabelle is kissing me, I said to myself. She was tracing a circle around my mouth, in each corner, two staccato notes of music on my lips; then her mouth pressed against mine once more, hibernating there. My eyes were wide with astonishment beneath their lids, the seashells at my ears were whispering too loud. Isabelle continued: we climbed rung after rung down into a darkness below the darkness of the tram depot. She had made her honey on my lips, the sphinxes were drifting into sleep again. I knew that I had needed her before we met. Isabelle thrust back her hair which had been sheltering us.

'Do you think she's asleep?' she asked.

'The new monitor?'

'She's asleep,' Isabelle decided.

'She's asleep,' I said too.

'You're shivering. Take off your dressing-gown.'

She opened the bedcovers.

'Come in without the light,' Isabelle said.

She lay down against the partition, in her bed, at home. I took off my dressing-gown, I felt I was too new on the rug of an old world. I had to get into bed with her quickly because the floor seemed to be giving away under me. I stretched myself out along the edge of the mattress: prepared to escape like a thief in the night.

'You're cold. Come close to me,' Isabelle said.

A sleeper coughed, trying to separate us.

She was already holding me, I was already held, we were already torturing one another, but the cheerful foot touching mine, the ankle rubbing against my ankle, reassured us. My nightgown occasionally brushed against me as we clutched one another and rolled back and forth. We stopped. Memory and the dormitory about us returned. Isabelle switched on the torch: she wanted to see me. I took it back from her. A wave carried her away and she sank down into the bed, then rose up again, plunged her face toward me, and held me to her. There were roses falling from the girdle she put around me. I fastened the same girdle around her.

'The bed mustn't make a noise,' she said.

I felt for a cool place on the pillow, as though that would be the place to keep the bed silent. I found a pillow of blonde hair. Isabelle pulled me on top of her.

We were still hugging each other, we both wanted to be swallowed up by the other. We had stripped ourselves of our families, the rest of the world, time, and light. As Isabelle lay crushed over my gaping heart I wanted to feel her enter it. Love is a harrowing invention. Isabelle, Violette, I thought to myself, trying to become accustomed to the magic simplicity of the two first names.

She swathed my shoulders in the white softness of her arms as though in a fur, she put my hand in the furrow between her breasts, on top of her muslin nightgown. The enchantment of my hand under hers, of my neck and shoulders clothed with her arm. And yet my face was alone: my eyelids were cold. Isabelle knew they were. Her tongue began to press against my teeth, impatient to make me warm all over. I shut myself up, I barricaded myself inside my mouth. She waited: that was how she taught me to open into flower. She was the hidden muse inside my body. Her tongue, her little flame, softened my muscles, my flesh. I responded, I attacked, I fought, I wanted to emulate her violence. We no longer cared about the noise we made with our lips. We were relentless with each other; then, becoming quieter, methodically, both together, we began drugging each other with our saliva. After the exchange of so much moisture, our lips parted despite themselves. Isabelle let herself fall into the hollow of my shoulder.

'A train,' she said to regain her breath.

There was something crawling in my belly. I had an octopus inside me.

Isabelle with a childish finger on my lips was tracing the outline of my mouth. The finger dropped down on to my neck. I seized it, I drew it across my eyes.

'They're yours,' I said.

Isabelle didn't speak. Isabelle didn't move. If she were asleep it would be over. Isabelle was once more as she had always been. I no longer trusted her. I should have to leave. This was her cubicle, not mine. I was unable to move: we hadn't finished. If she were asleep, then she had lured me there on false pretences.

Make her not be asleep among distant stars. Make the darkness not engender darkness in her.

Isabelle was not asleep!

She lifted my arm, my thigh grew pale. I felt a cold thrill of pleasure. I listened to what she took, to what she was giving, I blinked with gratitude: I was giving suck. Isabelle moved suddenly to another place. She was smoothing my hair, she was stroking the night out of my hair so that it ran all down my cheeks. She stopped, she created an intermission. Brow pressed against brow, we listened to the undertow; we were giving ourselves back to the silence, we were giving ourselves up to it.

A caress is to a shudder what twilight is to a lightning flash. Isabelle was dragging a rake of light from my shoulder to my wrist; she passed with her five-fingered mirror over my throat, over the back of my neck, over my back. I followed the hand, I could see under my eyelids a neck, a shoulder, an arm that didn't belong to me. She was raping my ear with her tongue as earlier she had raped my mouth. The artifice was shameless, the sensation strange. I grew cold again, this refinement of bestiality made me fearful. Isabelle found my head again, she held me by the hair and began again. I was disturbed by this fleshy icicle, but Isabelle's self-confidence reassured me.

Robert Musil

1880–1940

The Austrian novelist Robert Musil was born in Klagenfurt and educated at a military academy (the setting for his 1906 novel Young Törless, *dealing with sadism and homosexuality) before studying psychology and philosophy in Berlin, and fighting in the German army during the war. Musil is remembered primarily for his huge, satirical novel* The Man Without Qualities *(1930–43), set at the outbreak of war in Imperial Vienna, and often compared to the work of Joyce and Proust.*

From **The Perfecting of A Love**. *Trans. Eithne Wilkins and Ernst Kaiser*

But now, in this moment when it all came back to her, it carried her right to the end of whatever possibilities of real love, real union, there were in this transparently thin, glimmeringly vulnerable world of illusion – of illusions without which life could not be maintained: all the dream-dark straits of existing solely by virtue of another human being, all the island solitude of never daring to wake, this insubstantiality of love that was like a gliding between two mirrors behind which nothingness lay. And here in this room, hidden behind her false confession as behind a mask, and waiting for the adventure that she would experience as though she were someone else, she knew the wonderful, dangerous intensification of feeling that came with lying and cheating in love. She felt herself stealthily slipping out of her own being, out into some territory beyond anyone else's reach, the forbidden territory, the dissolution of absolute solitude – entering, for the sake of greater truthfulness, into the void that sometimes gapes for an instant behind all ideals.

And then suddenly she heard a furtive tread, a creaking first of the stairs and then of the floorboards outside her door, a faint creaking under the weight of someone who had stopped there.

Her eyes turned towards the door. How strange that there outside, behind those thin panels, there was another human being, standing motionless . . . And on each side of this indifferent, this accidental door tension rose high as behind a dam.

She had already undressed. Her clothes lay on the chair by the bed, where she had just flung them, and from them the vague scent of what had been next to her body rose and mingled with the air of this room that was let one day to this person, the next day to another. She glanced round the room. She noticed a brass lock hanging loose, on a chest of drawers. Her gaze lingered on a small threadbare rug, worn thin by many footsteps, at the side of her bed. Suddenly she could not help thinking of all the bare feet that had stepped on this rug, permeating it with their smell, and how this smell was given off again and entered into other people's being, a familiar, protective smell, somehow associated with childhood and home. It was an odd, flickering, double impression, now alien and abhorrent, now fascinating, as if the self-love of all those strangers were a current flowing into her and all that was left of her own identity were a passive awareness of it.

And all the while that man was there, standing on the other side of her door, his presence known to her only through the faint, hardly detectable sounds that he could not help making.

Then she was seized by a wild urge to throw herself down on this rug and kiss the repulsive traces of all those feet, exciting herself with their smell like a bitch on heat. But this was no longer sexual desire; it was something crying within her like a small child, howling like a high wind.

Suddenly she knelt down on the rug. The stiff flowers of the pattern loomed larger, spreading and intertwining senselessly before her eyes, and over them she saw her own heavy thighs, a mature woman's thighs, hideously arched and without meaning, yet tense with an incomprehensible gravity. And her hands lay there before her on the floor, two five-limbed animals staring at each other.

All at once she remembered the lamp in the passage there outside and the horribly silent moving circles it cast upon the ceiling, and the walls, the bare walls, remembered the emptiness out there and then again the man who was standing there, faintly creaking sometimes as a tree creaks in its bark, his urgent blood in his head like the thicket of the leaves. And here she was on her hands and knees, only a door between her and him. And still she felt the full sweetness of her ripe body, felt it with that imperishable remnant of the soul that stands quietly, unmoved, beside the ravaged body even when it is broken open and disfigured by the infliction of devastating injuries – that stands beside it, in grave and constant awareness and yet averted from it, as beside the body of a stricken beast.

Then she heard the man outside walking cautiously away. And even through the turmoil in her rapt senses she realised: all this was betrayal itself, greater and weightier than the mere lie.

Slowly she began to rise on her knees, spellbound by the baffling thought that by now it might all have really happened, and she trembled like someone who has escaped from danger by mere chance, not by any effort of his own. She tried to picture it. She saw her body lying underneath that stranger's body, saw it with a lucidity that branches out into every smallest detail, like spilt water seeping into every cranny. She felt her own pallor and heard the shameful words of abandonment and saw above her the man's eyes, holding her down, hovering over her, like the outspread wings of a bird of prey. And all the time she was thinking: '*This* is betrayal!' And now she pictured herself at home again after all this and how he would say: 'I can't feel you from inside. . . . ' And she had no answer but a helpless smile, a smile that tried to say: 'Believe me, it was not meant against us. . . . '

And yet there was one knee still pressed against the floor – a senseless, alien thing – and she felt her very existence in it, inaccessible, with all the forlorn, defenceless frailty there is in the ultimate human potentialities that no word can hold fast and no return can ever weave into the pattern of life as it once has been.

She was empty of thought. She did not know if she was doing wrong. Everything turned into strange and lonely grief – and the grief itself was like another room around her, enclosing a gentle darkness, a diffuse, floating room, softly rising in the air. And then gradually she perceived a strong, clear, indifferent light shining from above. In it she saw everything she did, her own gestures of surrender, and the abandonment of her innermost being, torn out of her in ecstasy, all that in its enormity seemed so real and yet was mere appearance. . . . There it lay, crumpled, small, and cold, all its relevance lost, far, far below her. . . .

And after a long time it seemed to her as if a cautious hand were again trying the door, and she knew he was there outside, listening intently. A whirling dizziness took hold of her, almost forcing her to creep to the door on all fours and draw back the bolt.

But she remained crouching on the floor in the middle of the room. Once again something held her back – a sense of her own sordidness, the atmosphere of the past. Like a single, violent thrust cutting her sinews, there was the thought that perhaps it was all nothing but a relapse into her past. She raised her hands above her head. 'Oh my beloved, help me, help me!' she cried out in her thoughts, and felt the cry was true. And yet it was only a soft, caressing thought: 'We moved towards each other, mysteriously drawn through space, through all the years . . . and now, by sad and hurtful ways, I enter into you.'

And then there was stillness, a great expanse: strength that had been painfully dammed up now pouring in through the breaches in the walls. Like a quiet, mirroring pool of water her life lay there before her, past and future united in the present moment. There are things one can never do – one does not know why. Perhaps those are the most important things? Indeed one knows they are the most important things. And one knows: a deadly languor lies upon life, one feels the stiffness and numbness of it as in frozen fingers. And sometimes again it loosens its hold, dissolves like snow and ice on meadows – one marvels, one is a sombre brightness expanding far, far away. But life, one's own hard and bony life, one's irrevocable life, resumes its callous grip – somewhere the links close – one does nothing at all.

Suddenly she rose to her feet, and the thought that now she *must* do this drove her soundlessly forward. Her hands drew the bolt back. There was no sound. The door did not move. And then she opened the door and looked out into the passage: there was no one there. In the dim light from the lamp the bare walls stared at each other through empty space. He had gone without her hearing it.

She went to bed, her mind full of self-reproaches. And, already on the borders of sleep, she thought: 'I am hurting you.' But at the same time she had the strange feeling: 'It is you who do whatever I am doing.' And sinking towards oblivion she knew: 'We are casting away everything that can be cast away, to hold on to each other all the more tightly, to wrap around us closely what no one can touch.' Then for an instant, thrown up into wakefulness, she thought: 'This man will triumph over us. But what is triumph?'

Sinking back into sleep, her thoughts slid down along that question into the depths and her bad conscience accompanied her like a last caress. A vast egoism, deepening and darkening the world, rose over her as over someone dying. Behind closed eyes she saw bushes and clouds and birds, and she became quite small among them, and yet it all seemed to be there only for her sake. And then there was the moment of closing up, of shutting out everything alien; and on the threshold of dream there was perfection, a great and pure love mantling her in a trembling light, dissolution of all apparent contradictions.

The visitor did not return. She slept undisturbed, her door unlatched – quiet as a tree on a meadow.

With the next morning a mild, mysterious day began.

Gore Vidal

b. 1925

The American novelist and polemicist Gore Vidal was born in New York into a patrician Democrat family. His work includes the historical novels Washington DC *(1967),* 1876 *(1976) and* Lincoln *(1984), and the transexual satire* Myra Breckenridge, *all trenchant commentaries on American public and private mores. In 1960, Vidal stood as a Democrat-Liberal candidate for Congress. He now lives in Italy.*

From **Myra Breckinridge** (1968)

'Do you . . . ' He began tentatively, looking down at me and the loose-stemmed rose that I held in my hand.

'Do I what?'

'Do you want me to . . . well, to ball you?' The delivery was superb, as shy as a nubile boy requesting a first kiss.

I let go of him as though in horror. 'Rusty! Do you know who you're talking to?'

'Yes, Miss Myra. I'm sorry. I didn't mean to offend you. . . . '

'What sort of woman do you think I am?' I took the heavy balls in my hand, as an offering. 'These belong to Mary-Ann, and no one else, and if I ever catch you playing around with anybody else, I'll see that Mr. Martinson puts you away for twenty years.'

He turned white. 'I'm sorry. I didn't know. I thought maybe . . . the way you were . . . doing what you were doing. . . . I'm sorry, really.' The voice stopped.

'You have every reason to be sorry.' Again I let him go; the large balls swung back between his legs, and continued gently to sway, like a double pendulum. 'In any case, if I had wanted you to – as you put it – "ball me," it's very plain that you couldn't. As a stud, you're a disaster.'

He flushed at the insult but said nothing. I was now ready for my master stroke. 'However, as a lesson, I shall ball you.'

He was entirely at sea. 'Ball *me?* How?'

'Put out your hands.' He did so and I bound them together with surgical gauze. Not for nothing had I once been a nurses' aide.

'What're you doing that for?' Alarm growing.

With a forefinger, I flicked the scrotal sac, making him cry out from shock. 'No questions, my boy.' When the hands were firmly secured, I lowered the examination table until it was just two feet from the floor. 'Lie down,' I ordered. 'On your stomach.'

Mystified, he did as he was told. I then tied his bound hands to the top of the metal table. He was, as they say, entirely in my power. If I had wanted, I could have killed him. But my fantasies have never involved murder or even physical suffering for I have a horror of blood preferring to inflict pain in more subtle ways, destroying totally, for instance, a man's idea of himself in relation to the triumphant sex.

'Now then, up on your knees.'

'But . . . ' A hard slap across the buttocks put an end to all objections. He pulled himself up on his knees, legs tight together and buttocks clenched shut. He resembled a pyramid whose base was his head and white-socked feet, and whose apex was his rectum. I was now ready for the final rite.

'Legs wide apart,' I commanded. Reluctantly, he moved his knees apart so that they lined up with the exact edges of the table. I was now afforded my favourite view of the male, the heavy rosy scrotum dangling from the groin above which the tiny sphincter shyly twinkled in the light. Carefully I applied lubricant to the mystery that even Mary-Ann has never seen, much less violated.

'What're you doing?' The voice was light as a child. True terror had begun.

'Now remember the secret is to relax entirely. Otherwise you could be seriously hurt.'

I then pulled up my skirt to reveal, strapped to my groin, Clem's dildo which I borrowed yesterday on the pretext that I wanted it copied for a lamp base. Clem had been most amused.

Rusty cried out with alarm. 'Oh, no! For God's sake, don't.'

'Now you will find out what it is the girl feels when you play the man with her.'

'Jesus, you'll split me!' The voice was treble with fear. As I approached him, dildo in front of me like the god Priapus personified, he tried to wrench free of his bonds, but failed. Then he did the next best thing, and brought his knees together in an attempt to deny me entrance. But it was no use. I spread him wide and put my battering ram to the gate.

For a moment I wondered if he might not be right about the splitting: the opening was the size of a dime while the dildo was over two inches wide at the head and nearly a foot long. But then I recalled how Myron used to have no trouble in accommodating objects this size or larger, and what the fragile Myron could do so could the inexperienced but sturdy Rusty.

I pushed. The pink lips opened. The tip of the head entered and stopped.

'I can't,' Rusty moaned. 'Honestly I can't. It's too big.'

'Just relax, and you'll stretch. Don't worry'

He made whatever effort was necessary and the pursed lips became a grin allowing the head to enter, but not without a gasp of pain and shock.

Once inside, I savoured my triumph. I had avenged Myron. A lifetime of being penetrated had brought him only misery. Now, in the person of Rusty, I was able, as Woman Triumphant, to destroy the adored destroyer.

Holding tight to Rusty's slippery hips, I plunged deeper. He cried out with pain.

But I was inexorable. I pushed even farther into him, triggering the prostate gland, for when I felt between his legs, I discovered that the erection he had not been able to present me with had now, inadvertently, occurred. The size was most respectable, and hard as metal.

But when I plunged deeper, the penis went soft with pain, and he cried out again, begged me to stop, but now I was like a woman possessed, riding, riding, riding my sweating stallion into forbidden country, shouting with joy as I experienced my own sort of orgasm, oblivious to his staccato shrieks as I delved that innocent flesh. Oh, it was a holy moment! I was one with the Bacchae, with all the priestesses of the dark bloody cults, with the great goddess herself for whom Attis unmanned himself. I was the eternal feminine made flesh, the source of life and its destroyer, dealing with man as incidental toy, whose blood as well as semen is needed to make me whole!

There was blood at the end. And once my passion had spent itself, I was saddened and repelled. I had not meant actually to tear the tender flesh but apparently I had, and the withdrawing of my weapon brought with it bright blood. He did not stir as I washed him clean (like a loving mother), applying medicine to the small cut, inserting gauze (how often had I done this for Myron!). Then I unbound him.

Shakily, he stood up, rubbing tears from his swollen face. In silence he dressed while I removed the harness of the dildo and put it away in the attaché case.

Not until he was finally dressed did he speak. 'Can I go now?'

'Yes. You can go now.' I sat down at the surgical table and took out this notebook. He was at the door when I said, 'Aren't you going to thank me for the trouble I've taken?'

He looked at me, face perfectly blank. Then, tonelessly, he murmured, 'Thank you, ma'am,' and went.

And so it was that Myra Breckinridge achieved one of the great victories for her sex. But one which is not yet entirely complete even though, alone of all women, I know what it is like to be a goddess enthroned, and all-powerful.

Terry Southern

b. 1926

and Mason Hoffenburg

An American novelist and screenwriter, Terry Southern was born in Texas and educated in Chicago. His novels include Candy *(written with Mason Hoffenberg), a reworking of Voltaire's* Candide *which set out to satirize pornography, and* Blue Movie *(1970). He also collaborated on the screenplays for* Barbarella *(1968) and* Easy Rider *(1969).*

From **Candy** (1968)

'No, resume the basic yoga position', said Grindle, 'and I will continue with the instruction.'

Candy lay back again with a sigh, closed-eyed, hands joined behind her head, and Grindle resumed his fondling of her sweet-dripping little fur-pie.

'Does the tingling sensation you referred to before continue, or increase?' he asked, after a moment or so.

' . . . I'm afraid so,' said the girl sadly, panting a little.

'And do you experience feelings of creamy warmth and a great yielding sensation?' demanded Grindle.

'Yes,' Candy sighed, thinking he was surely psychic.

'Never mind your crass and absurdly cheap philistine materialist associations with it,' said Grindle crossly, as he adjusted her legs again and ranged himself just above her. 'Put those from your mind – concentrate on your *Exercise Number Four*, for always remember that we must bring *all* our mystical knowledge to converge on the issue at hand – even as does the tiger his strength, cunning and speed.'

'Now I am inserting the member,' he explained, as he parted the tender quavering lips of the pink honeypot and allowed his stout member to be drawn into the seething thermal pudding of the darling girl.

Nègre en chemise Anonymous

'Oh my goodness,' said Candy, squirming her lithe and supple body slightly, though remaining obediently closed-eyed and with her hands clasped tightly behind her head.

'Now I shall remove the member,' said Grindle, ' . . . not all the way but just so, there, and in again. You see? And again so, I will repeat this several times – while you do your *Exercise Number Four.*'

'Gosh,' said Candy, swallowing nervously. ' . . . I don't think I can concentrate on it now.'

'Oh, yes,' said Grindle, encouraging her hips with his hands, setting them into the motion of the Cosmic Rhythm Exercise she had practised earlier in the rec-tent. And when she had satisfactorily achieved the motion, Grindle said: 'Now this, you see, approximates the so-called "sexual act".'

'I *know* it,' said Candy fretfully, greatly disturbed by the thought.

'I shall presently demonstrate still another mastery of glandular functions,' claimed great Grindle, 'that of the so-called *orgasm* or *ejaculation.*'

'Oh please,' said the adorable girl, actually alarmed, 'not . . . not inside me . . . I . . . I . . . '

'Don't be absurd,' said Grindle breathing heavily, 'naturally in willing the chemistry of the semen, I would eliminate the impregnating agent, spermatozoa, as a constituent – for it would be of no use to our purpose here you see.'

'Now then,' he continued after a moment. 'tell me if this does not almost exactly resemble the philistine "orgasm"?'

'Oh gosh,' murmured the darling closed-eyed girl, biting her lips as the burning member began to throb and spurt inside her, in a hot, ravaging flood of her precious little honey-cloister whose bleating pink-sugar walls cloyed and writhed as though alive with a thousand tiny insatiable tongues, ' . . . and how!'

Anaïs Nin

1903–1977

A French-born writer of Spanish-Cuban descent, who lived alternately in Paris and New York, Nin's fiction includes House of Incest *(1936),* A Spy in the House of Love *(1954), and the collection* Delta of Venus, *a reissue of her early pornographic writings. Her published diaries and correspondence with Henry Miller give vivid accounts of Parisian literary life in the 1930s.*

From **Delta of Venus** (1969)

Then he saw Martha as a woman for the first time. He had always considered her a child. What he saw was a voluptuous body, clearly outlined in the kimono, moist hair, a fevered face, a soft mouth. She waited. The expectancy in her was so intense that her hands fell to her sides, and the kimono opened and revealed her completely naked body.

Then John saw that she wanted him, that she was offering herself, but instead of being stirred, he recoiled. 'Martha! Oh, Martha!' he said, 'what an animal you are, you are truly the daughter of a whore. Yes, in the orphanage everybody said it, that you were the daughter of a whore.'

Martha's blood rushed to her face. 'And you,' she said, 'you are impotent, a monk, you're like a woman, you're not a man. Your father is a man.'

And she rushed out of his room.

Now the image of John ceased to torment her. She wanted to efface it from her body and her blood. It was she who waited that night for everyone to fall asleep so she could unlock the door to Pierre's room, and it was she who came to his bed, silently offering her now cool and abandoned body to him.

Pierre knew that she was free of John, that she was his now, by the way she came into his bed. What joy to feel the soft youthful body sliding against his body. Summer nights he slept naked. Martha had dropped her kimono and was naked too. Immediately his desire sprang up and she felt the hardness of it against her belly.

Her diffuse feelings were now concentrated in only one part of her body. She found herself making gestures she had never learned, found her hand surrounding his penis, found herself gluing her body to his, found her mouth yielding to the many kinds of kisses Pierre could give. She gave herself in a frenzy, and Pierre was aroused to his greatest feats.

Every night was an orgy. Her body became supple and knowing. The tie between them was so strong that it was difficult for them to pretend otherwise during the day. If she looked at him, it was as if he had touched her between the legs. Sometimes in the dark hall they embraced. He pressed her against the wall. At the entrance there was a big dark closet full of coats and snow shoes. No one ever entered there in the summer. Martha hid there and Pierre came in. Lying over the coats, in the small space, enclosed, secret, they abandoned themselves.

Pierre had been without sexual life for years, and Martha was meant for this and only came to life at these moments. She received him always with her mouth open and already wet between the legs. His desire rose in him before he saw her, at the mere idea of her waiting in this dark closet. They acted like animals in a struggle, about to devour each other. If his body won and he pinned her down under him, then he took her with such a force that he seemed to be stabbing her with his sex, over and over again, until she fell back exhausted. They were in marvellous harmony, their excitement rising together. She had a way of climbing over him like an agile animal. She would rub herself against his erect penis, against his pubic hair, with such frenzy that he panted. This dark closet became an animal den.

They sometimes drove to the abandoned farmhouse and spent the afternoon there. They became so saturated with lovemaking that if Pierre kissed Martha's eyelids she could feel it between her legs. Their bodies were charged with desire, and they could not exhaust it.

John seemed a pale image. They did not notice that he was observing them. The change in Pierre was apparent. His face glowed, his eyes looked ardent, his body became younger. And the change in her Voluptuousness was inscribed all over her body. Every move she made was sensual – serving coffee, reaching for a book, playing chess, playing the piano, she did every-thing caressingly. Her body became fuller and her breasts tauter under her clothes.

John could not sit between them. Even when they did not look at each other or speak to each other, he could feel a powerful current between them.

Monique Wittig

b. 1935

The French writer and theorist Monique Wittig was born in Alsace, and since 1976 has been resident in the US. Her first novel, L'opoponax *(1964), employed innovative narrative techniques to describe the experience of childhood. Other works include* Le Corps Lesbien *(1973) and a reworking of Dante,* Virgile, Non *(1985), both dealing with radical feminist and lesbian themes.*

From **Les Guerillères** (1969). *Trans. David Le Vay*

The women say that the feminary amuses the little girls. For instance three kinds of labia minora are mentioned there. The dwarf labia are triangular. Side by side, they form two narrow folds. They are almost invisible because the labia majora cover them. The moderate-sized labia minora resemble the flower of a lily. They are half-moon shaped or triangular. They can be seen in their entirety taut supple seething. The large labia spread out resemble a butterfly's wings. They are tall triangular or rectangular, very prominent.

They say that as possessors of vulvas they are familiar with their characteristics. They are familiar with the mons pubis the clitoris the labia minora the body and bulbs of the vagina. They say that they take a proper pride in that which has for long been regarded as the emblem of fecundity and the reproductive force in nature.

They say that the clitoris has been compared to a cherry-stone, a bud, a young shoot, a shelled sesame, an almond, a sprig of myrtle, a dart, the barrel of a lock. They say that the labia majora have been compared to the two halves of a shellfish. They say that the concealed face of the labia minora has been compared to the purple of Sidon, to tropic coral. They say that the secretion has been compared to iodized salt water.

They say that they have found inscriptions on plaster walls where vulvas have been drawn as children draw suns with multiple divergent rays. They say that it has been written that vulvas are traps vices pincers. They say that the clitoris has been compared to the prow of a boat to its stem to the comb of a shellfish. They say that vulvas have been compared to apricots pomegranates figs roses pinks peonies marguerites. They say these comparisons may be recited like a litany.

Yasunari Kawabata

1899–1972

The Japanese novelist Yasunari Kawabata was born in Osaka and educated at the Tokyo Imperial University. A reserved man, he was nevertheless a leading figure in Japanese literary culture, an early champion of Mishima, and the first Japanese writer to receive the Nobel Prize (1968). His novels – including The Scarlet Gang of Asakusa *(1929–30),* Snow Country *(1935–47) and* Meijin *(1954) – are marked by a melancholy lyricism, dealing with themes of alienation and homelessness.*

From **The House of the Sleeping Beauties** (1969).
Trans. Edward G. Seidensticker

He was not to do anything in bad taste, the woman of the inn warned old Eguchi. He was not to put his finger into the mouth of the sleeping girl, or try anything else of that sort.

There was this room, some four yards square, and the one next to it, but apparently no other rooms upstairs; and, since the downstairs seemed too restricted for guest rooms, the place could scarcely be called an inn at all. Probably because its secret allowed none, there was no sign at the gate. All was silence. Admitted through the locked gate, old Eguchi had seen only the woman to whom he was now talking. It was his first visit. He did not know whether she was the proprietress or a maid. It seemed best not to ask.

A small woman perhaps in her mid-forties, she had a youthful voice, and it was as if she had especially cultivated a calm, steady manner. The thin lips scarcely parted as she spoke. She did not often look at Eguchi. There was something in the dark eyes that lowered his defences, and she seemed quite at ease herself. She made tea from the iron kettle on the bronze brazier. The tea leaves and the quality of the brewing were astonishingly good, for the place and the occasion – to put old Eguchi more at ease. In the alcove hung a painting by Kawai Gyokudō, probably a reproduction, of a mountain village warm with autumn leaves. Nothing suggested that the room had unusual secrets.

'And please don't try to wake her. Not that you could, whatever you did. She's sound asleep and knows nothing.' The woman said it again: 'She'll sleep on and know nothing at all, from start to finish. Not even who's been with her. You needn't worry.'

·   ·   ·

It was the crimson velvet curtains. The crimson was yet deeper in the dim light. It was as if a thin layer of light hovered before the curtains, as if he were stepping into a phantasm. There were curtains over the four walls. The door was curtained too, but the edge had been tied back. He locked the door, drew the curtain, and looked down at the girl. She was not pretending. Her breathing was of the deepest sleep. He caught his breath. She was more beautiful than he had expected. And her beauty was not the only surprise. She was young too. She lay on her left side, her face toward him. He could not see her body – but she would not yet be twenty. It was as if another heart beat its wings in old Eguchi's chest.

Her right hand and wrist were at the edge of the quilt. Her left arm seemed to stretch diagonally under the quilt. Her right thumb was half hidden under her cheek. The fingers on the pillow beside her face were slightly curved in the softness of sleep, though not enough to erase the delicate hollows where they joined the hand. The warm redness was gradually richer from the palm to the fingertips. It was a smooth, glowing white hand.

'Are you asleep? Are you going to wake up.' It was as if he were asking so that he might touch her hand. He took it in his, and shook it. He knew that she would not open her eyes. Her hand still in his, he looked into her face. What kind of girl might she be? The eyebrows were untouched by cosmetics, the closed eyelashes were even. He caught the scent of maidenly hair. After a time the sound of the waves was higher, for his heart had been taken captive. Resolutely he undressed. Noting that the light was from above, he looked up. Electric light came through Japanese paper at two skylights. As if with more composure than was his to muster, he asked himself whether it was a light that set off to advantage the crimson of the velvet, and whether the light from the velvet set off the girl's skin like a beautiful phantom; but the colour was not strong enough to show against her skin. He had become accustomed to the light. It was too bright for him, used to sleeping in the dark, but apparently it could not be turned off. He saw that the quilt was a good one.

He slipped quietly under, afraid that the girl he knew would sleep on might awaken. She seemed to be quite naked. There was no reaction, no hunching of the shoulders or pulling in of the hips, to suggest that she sensed his presence. There should be in a young girl, however soundly she slept, some sort of quick reaction. But this would not be an ordinary sleep, he knew. The thought made him avoid touching her as he stretched out. Her knee was slightly forward, leaving his legs in an awkward position. It took no inspection to tell him that she was not on the defensive, that she did not have her right knee resting on her left. The right knee was pulled back, the leg stretched out. The angle of the shoulders as she lay on her left side and that of the hips seemed at variance, because of the inclination of her torso. She did not appear to be very tall.

The fingers of the hand old Eguchi had shaken gently were also in deep sleep. The hand lay as he had dropped it. As he pulled his pillow back the hand fell away. One elbow on the pillow, he gazed at it. As if it were alive, he muttered to himself. It was of course alive, and he meant only to say how very pretty it was; but once he had uttered them the words took on an ominous ring. Though this girl lost in sleep had not put an end to the hours of her life, had she not lost them, had them sink into bottomless depths? She was not a living doll, for there could be no living doll; but, so as not to shame an old man no longer a man, she had been made into a living toy. No, not a toy: for the old men, she could be life itself. Such life was, perhaps, life to be touched with confidence. To Eguchi's farsighted old eyes the hand from close up was yet smoother and more beautiful. It was smooth to the touch, but he could not see the texture.

It came to the old eyes that in the earlobes was the same warm redness of blood that grew richer toward the tips of the fingers. He could see the ears through the hair. The flush of the earlobes argued the freshness of the girl with a plea that stabbed at him. Eguchi had first wandered into this secret house out of curiosity, but it seemed to him that men more senile than he might come to it with even greater happiness and sorrow. The girl's hair was long, possibly for old men to play with. Lying back on his pillow, Eguchi brushed it aside to expose her ear. The sheen of the hair behind the ear was white. The neck and the shoulder too were young and fresh. They did not yet have the fullness of woman. He looked around the room. Only his own clothes were in the box. There was no sign of the girl's. Perhaps the woman had taken them away, but he started up at the thought that the girl might have come into the room naked. She was to be looked at. He knew that she had been put to sleep for the purpose, and that there was no call for this new surprise; but he covered her shoulder and closed his eyes. The scent of a baby came to him in the girl's scent. It was the milky scent of a nursing baby, and richer than that of the girl. Impossible – that the girl should have had a child, that her breasts should be swollen, that milk should be oozing from the nipples. He gazed afresh at her forehead and cheeks, and at the girlish line from the jaw down over the neck. Although he knew well enough already, he slightly raised the quilt that covered the shoulder. The breast was not one that had given milk. He touched it softly with his finger. It was not wet. The girl was approaching twenty. Even if the expression babyish was not wholly inappropriate, she should no longer have the milky scent of a baby. In fact it was a womanish scent. And yet it was very certain that old Eguchi had this very moment smelled a nursing baby. A passing spectre? However much he might ask why it had come to him, he did not know the answer; but probably it had come through the opening left by a sudden emptiness in his heart. He felt a surge of loneliness tinged with sorrow. More than sorrow or loneliness, it was the bleakness of old age, as if frozen to him. And it changed to pity and tenderness for the girl who sent out the smell of young warmth. Possibly only for purposes of turning away a cold sense of guilt, the old man seemed to feel music in the girl's body. It was a music of love. As if he wanted to flee, he looked at the four walls, so covered with velvet that there might have been no exit. The crimson velvet, taking its light from the ceiling, was soft and utterly motionless. It shut in a girl who had been put to sleep, and an old man.

'Wake up. Wake up.' Eguchi shook at the girl's shoulder. Then he lifted her head. 'Wake up. Wake up.'

·   ·   ·

As he withdrew his hand, her head turned gently and her shoulder with it, so that she was lying face up. He pulled back, wondering if she might open her eyes. Her nose and lips shone with youth, in the light from the ceiling. She brought her left hand to her mouth. She seemed about to take the index finger between her teeth, and he wondered if it might be a way she had when she slept; but she brought it softly to her lips, and no further. The lips parted slightly to show her teeth. She had been breathing through her nose, and now she breathed through her mouth. Her breath seemed to come a little faster. He wondered if she might be in pain, and decided she was not. Because the lips were parted, a faint smile seemed to float on the cheeks. The sound of waves breaking against the high cliff came nearer. The sound of the receding waves suggested large rocks at the base of the cliff. Water caught behind them seemed to follow after. The scent of the girl's breath was stronger from her mouth than it had been from her nose. It was not, however, the smell of milk. He asked himself again why the smell of milk had come to him. It was a smell, perhaps, to make him feel woman in the girl.

Jorge Amado

b. 1912

The Brazilian novelist Jorge Amado was born in the north-east province of Bahia, which provides the setting for much of his work. His early novels, such as Carnival Land *(1932),* Cacau *(1933), and the epic* The Violent Land *(1942), describe the class struggle on the cocoa estates in more or less stark Marxist terms, whereas later novels like* Shepherds of the Night *(1966) are witty and picaresque folk-tales.*

From **Dona Flor and Her Two Husbands:** 'Cooking School of Savour and Art' (1969). *Trans. Federico de Onis*

DONA FLOR'S RECIPE FOR MARINATED CRAB

INGREDIENTS (*for 8 servings*)

1 cup of coconut milk, without water
1 cup of dendê oil
2 pounds of tender crabs

SAUCE
3 cloves of garlic
salt to taste
juice of one lemon
a pinch of coriander
a sprig of parsley

a shallot
2 onions
½ cup of olive oil
a red pepper
1 pound of tomatoes

GARNISH
4 tomatoes
1 onion
1 red pepper

PROCEDURE

Grate two onions, crush garlic in mortar;
Onion and garlic do not smell badly, ladies,
They are fruits of the earth, perfumed.
Mince the coriander, the parsley, several tomatoes,
The shallot and half the pepper.
Mix all with the olive oil
And set aside this sauce
Of aromatic flavour.
(Those silly women who dislike the smell of onion,
What do they know about pure smells?
Vadinho liked to eat raw onion
And his kisses were like fire.)
Wash the crabs whole in lemon juice,
Wash them well, and then a little more,
To get out all the sand without taking away the taste of the sea.
Then season them, dipping them, one by one,
In the sauce, and put them in the skillet,

Each separate, with its seasoning.
Spread the remaining sauce over them
Slowly, for this is a delicate dish!
(Alas, it was Vadinho's favourite dish!)
Select four tomatoes, one pepper, one onion,
And slice them over the crabs
As a garnish.
Let them stand at room temperature for two hours
To absorb the flavour. Then put the skillet on the stove.
(He went to buy the crabs himself,
He was an old customer at the Market . . .)

When almost done, and only then,
Add the coconut milk, and at the very end
The dendê oil, just before removing from the stove.
(He used to go and taste the seasoning every minute,
Nobody had a more delicate palate.)

There you have that exquisite dish, of the finest cuisine,
Whoever can make it can rightfully boast
Of being a first-rate cook.
But, lacking the skill, it is better not to try it,
For everyone was not born a kitchen artist.
(It was Vadinho's favourite dish,
I will never again serve it at my table.
His teeth bit into the crab,
His lips were yellow with the dendê oil,
Alas, never again his lips,
His tongue, never again
His mouth burning with raw onion!)

Alexander Trocchi

1925–1984

Alexander Trocchi was a Scottish homosexual poet and novelist. His work includes a fake fifth volume of Frank Harris's My Life and Loves *and a pornographic autobiography,* Young Adam.

'For John Donne: Master Metaphysical' (1972)

Hear! this is what I
shall do to your body,
I shall play it as
a loved instrument
in touching it at deeps

touch you, my love
and gratify yr shyest intimations
of a perfect sexuality
in concrete terms
absorb at you

in me, round you
with all of spring & grass
our bright and coloured panoply!
Hear this: is what I
do to you. I mould
the very matter of yr
body's argument
a sweeter heroin
at yr crotch

to hard, my hot intent.
Take lips to suck
at short-haired places
still garlanded
with passion's traces

(Just a moment till
I undo my braces)

Nadine Gordimer

b. 1923

Nadine Gordimer was born in Springs, a small mining town near Johannesburg in South Africa, of immigrant Jewish parents. Her first short story was published in a South African magazine when she was only fifteen. Her first collection of short stories, Face to Face, *was published ten years later in 1949. She has now published ten novels and eight collections of short stories, as well as a few volumes of literary criticism. In 1991 Nadine Gordimer was awarded the Nobel Prize for Literature.*

From **The Conservationist** (1974)

Golden reclining nudes of the desert.
    Montego Bay. Shahara. Kalahari. Namib.
    There are beaches of black sand where he has been to.
    Wherever he has come from, there are hours on the way home over Africa when there is nothing down there. Sometimes it's at night and all you are aware of is perhaps a wave or two of turbulence, a heave from the day's heat, even at thirty thousand feet. Sometimes it's a day flight, clear, and even at thirty thousand feet you can squint down from the window-seat at long intervals and see it there, soft lap after lap of sand, stones, stones in sand, the infinite wreckage not of a city or a civilization but the home that is the earth itself. Sometimes there is a sandstorm down where you can't see, and even thirty thousand feet up the air is opaque. The plane is privately veiled, hidden in sand, buried in space. Nothing is disclosed.
    Once this winter he had to take a tourist class booking because – such is the number of people like himself travelling about the world on expense account – first class was full. At least he had a vacant seat beside him, in the tourist cabin. But at Lisbon a Portuguese family came aboard and after sulky looks between the two daughters who both wanted to sit with mama, one of them had to take the seat. So that was the end of his intention to lift the dividing arm and spread himself for sleep. It was midnight. She was a subdued girl, not pretty, nor perfumed beside him when the cabin lights were lowered and conversations gave way to hen-house shufflings. She had not said good evening, just looked at him with cow-eyes, someone who never got her own way, resigned to any objections that might be made as she approached the seat. When the hostess offered rugs she opened her thin mouth in a soundless mew of thanks. He was aware that she twisted her body, several times, to look back where mama and sister were

sitting some rows away but she couldn't have been able to see much. He could hear her swallow, and sigh, as if they were in bed together. He was not comfortable, although he had the advantage of the angle of window and seat to wedge the postage-stamp pillow against; of course she had settled her forearms along the armrests and he could not lean the other way without crowding her. She had the light soft rug drawn up to her thigh. Touched and drew almost away, touched and drew almost away, as she breathed, he supposed. He pushed it off and as he did so the side of his hand brushing a hand – hers, now lying, apparently, loosely against her thigh parallel with his – made of the movement a gesture of rejection: to excuse himself he corrected the movement into an impersonally polite one of replacing slipping covering.

Who spoke first?

Was it at all sure that it was he? Here in the dark (only dim, if he opened his eyes; the centre panels of light were off and it was the tiny reading bulb, no bigger than the light in the tail of an insect, of someone a few seats back that gave shape to what was next to him) here in the dark a hand lies half curled against a thigh. The thigh is crossed (he guesses) over another, or its inner side swells laid against a second identical to it.

– *And if another hand should move over the thigh, from the outer side, near the knee somewhere* (her body takes up the narrative), *up and inwards at the same time, it will meet the parallel lines of the two thighs where, like two soft bolsters or rolls of warm dough, they feel the pressure of their own volume against each other.* –

They are covered with something – stockings, I suppose, I didn't see when she seated herself, I didn't bother to look.

– *The hand may be cool or it may feel warm. The thighs may freeze against it, tendons flexed rigid, or maybe they will lie helpless, two stupid chunks of meat, two sentient creatures wanting to be stroked.* –

The plane was a hospital ward where the patients had not entirely settled for the night yet, the attendant with her blonde chignon passed silently down the rows in surveillance and the exchange stopped until she had gone, the hand waiting quietly on the thigh. Then, despite the fact that there was still the occasional movement that showed others were still awake, and an old man strolled slowly by on his way to the lavatory, the hand took up the thread of communication as happens when interruption cannot really disturb the deep level of pre-occupation at which it has been established. It was his left hand, which had been farthest away from him and closest to the other being, anyway, and he did not have to shift his position leaning against the angle of seat and window. Under the rug the hand found the edge of the very short skirt and there was a pause, quite delicate and patient, until the answer – she lifted her weight just enough to release the material so that he could glide his hand (yes, there were stockings) beneath it and push it up with his wrist as the hand rose.

An inquiry into what kind of flesh this was, to what milieu it belonged: as might have been expected, travelling well-chaperoned with a mother and sister, it was clothed in more than the usual garments for girls of the same age and more independent sophistication. A lining of some kind beneath the skirt, and beneath that, so surprising that they baffled him for a moment, at the top of the stockings those bumps of metal and rubber fasteners that lead by elastic straps somewhere up to the body. For years now women wore flimsy stockings and pants of a piece; there was something identifiably duenna'd about the suspenders and the belt they implied. His stranger's hand, man's hand, opened a forefinger and hooked it under the stocking-top and touched flesh.

In the cosy dark of other presences, in the intimacy like the loneliness of the crowd, the feel of flesh is experienced anew, as the taste of water is recognized anew in the desert. The finger went against the grain of fine down – yes, the flesh admits that it belongs to the Latin races, often hairy – and reached the warmth of the two legs pressed together. The skin was tacky, almost damp. It clung to his fingers with a message of excitement and pleasure. He felt how she kept her head absolutely still and knew he was forbidden to look at her face. Tucked, sucked in between the neatly parallel thighs his finger stirred only very slightly, just a murmur. He did not know its exact position in relation to the knees and the limits of the body; much higher than half-way, he guessed, because of the fullness of the thighs. The finger was in no hurry to broach the question; the thighs must be anticipating that it was coming. Even if they had never answered it before (neither she nor the sister looked more than sixteen or seventeen) they knew it had come now, whatever time this was – an hour between the hour of Europe and the hour of Africa, not registered on any watch glowing on passengers' wrists in the quiet dark – and whatever place this was: passengers are not disturbed by flight information while they sleep. It could have been the last of Europe or was Africa, already, they were unaware of passing over. She need not be afraid of wanting what was happening because it was happening nowhere. The other three fingers fluently joined the forefinger between the thighs and then unexpectedly (it must have been, for her) lost coherence and freeing themselves all the fingers trailed back and forth over the mound of one thigh, under the stocking but without unfastening the suspender, because the hand liked its confinement beneath a web. Then the fingers curled – she must have felt the tips if not the nails drawing in – and found, of course, another ridge of material that gave easily, in fact care had to be taken not to let it snap back against the skin – a crinkly edging round the leg of panties of some tight stretchy weave. If she had been sitting more upright, this was where the crease of juncture of thigh and body would have been. But she was lying as fully stretched under her rug as the seat on its reclining ratchet would allow, and his fingers recognized the juncture only by the different texture of the skin, a sudden grainless smoothness, silky and hot.

This time the question was differently phrased, that's all, but it must have been understood all the same: there was no rejoinder of change of position. The thighs, he could feel where the heel of his palm rested a moment on them, continued to clasp excitedly against nothing. His finger, just the one forefinger again (an appreciative monologue) roamed amid the curly hair in no hurry, delicately burrowed beneath this soft second rug as it was already concealed by the first and – suddenly – found itself tongued by a grateful dog. That was exactly what it felt like – delightful, fluttering, as innocent as the licking of a puppy; although it was he who was stroking movement along this wet and silky lining of her body, he had the impression it was his finger that was being caressed, not the finger that was doing the caressing. Now and then, quite naturally, he encountered the soundless O of the little mouth that made no refusal. As the night wore on – oh God knows how long it went on – the finger was able to enter, many times. At first he himself was magnificently tense, not only his sex but his whole body and legs, arms, neck, huge in the seat, swollen into unusual awareness of the bounds of himself, but later there were even moments when he must have been so fatigued he dozed, his finger inside her.

He woke with amazement: in the tunnel of seat-backs, the dim curving walls, the very faint creaking that was all there was to indicate that the sensation of motionlessness was in fact the nest of extreme speed – just as the extreme intimacy, his hand, finger still inside the body beside him, laved with it, was the extreme of detachment.

The gradual coming into the light of a morning somewhere did not bring an end. He could not leave her and she could not let him go. The only thing he could not get her to do was touch him; her rather plump and quite womanly hand went limp and stiff-wristed when he tried to carry it over to himself; she would not. Soon it was light, anyway, the lights went up brutally on the sleepers as prisoners are forced awake, and he took his weary hand back in good time before the trays of synthetic fruit juice arrived. The hand smelled of the body it had just left. The girl waited for him to take a plastic cup of juice and then took hers, with the same soundless thank you to the hostess. They did not speak; she emptied the cup thirstily (yes, my girl, lust dries the mouth), put the soft rug aside and went up the aisle. When she returned, she had to stand a moment before taking her seat because some-one was blocking the aisle, and he looked up and met her gaze, her pale, thick-skinned face with heavy eyebrows arched, hopeless, acceptingly. A stranger's face as the face of a woman with whom one has lived so long one doesn't see it anymore, becomes once again closed, a stranger's.

She carefully put back the rug over herself.

He had pushed up the eyelid of blind in his oval porthole. The reluctantly-awakened plane drifted to half-sleep again. Orange searchlights of rising sun pierced from window across to window in the prostrate humming silence. It all began again, uncanny in the daylight. Down there below reddish eddyings of the upper air and the glint of wing flashing monotonously at him, sand was an infinite progression of petrified sound-waves. It flowed on and on, echoing itself since there was no organic renewal by which life could be measured. On and on, shimmering, fading, paling, deepening nothing. His gaze was carried on it while he continued to stroke, fondle, dabble, on and on, all the way, caressing her all the way. The desert became forests, savannah, mine-dumps. At Johannesburg when he handed down a pink coat and a package of something that looked like a plant laced up in plastic, he spoke: – You are on holiday? – She answered that she and her mother and sister were coming to live with her uncle. Her English was strongly accented but quite intelligible. He said – Oh you'll like it there, in Durban. At the sea. – Her mother, moving with the other daughter along the queue in the aisle, nodded a faint and humble acknowledgment of the help he had given with hand-luggage.

He had washed his hands; used his electric razor; her hair was combed. The same clerk always came along with the driver to fetch him from the airport; he saw waiting at the barrier the respectfully alert, cocky young face, the sideburns and striped shirt advertised as correct wear for budding executives. An immigration official recognized him and waved him through ahead of the other sheep. The plant was being taken out of its wrapping at customs – of course, you can't bring in live plants from other countries. There was the usual making of conversation with the clerk in the car. – Good trip, this time, sir? Everything all right? –

– My knees need a week to straighten out, that's all. I had to travel tourist. Cramped as all hell. –

Her fluid on his hand as one says a man has blood on his hands. She screamed, or got up and told her mother. What an insane risk. A prosecution for 'interfering' with a young girl; yes, *crimen injuria*. That was the name; the girl had no name. A TAP mohair rug. Who would have thought it. Not without tenderness, but who is ever to know that is part of the scandal – perhaps even of rape and murder? – sometimes the only tenderness possible. A man in his position would never be free of tittering disgrace. Never. Silence in the boardroom, change of conversation at the dinner-table when his name came up, and the young daughter of the house not told the reason, because she had known him as a family friend since she was a child along with his son. An insane risk. Nothing will ever be disclosed. It was so easy, and god knows who the stranger was and where, in these streets or those, this town or that, she may anytime be quite near, with the mother and sister and whole clan those people have, guarding young girls.

Adrienne Rich

b. 1929

The American poet and essayist Adrienne Rich was born in Baltimore and educated at Radcliffe. In her collections of poems – including Change of World *(1951),* The Dream of a Common Language *and* A Wild Patience Has Taken Me This Far *(1981) – she has increasingly identified herself as a radical feminist and lesbian.* Of Woman Born *(1976) is a study of the politics of motherhood.*

'The Floating Poem, Unnumbered' (The Dream of a Common Language, 1978)

Whatever happens with us, your body
will haunt mine – tender, delicate
your lovemaking, like the half-curled frond
of the fiddlehead fern in forests
just washed by sun. Your traveled, generous thighs
between which my whole face has come and come –
the innocence and wisdom of the place my tongue has found there –
the live, insatiate dance of your nipples in my mouth –
your touch on me, firm, protective, searching
me out, your strong tongue and slender fingers
reaching where I had been waiting years for you
in my rose-wet cave – whatever happens, this is.

Marguerite Duras

b. 1914

The French novelist, dramatist, scriptwriter and film-maker Marguerite Duras was born in French Indochina (Vietnam), coming to Paris in 1931 to study law and political science. Her work, including the 1958 novel Moderato Cantabile *and the play and filmscript* Hiroshima mon amour *(1960), has always been concerned with issues of sexual desire, love and death, and has increasingly moved away from structured narrative.*

From **The Lover** (1984). *Trans. Barbara Bray*

It happened very quickly that day, a Thursday. He'd come every day to pick her up at the high school and drive her back to the boarding school. Then one Thursday afternoon, the weekly half-holiday, he came to the boarding school and drove off with her in the black car.

It's in Cholon. Opposite the boulevards linking the Chinese part of the city to the centre of Saigon, the great American-style streets full of trams, rickshaws and buses. It's early in-the afternoon. She's got out of the compulsory outing with the other girls.

It's a native housing estate to the south of the city. His place is modern, hastily furnished from the look of it, with furniture supposed to be ultra-modern. He says: I didn't choose the furniture. It's dark in the studio, but she doesn't ask him to open the shutters. She doesn't feel anything in particular, no hate, no repugnance either, so probably it's already desire. But she doesn't know it. She agreed to come as soon as he asked her the previous evening. She's where she has to be, placed here. She feels a tinge of fear. It's as if this must be not only what she expects, but also what had to happen especially to her. She pays close attention to externals, to the light, to the noise of the city in which the room is immersed. He's trembling. At first he looks at her as though he expects her to speak, but she doesn't. So he doesn't do anything either, doesn't undress her, says he loves her madly, says it very softly. Then is silent. She doesn't answer. She could say she doesn't love him. She says nothing. Suddenly, all at once, she knows, knows that he doesn't understand her, that he never will, that he lacks the power to understand such perverseness. And that he can never move fast enough to catch her. It's up to her to know. And she does. Because of his ignorance she suddenly knows: she was attracted to him already on the ferry. She was attracted to him. It depended on her alone.

She says: I'd rather you didn't love me. But if you do, I'd like you to do as you usually do with women. He looks at her in horror, asks, Is that what you want? She says it is. He's started to suffer here in this room, for the first time, he's no longer lying about it. He says he knows already she'll never love him. She lets him say it. At first she says she doesn't know. Then she lets him say it.

He says he's lonely, horribly lonely because of this love he feels for her. She says she's lonely too. She doesn't say why. He says: You've come here with me as you might have gone anywhere with anyone. She says she can't say, so far she's never gone into a bedroom with anyone. She tells him she doesn't want him to talk, what she wants is for him to do as he usually does with the women he brings to his flat. She begs him to do that.

He's torn off the dress, he throws it down. He's torn off her little white cotton panties and carries her over like that, naked, to the bed. And there he turns away and weeps. And she, slow, patient, draws him to her and starts to undress him. With her eyes shut. Slowly. He makes as if to help her. She tells him to keep still. Let me do it. She says she wants to do it. And she does. Undresses him. When she tells him to, he moves his body in the bed, but carefully, gently, as if not to wake her.

The skin's sumptuously soft. The body. The body's thin, lacking in strength, in muscle, he may have been ill, may be convalescent, he's hairless, nothing masculine about him but his sex, he's weak, probably a helpless prey to insult, vulnerable. She doesn't look him in the face. Doesn't look at him at all. She touches him. Touches the softness of his sex, his skin, caresses his goldenness, the strange novelty. He moans, weeps. In dreadful love.

And, weeping, he makes love. At first, pain. And then the pain is possessed in its turn, changed, slowly drawn away, borne towards pleasure, clasped to it.

The sea, formless, simply beyond compare.

Grace Nichols

b. 1950

Grace Nichols, Caribbean poet, novelist and children's story writer, was born and educated in Guyana. She moved to England in 1977 and won the Commonwealth poetry prize in 1983. Nichols is widely praised for both her commitment to black women's issues and her variety of linguistic styles. .

From 'Invitation' (1984)

Come up and see me sometime
Come up and see me sometime

My breasts are huge exciting
amnions of watermelon
　your hands can't cup
my thighs are twin seals
　　fat slick pups

there's a purple cherry
below the blues
　of my black seabelly
there's a mole that gets a ride
each time I shift the heritage
of my behind

Come up and see me sometime

Richard Ntiru

b. 1946

The Ugandan poet Richard Ntiru studied literature at Makerere University in Kampala, and published his first book of poems, Tensions, *in 1971. A leading figure in Ugandan culture, he is active in promoting and organizing the arts, including literature and drama.*

From 'Rhythm of the Pestle'

Listen – listen –
listen to the palpable rhythm
of the periodic pestle,
plunging in proud perfection
into the cardial cavity
of maternal mortar
like the panting heart
of the virgin bride
with the silver hymen,
or the approaching stamp
of late athleting cows
hurrying home to their bleating calves.

At each succeeding stroke
the grain darts, glad to be scattered
by the hard glint
of the pestle's passion.

During the aerial suspension
of the pendent pestle
the twice-asked, twice-disappointed girl
thinks of the suitor that didn't come,
of her who dragged her name through
　ashes
uncleansed by the goat-sacrifice,

of her bridal bed
that vanished with the ephemeral
   dream,
of her twin firstlings
that will never be born,
and her weltering hands
grip, grip, rivet hard
and downright down
comes the vengeance pestle.

Pat Califia

b. 1954

The American writer Pat Califia was born in Texas, educated at the San Francisco State University, and now lives in Los Angeles. Describing herself as a 'radical pervert', her books include The Lesbian S/M Safety Manual (*1988*), Macho Sluts *and* Doc and Fluff (*1990*).

From **Macho Sluts**: 'A Dash of Vanilla' (1989)

I hate this feeling. . . .

My neck really hurts. I'm having trouble holding my head up. Sweat is running down my forehead and I can't wipe it off, so it runs into my eyes and stings. My hands are completely numb, and so are my forearms, all the way up to the elbow. I can't tell if I am still gripping your labia or not. I can only tell by the shape of your clit in my mouth just how far back I'm still managing to keep them. I am angry with you because you are taking so long, angry because you leave me alone down here, with no idea what is going on with you, if you are enjoying it or not, no indication of how close you are, how much longer it's going to take. I want to shout, '*Are you ever going to come?*' I desperately need some help, and I begin to whisper, 'please, please,' sometimes loud enough for you to hear me. Any kind of groan or sigh you make is of life-or-death importance to me now and keeps me going for a few more minutes. But I feel as if I am hanging from a cliff face by my skinned and bleeding palms, and I know I cannot hold on to the bare rock for much longer. . . .

Still I work on and on, mechanically, softly, like the Colorado River carving the Grand Canyon one eon at a time, like a bird flying across the ocean that can't stop no matter how tired she is because there is no place to land. Save me, give it to me, help me, seize my head between your thighs and drown me! Come, come!

Sometimes, not all the time, at a time I am never able to predict and for reasons I still do not understand, you promise me a miracle. You begin to talk to me. After your long silence, it feels very odd, being talked to. I pay close attention to what you have to say. It must be important if you can't keep quiet any more.

'Oh, lover,' you say, 'I'm going to come. Can you feel it? Lover!'

Now I am moving fast and sloppy, but it doesn't matter, you will come now no matter what I do, and anyway we are finally in sync, finally in this together . . . shove my fingers into you, past your locked thighs, just as you begin to come. After the shouting, you lie very still, like someone who has fainted. I am still terribly excited. As soon as your thighs relax a little, I push my hand between them, put my fingers up to feel how wet you are, and slide them in. You always say, 'No. No, lover, don't.'

And I say, 'Why? Why not? I want it. You can't stop me. Give it to me.' Then I fuck you. You don't like it, but it makes you come anyway, you can't help it, you jerk and throb around my hand and lock me between your thighs once more, and come until you're screaming obscenities at me, it feels so good to you. If I can, I fuck you yet again, and this time you really protest. It's too much, you're too tired, you're sore. But I am adamant. I've worked so hard to get you to this place, thrown open to me, responding with these free and easy, quick and intense orgasms, that I have to use your pussy as often as you will let me take it. It's what I want myself, for you to pin me down and fuck me, but coming has left you too enervated to struggle with me, so I fuck you instead and like it just as much as coming myself. Besides, this is the only time you can come when I fuck you, right after you've been eaten into an orgasm. You love to get fucked and will take literally hours of it, but never give in and come completely around me, come until you are satisfied. . . .

Yes, it's difficult to make you come. You are difficult in other ways, too. You expect me to do things for you that I think people should do for themselves. I try anyway, and in return you hurt my feelings by complaining that I don't take good enough care of you. My desire for you is desperate, as if making you respond in bed could make up for all the things that go wrong elsewhere and give me back what I lose when you make a contemptuous remark about something I love or tell a story that is supposed to prove you will always be better than me at everything I care about doing well. I take it because I love you. But making love to you barely salvages my self-esteem, and keeps me addicted to you. Anybody could do this for you.

I will know I don't love you any more, that the anger has outweighed the lust, when I stop myself from taking that first puppy-lick, ice-cream-cone-lick, you-are-the-most-desirable-woman-in-the-world-lick that leads to two hours of being muzzled by your cunt, my tongue chasing itself around your clit, aching to have your wet and coming cunt plastered across my nose and mouth, my neck in the scissors of your thighs, hurting for those few seconds when I don't need to breathe or think or remember my name or my pride.

It's so difficult to make you come that only three of your lovers have been able to do it. Did any of them have the stamina to eat you twice in one night? How would you like to come again?

Alina Reyes

b. 1956

Alina Reyes was born in Soulac-sur-Mer, south-west France. The Butcher was inspired by a holiday she spent in her home town while in her mid-teens, when she worked as a cashier in the local butcher's shop. A great admirer of fantasy writers such as Kafka, Poe and Cortazar, Alina Reyes took her pseudonym from Cortazar's novel La Lointaine ou le Journal d'Alina Reyes. *She now lives and works in Paris, and her second novel,* Lucie's Long Voyage, *was published in 1992.*

From **The Butcher** (1988). *Trans. David Watson*

The blade plunged gently into the muscle then ran its full length in one supple movement. The action was perfectly controlled. The slice curled over limply onto the chopping block.

The black meat glistened, revived by the touch of the knife. The butcher placed his left hand flat on the broad rib and with his right hand began to carve into the thick meat once again. I could feel that cold elastic mass beneath the palm of my own hand. I saw the knife enter the firm dead flesh, opening it up like a shining wound. The steel blade slid down the length of the dark shape. The blade and the wall gleamed.

The butcher picked up the slices one after the other and placed them side by side on the chopping block. They fell with a flat slap – like a kiss against the wood.

With the point of the knife the butcher began to dress the meat, cutting out the yellow fat and splattering it against the tiled wall. He ripped a piece of greaseproof paper from the wad hanging on the iron hook, placed a slice in the middle of it, dropped another on top. The kiss again, more like a clap.

Then he turned to me, the heavy packet flat on his hand he tossed it onto the scales.

The sickly smell of raw meat hit my nostrils. Seen close up, in the full summer morning light which poured in through the long window, it was bright red, beautifully nauseating. Who said that flesh is sad? Flesh is not sad, it is sinister. It belongs on the left side of our souls, it catches us at times of the greatest abandonment, carries us over deep seas, scuttles us and saves us; flesh is our guide, our dense black light, the well which draws our life down in a spiral, sucking it into oblivion.

The flesh of the bull before me was the same as that of the beast in the field, except that the blood had left it, the stream which carries life and carries it away so quickly, of which there remained only a few drops like pearls on the white paper.

And the butcher who talked to me about sex all day long was made of the same flesh, only warm, sometimes soft sometimes hard; the butcher had his good and inferior cuts, exacting and eager to burn out their life, to transform themselves into meat. And my flesh was the same, I who felt the fire light between my legs at the butcher's words.

There was a slit along the bottom of the butcher's stall where he stuck his collection of knives for cutting, slicing and chopping. Before plunging one into the meat the butcher would sharpen the blade on his steel, running it up and down, first one side then the other, against the metal rod. The sharp scraping noise set my teeth on edge to their very roots.

The rabbits were hung behind the glass pane, pink, quartered, their stomachs opened to reveal their fat livers – exhibitionists, crucified martyrs, sacrificial offerings to covetous housewives. The chickens were suspended by the neck, their skinny yellow necks stretched and pierced by the iron hooks which held their heads pointing skywards; fat bodies of poultry with grainy skin dangling wretchedly, with their whimsical parson's noses stuck above their arseholes like the false nose on a clown's face.

In the window, like so many precious objects, the different cuts of pork, beef and lamb were displayed to catch the eye of the customer. Fluctuating between pale pink and deep red, the joints caught the light like living jewels. Then there was the offal, the glorious offal, the most intimate, the most authentic, the most secretly evocative part of the deceased animal: flabby, dark, blood-red livers; huge, obscenely coarse tongues; chalky, enigmatic brains; kidneys coiled around their full girth, hearts tubed with veins – and those kept hidden in the fridge: the lights for granny's cat because they are too ugly; spongy grey lungs; sweetbread, because it is rare and saved for the best customers; and those goats' testicles, brought in specially from the abattoir and always presented ready wrapped, with the utmost discretion, to a certain stocky gentleman for his special treat.

About this unusual and regular order the boss and the butcher – who treated most things as an excuse for vulgar asides – never said a word.

As it happens I knew that the two men believed that the customer acquired and maintained an extraordinary sexual power through his weekly consumption of goats' testicles. In spite of the supposed benefits of this ritual they had never ventured to try it themselves. That part of the male anatomy, so often vaunted in all kinds of jokes and comments, nevertheless demanded respect. It went without saying that one could only go so far before trampling on sacred ground.

Those goat's testicles did not fail to excite my imagination. I had never managed to see them – had never dared ask. But I thought about that chubby pink packet and about the gentleman who carried it away without a word, after paying, like everyone else, at my till (the testicles were sold for some derisory sum). What was the taste and texture of these carnal relics? How were they prepared? And above all, what effect did they have? I too tended to attribute extraordinary properties to them, which I thought about endlessly.

Leslie Dick

b. 1954

Leslie Dick is an American novelist and short-story writer. She has lived in London since 1965. Her first novel, Without Falling, *was published in 1987, and her second,* Kicking, *in 1992.*

From **Minitel 3615** (1989)

It was a love affair by electronics, a love affair by MINITEL, the Paris computer system that offers interactive communication between users, who type texts onto their computer screens, these texts transmitted instantly from monitor to monitor, through the telephone lines of the city. An abstract, immaterial love affair, therefore, a literary love affair, epistolary without the literal object, no pen, ink, or paper, only an ephemeral alphabet written in white light against a plain grey screen. The MINITEL system is low tech: you can book theatre tickets, or find out railway timetables, you can check your bank balance and then, you can give in, accept the invitation posed by incessant, all-pervasive advertising, and dial 3615, the number that lets you into the network of lovers, those who pursue sexual gratification through the exchange of texts, only. No kiss, no touch; no object: no letter, or scrap of silk; no image, no voice, even; no trace of the body. The body vanishes, leaving a flickering screen, rows of words inscribed in fugitive white light.

Desire Me Allen Jones

C: Hello. Edward?

E: You speak English? – or write English?

C: That's right.

E: Good. We can do it in English, then.

C: Excellent.

E: Begin.

C: How?

E: Any way you please.

C: Do you know the 3615 poster, the big one at the corner of rue Malher and rue St Antoine? The one of the very young girl, the girl with dark hair?

E: The one that's repeated all along the tunnels at the Bastille?

C: Yes. That's me. Catherine.

E: That's how I imagine you. A libertine child, the child who read James Bond at the age of seven, Fanny Hill at nine, and was deep in Philosophy in the Bedroom and Henry Miller at eleven.

C: But of course!

E: The intellectual, precocious, clever child, the voracious reader, sneaking these forbidden books off her parents' shelves. Your parents are absent, uninterested, preoccupied, and would possibly be amused, if they knew – until they discovered the extent of your depravity, how every afternoon after school you lounge, like those girls in Balthus paintings, your skirt falling back over your skinny thigh, book in hand, eyes racing, racing over the page, and then moving more slowly, desultory. Eleven years old, lying on the sofa – and already too old, corrupt, fascinated. Hooked. That's how I picture you, Catherine.

C: Yes.

E: The apartment was rather large; long rooms with windows opening onto narrow balconies, thin white light reflecting off pale stone, Paris light, reflecting back on the white walls of these rooms. There were paintings on these walls, and the parquet creaked in places. You remember – a specific set of sounds, the familiar sounds of different people moving through this space, these rooms and corridors. The woman who cooked and cleaned and kept an eye on you. Your mother with her luncheon appointments, her shopping, her endless telephoning. Your father so beautiful, with his dark hair falling across his forehead. Every day he shut himself into his study; he would eat his lunch off a tray that was left outside his room, in the corridor, and invariably he would walk for an hour after lunch, to clear his head, he said. You remember, perhaps, one afternoon when you got up from your nap, and walked down the corridor. You could hear Ariette singing quietly to herself, working in the kitchen. You wanted to ask your father the meaning of a word in a book you were reading. He was not in his study. You went to the bedroom, your parents' room. You looked through the keyhole, your dress falling forward as you bent down to look. Your legs were bare, and they began to shake slightly, as your heart pounded, watching your father fucking your mother. She was pale, naked, absolutely passive, flat – her arms were stretched wide, he held them out, flat, as his body moved over her. You saw, you understood, you wanted that – that precisely, to become him, to become her – to lie on a bed in the afternoon, the shutters drawn across the windows, a sense of the busy city traffic below, the white reflected light of Paris outside, autumn, and you, and

Ariette, carrying on your normal afternoon, and here, in this shadowed room, this excess of passion enacting itself. As you watched, your mother didn't move, it was as if she were dead, but her mouth was open, a series of little 'Oh!s' came out of this mouth, and you felt your vagina flicker. This was what you wanted, precisely this.

C: Perhaps. Go on.

E: The next afternoon, you were alone, reading, as always. Your parents had gone to the country, to stay with friends, without you. Ariette was asleep, sound asleep, in her room. Taking a glass of apricot juice from the fridge, you'd looked in and seen her sleeping there. You were reading, and as you read you rocked back and forth gently in your chair, as was your habit. You sat with one pale, bare leg folded under you, your foot tucked under you, and rocked gently. Now you associate the flood of words in your mind, reading, that pressing flow, moving onward, reading this, now, with the rising pleasure, as you gently rocked back and forth. But the book was surprising: suddenly it described a scene of petticoats, white thighs, a thin leather riding whip across those thighs. Your fingers longed to touch yourself, you remember your mother lying flat, so thin and pale, her arms held outstretched, held down by the man with the beautiful body. She could not touch herself. You can. Reading the scene over and over, picturing the woman's pale legs, her skirts pulled up, the fine whip coming down, you put your hand under your skirt, down into your knickers, and slip your middle finger easily between those lips. With your other hand you stroke your mouth, leaning forward over the book, which lies flat on the table. You come. You think, as the rush recedes, you think, that is what I want. To be the thighs, the whip, the eyes, watching, the woman leaning over, who cannot see. The hand that holds the whip, the thighs that feel it. That is what I want.

C:

E: I'm still here.

C: Do you want to make a date?

E: Do you mean here, on the machine? Or in real life?

C: The machine is better than real life, don't you think? We could arrange the time, and meet.

E: Yes.

C: Every afternoon at half past five, perhaps, a conversation in writing. An exchange, of some sort.

E: Not at the weekends.

C: All right.

E: I'm afraid I can't make it tomorrow. Wednesday.

C: Till then.

Angela Carter

1940–1992

Angela Carter, an English novelist and short-story writer, was born in Eastbourne and educated at Bristol University. Carter's work often explores erotic and aggressive fantasy through the reworking of myth and fairy-tale, combining Gothic elements with exuberant comedy. Her novels include Nights at the Circus *(1984) and* Wise Children *(1991), her screenplays* The Magic Toyshop *(1967) and* Company of Wolves.

From **The Woman Who Married Her Son's Wife** (1990)

Once there lived an old woman who desired her son's pretty young wife. This son was a hunter who often would be gone for many days at a time. Once, while he was gone, the old woman sat down and made herself a penis out of sealbone and skins. She fastened this penis to her waist and showed it to her daughter-in-law, who exclaimed: 'How nice . . . ' Then they slept together. Soon the old woman was going out to hunt in a big skin kayak, just like her son. And when she came back, she would take off her clothes and move her breasts up and down, saying: 'Sleep with me, my dear little wife. Sleep with me . . . '

It happened that the son returned from his hunting and saw his mother's seals lying in front of the house. 'Whose seals are these?' he asked of his wife.

'None of your business,' she replied.

Being suspicious of her, he dug a hole behind their house and hid there. He figured that some hunter was claiming his wife in his absence. Soon, however, he saw his mother paddling home in her kayak with a big hooded seal. Mother and son never caught anything but big hooded seals. The old woman reached land and took off her clothes, then moved her breasts up and down, saying: 'My sweet little wife, kindly delouse me . . . '

The son was not pleased by his mother's behaviour. He came out of hiding and struck the old woman so hard that he killed her. 'Now,' he said to his wife, 'you must come away with me because our home place has a curse on it.'

The wife began to quiver and shake all over. 'You've killed my dear husband,' she cried. And would not stop crying.

Nicholson Baker

b. 1957

An American novelist, born in New York, Baker's novels include The Mezzanine *(1988),* Room Temperature *(1990) and* Vox, *wittily digressive works describing the minutiae of, respectively, an office worker's lunch hour, a father feeding his baby girl, and sexual obsession over the phone.*

From **Vox** (1992)

' . . . from the point where I've scheduled my orgasm I have to gauge exactly, depending on how close to coming I think I am – so if I'm very close to coming I only go back a paragraph, but if it looks like it'll be a while I may even read the whole scene or the whole letter that's *before* the letter I'm interested in and then go on and read the letter I'm interested in and then go on and read the letter I'm interested in. And sometimes I misjudge, and I start to get close to coming when the big moment of the story is still on the next page, and I have to race ahead looking for the words I need, or sometimes the opposite happens and I'm crowding up to the big moment of the story and my orgasm is dawdling, not all the precincts are reporting yet, and so I have to read the chosen come-sentence very slowly, syllable by syllable, "up . . . and . . . down . . . on . . . his . . . fuck . . . pole . . . "'

'So if you walked into a room,' he said, 'and there was an armchair, and a table, and on one end of the table was a TV and a VCR and an X-rated tape, and at the other end of the table was some book of Victorian pornography, what would you choose?'

'The Victorian pornography, no question.'

'That's incredible to me.'

'You'd choose the tape, right?' she asked.

'That or possibly the armchair itself. Not the book.'

'The classic opposition,' she said.

'True, but no – actually, it's interesting. Because I've heard for so long about those studies that say that women like stories and men like pictures I've started to feel lately that stories *represent* women and are therefore sexually charged for me, and in fact that's what got me so hot at Bonnie's Books that time, the idea that I was peeping in on a women's preserve. I think I *am* slowly starting to understand why in general people would prefer written porn. It gives your brain a vaginal orgasm rather than a clitoral orgasm, so to speak, whatever that means. I read one story in some men's magazine once, years ago, in the first person, written by a woman, or probably not, but written at least with the pretence that a woman was telling the story, about a sixteen-year-old girl who goes swimming in a neighbour's pool and of course her frans are still somewhat new and unfamiliar to her, and she'd forgotten that her top from last year was flimsy and inadequate to the demands that were made on it, and presto it comes off after she's swum a lap, and she's *so* embarrassed and apologetic, but Mr. Grunthole reassures her that she needn't be ashamed, he doesn't mind if she swims without her top, and so on, and so on, and even though it was a totally conventional and undistinguished story, the fact that it was written in the voice of this girl, so I could peep in on her mixed feelings when her top came off, did give me a huge . . . an unexpectedly large return on my investment. I guess insofar as verbal pornography records thoughts rather than exclusively images, or at least surrounds all images with thoughts, or something, it can be the hottest medium of all. Telepathy on a budget. But still honestly I need the images. For instance of you there in the shower. I mean, when you come are your legs slightly apart?'

'Yes.'

'And do you have one of those legendary Water Pik shower-massage showerheads?'

'I do, but I don't use it with any of the special settings. It was installed already when I moved in. It's useful for cleaning the tub. But when I'm – I don't hold it or put it between my legs or anything, I just treat it as a regular showerhead. What I do is . . . '

'Yes?'

'When I start to come?'

'Yes?'

'I – '

'Yes?'

'I open my mouth and let it fill with water. The feeling of the water overflowing my mouth . . . You there?'

'*Don't* stop talking.'

'But that's all,' she said.

'You were in the shower, yesterday night, and the water was coursing onto your face and falling down from one part of you to another, like balls in a pinball machine, and your eyes were closed. What was in your mind? Oh I'd like to . . . '

'Excuse me? You're murmuring.'

'I said I'd like to *clk*,' he said.

'*What?*'

'Sorry, I occasionally have a problem with involuntary swallowing. I said I'd like to . . . put my hands on your thighs, very high up, and hold them apart and cover your whole mound with my mouth and just breathe on you, through the fabric of your underpants.'

'Ooch.'

'Are your legs apart right now?'

'They're crossed at the ankle on the coffee table.'

'That will have to do,' he said. 'Tell me what was in your mind in the shower last night.'

'I honestly don't think I remember. And anyway the things I think of go by so fast. And it's not like all I do is come and come. Very often in the shower I remember some embarrassing moment, or some dumb thing I've said, and I curse it out, I say, "Get away from me, stinker." For instance, I might remember this time after I'd come back from a party when I was quite drunk, so drunk that I started to feel that I was going to be sick, but this person was in my bathroom, washing their face, brushing their teeth, humming happily away, and I moaned, I was leaning against the door, I knocked politely, I made these feeble scrabbling sounds, but this person had used the hook and eye on the inside because the latch didn't work on that door, and he was just too pleased with the world to hear me, or thought I was joking, saying hello by knocking, and so I was sick on my own bathroom door.'

'Oh, terrible.'

'Sorry to be gross. Fortunately it was just the usual fruit punch.'

Source notes

Every effort has been made to trace the copyright holders of material in this book. The publishers apologize if any material has been used without permission and would be pleased to hear from anyone who has not been consulted.

The editor and publisher would like to thank the following for allowing the reproduction of copyright material:

Page 29 from *The Sumerians: their History, Culture and Character* by Samuel Noah Kramer (University of Chicago Press 1964); page 30 from *Inanna* by Diane Wolkstein and Joseph Kramer (Harper & Row 1983); page 35 from *The Literature and Mythology of Ancient Egypt* by Joseph Kaster (Penguin 1970); page 36 from the *Iliad* by Homer translated by E.V. Rieu (Penguin Classics 1950), translation copyright © the Estate of E.V. Rieu 1950; page 37 from *The Seduction* by Archilocus translated by Kenneth McLeish, copyright © Kenneth McLeish 1993; page 38 from *The Golden Lyre: the Themes of the Greek Lyric Poets* by David A. Campbell (Duckworth 1983); page 38 from *Sappho: Poems and Fragments* by Josephine Balmer (Ballantine 1970); page 38 from *The Constraints of Desire* by John D. Winkler (Routledge 1990); page 39 Asklepiades translated by Kenneth McLeish, copyright © Kenneth McLeish 1993; page 39 from *Eros the Bitter Sweet* by Anne Carson, copyright © 1966 and reprinted by permission of Princeton University Press; page 40 from the Authorized Version of the Bible (King James Bible), the rights in which are vested in the Crown, reproduced by permission of the Crown's Patentee, Cambridge University Press; page 43 from the *Greek Anthology* (Meleager and Automedon) translated by Kenneth McLeish, copyright © Kenneth McLeish 1993; page 44 from *The Poems of Catullus* translated by Peter Whigham (Penguin Classics 1966), translation copyright © Peter Whigham 1955; page 45 from the *Aeneid* by Virgil, translated by Kenneth McLeish, copyright © Kenneth McLeish 1993; page 47 from *The Elegies* by Propertius translated by Kenneth McLeish, copyright © Kenneth McLeish 1993; page 48 from *Amores*, Book 111 by Ovid translated by Kenneth McLeish, copyright © Kenneth McLeish 1993; page 50 from *Metamorphoses* by Ovid translated by Mary M. Innes (Penguin Classics 1955), copyright © Mary M. Innes 1955; page 53 from *The Satyricon* by Petronius translated by J.P. Sullivan (Penguin Classics 1965, 3rd revised edition 1986), translation copyright © J.P. Sullivan 1965, 1969, 1974 1986; page 55 from *Epigrams* by Martial, translated by James Michie, copyright © James Michie; pages 56, 76, 81, 122 and 248 from *Women Poets of China*, copyright © Kenneth Rexroth and Ling Chung 1972, reprinted by permission of New Directions Publishing Corporation; page 56 from the *Greek Anthology* translated by Kenneth McLeish, copyright © Kenneth McLeish 1993; page 57 from *The Golden Ass* by Apuleius translated by Robert Graves,

Bibliography of secondary sources

Adams, J.N., *The Latin Sexual Vocabulary*, London 1982.

Alexandrian, *Histoire de la littérature érotique*, Paris 1989.

Apollinaire, Guillaume, *et al.*, L'Enfer de la Bibliothèque Nationale: *Incono-Bio-Bibliographie descriptive, critique et raisonnée, complète à ce jour de tous les ouvrages composant cette célèbre collection avec un index alphabètique de titres et noms d'auteurs*, Paris 1919.

Aries, Philippe, *The Hour of our Death*, Harmondsworth 1983.

Armstrong, Nancy, *Desire and Domestic Fiction*, London 1987.

Arts Council, *The Obscenity Laws*, London 1969.

Ashbee, Henry Spencer (pseudonym Pisanus Fraxi), *Catena librorum tacendorum*, London 1885; *Centuria librorum absconditorum*, London 1879; *Index librorum prohibitorum*, London 1877.

Atkins, John, *Sex in Literature* (4 vols), London 1970–82.

Aubrey, John, *Brief Lives*, London 1949.

Barthes, Roland, 'The Metaphor of the Eye' in George Bataille, *Story of the Eye*, Harmondsworth 1982.

Bataille, Georges, *L'Érotisme*, Paris 1957.

Bettelheim, Bruno, *The Uses of Enchantment*, Harmondsworth 1986.

Bhatacharyya, N.N., *A History of Indian Erotic Literature*, London 1975.

Bloch, Iwan (pseudonym Eugen Duhren). 'Ethnological & cultural studies of the sex life in England: as revealed in its erotic and obscene literature and art', New York 1972.

Boardman, Jasper Griffin and Oswyn Murray (eds), *The Oxford History of the Classical World*, Oxford 1986.

Bogin, Meg, *Women Troubadours*, New York 1976

Bold, Alan, *The Sexual Dimension in Literature*, London 1982.

Boswell, John, *Christianity, Social Tolerance and Homosexuality*, Chicago 1980.

Boyle, Nicholas, *Goethe: The Poet and the Age*, Vol 1: *The Poetry of Desire*, Oxford 1991.

Bremmer, Jan (ed), *From Sappho to de Sade*, London 1991.

Bristow, Edward J., *Vice and Vigilance: Purity movements in Britain since 1700*, Dublin 1977.

Brown Peter, *The Body and Society*, New York 1988.

Buchen, Irving (ed), *The Perverse Imagination: sexuality and literary culture*, New York 1970.

Campbell, David A., *The Golden Lyre: The Themes of the Greek Lyric Poets*, London 1983.

Carson, Ann, *Eros the Bittersweet*, Princeton 1986

Carter, Angela, *The Sadeian Women: An Exercise in Cultural History*, London 1979.

Chandos, John (ed), *To deprave and corrupt*, London 1962.

Chester, Gail and Dickey, Julienne, *Feminism and Censorship*, London 1988.

Clark, Kenneth, *The Nude*, London 1960.

Craig, Alec, *The Banned Books of England and Other Countries: A Study of the Conception of Literary Obscenity*, London 1962.

Croft-Cooke, Rupert, *Feasting with Panthers: A New Consideration of Some Late Victorian Writers*, London 1967.

Curll, Edmund, *Post-office intelligence*, London 1736.

Deakin, Terence, *Catalogi librorum eroticorum: A critical bibliography of erotic bibliographies and book-catalogues*, London 1964.

Derrida, Jacques, *Of Grammatology*, Baltimore 1976.

Dijkstra, Bram, *Idols of Perversity: Fantasies of Feminine Evil in Fin-de-Siècle Culture*, New York 1986.

Dover, K.J., *Greek Homosexuality*, New York 1980.

Dronke, Peter, *Medieval Latin and the Rise of the European Love Lyric*, Oxford 1968.

Drummond, D.A. and Perkins G., *Dictionary of Russian Obscenities*, Oakland 1987.

Dworkin, Andrea, *Pornography: men possessing women*, London 1981.

Elias, Norbert, *The Civilizing Process*, New York 1978.

Ellis, Albert and Abarbanel, Albert, *The Encyclopaedia of Sexual Behaviour* (2 vols), New York 1961.

Faderman, Lillian, *Surpassing the Love of Men: love between women from the Renaissance to the present*, London 1985; *Odd Girls and Twilight Lovers: A History of Lesbian Life in Twentieth-Century America*, London 1992.

Faust, Beatrice, *Women, Sex, and Pornography*, London 1980.

Ferrante, Joan (ed), *In Pursuit of Perfection: Courtly Love in Medieval Literature*, London 1975; *Woman as image in medieval literature from the twelfth century to Dante*, London 1975.

Fiedler, Leslie, *Love and Death in the American Novel*, London 1967.

Foucault, Michel, *The History of Sexuality* (Vol 1), London 1979; *The Use of Pleasure* (Vol 2), London 1986.

Foxon, David, *Libertine Literature in England 1600–1745*.

Freud, Sigmund, 'On Narcissism: an introduction' and 'Beyond the Pleasure Principle' in *The Pelican Freud Library* (Vol 2), Harmondsworth 1984; 'Jokes and their Relation to the Unconscious' in *The Pelican Freud Library* (Vol 6), Harmondsworth 1976; 'Three Essays on the Theory of Sexuality' in *The Pelican Freud Library* (Vol 7), Harmondsworth 1977.

Friday, Nancy, *My Secret Garden*, London 1975.

Fryer, Peter (ed) *The man of pleasure's companion: a nineteenth-century anthology of amorous entertainment*, London 1968; *Mrs Grundy: Studies in English Prudery*, London 1963; (ed) *Forbidden Books of the Victorians*, London 1970.

Furber, Donald, and Callahan, Ann, *Erotic love in literature from medieval legend to romantic illusion*, New York 1981.

Gay, Peter, *The Bourgeois Experience: Victoria to Freud*, New York 1984.

Gelb, Norman, *The Irresistible Impulse: An evocative study of erotic practices and notions through the ages*, London 1979.

Ginzburg, Ralph, *An Unhurried View of Erotica*, New York 1958.

Grant, Michael, *Erotic Art in Pompeii*, London 1975.

Graves, Robert, *The Greek Myths* (2 vols), Harmondsworth 1960.

Green, Jonathon, *The Encyclopedia of Censorship*, New York 1990.

Griffin, Susan, *Pornography and Silence*, New York 1981.

Hagstrum, Jean H., *Sex and Sensibility: ideal and erotic love from Milton to Mozart*, London 1980; *The Romantic Body: Love and Sexuality in Keats, Wordsworth and Balke*, Knoxville, Tenn. 1985.

Haight, Anne Lyon and Grannis, Chandler B., *Banned Books: informal notes on some books banned for various reasons at various times in various places*, New York 1978.

Halperin, David M., *One Hundred Years of Homosexuality and Other Essays on Greek Love*, New York 1989.

Halperin, David M., Winkler John J. and Zeitlin, Froma I. (eds), *Before Sexuality: The Construction of the Erotic Experience in the Ancient Greek World*, Princeton 1989.

Harrison, Fraser, *The Yellow Book*, London 1982.

Hoffmann, Frank, An *Analytical Survey of Anglo-American Traditional Erotica*, Ohio 1973.

Home Office, *Report of the Committee on Obscenity and Film Censorship*, London 1979.

Hughes, Douglas A., *Perspectives on Pornography*, New York 1970.

Hurwood, Bernhardt J., *The Golden Age of Erotica*, London 1968.

Huysmans, J.K., *Against Nature*, Harmondsworth 1959.

Hyde, H. Montgomery, *A History of Pornography*, London 1964.

Jenkyns, R., *Three Classical Poets: Sappho, Catullus and Juvenal*, Cambridge, Mass. 1982.

Johns, Catherine, *Sex or Symbol: Erotic Images of Greece and Rome*, London 1982.

Johnson, Wendell Stacey, *Sex and Marriage in Victorian Poetry*, Ithaca 1975.

Jones, Roger and Penny, Nicholas, *Raphael*, London 1983.

Kaplan, Cora, *Sea Changes: Culture and Feminism*, London 1987.

Kaplan, Louise J., *Female Perversions*, London 1991.

Kaster, Joseph (ed), *The Literature and Mythology of Ancient Egypt*, London 1970.

Keach, William, *Elizabethan Narratives: Irony and Pathos in the Ovidian Poetry of Shakespeare, Marlowe and their contemporaries*, Hassocks 1977.

Kearney, Patrick J. *The Private Case: an annotated bibliography of the private case erotica collection in the British (Museum) Library*, London 1981.

Kendrick, Walter, *The Secret Museum: Pornography in Modern Culture*, New York 1991.

Khan, Masud R., *Alienation in Perversions*, London 1989.

Kramer, Samuel Noah, *From the Tablets of Noah*, London 1956; *History Begins at Sumer*, London 1958; *The Sumerians: Their History, Culture and Character*, Chicago 1964.

Kronhausen, Eberhardt and Phyllis, *Erotic Fantasies*, New York 1970.

Laqueur, Thomas, *Making Sex: Body and Gender from the Greeks to Freud*, London 1991.

Lawrence, D.H., 'Pornography and Obscenity', 'À Propos of Lady Chatterley's Lover' in *Phoenix* (vols 1 and 2), London 1929, 1930.

Legman, Gershon, *The Horn Book: studies in erotic folklore and Bibliography*, London 1970.

Lever, J.W., *The Elizabethan Love Sonnet*, London 1956.

Levi, Peter, *The Pelican History of Greek Literature*, London 1985.

Lewis, C.S., *Four Loves*, London 1960; *The Allegory of Love*, London 1936.

Lewis, Roy Hanley, *The Book Browser's Guide to Erotica*, Newton Abbot, 1981.

Longford, Lord, *Pornography: The Longford Report*, London 1972.

Loth, David, *The Erotic in Literature: A Historical Survey of Pornography as Delightful as it is Indiscreet*, London 1962.

Luck, George, *The Latin Love Elegy*, London 1955.

MacCormack, Robert M. and Struthers, Marilyn, *Nature, Culture and Gender*, Cambridge 1980.

McNaron, Toni A.H., *The Sisterbond*, New York 1985.

Marcade, Jean, *Roma Amor: Erotic elements in Etruscan and Roman Art*, London 1961.

Marcus, Steven, *The Other Victorians: a study of sexuality and pornography in mid-nineteenth-century England*, London 1966.

Marcuse, Herbert, *Eros and Civilisation: A Philosphical Inquiry into Freud*, London 1966.

Marcuse, Ludwig, *Obscene, The History of an Indignation*, London 1965.

Marks, Elaine and Courtivron, Isabelle de, *New French Feminisms: An Anthology*, Brighton 1981.

Matusak, Susan, *Bibliography of the eighteenth-century holdings of the Institute for Sex Research*, Bloomington, Indiana 1975.

Meese, Edwin, *The Report of the Attorney General on Pornography*, New York 1972.

Melville, Robert, *Erotic Art of the West*, London 1973.

Michelson, Peter, *The Aesthetics of Pornography*, New York 1971.

Miller, Henry, *Defence of the Freedom to Read*, Oslo 1959.

Molyneux, Maxine and Casterton, Julia, 'Looking Again at Anaïs Nin' in *The Minnesota Review*, Minnesota 1980.

Montefiore, Jan, *Feminism and Poetry*, London 1985.

Moore, H.T. (ed), *Sex, Literature and Censorship*, London 1955.

Nobile, Philip (ed), *The New Eroticism: theories, vogues & canons*, New York 1970.

Ogilvie, R.M., *Roman Literature and Society*, London 1980.

Orwell, George, *Inside the Whale and other Essays*, London 1940.

Page, Denys L., *Sappho and Alcaeus*, Oxford 1955.

Parker, Rozsika and Pollock, Griselda, *Old Mistresses: Women, Art and Ideology*, London 1981.

Partridge, Eric, *Shakespeare's Bawdy*, London 1968.

Paulhan, Jean, 'The Marquis de Sade and His Accomplice' in de Sade, Justine, *Philosophy in the Bedroom, Eugenie de Franval and other writings*, New York 1966; 'A Slave's Revolt: An Essay on the Story of O', London, 1990.

Pearsall, Ronald, *The Worm in the Bud: the world of Victorian sexuality*, London 1967.

Peckham, Morse, *Art and Pornography*, New York 1971.

Perkins, Michael, *The Secret Record: Modern Erotic Literature*, New York 1976.

Perrin, Noel, *Dr Bowdler's Legacy: a history of expurgated books in England and America*, New York 1969.

Perry, Anthony T., *Erotic Spirituality: the Integrative Tradition from Leone Ebreo to John Donne*, Alabama 1980.

Peterson, Karen and Wilson, J.J., *Women Artists*, New York 1976.

Petersson, Robert T., *The Art of Ecstasy: Saint Teresa, Bernini and Crashaw*, London 1970.

Petroff, Elizabeth Alvilda (ed), *Medieval Women's Visionary Literature*, Oxford 1986.

Phelps, Guy, *Film Censorship*, London 1974.

Porter, Cathy, *Alexandra Kollontai*, London 1980.

Porter, Roy and Rousseau, G.S. (eds), *Sexual Underworlds of the Enlightenment*, Manchester 1988.

Postgate, Raymond, *That Devil Wilkes*, London 1930.

Quetel, Claude, *History of Syphilis*, Oxford 1990.

Quevedo, Raymond, *Attila's Kaiso: a short history of Trinidad Calypso*, St Augustine, Trinidad 1983.

'Reage, Pauline' (pseudonym), *The Story of O*, London 1990; 'Who is Jean de Berg?' in de Berg, Jean, *The Image*, Paris 1956.

Reisner, Robert G., *Show Me the Good Parts: the reader's guide to sex in literature*, New York 1964.

Rembar, Charles, *The End of Obscenity*, London 1969.

Rimer, J. Thomas, *A Reader's Guide to Japanese Literature*, New York 1988.

Robertson, Geoffrey, *Obscenity*, London 1979; *Freedom, the Individual and the Law*, London 1989.

Rolph, C.H. (ed), *The Trial of Lady Chatterley*, London 1990; *Does Pornography Matter?* London 1961.

Rose, Alfred (pseudonym Rolf S. Reade), *Register of Erotic Books* (2 vols), New York 1936.

Sabbah, Fatna A., *Women in the Muslim Unconscious*, Oxford 1984.

Saikaku, Iharu, *Five Women Who Loved Love*, London 1962.

Segal, Lynne and McIntosh, Mary, *Sex Exposed: Sexuality and the Pornography Debate*, London 1992.

Selkirk, Errol, *Erotica for Beginners*, London 1991.

Shahar, Shulamith, *The Fourth Estate: A History of Women in the Middle Ages*, London 1983.

Showalter, Elaine, *Sexual Anarchy: Gender and Culture at the Fin de Siècle*, London 1991.

Singer, Irving, *The Nature of Love 1: Plato to Luther*, Chicago 1984.

Smallwood, Angela, *Fielding and the Woman Question: the novels of Henry Fielding and the Feminist Debate 1700–1750*, Harvester 1989.

Sontag, Susan, 'The Pornographic Imagination' in *Styles of Radical Will*, London 1967.

Spender, Dale, *Mothers of the Novel: 100 Good Women Novelists before Jane Austen*, London 1986.

Steinem, Gloria, 'Erotica vs. Pornography' in *Outrageous Acts and Everday Rebellions*, London 1984.

Steiner, George, 'Night Words: High Pornography and Human Privacy' in *Encounter*, New York Oct. 1965; *Language and Silence*, Harmondsworth, 1979.

Stoller, Robert J., *Perversion: The Erotic Form of Hatred*, London 1977; *The Dynamics of Erotic Life*, London 1979.

Straus, Ralph, *The Unspeakable Curll*, London 1927.

Tannahill, Reay, *Sex in History*, London 1980.

Tate Gallery, *Fuseli*, London 1975.

Theweleit, Klaus, *Male Fantasies* (2 vols), Oxford 1991.

Thomas, Donald, *A Long Time Burning: The History of Literary Censorship in England*, London 1969.

Thompson, Roger, *Unfit for Modest Ears: A Study of Pornographic, Obscene and Bawdy Works written or published in England in the second half of the Seventeenth Century*, London 1979.

Tilly, Andrew, *Erotic Drawings*, Oxford 1986.

Topsfield, L.T., *Troubadours and Love*, Cambridge 1975.

Vatican, *Index Librorum Prohibitorum*, Rome 1938.

Vidal, Gore, 'Pornography' in *Collected Essays 1952–1972*, London 1974.

Wagner, Peter, *Eros Revived: Erotica of the Enlightenment in England and America*, London 1990.

Warner, Keith Q., *The Trinidad Calypso*, London 1982.

Warner, Marina, *Alone of All Her Sex: the Myth and Cult of the Virgin Mary*, London 1976.

Webb, J. Barry, *Shakespeare's Erotic Word Usage*, London 1899.

Webb, Peter (ed), *The Erotic Arts*, London 1975.

Wedeck, Harry E., *Dictionary of Erotic Literature*, London 1963.

Williams, Linda, *Hard Core*, London 1990.

Winkler, Irvine, *The Constraints of Desire: The Anthropology of Sex and Gender in Ancient Greece*, London 1990.

Wolkstein, Diane and Kramer, Samuel Noah, *Inanna Queen of Heaven and Earth*, New York 1983.

Yellow Silk, *Journal of Erotic Arts*, Albany 1983–1992.

Young, Wayland, *Eros Denied*, London 1968.

Zall, Paul, *Ben Franklin Laughing: anecdotes from original sources by and about Benjamin Franklin*, London 1980.

Index

The figures in **bold** type are page references for authors or works that have been anthologized in this collection.